FLAMES

#1 FLAMES OF WINTER SERIES

BY BREE WOLF

WOLF PUBLISHING

Flames of Winter by Bree Wolf

Published by WOLF Publishing UG

Copyright © 2022 Bree Wolf
Text by Bree Wolf
Paperback ISBN: 978-3-98536-131-1
Hard Cover ISBN: 978-3-98536-132-8
Ebook ISBN: 978-3-98536-130-4

WOLF Publishing - This is us:

Two sisters, two personalities.. But only one big love!

Diving into a world of dreams..
      ...Romance, heartfelt emotions, lovable and witty characters, some humor, and some mystery! Because we want it all! Historical Romance at its best!

Visit our website to learn all about us, our authors and books!

Sign up to our mailing list to receive first hand information on new releases, freebies and promotions as well as exclusive giveaways and sneak-peeks!

WWW.WOLF-PUBLISHING.COM

Also by Bree Wolf

Flames of Winter Series

Some stories can be told in one book. Others cannot. This is one of those stories.

In the Flames of Winter series by USA Today bestselling and award-winning author BREE WOLF, a young English miss dares to break society's strict rules as she flees from her parents' house the night before her wedding. This one decision ends up leading her from one adventure into the next...and, of course, into the arms of a fiercely protective highlander. He may not be a peer, but he is the one man she never knew she always wanted.

   #1 Flames of Winter

   #2 Shield of Fire

   #3 Out of Smoke and Ashes

   #4 On the Wings of Cinders

FLAMES

of Winter

Chapter One

A LADY'S CHOICE

London, January 1804 (or a variation thereof)

*O**h, this is a mistake!***
With her arms wrapped around herself, Sarah Mortensen, second daughter to Baron Hartmore, stood shivering in her chamber, eyes wide and trying to see out into the dark of night. Blackness engulfed London, and she could hardly make out the delicate frost crystals upon the windowpane in front of her. Shadows seemed to linger everywhere, and yet she could barely make out any light. Did shadows not need light to exist?

Tightening her hands upon her arms, Sarah shook her head, trying to clear it, trying to focus her thoughts. This night, more than ever, she needed her wits. She needed every ounce of self-control she could muster. She needed to be brave.

I've never been brave in my life!

Sarah swallowed hard, her wide eyes looking back at her from the reflection upon the window. What she saw sent an icy chill down her back. Was that truly what she looked like? A thin, shivering creature with fearful eyes and a bowed head? Indeed, the mere thought of being brave seemed ludicrous.

Oh, this is such a big mistake!

Sarah could feel every inch of herself shivering, and she knew it was not the cold floorboards beneath her bare feet or the icy chill that lingered about the room despite the fire in the grate that made her limbs tremble. No, it was fear that held her in its grip. Plain and simple. Sarah knew fear. She knew what it meant to feel terrified, to be frozen in place, unable to move, unable to act. Yes, fear was a familiar concept. Always had been. How on earth had she ever thought she could do this? She had to have been raving mad to believe so!

Willing a deep breath down into her lungs, Sarah closed her eyes and listened. She strained her ears, uncertain what she hoped to hear.

Silence met her.

The house was asleep.

And so was everyone in it.

Now...was the time to act.

Panic shot through Sarah, and she felt her fingernails dig painfully into her flesh. "I can't do this," she whispered, listening to the soft sound of her words as it echoed gently through her chamber. "I can't do this."

Opening her eyes, Sarah's gaze fell on the sturdy wooden trunk in the corner. Within were her clothes and books and other personal belongings, Sarah was to take with her upon the morrow when a new chapter of her life would begin.

Tomorrow.

Her wedding day.

"I can't do this," Sarah whispered once more. Only this time, her words held a different meaning. She no longer thought of the plan that was to set her free but instead of the prison that awaited her. No, she could not marry Lord Blackmore. The thought was worse than any other she had ever entertained, even worse than the idea of stealing away into the night.

Move! Now! Sarah commanded herself silently, and to her utter surprise, her body finally complied.

Willing her thoughts on the task at hand, Sarah moved quietly through her chamber. She retrieved the clothes she had hidden underneath her mattress and hurried to pull them on. Trembling fingers moved to pull woolen socks over her feet and a simple dress of sturdy fabric over her head. She slipped into heavy winter boots, barely able to tie the straps.

When she lifted her head and straightened, Sarah once more spotted her own reflection. It was not clear but rather blurred and faint. Yet with her white nightgown now hidden beneath the darker garments she had donned, she no longer looked so pale, so ghostlike, as though she were nothing but a phantom drifting through the house. No, she was a woman of flesh and blood, and she knew if she did not save herself, no one else would.

Sarah almost scoffed at the notion. After all, she had grown up with thoughts of dashing heroes and gallant gentlemen, always rushing to a lady's rescue. Only the world had never truly been that place, had it? Those had only been stories. Dreams perhaps. Things whispered to young ladies who knew nothing of the truth, of the world they lived in. Sarah had been one of them long ago but not too long ago. She still remembered well what it felt like to have faith. Now, though, she could only shake her head at herself.

"I was a fool," she muttered and then turned away from her reflection. She reached for the heavy woolen winter cloak concealed beneath another corner of her mattress. Its hood fell deep into her face, and as Sarah pulled the warm fabric tight around her shoulders, she seemed to almost disappear inside it. Perhaps that was good. Perhaps no one would notice her this way.

As she stepped toward her door, Sarah paused at her vanity. From the top drawer, she withdrew a small sheet of parchment, words scrawled upon it in crude penmanship. No matter how hard Sarah could have tried, she could never have produced such a letter. Indeed, alone, she would never even have dared to think of such an outrageous plan.

Fortunately, she was not alone. It was a thought that gave her strength, if only for a moment. But it was enough. Enough for her to place the ransom note upon her vanity and then move swiftly toward the door.

Again, Sarah hesitated, only this time to listen. Her senses reached out, and she could almost hear the faint ticking of a clock downstairs.

Beyond that no sound reached her ears. And so, Sarah tentatively opened the door and stepped out into the dark corridor. She looked up and down it and then quickly urged herself onward.

Oh, this is a monumental mistake! Yet...what choice do I have?

With her heart hammering in her chest, Sarah hastened toward the back staircase, for the first time relieved that her father could no longer afford a large household staff. With every Season that passed, fewer and fewer servants were in their employ, a circumstance that now granted Sarah the opportunity to move unseen through the house.

It was not even *their* house. Not the one Sarah had spent her youth in. Long ago, she had been blissfully oblivious to the hard times that awaited her family. However, life had caught up with her, with them all. Her father's gambling debts had eventually forced them to sell their townhouse and move to a smaller, rented one in a lesser neighborhood.

And now, they were forcing her into marriage.

No!

That one word continued to echo through Sarah's head as she silently slipped downstairs. Her eyes moved over the darkened walls and shadowed doors, her heart tensing again and again whenever her mind conjured someone who was not truly there. By the time she finally reached the back entrance, her breath was coming fast and bright spots began to dance in front of her eyes.

I can't do this! Sarah thought frantically. *I'm not brave! I've never been brave! I should turn back. I should—*

No!

Her fingernails dug into her palms as she forced her head up, her teeth gritted hard against the wave of panic that washed over her. Standing in front of the door that would lead her outside, Sarah closed her eyes and willed another deep breath into her body. She needed to stay calm. She needed to stay in control. Everything had been planned. She could not falter now. After all, there were good reasons why she was doing this, why she was defying her father, why she was risking...everything.

Not that I can think of any right now! a voice whispered in the back of Sarah's mind, and she almost chuckled at the absurdity of that thought.

The old grandfather clock in the drawing room chimed loudly, and for a second, Sarah swore her heart stopped. It seemed to jump into her throat, squeezing the air from her lungs, as though trying to flee her body.

Not daring to think another thought, Sarah slipped her trembling hands into the mittens and then stepped through the door, across the threshold and into a life that would now forever be different.

The icy night wind instantly wiped Sarah's mind clear, its chilled fingers reaching inside her hood and underneath her cloak, making her tremble again—only this time with cold.

Sarah welcomed it.

Pulling the hood deeper into her face, Sarah moved slowly, sneaking from shadow to shadow. Snow had fallen earlier in the night, and yet its scent had been lingering upon the air for days now, like a promise soon to be fulfilled. Sarah could smell the chill, the freshness, the scent of something upon the horizon. If only it had remained a mere promise for another few hours, Sarah thought, uncertain how tracks might affect their plan. With snow covering the ground, would someone be able to follow them? Would they be found then?

Another shiver shot through Sarah at that thought. Indeed, how many other things could go wrong? How many things had they not thought of? *She* had certainly not thought of anything. She could have never thought of such a plan, let alone pulled it off. No, it had been *her*.

Grandma Edie as everyone called her.

Hiding in the shadow of a large bush, Sarah looked out at the deserted street. Streetlamps lit the night here and there, but darkness seemed to linger like a heavy blanket upon the world. She knew she ought not, and yet Sarah could not help but wonder what else or who else might be hiding in all the other shadows nearby. Could someone be there? Watching her? Waiting for her to reveal herself?

Women of the *ton* were not supposed to leave the house on their own, let alone at night. It had always seemed like a sensible rule to Sarah, but here she was, daring fate by leaving the safety of her home. Yet home no longer promised safety, did it?

If she did not leave now, she would still be forced to leave her family's home upon the morrow. Her wedding day. She would become Lord Blackmore's wife, a man she had known all her life...and feared all her life. She had only ever known him as an acquaintance of her father's, and yet in recent weeks he had come to look at her differently. In a way that made her shudder and fear him even more. A small part of Sarah could still not believe that her father was truly handing her to such a man in order to pay off his gambling debts. Did he truly not feel anything for her? Did he not see the daughter he had held in his arms as a babe when he looked at her? Was there no part of him that felt compelled to protect her?

Sarah knew the answer to all of these questions. Only she wished it were not so. Always had she wanted a family like the Whickertons. Once they had been neighbors. Once she had shared everything with their daughters, Christina especially. Sarah had almost felt like one of them. Only once grown up, she had been forced to realize that there was one marked difference between them.

Her life was not her own.

And neither were her choices.

Well, this is *my choice,* Sarah reminded herself as her gaze swept up and down the deserted street. Always had she been the dutiful daughter, always concerned with doing the right thing, fearing her father's anger and her mother's disappointment. Even despite everything that had happened, she could not completely ignore the stab of guilt she felt at the thought of betraying them. Because what she was doing right here in this moment was a betrayal, plain and simple. As her father's daughter she ought to heed his words, his decision and bow her head. Yet for the first time in Sarah's life, she could not.

Out of the corner of her eye, Sarah spotted a carriage idling a good distance down the street. It almost seemed like a shadow itself, no markings of any kind setting it apart from the dark night surrounding it. Was this it? Sarah wondered. *If the carriage is unmarked, how will I know if this is truly the one? How can I be certain?*

Still, she could not remain. She could not simply stay here in the shadows as they would vanish once the sun rose in the east. The day would come and take away this one chance. If she was to act, it had to be now.

Gathering her courage, Sarah stepped out of her hiding place and marched down the street. Her legs felt stiff, and her hands still trembled. Her cheeks burned with the cold, and the tip of her nose felt like an icicle. With each step she took closer toward the carriage, Sarah's panic grew. Doubt and fear returned, urging her to turn and run. It was an instinct, no more, but it was a powerful one. One not easily ignored.

And then Sarah could make out the dim outline of a large, sturdy horse, its coat as black as the night. It tossed its head, plumes of breath billowing from its nostrils as it waited, perhaps annoyed with her slow approach. A man sat atop the box of the carriage. He, too, looked like a shadow, a phantom not from this world. A heavy black coat hid his large frame, and his hat was pulled deep into his face. Even the hands that held the reins were shrouded in black leather gloves. Indeed, he did not strike her as one of the Hackney drivers found all over London. Was his disguise part of Grandma Edie's plan? Sarah did not know. She had not thought to ask for more details, only now realizing how little she truly knew.

You're a fool, Sarah chided herself. Perhaps her father was right. Perhaps women truly did not possess the mental faculties to lead their own lives. Or was it only her? Was she somehow deficient? After all, at the mature age of three-and-twenty, she had never once received a marriage proposal.

Not a true one, at least.

Sarah's feet drew to a sudden halt when the man upon the box shifted, his head slightly turning toward her. *Is he looking at me? Is this the right carriage? What if—?*

Jumping off the box in one fluid motion, the man reached out to open the carriage door. He moved without sound, without a single word leaving his lips, and yet Sarah could not shake the feeling that he was watching her. She wished she could see his eyes. Eyes spoke to one's soul, did they not? Perhaps if she could look into his eyes, she would feel reassured. Or perhaps not? After all, what kind of man would pose as a kidnapper? Was he trustworthy? Would she be safe in his presence?

As Sarah hesitated, the man gave a slight nod of the head, as though encouraging her to step forward and enter the carriage. He did not approach her, though, did not reach toward her in any coercive manner, and Sarah breathed a sigh of relief.

The freezing night air chilled a path down into her body, and for a moment, Sarah felt compelled to look over her shoulder, back at the house she had called home this past year. Only she did not.

There was no other course of action. She could not go back. She could only go forward. And so, carefully, slowly, Sarah approached the carriage. She tried to keep her gaze fixed upon the carriage door or the tips of her feet, and yet they continued to stray to the man still holding open the door for her. He made her nervous. He made her want to turn and run. He also promised a way out.

As though sensing her unease, the man moved back a step, his right arm now stretched to the fullest as he continued to hold the door for her.

Sarah almost smiled at him, but then quickly slipped inside, seating herself on the cushioned bench within. Only a moment later, the door fell closed with finality, leaving Sarah in the shadowed interior. She did not hear his footsteps as he moved back toward the box, but she knew he was climbing on when she felt the carriage sway slightly.

'You foolish girl!' Her mother's berating voice rang loud and clear in her head, and Sarah cringed. 'You've done it now! You've ruined us all!'

And then the carriage began idling down the road, turning away from the streets Sarah knew, heading north.

The urge to fling herself out of the carriage and make a run for it remained strong within her, and Sarah tightened her hands upon the thick woolen blanket she had found beside her on the seat. For a long time, she sat there in the dark, every muscle tense to the point of breaking, like a cornered animal waiting to be attacked.

Yet...nothing happened.

The carriage proceeded to roll down the street and, turning a corner here and there, moved farther and farther away from the place where Sarah belonged.

Where she was supposed to be.

Where she should have stayed.

Kate had.

Though unwilling as well, Sarah's elder sister Katherine had married according to their parents' wishes. She had known her place, accepted it and, with it, Lord Birchwell's marriage proposal. Still, Sarah doubted her sister was anywhere near as happy as their mother always insisted she was. Sarah felt it like a weight in her stomach. Something was wrong. Somehow, she was certain that Kate was far from happy. Or was she wrong? Was that only her fear talking?

As the carriage rumbled along, Sarah sat trapped within, her attention free to dwell upon all she feared. Was she truly better off in a carriage with a stranger? Young women married every day, and it was not the end of the world, was it? As much as she abhorred the thought of marrying Lord Blackmore, perhaps her father had been wise to make this choice for her.

Sarah shuddered, knowing her own thoughts to be wrong. As much as she had always done her utmost to do as was expected of her, to be the dutiful daughter and comply with all her parents' wishes, her parents, in turn, had never truly cared for her happiness, had they? It was a sad truth that Sarah had ignored for far too long.

Until it had been almost too late.

No, she thought to herself. *I have every right to save myself...or to try and do so, at least. Have faith! Nothing will go wrong. After all, Grandma Edie was not known to be wrong. Ever!*

As they left London behind, Sarah prayed that this daring adventure would not prove to be the exception to the rule.

Chapter Two

OUT ON THE ROAD

Guiding the softly swaying carriage out of London, Keir MacKinnear, second son to the Laird of Clan MacKinnear in the Scottish Highlands, wondered about the young lady he had been sent to *kidnap*. Quite unexpectedly, she had looked familiar. Granted, he had only caught a brief glimpse of her face, but it had been enough to stir a faint memory within him. He was almost certain he had seen her wide blue eyes before. If only he could recall where. Unfortunately, the memory proved rather elusive.

With practiced ease, Keir directed the black gelding down the road, while his gaze scanned their surroundings. It did not appear anyone had taken note of the young lady's disappearance, but one could never be too careful. Still, the quiet calm surrounding them was reassuring. It reminded him of home, the vast endlessness of the Highlands where one could spend a whole day in the saddle and not meet a soul. Of course, as soon as Keir gazed over his shoulder, he could still spot the faint outlines of London, tiny lights flickering here and there.

More distance was needed, and so they continued down the road for another hour or two. Fortunately, nothing changed. Everything remained quiet as the wind howled around them, shaking the carriage, and threatening to rip the hat from his head. He hoped the young lady inside was well. After all, she had seemed rather terrified upon approaching him. It had not only been the wide set of her eyes but the way she had seemed like a spooked deer, ready to bolt at a moment's notice. She had looked frighteningly pale, staring at him with wide unblinking eyes, as though at any moment he might seize and devour her.

Keir sighed. In his experience, those afraid of life were just as afraid of living. Was she running away from something? Or running toward something?

He rather doubted it was the latter.

In truth, Grandma Edie had told him very little, as the woman was wont to do. She liked to hold all the strings in her hands, sharing only what she deemed necessary with those around her.

Keir chuckled. In the short time he had known her, he had come to admire her greatly. Although not related by blood, the Dowager Lady Whickerton felt like family. She had once been his own grandmother's dearest friend, and although the two families had made their homes far apart from one another—one in London and the other in the Scottish Highlands—their hearts had always remained close. And then, roughly half a year ago, Grandma Edie had asked for him, asked for his help in aiding a friend.

And Keir had complied, for he, too, had been in need of something.

A distraction.

An adventure.

Yet never in his wildest dreams could he have seen *this* coming. Aye, the Dowager Lady Whickerton had always been rather daring—according to his own grandmother—and equally meddlesome. Of course, she had not come out directly with her plan. It had been some time before Keir had realized that he was meant to *kidnap* someone. Of course, following that revelation, he had asked questions...to which he had only received rather vague answers.

He grinned. Truly, Grandma Edie had perfected the art of speaking without revealing a thing.

Sighing, Keir clicked his tongue, and the gelding picked up his pace. The carriage rumbled along across the frozen snow-covered ground, and once again, Keir wondered how his passenger was faring. Were her eyes still as wide as before? Or had she even fallen asleep? Somehow, Keir could not imagine it to be so. Generally, he was an excellent judge of character, and the young lady struck him as someone who was far from used to putting even a toe out of line. Why then was she here tonight? What had prompted her to leave the safety of her home and venture out into the unknown?

According to Grandma Edie, she was to be married soon, and to an old man, no less. Indeed, the practices of the *ton* seemed odd to him. However, they did not to everyone else. Very few people married for love. Most sought a match based on other reasons. What then had made a difference for this young woman? What had made her break with tradition?

The scent of snow lingered upon the air, and Keir wondered how soon the sky would open up again, blanketing the world anew. This early in the year, days were still short and sunrise hours away. He squinted into the darkness, grateful for the sliver of moon that barely illuminated the ground in front of them. Yet in the distance, a large shadow loomed upon the horizon, and he knew they were drawing closer to their destination.

The woods.

After all, where did one hide a well-bred young lady during a feigned abduction? Keir chuckled. Apparently, in the woods. Not that he had any experience in such matters. He doubted anyone truly did. With the exception of Grandma Edie, perhaps. He would not put anything past that woman.

And he meant that as a compliment.

Without any delays, they were making good time, and Keir hoped that everyone else involved in this rather unusual plan had been equally successful. As they drew closer to the darkened shape of the woods, Keir spotted his two horses tied to a branch. He hoped they had not been left there too long ago, considering the cold that night. *The poor beasts!*

Flicking the reins, Keir directed the black gelding to a hidden spot in a small grove and then jumped to the ground. He quickly brushed down the snorting creature and then wrapped a thick blanket around him to keep him warm until someone else would come and take the carriage back to London. After all, it must not be found here!

As he turned, Keir's gaze fell on the young woman, peeking tentatively out of the open carriage door. She seemed to contemplate stepping down but could not quite work up the nerve. The look upon her face spoke of confusion as her eyes swept their surroundings. *Aye, she does look familiar!*

"Step down, lass," Keir said to her, gesturing toward the two horses that would see them safely away. "We mustna linger here too long."

Instead of doing as he had asked, the young woman suddenly stared at him with wide, unblinking eyes. Her hand remained upon the door handle as though frozen, her body crouched on the carriage seat.

Keir paused. "Are ye all right?" He stepped closer, then on impulse spun around, thinking she had spotted someone beyond his shoulder. Swiftly, he drew the dagger at his belt, which had thus far been hidden beneath the folds of his large overcoat.

Fortunately, his gaze found no one.

Slowly, Keir's pulse slowed, and he resheathed his dagger. Then he turned back to the young woman, who was still staring at him as though he was some kind of wood sprite risen from the ground beneath his feet. "Are ye all right, lass?" Keir asked yet again, approaching her slowly.

Still seated upon the cushioned seat inside the carriage, her hand resting upon the half-open door, the young woman swallowed hard. Despite the shadow that fell over her face from the hood she had drawn low, she looked almost frighteningly pale, as though she might faint at any moment.

Keir stilled his feet, regarding her curiously. "There is no reason to fear me," he told her calmly, then he removed the hat from his head, hoping that seeing his face might somehow reassure her.

Unfortunately, the opposite was the case. Her eyes widened even more, and he could see a shudder go through her as her gaze swept over him. Keir knew he looked different from the English gentlemen she was no doubt used to. After all, he had always kept his hair rather long, down to his shoulders, sometimes tied in the back, sometimes loose. A few strands upon his temples were braided and pulled back, keeping hair out of his face.

Those little braids had been his sister's doing, and now that she was gone, Keir could not seem to bring himself to wear his hair in any other fashion.

Caught off guard by the thought of Yvaine, Keir cleared his throat, firmly pushing the memories away. "I assure ye, ye have nothing to fear from me. I give ye my word." He waited for a moment, for his words to sink in, and then he stepped closer, his hand reaching toward the door.

Straightening in her seat, the young woman let her hand fall from where it rested upon the door handle. She watched him carefully, warily; however, her eyes were no longer the size of plates.

Keir held out his hand to her. "Come, lass. We have to go."

Heaving a deep sigh, she inched forward, gathering up her skirts before alighting from the carriage. She clasped the door frame as well as the door to steady herself, ignoring his proffered hand.

Keir chuckled. "Let me ready the horses, and we'll be off." He nodded past her shoulder toward the two mounts, one a chestnut-colored mare and the other a bay gelding, their coats perfectly suited to the colors of the woods.

The moment Keir made to stride toward them, the young woman suddenly staggered backwards and all but fell into his arms. He could not see her face but heard the sharp intake of breath as she stared toward the two mounts, her hands clasped together tightly. Faint sounds drifted from her lips that sounded like, "No! No! No! No!"

The young lady was a delicate thing, slender, her limbs trembling, her heart beating fast against his own as Keir held her, her back to his chest, her gaze still directed at the horses. "They're quite friendly, I assure ye. Ye needna worry." Frowning, he tried to look down into her face but only caught a glimpse of her profile in the near darkness.

Swallowing hard, audibly, she shook her head, then tried to retreat, only now realizing that she all but stood in his embrace, his hands upon her arms, holding her upright. Instantly, she spun around, freeing herself, her eyes once again as round as plates. She swayed upon her feet and flailed her arms until Keir reached out to steady her.

The moment she regained her balance, though, he released her, taking a step back. He held up his hands in appeasement but locked his gaze with hers. "Do ye not know how to ride?" he asked carefully, wondering how the dowager countess could have missed this. After all, the lady was usually well-informed.

The young lady shook her head; however, the gesture did not seem to be an answer to his question but rather a general refusal to approach the horses.

Keir exhaled a slow breath, knowing there was no other way. "We canna take the carriage," he tried to reason with her. "To ensure that we're not followed, we need to go off-road."

For a moment, the young lady closed her eyes, a look of resignation coming to her face. She looked desperately forlorn, as though all strength had suddenly deserted her.

"What's yer name, lass?" Keir asked gently.

Her eyes opened, and for a moment, she seemed to eye him cautiously, doubtfully. Her gaze swept him from head to toe, no doubt taking in his rather rugged appearance, heavy boots and coat, a dagger and pistol upon his belt, his hair unfashionably long. Keir mused that he quite possibly looked like a true highwayman and chuckled.

Instantly, her eyes grew round again, and she began backing away.

What a frightened little deer! Keir thought, watching her retreat… which—clearly unbeknownst to her—carried her closer and closer to the horses.

With the cloak drawn tightly around her, the young woman continued to move backward, her gaze fixed upon him, as though expecting an imminent attack.

"Listen," Keir said carefully, before glancing up and down the road, "ye need to make a choice." He paused, holding her gaze as best as he could in the dark. "Either we continue on on horseback," his gaze drifted past her shoulder to the horses, "or I'll take ye back to London in the carriage." His brows rose meaningfully.

Her jaw began to tremble as her gaze was drawn to the road, the road back to London. Then she looked back at him, clearly torn, her eyes now glittering in the faint moonlight, as though tears clung to her lashes. Her chest rose and fell quickly, and Keir sensed she was close to breaking down. If one more thing were to—

Her booted foot stepped on a twig. It snapped in half, and the sound all but shattered the stillness of the night. Instantly, the mare tossed her head and neighed her disapproval.

As the young lady spun around in terror, Keir lunged forward. He saw her clasped hands pressed to her chest as she inhaled a shocked breath. Then her eyes rolled backwards, and her knees gave in.

The moment she sank to the ground, Keir caught her in his arms, gently easing her down to the forest floor. Her hood fell back, revealing her soft features, finally relaxed as her eyes lay closed. Her fair tresses had been braided down her back, giving her a stern expression. Only a few wisps of hair seemed to refuse obedience, curling along her temples in determined resistance.

Keir smiled. "What is it ye fear so, little wisp?" he murmured, pulling the cloak tighter around her against the cold. Then he looked up, his gaze moving from the carriage to the two waiting horses. "There's nothing for it." He pushed to his feet and strode over, removing the heavy blankets from both animals and storing them inside the carriage. Then he untied both their reins and led them over to where the young lady lay upon the ground.

Kneeling down beside her, Keir hoisted her up into his arms. "Ye weigh almost nothing, little wisp," he murmured, shifting her easily as he approached the bay gelding. "'Tis almost as though ye're not truly here." Indeed, she had not spoken a word to him, her face continually covered by the large hood, her body wrapped in a dark cloak. It was only too easy to believe her an apparition, someone he had merely imagined, someone who had never truly been here.

As Keir stepped onto a conveniently located tree stump and then pulled himself—and her!—up and into the saddle, her soft weight and gentle warmth made him wonder who she was. Aye, she was real, a woman of flesh and blood. She had had a life. One that had taught her to be wary, if not downright afraid. And yet courage still beat in her heart, or she would not be here.

In this moment.

With him.

Settling her in front of him, her head resting against his shoulder, Keir urged the gelding onward, away from the road and into the forest.

A click of his tongue made the mare follow. "I'll see ye safe, little wisp," he murmured as he looked down into the young woman's face. "I promise ye."

The desire to protect her swelled in Keir's chest, and he held her closer, wondering why she had no one else to do this for her. Truly, it seemed it had been her own family, her parents, who had forced her to make this impossible choice. A choice that had made her run from her own home in the middle of the night.

As the gelding picked his way deeper into the forest, Keir wondered what awaited him in the coming days. How soon could this situation be resolved? How long was this *abduction* going to take? Of course, he could not say. Perhaps a sennight? Surely not a fortnight? After all, how long did it take to pay a ransom?

A soft sigh drifted from the young woman's lips, and she seemed to huddle closer, seeking his warmth. Yet her eyes remained closed, her mind still oblivious to where she was and where they were going.

Keir frowned, wondering what she would say and how she would react when she came to, finding herself not only in his arms but also upon the back of a horse. Clearly, that thought alone terrified her.

As did many others.

"Why did ye not tell me the lass was afraid of horses?" Keir thought out loud, remembering the moment the dowager countess had explained in great detail all the individual steps of this night. "Surely, ye must've known." He chuckled, wondering if the lady had had an ulterior motive. However, he could not think of a single reason to keep this information from him.

Breathing in deeply of the night air, Keir smiled down at the young woman in his arms. "Well, this ought to be interesting."

Chapter Three

IN THE HANDS OF HER KIDNAPPER

The first thing Sarah became aware of was the soft swaying from side to side, and for one far-away, distracted moment, she wondered if she was perhaps on a ship or boat of some kind. However, why would she be on a boat? No, the last thing she remembered was—

Her eyes flew open, and she jerked upright, panic clawing at her heart as she felt her feet dangling in the air. For a terrifying moment, Sarah felt nothing to hold on to, nothing to keep her steady. There was only darkness around her, interspersed by faint shimmers of light here and there, but nothing tangible.

And then suddenly arms came around her. Out of the dark. Out of nowhere. They wrapped her in a tight embrace, pulling her back against something warm.

For a moment, Sarah tried to resist, but anything was better than this sense of falling, of spinning, of having no control. It reminded her too much of—

Sarah pinched her eyes shut, willing away the memories, the pain, the fear. She felt her fingers curl into something soft, a thick fabric, a bit coarse but warm and sturdy. Her mind was still spinning, and yet it picked up whispered words nearby. She could not make them out, could not understand them, but they sounded soothing, and she felt herself relax.

"Aye, that's better," a deep, rumbling voice said only inches from her ear. "Take a deep breath, little wisp. All will be well."

Sarah froze the moment her addled mind picked up words she could make sense of, words that held meaning. She blinked her eyes, tension holding her body almost rigid. And then slowly, she lifted her head.

In the dark, Sarah could barely see anything at first. Her eyes blinked once, then twice, before the outline of another person took form right in front of her.

Below a wide-brimmed hat, she found a face she had only glimpsed before. It was angular with a strong jaw and eyes as dark and compelling as the dead of night. Although dark hair framed his face, no beard hid its lower half. Still, the man was not clean-shaven.

My kidnapper! Her mind supplied helpfully. Or rather unhelpfully, for the mere thought sent her into another panic.

'See, what you did?' Her mother's voice chimed in her head. 'This is the kind of man we were protecting you from.'

Pushing hard against her kidnapper's chest, Sarah tried to squirm away, desperate for more distance between them. She dimly recalled seeing him seated atop the unmarked carriage down the street from her parents' rented townhouse. She remembered thinking, what kind of man would volunteer to pose as a kidnapper? Was he truly a criminal? Someone with no morals whatsoever? And why was he holding her?

"Ye might want to cease yer struggles, little wisp," he said in that deep, rumbling voice of his, his words heavily accented, "or ye'll fall off the horse."

At his words, Sarah instantly stilled. *Horse?*

Her heart seemed to pause in her chest as she swept her gaze sideways, her eyes slightly squinted to see through the dark. And then she spotted the ground far below to the right and left of a horse's neck. The creature's ears flicked from side to side, and she could see a plume of its breath as it tossed its head and snorted.

Shock and disbelief surged through Sarah, and as though to taunt her, her body instantly went slack. It was as though her muscles no longer knew what to do. She felt herself tilt and slide; the ground coming closer and closer, and she found herself unable to prevent it. She knew she would fall. She knew the pain that awaited her; she knew—

Again, strong arms wrapped around her, pulling her back, back into a tight embrace, preventing her fall and keeping her upright. Sarah knew she ought to resist, and yet she still did not possess the power to move. She could not prevent her kidnapper from gathering her against his chest, one arm wrapped around her back while the other urged her head against his shoulder. "Hush, little wisp. All will be well," he murmured in her ear, his left hand brushing up and down her arm in a soothing gesture.

Sarah felt all but paralyzed, her mind overwhelmed and her body unable to function. She was atop a horse! A horse! And on top of that, she was settled in the arms of a stranger! A kidnapper! A criminal!

Oh, how had things gone so horribly wrong? She should never have agreed to this. It had been a ludicrous idea to begin with, and she should have rejected it right away. Why had she not? Had she truly believed this would prove the solution to her troubles? *Oh, what a fool I am!*

Moments passed before Sarah realized that her body no longer felt tense and rigid. In fact, to her utter shame, she lay rather comfortably in the stranger's arms. Her breath had evened, and she could once more hear him whispering soft words to her, words in a language she could not understand. His hand still traveled up and down her arm before it suddenly stilled and moved higher.

Sarah held her breath as she watched him reaching for her, the tips of his fingers so close to her cheek that she could almost feel him. Only he did not touch her face, but instead he pulled a stray curl away that had gotten caught in her lashes. He ran it through his fingers, and she could hear an amused chuckle drift from his lips before he gently tugged it back into her hood.

Little wisp.

Was that not what he had called her? Sarah wondered as she tried to work up the courage to meet his eyes. Why had he called her that?

She did not know, and yet all of a sudden those two words continued to echo through her head.

"Ye needna be afraid of me, little wisp," he spoke then. "I promise I shallna bite ye." Humor swung in his voice, and without thinking, Sarah lifted her gaze to see if he was smiling.

The moment their eyes locked, Sarah felt her insides do something utterly unexpected. She knew not how to explain it; her reaction to the man made all her years of conversation training fail her. She felt utterly incapable of stringing even two words together, her mind too over-whelmed and her body too weak. Obviously, she ought to insist he set her down, but no words would fall from her lips. All she did was lie there, in his arms, staring up into his eyes.

Although his eyes remained shrouded in darkness, the corners of his mouth once more twitched in amusement, offsetting his frighten-ingly dangerous presence. With sudden clarity, Sarah remembered the swiftness with which he had spun around and drawn the dagger at his belt. The sight had frightened her nearly witless, making her realize she was far away from home, all alone, in the middle of the night, in the company of a very dangerous man.

"Ye can speak, can ye not?" her kidnapper suddenly asked, a slight frown drawing down his brows as his gaze swept over her face.

Sarah swallowed. She felt her lips part and her mind form words, and yet none flew off her tongue. The words remained stuck in her throat, no sound drifting out into the snowy night air.

Her kidnapper waited patiently, that hint of amusement still upon his face as the right corner of his mouth twitched. "One word?" he asked teasingly, as though they had sat down to negotiate the points of an agreement.

Sarah's pulse beat wildly in her veins. She could even hear it in her ears, like a hammer pounding nails. She wanted to speak, had every intention of saying *something* but—

A wicked spark suddenly lit up her kidnapper's face. "Perhaps a kiss will do the trick." Then he dipped his head—but only a fraction.

Still, Sarah flinched, and all but felt her jaw drop and her eyes widen in shock. Her hands came up defensively as she once again pushed away from him.

In response, her kidnapper feigned a look of dismay, his embrace still not allowing her to escape...or fall. "Now, I'm hurt, little wisp. No lass has ever reacted to the offer of a kiss quite like that."

Involuntarily, Sarah's gaze drifted to his lips and her mind conjured the image of a kiss.

"That's more like it," her kidnapper remarked with a chuckle.

Belatedly, Sarah realized that her gaze was locked upon his mouth, and she blushed profusely. *Oh, how humiliating!* Never in her life had Sarah felt quite so...so...

Oh, she had never felt quite at ease in a ballroom. Or in the company of a gentleman. Perhaps it had been her parents' pressuring her into securing a good match. Or perhaps it had been *her* all along. Sarah had always tried her utmost to smile at and converse with potential suitors, but it had never come easy to her. From the fact that, in all her years, she had never received even a single honest marriage proposal, Sarah knew that her ability to attract the opposite sex fell far short of that of other young ladies. Thus, the only attention any *gentleman* had ever paid her had been unwanted.

Sarah shuddered at the memory of Lord Blackmore's last visit to their house. It had been that night that had made her realize she could not be his wife, that she had to accept whatever risk necessary in order to escape such a fate.

"Are ye all right?" her kidnapper asked, his tone surprisingly gentle. His gaze lingered upon her face, as though trying to guess her thoughts. Then he exhaled slowly, and his hold on her lessened, allowing a little more distance between them. "Would ye rather ride the mare?"

The mere mention of riding on a horse sent a fresh jolt of panic through Sarah, and her hands instinctively reached for the man holding her. Her hands dug into his coat, her fingers curling around the sturdy fabric, as her gaze flew sideways, for the first time taking note of the second horse following close by.

"Hush, little wisp," her kidnapper murmured as his hands settled upon her shoulders. "Look at me."

Sarah blinked, then focused her gaze upon his. Her breathing came fast, and for a moment, she feared she would pass out again.

"In and out. Slowly. Aye, just like that."

Bit by bit, Sarah's vision cleared. She could feel her breathing even, grateful for the steadying hands upon her shoulders. Oh, how she hated this loss of control! This inability to calm herself! With time, she had learned to accept the sight of a horse or even riding in a carriage—then, at least, she did not see the horse, her gaze stubbornly focused out the window. Still, riding on horseback was an entirely different matter!

And yet...

Feeling like an absolute dimwit, Sarah suddenly all but jumped into her kidnapper's arms when she remembered that she was *already* seated atop a horse!

Amusement rumbled in his throat, and she felt his arms come around her, his hands brushing up and down her back. "Dunna worry, little wisp. I dunna mind holding ye a bit longer."

Momentarily distracted by the man's odd insistence on calling her *little wisp*, Sarah pulled back and looked up into his eyes. Her lips parted and...yes, she meant to ask why he did so. She truly and honestly did.

Only once again, no words materialized. She often found them absent in challenging moments, and this, right here, was definitely a challenging moment.

At least, for Sarah.

"We should continue on," her kidnapper murmured, his dark eyes thoughtful as he gazed down at her. "All right?"

Swallowing, Sarah nodded.

His hands once more settled upon her shoulders, urging her to turn until she sat with her back against his chest. His arms came around her, holding the reins, before he clicked his tongue, and they were off again.

At the soft swaying from side to side, Sarah pinched her eyes closed. Her heartbeat instantly accelerated, and she began to feel dizzy.

"Slowly, little wisp," her kidnapper murmured beside her ear, his warm breath tickling her skin. "In and out."

With her hands clutching the horse's mane, Sarah concentrated on her breathing, tried her best to remain calm. Only—

"The mare's name is Autumn," her kidnapper explained rather unexpectedly. "'Tis a fitting name. Ye'll see as soon as the sun rises. Her coat reminds me of the time the first leaves fall at the end of summer." His voice drifted on the air like a leaf, gentle and weightless like a snowflake, that Sarah felt carried along. "She is a sweet one, very even-tempered, but she'll bite ye if ye dunna treat her with respect." Pride rang in his voice, and once again Sarah wondered about the man seated behind her. "Aye, trust isna a thing easily come by. It must be earned, and before she'll trust ye, ye'll have to prove to her that ye mean her no harm, that she's safe with ye. Until that moment, she will eye ye warily and act skittish around ye, never quite sure what to expect."

Out of the corner of her eye, Sarah spotted the vague outline of the mare, of Autumn. She listened to her kidnapper's words and felt strangely affected by them. Indeed, somehow it almost felt as though he spoke not of the horse but of her. Did she not feel like that as well? Had she not also learned to be wary, to not place her trust in another easily? A part of Sarah still wished she had never learned that lesson. Unfortunately, it had been necessary. The world was not a safe place, and people, in general, could not be trusted. She knew that by now. Yes, she was safer knowing it. And yet, a part of her wished she could have simply continued on believing that all people were good, just as she had as a child.

"Scout here is different," the man behind her continued on, his voice even and soothing as before, and Sarah got the distinct feeling that he was speaking for her benefit alone, not to convey information but to set her at ease. "He is always eager for adventure and rarely shies away from anything." He chuckled, then reached past her to pat the horse's neck. "Even if it gets him in trouble sometimes. He likes to run and feel the sun on his back, never quite happy in the stable as he always longs for fresh air and the far horizon."

Sarah tried to imagine such a day of freedom and endlessness. In her mind, she saw Scout racing across the fields, chasing the horizon. She all but felt his heart beat with eagerness, his legs moving with such strength that he flew through the air. She felt his joy and his contentedness, and for one brief moment, Sarah wished she could be like that as well.

The man behind her exhaled a slow breath. "They're not so different from us," he murmured, and this time Sarah knew he was speaking to her. "They, too, have dreams and fears. Like people, they want to be seen for who they are, not one of many."

For the first time that night, Sarah truly did not know what to think. Deep down, she realized that the stranger understood her fears and was doing his utmost to alleviate them. He was trying to help in a way that no one ever had before. Was that possible? Or was she simply imagining this? Perhaps she was trying to see something in him to put herself at ease, to not fear him anymore. After all, if he was a criminal with no morals and no decency, what would that mean for her?

Of course, Sarah trusted Grandma Edie's judgment. She trusted the Dowager Lady Whickerton would never put her in harm's way. That was the reason why Sarah had agreed to this outrageous plan, and yet sometimes plans did go wrong, did they not?

For a long time, they continued on through the forest, and Sarah felt her mind linger upon her kidnapper's words. Her gaze drifted from the horse she sat upon to the one following close behind, and she tried to imagine their hearts and souls. She tried to see them as they were, the way he had suggested. It kept her calm, kept her panic at bay. No longer were her thoughts overwhelming, threatening to drown her, but instead they felt manageable if she focused her mind, concentrated on breathing evenly and kept her thoughts distracted.

Still, Sarah was very much aware of the large man seated behind her. Even though she could not see him or, at least, see more than the lower half of his arms and his hands as they held the reins, she sensed his presence. He, too, had fallen into silence, and yet the sound of his voice continued to echo through her head. At first, she tried to maintain a certain distance between them and tried to sit upright, her hands clasping the horse's mane. Still, fatigue eventually got to her, and she slowly sank back until she was once again cradled in his arms, the back of her head resting against his shoulder. Every once in a while, her eyes would close, and time would slip from her grasp.

Whenever she woke, that first moment of consciousness once

again brought on panic. However, it passed quickly as she recalled what had happened that night and where she was. It was no longer fear she felt but rather unease and uncertainty, concern, certainly, and discomfort. Sarah preferred those to that numbing sense of terror she knew so well. Still, questions about her kidnapper continued to circle through her mind, and she wished she had something else to focus her thoughts on.

Eventually, the sun rose, light filtering through the trees surrounding them, sheltering them. At first, it was no more than a soft glow, warm and comforting as it reached through the frozen canopy above. Then it grew in brightness until day had truly arrived, and Sarah could see Autumn's beautiful coat with her own eyes. Indeed, her kidnapper had spoken true, the horse's color did remind Sarah of the first leaves of autumn.

"We should stop here," the stranger said as they reached the edge of the forest, and her eyes fell upon a small stream. "We'll have a bite to eat and then move on."

Sarah was not sure what to say or if she would even be able to say anything. Fortunately, it seemed a reply from her was not necessary, not expected.

Pulling Scout to a halt, her kidnapper swung himself out of the saddle, his hands grasping her arms as he did so, keeping her upright. And then his feet were on the ground and he was looking up at her, one hand still upon her arm as he held the other one out to her. "Trust me, little wisp," he said with that teasing note in his voice that was slowly starting to sound familiar to Sarah's ears. "I promise I shall not let ye fall."

Swallowing hard, Sarah forced her head sideways, willed her eyes not to drop to the ground but to meet his instead. They were a startling blue, deeply compelling and yet filled with such mirth that Sarah almost smiled. Indeed, her heart seemed to respond to him in ways she had not expected. After all, he was a criminal, was he not? How was it possible that he set her at ease so easily? Was she such an awful judge of character? Yes, perhaps she was simply misreading him. Never had she been able to tell what people were thinking. Never had she been able to see beyond their smiles and uncover what truly lay in their hearts.

Sarah sighed and dropped her gaze, reminding herself to be more careful, reminding herself not to trust an easy smile.

"I shall have to earn yer trust then," the man suddenly said, as though reading her thoughts.

Sarah's head snapped up, and she stared at him when he suddenly moved forward, his hands grasping her waist and then lifting her out of the saddle. For one terrifying moment, Sarah felt reminded of when she had woken the night before, finding herself on top of a horse, her feet dangling in the air. And then, solid ground was beneath her feet, and she exhaled the breath she had been holding.

However, before she could gather her wits again, the man grasped her chin between two fingers, tilting it upward until their eyes met once more. He simply looked at her then, no words falling from his lips as they stood in silence.

Out of nowhere, something familiar descended upon Sarah's mind, as though she had found herself in precisely this moment before. How could that be? Of course, it could not. She had never met this man in her life. How could she have? After all, she had never before ventured away from upper society, and he certainly had never set foot into it. Perhaps it was simply her mind trying to reassure her. Yes, that had to be it.

"Are ye hungry, lass?" her kidnapper asked when he finally released her chin and turned away toward Scout's saddle bags. "Though I'm afraid I canna offer ye any more than a piece of bread and a chunk of cheese." He glanced at her, still rummaging through the bag. "We canna stay for long, but ye should try and move yer legs a wee bit." He put a crust of bread and a piece of cheese into her hands and then nodded toward the stream. "Only a few minutes."

Sarah nodded obediently, then turned and walked toward the stream. Her legs instantly protested, her back aching, as she set one foot in front of the other. Gritting her teeth against the pain that shot up and down her body, Sarah forced herself to move forward, to continue on. She did feel hungry, and yet the thought of eating almost turned her stomach. Still, she nibbled a little upon the crust of bread, realizing that she was truly hungry once the food found its way into her stomach. Then, she ate with more vigor, finishing both bread and cheese before she even reached the stream.

There, at the snowy riverbank, she knelt down and washed her hands in the icy waters, splashing some on her face. It felt invigorating but freezing nonetheless. Sitting back, she looked out across the land, seeing a wide clearing bordered by forests on all sides. She could not spot a road anywhere nor another soul nearby.

Sarah paused. Was he still here? Indeed, for a moment, she truly felt like the last person on this earth. As far as the eye could see, there was no one there, no sign of human life, only snow and trees and the wind swaying the branches gently. The sun shone so brightly that the cold air felt like it did not quite belong. Everything Sarah's eyes touched upon whispered of warmth. Only the bare trees, leafless in the middle of winter, betrayed the season.

A shadow fell over Sarah, and she spun around, her heart hammering in her chest. It was her kidnapper standing behind her, the sun illuminating him in a way that took her breath away. More than anything, Sarah wanted to know who he was and how he came to be here, but once again her thoughts would not make it past her lips. Would she ever be able to speak to him?

She doubted it very much.

"We need to leave, lass," he said, holding out his hand to her.

Sarah nodded, her eyes drifting to his outstretched hand. It was no more than a mere offer, but it made her feel uneasy. So instead of accepting it, she pushed to her feet on her own, unable to meet his eyes. She wondered if he would say anything as she made her way back toward the horses. Yet he did not. He simply followed her, not saying a word.

And then, Sarah stood in front of Scout and Autumn, her gaze shifting back and forth between the two horses. Indeed, she stood closer to a horse than she had in a long time, but her feet would not take another step. She saw Autumn's chestnut coat and Scout's bay color, and she saw they were not simply *horses*, but souls as unique as her own. Only the memories still lingered, tightening her heart and squeezing the air from her lungs.

All of a sudden, the stranger stood behind her. She could feel his warmth nearby, so close. She could sense him looking down at her over her shoulder, his eyes tracing the lines of her face. What was he thinking? Sarah wondered. Was he laughing about her on the inside? Was he shaking his head about her, about her foolishness, her silly fears? Or was he annoyed with her?

Sarah knew she was stuck. Yes, she needed to get on one of the horses because they needed to continue their journey. She could not stay here. She would no doubt freeze to death once night fell. Someone might come upon her here. Yes, she definitely needed to get onto one of the horses. But which one? Was she to ride Autumn all by herself? Or get back up onto Scout with the man seated behind her? Neither option seemed appealing. In fact, both options were terrifying.

Riding Autumn, she would, at least, be free of the man's presence, the feel of his touch. It still made her uneasy, in part because...it did not. Yet, alone on Autumn, she would truly be...alone. If she chose Scout, at least, she would have her kidnapper's reassuring presence. However—

Stepping around her, the man swiftly pulled himself into Scout's saddle. Then he turned toward her, his blue eyes meeting hers, and held out his hand to her. "Come, lass. We need to be off."

Somewhere in the back of her head, Sarah wondered why he was no longer calling her *little wisp*. She did not know why but somehow it felt like a loss to her. In any case, these thoughts served, at least, as a minor distraction, for without thinking, Sarah took a step forward, held out her hand and then grasped his.

In her mind, she saw her mother cross her arms and shake her head at her. 'Are you truly forsaking everything you were raised to be?'

Chapter Four

A CABIN IN THE WOODS

Seating the young woman in front of him once more, Keir turned Scout north. Once again, she sat up straight as a rod, careful not to allow them to touch, flinching every time his arm brushed against hers. He chuckled at her efforts. "It will be another few hours until we reach our destination," he informed her. "There's nothing wrong with being comfortable, little wisp."

For a second, she stilled, as though something he had said had caught her by surprise. Then, her shoulders began to slump a little, as though she wanted to lean back against him, to accept his offer, but did not quite dare, did not quite know how to go about it.

Sensing her exhaustion, Keir reached out and his hand settled upon her shoulder, urging her back until her back once more rested against his chest. Her head came to lean against his shoulder, and for a moment, she seemed to close her eyes, exhaling slowly, her body still rigid. He could tell that she was fighting to relax the tight grip upon her muscles.

"I've always enjoyed spending time outdoors," Keir murmured, his lips close enough to her ear that there was no need for volume. "The feel of the sun's warmth. The soft touch of a summer's breeze. The powerful push of a raging storm." Keir smiled at the many wonderful memories he had gathered throughout his life. "Out here, 'tis quiet and peaceful. There are sounds, but they are different from people's voices. The soft trilling of a bird or chirping of a cricket. I enjoy being alone out here, and yet it doesna feel lonely or empty. Softness and harshness are at a unique balance here. One can truly explore one's own soul and character, push one's own body to its limits and see what one is made of."

As Keir had hoped, the young woman's body slowly relaxed as she listened to his words. A deep sigh drifted from her lips as she lifted her head off his shoulder, and her eyes took in their surroundings. Keir guessed she had never spent much time outside in nature. She had never known the tranquility that could be found here. Perhaps if she had, she would not be so lost right now. And lost she was.

Anyone could see that.

Never in his life had Keir met someone who knew so very little about who she truly was. Was she even aware of that fact? He wondered.

Keir could tell that his gelding was tiring. Yet the mare was not strong enough to carry them both, and so he allowed Scout to choose his own pace, giving him free rein.

After crossing the clearing, they returned into the forest. The familiar sounds of winter were everywhere, quieter than those of summer, but there, nonetheless. Keir spotted a few tracks now and then, but only those of animals and never once did he see evidence of a human presence.

That is reassuring!

As the sun rose high in the sky, they made their way onward, crossing another small stream before heading deeper into the thicket of the forest. Keir knew that few people ever ventured here. Yes, the occasional hunting party crossed through this area. However, never in winter. He had scoured the countryside for weeks to find the perfect spot for this very purpose. He had looked at many hideouts in this area, and the one that was slowly coming into view through the trees was the only one that served their purpose.

Amidst the trees stood a small house, a cabin, abandoned years before, with a shed on one side and a small grown-over vegetable patch on the other. A green clearing lay beyond it, fenced in for the horses or livestock that had once been here. Keir had traveled here several times throughout the last half year, making repairs and setting everything to rights. The roof had leaked in several places, and the door had been all but ripped off its hinges. Two of the windows had been broken and needed replacing, and the shed had been half destroyed when a tree had crashed down upon it during a storm. Also, some of the boards on the fence had needed replacing to ensure that neither Scout nor Autumn would venture off.

Now, however, everything was as it should be. A comfortable, small house with simple furnishings and a well-stocked pantry. Aye, all had been prepared, and Keir hoped that the young woman would finally find some peace here. No one could be this tense for such a prolonged time and not suffer from it.

"We're almost there," Keir told her, jolting her awake. "I'm sorry," he murmured, then pointed ahead through the trees. "Over there."

Her eyes followed his outstretched hand, and she breathed in deeply, holding it in for a heartbeat or two before exhaling slowly. Keir wished he knew what she was thinking, but from everything he knew about her—or ladies like her—he suspected that, unlike him, she would not see the snug comfort of the little house but rather its lack of luxury.

At least, they would not be here for very long.

Upon reaching the front yard, Keir slid out of the saddle, once again careful to steady the young woman before he helped her down to the ground. Her hands held on tightly to his arms, her fingers curled into the fabric of his coat, as she closed her eyes briefly, no doubt fighting a spell of dizziness, for she swayed upon her feet. "Go on ahead and inside, lass," Keir said to her when she finally opened her eyes, her balance restored. "I'll see to the horses." He released her, and she all but pushed away from him, something dark and fearful in her gaze once more.

Indeed, she seemed afraid of nearly everything. A bird trilled somewhere far off, and she flinched. Autumn tossed her head and snorted, and she flinched. At the same time, she looked utterly exhausted, not just her body but her mind as well. Keir could not help but wonder what she had been through.

Swallowing hard, the young woman finally nodded. Then she turned away, her eyes sweeping over the small house. Staring at it, she hesitated for a long moment but then took a step toward it.

Keir did not wish to linger, to watch her, thinking it might increase her unease. And so, he reached for the horses' reins and led them into the shed. There, he brushed them down, removing their bridles and saddles, before ensuring they—as well as the goat—had water and oats. Then he moved into the side room that served as a chicken pen, a small opening at the back allowing the birds to venture outside into a closed space, safe from predators. He poured them some grain and collected a few eggs in return.

Then he turned back toward the house.

Stepping inside, Keir shrugged out of his coat and hung it up on a peg just inside the door. His gaze moved toward the narrow staircase leading upstairs and then to the other side down the hallway toward the small parlor. Faint sounds drifted to his ears, and he frowned. Still, deep down he knew precisely what he was hearing.

The young woman was crying.

Never having been one to run from an uncomfortable situation, Keir left the eggs on the table in the kitchen before gathering some firewood from the corner by the back door and then headed into the parlor. The moment he stepped across the threshold, the young woman's head snapped up and she frantically tried to wipe the tears from her eyes.

The air in the house was cold, and his charge was huddled in a simple armchair by the fireplace, a cloak wrapped tightly around herself. Her face looked red and tear-streaked, and she kept her head bowed, unwilling to meet his eyes.

Keir strode over to the fireplace, set down the logs and gathered some kindling around them. "It'll be warm soon," he told her over his shoulder as he struck the flame and lit the dry tinder. "There are two bedrooms upstairs and a kitchen in the back." He blew on the flame, watching it spring to life. "Are ye hungry, lass?"

As expected, he received no answer. Only the sound of soft sniffles and trembling breaths drifted to his ears. Once the fire was lit, Keir rose to his feet and approached her.

With her head bowed, she sat there like a picture of misery, her hands in her lap, picking apart a tear-stained handkerchief. Yet the moment she sensed his approach, her hands clasped together until the tendons stood out white. Again, she refused to lift her head.

Kneeling down in front of her, Keir tried to look up at her face. He did not want her to be afraid. Least of all of him. "Ye have nothing to fear from me, lass," he told her for what felt like the hundredth time. When she still refused to look at him, he reached out and placed his right hand upon hers.

That, at least, elicited a response. Her eyes flew up, round as plates, and stared into his. Her breath came fast, and he could sense her impulse to retrieve her hands, to pull them out from underneath his.

"I'm here to protect ye," Keir told her, giving her hands a gentle squeeze before removing his own and giving her space. "I have given my word to see ye safe, and I've never once broken a promise given." Her wide blue eyes looked into his, tears clinging to her lashes, as she listened. "Will ye tell me your name? I'm Keir."

Keir dimly recalled Grandma Edie's insistence he not reveal his identity to the young woman. Although she was a family friend, Grandma Edie had shared that she was not one who knew how to keep secrets because she wore all her emotions on her face. It was an assessment that Keir could already agree with based on their limited acquaintance. Of course, he had not truly kidnapped her. Yet should any details of their plan ever become known, it would stir up trouble for him. Nevertheless, Keir doubted that simply giving her his first name could do any harm.

The ghost of a smile flitted across the young woman's face, and she once more dabbed her handkerchief to her eyes, an apologetic expression upon her face.

Returning her smile, Keir repeated, "Will ye tell me your name as well?"

Inhaling a deep breath, the young woman nodded ever so slightly. Her lips parted, and a soft sound emerged. Keir doubted that without knowing her name, anyone would have been able to make it out. Fortunately, Grandma Edie had provided that information while urging him not to let on what close connections Keir had to the Whickertons.

Keir was about to repeat the young woman's name when a stroke of ingenuity interfered. "Sally?" he asked, maintaining a straight face.

The young woman frowned, then shook her head. Again, she repeated her name, and again, it was only a whisper.

"Sandra?"

She shook her head, more vehemently this time. Then she spoke again…with a touch more volume.

Keir intentionally misunderstood. "Susan?"

This time, she rolled her eyes, and Keir almost smiled. "Sarah!" she insisted in a hushed whisper, but this time loud enough to be understood. "My name is Sarah!"

"'Tis a pleasure to meet ye, Sophie," Keir greeted her, and this time, he did smile.

For a moment, Sarah looked rather exasperated, ready to correct him again, when she suddenly stilled, her blue eyes staring into his, understanding slowly dawning there. Then she blushed profusely and quickly clasped both hands over her mouth, as though she had said something wrong. Perhaps she had not meant to give him her first name. After all, the *ton* liked to stand on ceremony. Perhaps she had merely been prompted by him offering his own. Whatever it was, she looked rather adorable with that flush on her cheeks, complementing the golden glow of her curls, her braid now in complete disarray. Still, it made her look wilder, freer, and that was something—Keir suspected —Sarah ought to pursue at all cost.

But then again, she was already doing that, wasn't she?

Fortunately, in that moment, another inhabitant of the small house chose to make an appearance.

Slinking around the door frame, the brown-gray cat with black stripes and a white line down his nose sauntered toward them like the master of the house, come to greet his guests. His amber eyes watched them with interest before he bumped his head against Keir's knee and then, in one fluid motion, jumped onto the armrest of Sarah's chair.

Sarah flinched—apparently, a completely normal reaction for the young woman—and stared at the cat.

"This is Loki," Keir introduced the feline and scratched him behind his ears. "He sort of came with the house." He chuckled, grateful to see Sarah recover quickly and hold out her hand for Loki to sniff it. "When I first came here, the place was in terrible disrepair. However, I suppose Loki found it comfortable enough and still considers it his home." He grinned at Sarah, and again, the ghost of a smile tickled the corners of her mouth. "I'm afraid there is no getting rid of him."

Sarah gently patted Loki, her breathing evening as she focused her thoughts away from herself.

"Are ye hungry?" Keir asked, and Sarah nodded shyly. "Good." He pushed to his feet. "Ye can help me in the kitchen." He stepped back and then held out his hand to help her up.

Sarah, however, eyed him warily, like someone constantly on their guard, uncertain if they would need to fight or flee at any moment. Then she rose without taking his hand, her eyes once again glued to the floor.

As Keir strode ahead of her into the kitchen, he thought, *I wonder what made her so fearful of life.* After all, no one was born expecting only the worst. No, that was something that was learned. He gritted his teeth against a wave of anger that abruptly rolled through him. After all, Sarah was not alone in this world. There ought to be those, standing to protect her. How was it that they had failed? Had they even tried?

Keir wondered if there was anything he could do to help her. Everyone deserved to feel safe and comfortable in their own skin.

Perhaps...

Chapter Five

A RUINED WEDDING

At the same time back in London

Albert Harris, Baron Blackmore, sat in his study behind his great-great-grandfather's antique mahogany desk, eyes fixed upon the note in his hands. No more than a few quickly scrawled words graced the parchment, and yet they possessed the power to ruin Albert's day. After all, today was supposed to be his wedding day.

And now, instead of taking a bride, he faced a most aggravating situation. How on earth had this happened? Gritting his teeth, Albert brought his clenched fist down hard upon his great-great-grandfather's desk, sending papers flying.

As though on cue, a knock came on the door.

"Enter!" Albert bellowed, dropping the note onto the desk. Exhaling slowly, he leaned back in his leather chair, steepling his fingers, elbows upon the smooth armrests.

His butler appeared in the door frame, face expressionless, and offered a respectful bow. "I apologize for the interruption, my lord. However, you have a visitor."

Slowly, Albert inhaled through his nose, then he ran a hand through his graying hair. "Who is it?" he demanded, annoyed with himself for losing control like this, for appearing weak in the eyes of another. It had been a long time since he had felt like this, and he did not care for it at all.

"Lord Hartmore is here to see you, my lord."

Albert's teeth ground together at the mention of the man's name. How dare he show his face here? "Show him in," Albert snapped, and his butler immediately hastened away to do his bidding. As always, that was something that pleased Albert greatly. He enjoyed the sight of others quaking before him, of them rushing to do as he demanded, of those sparks of fear in their eyes when he turned his hard gaze on them. Yes, that was what he lived for!

Only moments later, Lord Hartmore stepped across the threshold, his gaze unsteady and red blotches blooming on his neck and cheeks. "Good morning, Blackmore," the man greeted him as he stepped up to Albert's desk. "I apologize for this...inconvenience, and I assure you that...that..." He broke off, fidgeting with his hands.

Albert was not surprised. After all, the man could not assure him of anything. Was that not the very reason why Hartmore had promised him his daughter in marriage? Because he had nothing else to give? Not a penny to his name? Of course, Albert liked it that way. It granted him power, and he so enjoyed being the puppeteer, making others dance with only a tug on a string.

Leaning forward, Albert placed his hands upon the desk and fixed Hartmore with a threatening gaze. "How could you allow this to happen?" he snarled, then slowly pushed to his feet, all the while enjoying the way the other man trembled before him. No doubt, Hartmore feared that this would mean the end of their *arrangement*. "How could you allow her to be taken?" Here, he paused, watching Hartmore sweat with great satisfaction. Then he once more seated himself, leaning back comfortably in his chair and steepling his fingers thoughtfully. "Tell me what happened," he commanded. "Your note revealed far too little."

Hartmore had just opened his mouth to speak when another knock sounded on the door. An instant later, it was pushed open, and Albert looked up as his eldest son and heir, Anthony, stepped across the threshold. He paused when he saw Hartmore, the look upon his face distraught. "I just heard what happened." He looked from Hartmore to his father. "I'm so very sorry. Please, if there is anything I can do." His brown eyes shone with empathy, far too much empathy in Albert's opinion.

"Thank you," Albert replied in a curt tone, then gestured for the two men to seat themselves opposite him. "Now, Hartmore," he fixed his bride's father with a hard stare, "tell me what happened."

Hartmore shrugged. "We are not certain. There was no indication that anything like this might happen. Everything was as it should—"

"Stop your rambling!" Albert thundered, well aware of the disapproving frown that came to his son's face. Yes, far too much empathy! "You're wasting my time. What exactly happened?"

Hartmore swallowed, cast an almost pleading look at Albert's son and then once more looked down at his hands. "The maid found her bedroom empty this morning. At first, we believed she had simply risen early...in happy expectation of today," he looked up, a placating smile upon his face. "However, when we could not find her anywhere, we once more searched her room. On her vanity, we found...a note."

"A note?" Anthony inquired before Albert could snap at the man, once more, to finally get to the point. "From your daughter?"

Hartmore shook his head. "No, from whoever took her. It was no more than a few lines but..." He reached inside his coat pocket and withdrew a small piece of parchment. His pale eyes met Albert's before he handed the note across the desk.

Albert all but ripped it from his fingers, unfolding it quickly and scanning its contents.

We have your daughter. If you value her life, you will do nothing but wait for further instructions. You will alert no one to her disappearance with the exception of her future husband, Lord Blackmore.

Grinding his teeth, Albert crushed the note in his hand, seething anger rolling through his body. How dare they?

"What does it say, Father?" Anthony inquired in that gentle voice of his. It was by far the last thing Albert wanted to hear in that moment!

Ignoring his son, Albert glared at Hartmore. "They will be asking for ransom," he snarled, savoring what small delight he found in seeing the man cringe before him, "and they expect me to pay it. After all, all the world knows that you have absolutely nothing to your name. Your daughter was your last valuable possession, and now that she has been taken, you have nothing left."

Reaching for the crumpled-up note, Anthony read it quietly. "It is imperative that we keep this quiet."

"Ha!" Albert scoffed, once more pounding his fist onto the desk. "You are a fool if you believe it is not already all over London. After all, servants are notorious for spreading gossip."

Concern drew down Anthony's brows. "Still, they will not harm her because if they did, they'd lose their leverage. They want money, and so long as they believe we will pay, she is safe."

Hartmore followed the conversation with quiet attention, his eyes wide and fearful, marked with uncertainty. "You have my sincerest apology, Blackmore. I assure you I never meant for any of this to happen."

Albert fixed him with a hateful stare. "Quite frankly, Hartmore, I am tempted to refuse payment. After all, she is not yet my wife. If she were, this would not have happened."

"Father!" Anthony stared at him, an aghast look upon his face. "You cannot be serious! Surely, you cannot mean to abandon her to her fate."

Albert heaved a deep breath. Oh, he would like to do nothing better than precisely that! "No, I do not," he finally conceded. "If I were, society would skin me alive. No, I'm afraid I'm honor-bound to see to her safe return."

Hartmore exhaled a deep breath, relief palpable upon his face. Anthony, too, bore a similar expression, one Albert wanted to wipe off his son's face. Yet before he could say more, another knock came on the door. Again, his butler appeared. Only this time, he led a simply dressed man into the study as Albert had instructed.

"Mr. Smith," Albert greeted the man, gesturing for him to

approach, "how good of you to join us today." In a few short words, he explained the situation and instructed Mr. Smith to make further inquiries into his fiancée's whereabouts as well as the identity of the men who had removed her from her father's house without his permission.

Mr. Smith nodded obediently, a calculating expression in his narrowed eyes. Clearly, he was not a man moved by fancy, a fact Albert greatly appreciated. Indeed, he had used the man's assistance before and not regretted it. Mr. Smith was tall and burly, a scar slashing through the end of his right eyebrow, marking him as a man quite capable of handling himself.

After Mr. Smith had taken his leave, Albert turned to Hartmore. "Return home and inform me the instant you are contacted."

Hartmore scrambled to his feet, nodding eagerly. "Of course! Of course!" He stepped toward the door and then paused, looking back over his shoulder. "I thank you for your assistance in this matter." He nodded once more and then disappeared out the door.

With a heavy sigh, Albert leaned back in his chair, annoyed this matter had been forced upon him. Indeed, he had imagined this day quite differently.

"Are you certain this is wise, Father?" Anthony asked as he rose to his feet and then stepped around the desk, concern in his eyes. "After all, the note says to wait for further instructions and not involve anyone else in this matter. What if Mr. Smith is found out? What will then happen to Miss Mortensen?" Sighing, he shook his head. "I believe it would be safer for the lady if—"

Albert shot to his feet. "I refuse to bow down to these sniveling delinquents! I will find out who crossed me and I will make them pay!" He forced a slow breath down his throat and then retook his seat. "There is no harm in doing a little investigating, Son."

Sighing heavily, Anthony ran a hand through his hair. "I do hope you're right, Father. But what if they find out that you sent Mr. Smith to investigate them?" He stared down at his father, slowly shaking his head. "You are risking her life."

Albert could not help the grin that slowly spread across his features. "Then, at least, I won't have to pay her ransom."

Chapter Six

IN A KITCHEN WITH A SCOT

S tanding in the small kitchen, Sarah felt as though she had entered some sort of magical realm. Everything looked foreign and unfamiliar. Nothing sparked any sense of recognition. She had spent no time at all in a kitchen and did not have the slightest inkling how to prepare a meal. Yet clearly, that was precisely what was on her kidnapper's mind.

Keir, Sarah heard his name whispered somewhere in the back of her mind. He had given his first name freely, and somehow it had prompted her to give her own. What had she been thinking? *I truly am a fool, am I not?* And now, it was too late. Now, she could not insist he address her as Miss Mortensen, could she?

'You ought to!' Her mother's insistent voice snapped in her head. 'You are a baron's daughter, and he is a mere criminal. What are you thinking mingling far below your station?'

Sarah gritted her teeth, willing her mother's voice to retreat. After all, she knew very well that she was walking a very fine line, that she ought not be here. Her own doubts were enough. She did not need her mother's objections crowding her mind as well.

"Have ye ever been in a kitchen before?" Keir asked her, his tall frame dwarfing the small room. A teasing grin rested upon his features as he eyed her curiously, that blue gaze of his seeing far too much—in Sarah's humble opinion. Whenever he looked at her, a sense of unease teased her spine, as though he knew precisely what thoughts were running through her head no matter how hard she tried to hide them.

Looking up—if only for a brief moment—Sarah shook her head. He made her nervous, and yet whenever he looked at her, she felt an odd sense of relief. Criminal or not, she did not fear him. At least, not the way she feared her future husband.

"Wonderful!" Keir exclaimed, and as he smiled, dimples appeared at the corners of his mouth. "A blank canvas!" He held out his hand to her. "Come, I'll teach ye how to cook."

Sarah all but stared at his outstretched hand, her mind frozen while at the same time, countless thoughts raced through her head, far too many to sort and look at in great detail.

Again, his closeness overwhelmed her, and she felt herself instinctively move away. She also wondered who had taught him how to cook. After all, it was not generally considered men's work. Yet how would Sarah know? In her societal circle, neither men nor women pursued any kind of occupation.

All anyone had ever expected of her was to make a good match. Sarah heaved a deep sigh. She had not even been able to do that. And now that her father had procured her such a match—at least, according to society's standards—she had simply run off, refusing to do her duty.

As though on cue, her mother's voice snapped in her head, 'We raised you to be a proper, young lady, and this is how you treat your parents? Have you no decency?'

The full impact of what she had done suddenly came crashing down upon Sarah. She felt her knees buckle, no longer able to bear the weight of this burden. Tears shot into her eyes as she imagined her parents finding her gone, their thoughts at having their carefully laid-out plans overturned. After all, how often had they tried to arrange a match for her? How often had Sarah thought herself on the brink of matrimony? At least three times by her count.

Only each time something had interfered.

In truth, each time it had been the Whickertons, her old friends, refusing to abandon her to a loveless marriage. They had taken it upon themselves to prevent these marriages that Sarah had not wanted, that her parents had only orchestrated because they had needed them, because they had needed her future husband's fortune.

Remembering the ups and downs of the past two years, Sarah was beginning to feel faint. She could not remember a single day of peace, each and every one of them marked by this tension that held her rigid, her mind plagued by thoughts of what tomorrow might bring. *Fear! Yes, I know fear.*

"Are ye all right?"

Blinking her eyes, Sarah's head snapped up, and she found herself looking at her kidnapper. At Keir. Somehow he had all but materialized in front of her. She had not even taken note of his approach. Again, she blinked, realizing that his right hand was resting upon her shoulder, steadying her.

A part of Sarah flinched, uncomfortable with any kind of contact, while another remained perfectly calm. Indeed, Keir had a way of stepping closer without making her feel threatened. There was no ulterior motive lurking in his eyes, no sense of hidden agenda. Indeed, whenever she looked up at him and their eyes met, she got the distinct feeling that...he was truly concerned for her. Was that possible? He hardly knew her. She was nothing more than a task for him, a job to be undertaken, a way to earn a living. Surely, she was imagining that gentle expression upon his face. He was simply being polite, intent on keeping her safe as he had been tasked to do.

Retreating from him, Sarah felt his hand slide off her shoulder. Then she slowly shook her head, once more unable to force even a single word past her lips.

Keir remained where he was, a thoughtful expression in his blue eyes, and once again, Sarah thought he knew precisely how she felt. How was that possible?

"Come," he said, gesturing toward one of the two chairs placed around a small table in the center of the kitchen. "Sit." As she approached, he moved away, quickly disappearing into a small pantry off to the side. The moment Sarah seated herself, Keir strode back toward the table, a loaf of bread in his hands. "Ye needa eat something," he said with the certainty of someone who had never known an indecisive moment in his life.

When Keir drew the knife from his belt, Sarah froze, staring as he swiftly cut off a slice, then handed it to her.

With a trembling hand, Sarah reached out to take the piece of bread, feeling his gaze watching her. She wished she possessed the courage to look at him again, to see what he saw when he looked at her. Would she know simply by looking at his face? *Does he pity me? Does he think me a fool?* Perhaps it was better for her not to know. In all likelihood, she would not like the answer.

"Take yer time," Keir told her with a smile. "Loki shall keep ye company." As though his words had drawn the feline out of thin air, the striped cat jumped onto the table in that moment.

Sarah flinched, caught off guard but equally intrigued by the curious gleam in the creature's amber eyes.

Moving toward her, Loki lowered his head and sniffed her hand. Then he inspected the piece of bread she was holding, concluding with a little shake of his head that he did not care for it.

Keir chuckled. "Would a saucer of milk be more to yer liking, yer highness?" he asked the cat with a formal bow, mirth twinkling in his eyes.

Loki looked up, tilted his head sideways and sat back on his haunches, waiting.

Sarah watched with fascination as Keir provided a small bowl of milk for the cat, who then proceeded to devour it with great eagerness. "He is like a little king presiding over his kingdom," Keir remarked. "A rather mischievous king." Chuckling, he turned away and then rummaged through the kitchen. He lit a fire in the stove and then set a huge pot on top of it. After that, he disappeared outside, returning shortly with a bucket of water, which he refilled two or three times before the pot was completely full.

Nibbling on her slice of bread, Sarah alternately watched the cat and the man. Amusement teased the corners of her mouth, and yet she experienced a deep sense of disbelief. In an odd way, this moment seemed so ordinary, so normal, so every day that it should not strike her as odd at all. However, in quite another, it was the most unusual moment she had ever experienced.

So peaceful.

So harmonious.

Sarah wished she had the words to express what this moment meant to her. She wished...Keir would speak to her again. He had a way of speaking of ordinary things that made them seem important and meaningful. His voice had put her at ease before...even when she had been near a panic. Sarah did not know how he had done it, but she longed for the calm that had settled upon her.

If only I knew what to say! If only I could speak whenever I wish!

All her life, Sarah had only known polite conversation, trained to smile and nod and provide the occasional response to a gentleman's inquiry. She had never quite *spoken* to a man before, though, shared her thoughts and listened to his. Only what could the two of them possibly speak of? They were as different as night and day. Perhaps, once again, it was wise not to interact, to keep their distance from one another as much as possible.

With the slice of bread gone, Sarah was about to rise from the table and retire to her chamber when Keir suddenly spoke up. He still stood with his back to her, moving about the kitchen, as though he had spent his entire life here. "My mother taught me to cook. She always loved it, always knew how to turn a handful of ingredients into a mouthwatering meal." He chuckled, and yet Sarah did not miss the note of pride that rang in his voice. Was it possible for a criminal to be a family man? "Unfortunately for her, she only bore three sons. Of course, that didna stop her." He turned to look at her over his shoulder, a wide grin marking his features and revealing the dimples at the corners of his mouth. "I remember, one autumn afternoon, standing in the kitchen next to my eldest brother with our mother marching, like a general, up and down in front of us. I remember her eyes sweeping over the two of us in a way that I got the distinct impression that she was looking for something, even though she didna say a word, didna ask anything of us. And then she waved her hand and sent my brother away."

All thoughts of leaving were forgotten as Sarah sat and listened. She had always loved stories; first, conjuring them with her sister Kate and then later with her dearest friend, Christina, one of the Whickerton sisters. To this day, Christina was a wonderful storyteller, and yet at some point, she had all but given up on her stories, deciding to keep them a secret. Sarah still did not quite know why, what had prompted her to do so. Had Christina somehow received the impression that writing stories was not something a lady ought to do? Only Christina had never been one to bow her head to unwritten rules. After all, she had always been rather headstrong and willful.

As were most of the Whickertons.

"My mother then put a knife into my hands and told me to cut some vegetables," Keir continued as he moved toward the table, a basket of carrots in one hand and a knife in the other. "She told me of the wonderful stew we were about to make, spoke of all the ingredients we could add if we so chose." He shrugged, smiling down at her. "'Twas a wonderful afternoon, one I shall never forget."

Almost entranced, Sarah looked up at him. Indeed, she remembered not a single moment like that with her own mother or father. Always had they been distant, not interested in their two daughters.

'We've done all we could,' her mother's voice objected indignantly in her thoughts, 'given you all we had, and this is how you rep—'

"Here."

Sarah blinked at the carrots Keir set down in front of her. Then her gaze traveled to the knife he held out.

"Dunna worry. Ye'll do fine." Then he placed the knife upon the table and returned to his own preparations, all the while speaking of one ingredient or another. Some Sarah had never even heard of.

Completely overwhelmed, Sarah stared back and forth between the knife and the carrots. Never had she prepared a meal. Never had she used a knife such as this. And yet if she wanted to eat...

Tentatively, Sarah reached for the knife. It felt strange in her hand, its weight surprising. Loki eyed her suspiciously for a moment before he returned his attention to the bowl of milk. Inhaling deeply, Sarah set the blade upon the carrot...and then pushed down. It was surprisingly hard to cut off a piece, and soon, Sarah's full concentration was on the task before her.

"My brother canna tell a carrot from a potato," Keir remarked with a chuckle, "and my mother knew he would be miserable in a kitchen." His shadow fell over Sarah as he stepped up to the table. "Do ye have any siblings?"

Realizing that he had addressed her, Sarah stilled, her mind returning to focus on his words as she lifted her head to look at him. *What did he say? Siblings?*

Waiting patiently, Keir smiled at her, and Sarah realized he would not allow her to run from this. He wanted an answer, and he would not walk away until he had it.

Swallowing, Sarah nodded.

"A sister?"

Sarah nodded again.

"Did ye cook together?" Keir asked with a grin, his gaze darting to the rather thick and unevenly cut carrot pieces in front of her.

Feeling a slight blush creep up her cheeks, Sarah shook her head. *I'm no good at anything, am I?*

"Then what did ye do together?"

Sarah flinched. *Oh, dear! This is not a question requiring either a nod or a shake of the head!* "W-We..." She swallowed. "We em-embroidered and s-such."

His blue eyes narrowed as he leaned down and braced his hands on the table. "Did ye ride out together?"

Sarah froze, feeling all the warmth of this moment slip away.

Keir nodded, as though she had explained herself in great detail. "Were ye thrown?"

A shuddering breath left Sarah's lips as the memories returned, memories she had fought so hard to keep banished. Her hand tensed upon the knife, and her eyes pinched shut. She could feel her heart thunder inside her chest and wished she could simply run away from this moment.

"Ye're holding it too tightly," Keir murmured, somewhere near her. "Here, let me show ye."

The moment his hand touched hers, Sarah flinched.

Chapter Seven

A NEW WORLD

K eir knew he made Sarah nervous. The little wisp had made that abundantly clear from the very first. Yet she did not fear him. She was wary of him, felt uneasy when he approached, but she did not fear him.

He was certain of that, and so he decided to make use of that fact.

Moving behind the chair Sarah was seated on, Keir leaned forward and placed his hands upon hers—one was holding the carrot and the other the knife. The instant his fingertips brushed against her skin, Sarah flinched, drawing in a sharp breath.

"Loosen yer grip," Keir murmured softly, watching as his breath teased the little wisps of hair upon her right temple. "The blade willna hurt ye so long as ye respect it."

Her hand all but dropped the knife, but Keir gently kept his own wrapped around hers, urging her to remain and meet this challenge. He could feel her breath coming fast and watched as a deep flush slowly crept into her cheeks.

Keir chuckled. "Ye're blushing, little wisp," he teased, and the color of her cheeks darkened even more. "Am I making ye nervous?" He knew he was a beast for teasing her like this, but as far as he could tell, his nearness had served its purpose. Sarah clearly no longer thought of that moment of her past that instilled fear in her to this day.

Her focus had shifted to him.

"Try again," Keir urged in a gentle tone as he released her hands and straightened, moving his hands to the backrest of her chair. "Instead of simply pushing the blade down, make a sawing motion. Like this." He gave a quick demonstration, his hands moving through the air. "Try it."

Sarah's hands trembled slightly as she heeded his advice, her gaze fixed upon the items in her hands. Indeed, her posture seemed a touch rigid, as though she was trying very hard not to look at him.

Keir smiled. His little wisp was a sweet one, utterly innocent in the ways of the world, and yet daring enough to risk this adventure. She was vulnerable out here, alone with him; more vulnerable than she had ever been before, and she knew it. She would only feel safe so long as she trusted him. *But how can she?*

Moving back toward the workbench in the corner, Keir continued his own vegetable chopping. Onions, leeks, potatoes, a variety of herbs as well as the chicken, whose neck he had wrung on one of his trips to the well, were all added to the steaming pot upon the stove. Occasionally, he would look over his shoulder at Sarah, relieved to see that her blush was fading, and her hands were no longer tense. Her gaze was once more focused on the task before her, and he could no longer see a dark cloud above her head.

"A long time ago," Keir began, well aware that she appreciated his storytelling, "my elder brother gifted me a horse." At his words, Sarah paused briefly but then continued her work. "He used to love playing tricks on me, and he knew the horse was a wild one. Countless men had tried to ride it, to tame it, and all had failed, had barely managed to put a saddle upon it."

At the table, Sarah's hands had stilled, the knife almost forgotten. Her gaze was distant and not trained upon him, yet Keir thought she was listening intently.

"Of course, I'd heard the rumors, and so I knew to be wary. Only I wanted to meet this challenge. I did not want to give up and give my brother Duncan the satisfaction of surrender." He chuckled. "'Tis always been the way between us, to tease one another mercilessly but with good humor." He paused and then half turned to look at her over his shoulder. "Was it the same for ye and yer sister?"

Sarah blinked, and then her eyes flickered to meet his. He could see tears clinging to her eyelashes, the blue of her gaze reminding him of the sky before a storm. A deep sigh left her lips before she finally nodded, the ghost of a smile gracing her features. "Yes." It was one small word, and yet she spoke it with no hesitation, without the slightest hint of unease in her eyes.

Keir nodded, returning her smile, and then turned back to cutting the chicken into even pieces. As expected, Loki jumped up onto the workbench beside him. Now that his bowl of milk was empty, he was looking for further treats. "Here ye go, yer highness." Keir placed a small bowl with a few pieces of chicken in front of the feline. "I removed all bones," he said in a mockingly formal tone. "Just as ye instructed, yer highness."

Out of the corner of his eye, Keir saw a deep smile come to Sarah's face as she watched him and the cat. Aye, she was beautiful when she smiled and her eyes were not overshadowed by fear and the burdens of memories. *Aye, she's a bonny lass!*

"Well, getting back to my story," Keir said, meeting Sarah's eyes for a split second before turning back to his own work. "Whenever the stallion was out in the meadow, far away from people, he seemed perfectly fine and content. However, as soon as he was approached, he became wild. His ears would flatten back, and he would toss his head in a panicked manner, kicking up his hooves, as though fearing an attack was imminent." Keir sighed at the memory, for it had taught him not to judge others too quickly. What one saw on the surface was more often than not quite different from what lay underneath. "I spent days only watching him, trying to understand what he feared. My brother laughed every time he saw me, certain that any effort would be in vain. Countless people urged me to consider him a lost cause and be rid of him." Turning around, Keir leaned back against the workbench, his gaze seeking Sarah's, a wistful smile coming to his lips. "And then my sister said something to me that changed everything."

Clearly intrigued, Sarah leaned forward, her attention completely focused on his story, the look in her eyes eager. Keir could see that she wanted him to continue, and so, he waited.

One moment.

And then another.

"What...What did she say?" Sarah asked tentatively, her words barely audible, and yet the expression upon her face spoke volumes.

Keir exhaled a slow breath. "She was only a girl at the time, barely ten years old, but she told me something I never forgot." He paused, holding Sarah's gaze. "She said that everyone only ever thought of what they wanted from him, but no one ever thought to ask what he wanted." Remembering how Yvaine had stood before him that day, her face scrunched up in displeasure, righteous indignation flaring up in her green eyes, her own tousled fiery-red hair as wild as the horse's spirit.

Aye, his little sister had always been a force to be reckoned with.

Keir watched as Sarah's expression slowly stilled, as though time had stopped. One moment, her blue eyes were looking into his, and in the next, he knew that she no longer saw him. Clearly, Yvaine's words had touched her. Sarah knew how the stallion had felt all those years ago. She knew what it felt like not to be seen, not to be considered worthy of choice. Was that not precisely why they were here today? Why she had run from her home?

"I spent days sitting out in the meadow in the grass," Keir went on, watching Sarah's lashes flutter down to touch her skin, the look in her eyes suddenly no longer as faraway as before. "I didna look at him but kept my gaze turned toward the sea, toward the far horizon, Yvaine's words echoing through my mind." He smiled at her, seeing her need to hear the end of his story upon her face. "And then one day, he stood before me, his eyes watching me curiously before he lowered his head and nudged me with his nose."

A wide smile graced Sarah's face, and a lone tear spilled over and ran down her cheek. She quickly wiped it away and once again lowered her head, but Keir had seen how deeply she had been touched.

Keir reached for the bowl into which he had cut up the chicken and quickly snatched it up before Loki could get any ideas. Then he poured the contents into the steaming water in the pot. "How are the carrots coming?" he asked without looking over his shoulder. "When ye're finished, throw them in here."

As Keir stirred the stew, he heard a chair being pushed back. Tentatively, Sarah rose to her feet, and he could imagine her hands trembling as she held the cutting board. Then he heard the soft sound of her footfalls moving closer. He could sense her approach and wished he could see her face. As much as she tried to hide her anxieties, her fears, her face was incredibly expressive. Every thought, every emotion was written there. *She isna aware of that, is she?*

Coming to stand beside him, Sarah briefly glanced up at him before turning her attention to the bubbling stew. She carefully used the blade to push the carrots off the board and into the pot. As a bigger piece dropped in, soup splashed up and landed on the inner side of her left wrist.

Instantly, Sarah flinched, pulling back her arm.

Keir took the board as well as the knife from her hands and set them aside. Then he grasped her uninjured hand and pulled her forward toward the side door. "Wait here." He snatched up a bowl and then strode outside, just beyond the door. His gaze fell upon the glistening snow, and he scooped some of it into the bowl. Then he stepped back inside and closed the door.

Sarah stood waiting where he had left her, her right hand clasped around her left arm, her teeth worrying her lower lip as she looked down at the slight burn on her wrist. As he moved closer, she lifted her gaze, looking up at him. "I'm sorry."

Keir smiled at her as he crushed a bit of snow in his hand before placing it upon her wrist. "Ye're sorry? What for?"

A shiver went through Sarah at the feel of the cold snow upon her warm skin. "I...I should've been more careful. I should've–"

"Ye did very well," he assured her, drawing her back toward the table and then urging her to sit down. With the bowl set in front of her, he pulled up the other chair and sat opposite her. "Trying something new always comes with its own challenges." As the snow melted upon her arm, Keir added fresh snow from the bowl.

"Do you often kidnap people?" The moment these words left

Sarah's lips, her eyes grew wide with shock, and she clasped her uninjured hand over her mouth.

Keir chuckled, sensing her urge to retrieve her other hand as well. He held it gently but determinedly within his own, adding more packed snow when necessary. "Is that what ye think?" he asked, delighted that she had spoken so freely. "That I go about the countryside kidnapping people and demanding ransom?"

Still staring at him, Sarah shook her head, clearly terrified that she had offended him. "No! No! Of course not!" Again, she moved her head from side to side, her blue eyes as round as plates. "I only meant to ask... That is, I only—" Her breath came fast, and for a moment, it seemed as though her eyes would roll back into her head at any moment.

"Look at me, little wisp," Keir murmured gently, seeking her gaze. "Ask me anything ye wish. I assure ye I dunna mind." He reassuringly squeezed her hand. "The answer is no, I dunna often kidnap people." He grinned at her. "In fact, ye're the first and only one who has ever had the privilege of being my captive." He chuckled.

A slow breath rushed from her lungs, and Keir could see the hint of a smile tease the corners of her mouth. Her cheeks, however, were a flaming red once more.

With the last bit of snow now melted, Keir dipped a small cloth into the bowl, soaking it with the icy water. Then he gently wrapped it around Sarah's wrist, tying a quick knot. "There. That should keep it cool for a little while." He rose to his feet. "Come, while the stew boils, I'll show ye around."

With Loki rushing to take the lead, Keir and Sarah walked through the house. They moved quickly through the downstairs as there was not much more to see aside from the storage room toward the back. Then they headed to the upper floor, one door on either side of the narrow staircase. Keir gestured to the one on the left. "This one is yers," he told her, moving to open the door. "The dowager countess had clothes and such things purchased and brought here beforehand. Everything is inside, but please let me know if there's anything else ye require."

Keir watched as Sarah tentatively moved past him and stepped over the threshold, her large eyes taking in the sparse furnishings. The room held no more than a bed at the far wall, a small fireplace on the northern side as well as a wardrobe and a washing stand.

"Perhaps ye should change," Keir suggested, nodding toward the outfit she had worn for the past night and day. "Make yerself comfortable while I have a look around. I'll see ye at supper."

Sarah nodded, the expression upon her face tense once more. Somehow, the ease that had developed between them during his story had slowly slipped away. Keir regretted it.

Closing the door, Keir ventured back downstairs. He donned his heavy coat and then stepped outside. Darkness was slowly falling, and he quickly explored the immediate area around the house, ensuring that there were no signs of another having been in the vicinity. Fortunately, the snow-powdered ground looked untouched, his own footprints the only ones he found. On his way back, Keir stopped by the shed to see to the horses. They were dozing peacefully, tired after the long ride; Scout, in particular, having carried them both for so long. The goat that had provided the milk for Loki looked already half-asleep, not responding in the slightest when Keir patted her head.

After stomping the snow off his boots, Keir stepped back inside, grateful for the warmth that lingered in the rooms. He hung his coat upon a peg in the hall and then walked back into the kitchen, checking on the stew. It bubbled nicely, its mouthwatering aroma drifting through the kitchen, making Keir's stomach rumble. Aye, it was time for a hearty meal. He set the table for two and then, grinning, added yet another bowl as Loki jumped onto the table, a rather disapproving expression upon his features. How the feline managed that, Keir did not know. Never before in his life had he seen a cat capable of looking *disapproving*.

"Dunna bother sending for the executioner," Keir told the striped beast. "Here, yer highness, a bowl for ye as well. I assume ye do not insist upon a spoon, am I correct?" He chuckled, and looking up, he found Sarah standing in the door frame.

Chapter Eight

A GIANT STEP FOR A SHY ENGLISH LASS

Sarah did not know what to make of the sight before her eyes. In the days before the kidnapping, when she had received word from Grandma Edie detailing what would happen, Sarah had spent all her time wondering and worrying about everything but particularly about the man who had been tasked with kidnapping her. Of course, she had always trusted Christina's grandmother. Otherwise, she would never have agreed to this plan. However, in her mind, she had been unable to imagine a decent man agreeing to such a scheme. In her mind, he had always been a ruthless criminal. Clearly, her mind had led her astray.

'He is a criminal,' her mother's voice insisted, echoing Sarah's original thoughts. 'A man who does not know right from wrong. Look at what he has you doing, kitchen work! How dishonorable!'

Sarah cringed at her mother's criticism; yet it did not sting as much as it usually did. Try as she might, she could not see Keir as a truly wicked man. After all, she had known wicked men, one in particular, and Keir was nothing like him. And in truth, Sarah had not minded being included in the supper preparations. Indeed, it made her feel... capable...in a small way.

Seeing Keir now, jesting with the cat at the kitchen table, she could not help but wonder about his life. He had made it quite clear that kidnapping people was not his regular profession—if one could indeed call it a profession! *But then who could he be?*

His laughing blue eyes met hers, and he immediately beckoned her forward. "Hungry?" He gestured to the chair she had sat upon when cutting the carrots. "I suppose we better hurry," he glanced at Loki, "for his highness looks quite ravenous tonight." He winked at her.

For another heartbeat, Sarah remained where she was, unable to tear her eyes away. Indeed, the way Keir smiled made his entire face light up. Never before had she met another person who smiled as deeply as he did. Had he ever known gray clouds in the sky? It had to have been so, did it not? And yet when Sarah looked at him, she got the distinct impression that all he ever truly saw was sunshine. Was that possible? No one's life could ever truly be filled with only sunshine. Of course, there had to be rainy days. Days when storms raged.

"Is everything all right?"

Shaking off the daze that had settled upon her mind, Sarah stepped into the kitchen. "Yes," she managed to say, wondering at what point and why her voice had returned. She had barely taken note of it. All of a sudden, it had simply been there, faint, almost inaudible, but there, nonetheless.

Again, her gaze sought his face, trying to look deeper. It had been his doing, had it not? Somehow Keir had put her at ease. Somehow he had given her back her voice. *Did he do so on purpose? With the intention of helping me? Or is it something that simply comes naturally to him?*

Sarah did not know, but she wished she did.

Seating herself, Sarah watched as Keir filled their bowls, the aroma wafting up into her nostrils. She closed her eyes and savored the beckoning smell.

"Am I correct in assuming," Keir said to Loki in that feigned formal tone, "that yer highness is only interested in the chicken and not the vegetables?"

Sarah could not help the smile that came to her face, and she felt herself blush all over again when Keir's gaze shifted to her, his own smile as compelling as before.

Loki, on the other hand, remained as dignified as ever. At least, until chicken filled his bowl. At that point, he seemed to all but pounce on it like a cat cornering a mouse. Oddly enough, that comparison made Sarah wonder. After all, Loki *was* a cat, and yet she could not think of him as such.

Seated opposite one another at the table, they ate. The hot stew tasted wonderful, and Sarah savored every bite. It was completely different to what she was used to, and she could not recall ever enjoying a meal quite as she did this one.

As though reading her thoughts, Keir remarked, "It always tastes better when ye have prepared the meal yerself."

Sarah frowned. "All I did was cut the carrots."

"If ye had not, their flavor would be missing," Keir replied with a wink.

Sarah could not say why, but all of a sudden she felt completely at ease in this conversation. "If I had not, you would have. And done it better, I might add."

Keir chuckled. "Oh, can ye truly taste that the carrots were cut unevenly? What a fine palate ye must have!" He grinned at her before his expression grew earnest. "Aye, ye did not do much, but ye helped. Ye did well for yer first time cooking, and I'm certain the next time will be even better."

Unexpectedly, Sarah felt tears prick the backs of her eyes. *Indeed, I've done very little. It is barely noteworthy. In fact, it is not. And yet...*

Keir's watchful eyes swept over her features. "Ye dunna often receive compliments, do ye?" he asked, a touch of anger in his voice, as though he were outraged on her behalf.

Sarah wiped a tear from the corner of her eye. "I suppose I'm not truly good at anything. That's probably why—" She clamped her lips shut, shocked by how much she had almost revealed. *I ought not have spoken to him of this! Of my shortcomings as a woman! I should not have spoken to him at all!*

"Why what?" Keir inquired, gently blocking Loki's path with his arm as the feline strode closer to inspect Keir's bowl after having finished his own.

With her gaze focused on her own food, Sarah shook her head. "Nothing."

For a long moment, silence lingered, and Sarah wondered if Keir would press the matter or drop it, uncertain which she was hoping for.

"I suppose we should talk about what will happen next," Keir said instead of inquiring after the true meaning of her words.

Sarah looked up, grateful to see neither reproach nor disappointment upon his face. "I admit I know very little. At the time, it did not occur to me to ask for more. My mind was so preoccupied with..."

Keir nodded. "I understand," he said, and those two simple words made all the difference. "The dowager countess is not one who is terribly forthcoming with information, is she?"

A wide smile came to Sarah's face. "No. No, she's not." Then she frowned. "Do you know her?"

For a second, Sarah thought to see Keir tense, but then his usual good-natured smile reappeared. "Of course. After all, she was the one who hired me."

Sarah wanted to ask for more. She longed to know who he was and what his life usually looked like. How had Grandma Edie found him, known she could trust him, known that he would agree to this plan? Sarah wanted to ask all that and more but did not dare. It would be inappropriate, would it not? What Sarah had learned early on, before anything else, was what not to say! After all, women ought not have opinions of their own, ought not speak of things boring to a gentleman. In fact, women were only to speak when spoken to. How often had her father said these words?

Countless times, was the answer. Until they had become a part of Sarah, of who she was and how she saw herself.

"There is an inn not far from here," Keir continued on. "I shall travel there every other day and wait for instructions."

Sarah felt herself tense at the thought of being left behind here on her own.

"Dunna worry. Ye will be safe here, and I shall always be back before nightfall." His eyes lingered upon hers, a promise there that Sarah trusted without thinking twice about it. *How did this happen? After all, I met this man only the day before. How have I come to trust him?*

After supper, Keir gathered some firewood in his arms and carried it upstairs to her chamber. With a few quick movements, he had a fire going, as though he had conjured it out of thin air. The room began to warm, the soft orange glow of the dancing flames soothing to Sarah's rattled nerves.

Still, as Keir turned to leave, she stepped toward him, her words once more stuck in her throat.

"Is there anything ye need?" Keir asked, once again all but guessing her thoughts.

Sarah nodded. "Water," she whispered, glancing toward the empty pitcher on the wooden stand.

Smiling, Keir strode forward and reached for the pitcher. "I shall bring ye some," he told her as he made to leave. Then, however, he stopped in the doorway and looked back at her, a mischievous twinkle in his eyes. "And tomorrow I shall show ye how to fetch some for yerself."

Sarah stood and watched him walk downstairs. The thought of fetching her own water should be appalling to her. Her mother certainly would have been! Only Sarah was anything but. "I cut carrots today," she whispered to the empty room. It was a minuscule task, nothing worth mentioning, but it filled Sarah with pride. "And tomorrow I shall fetch my own water."

Smiling, she moved over to the window. Ice crystals clung to the windowpane, and her warm breath fogged up the glass momentarily. The night was dark, and yet everything down below glittered in the faint light of the moon. It looked beautiful and peaceful, and Sarah's mind drifted back to the night before. Then, too, she had stood by the window looking out.

Her window.

In her parents' townhouse.

Oddly enough, that moment seemed an eternity ago. It did not seem as though only a day had passed since. Sarah remembered well how frightened she had been, how nervous and uncertain. She remembered all the doubts that had run through her head, making her waver, making her question her decision. She had been so close to giving up, so close to changing her mind.

Sarah breathed in deeply, her eyes still sweeping across the snow-covered ground outside. *I am so relieved I did not! So very relieved!*

Sarah could hear the door down below open and saw a faint light spill out onto the snow. A moment later, Keir appeared, once again dressed in his long overcoat. He stalked through the snow and then disappeared around the side of the house. Sarah remembered how she had first caught a glimpse of him, high up on the carriage. She had been terrified of the stranger she did not know, of the stranger she had imagined him to be. Of course, her mind had conjured countless scenarios of how this plan would go horribly wrong. Sarah was used to worry. She had always done it, quite expertly actually. She knew how to drill down to her most paralyzing fears and make them come to life. She knew what to tell herself to lose her head and be frightened out of her mind. That was something she knew how to do well. It was not something that had ever served her in any way, of course. How could it?

"I cut carrots today," Sarah whispered to the night, wondering where that small step might lead her. And in that moment, for the first time, Sarah wondered about something else. Not something that frightened her but something that gave her hope. Once the ransom was paid and she returned home, would she still be the same woman she had been only the day before?

Keir once again appeared in her line of vision, carrying a bucket in his right hand. He moved quietly, reminding her of a feline stalking its prey without sound, his footprints in the snow the only proof that he had been there.

Yet again Sarah wondered about his life. *Where did he come from? And where will he go back to once all of this is over? He clearly has a family he cares about—two brothers and one sister.* She paused. Had Keir not told her that his mother had only born three sons? *How odd.* Sarah shrugged. *Perhaps I misunderstood. After all, a lot happened today.*

And still, although she knew next to nothing about him, he no longer seemed to her like the stranger he had been up on the box of the carriage. Something had changed. Perhaps it was the way he looked out for her or the way he looked *at* her. There was kindness in his eyes, but what she delighted in most was that sense of weightlessness that lingered about him, as though nothing could ever subdue his spirit. No doubt, he, too, had experienced moments of loss and pain. No one could walk this earth without experiencing them. Still, the way he smiled, the way his eyes would light up made her think that, perhaps long ago, he had made the decision to accept the pain but not let it darken the joy life offered. Sarah wished she had the strength to do so as well.

Indeed, the past two years had been marked by uncertainty, by fear. Sarah could barely remember a moment of pure joy, not overshadowed by something that haunted her. She had watched the Whickerton sisters fall in love and marry, sometimes standing right beside them and sometimes from afar. She had seen their joy and wished it could be hers as well. Yet with time Sarah had lost hope.

All she wanted now was to be safe from her parents' desperate matchmaking schemes. She did not want to be sold into marriage to pay her father's debts. Hopefully this plan, this kidnapping would ensure that no one—no one!—would ever seek her hand in marriage again, that she would be useless to her father. After all, Sarah was not that naïve to believe that her kidnapping could be kept quiet. Somehow people would find out. People always found out. And she would be ruined.

For good.

Then, at least, she would be safe.

Chapter Nine

WORLDS APART

The air felt crisp and fresh as Keir carefully picked his way through the snow. Another few inches had been added the night before, covering not only the house and shed but also obscuring every print that might have been left upon the ground. He crouched down to inspect a broken branch, relieved to see that it was not likely to have been broken by someone stalking through the underbrush. Indeed, the world seemed untouched. No one had been nearby. They were still safe.

Returning to the house, Keir stopped by the chicken pen to gather a few eggs and then fetched a cupful of milk from the old goat. As he strode across the yard, his gaze traveled upward to Sarah's window. Her curtains were still drawn, and he wondered if she was still abed.

When he had woken this morning, he had experienced a moment of disorientation. It had lasted little more than a second, but he remembered it well, that faint question lingering, reminding him he was not in a place he usually found himself in. He had slept in a new place, and a new bed, and his mind had needed a moment to catch up. *Is it the same for Sarah?* He wondered.

Stomping off the snow, Keir stepped inside and once more hung his coat on the peg by the door. For a moment, he stopped, eyes traveling up the stairs, and listened. Yet all remained quiet, and so he continued on into the kitchen.

To his surprise, Loki was nowhere to be found, and he wondered where the sneaky feline had gone. Rummaging through the kitchen, beginning to set the table, Keir continued to listen to sounds from above. Of course, after the night before, Sarah had in all likelihood needed a good night's sleep.

Still, Keir wondered if perhaps she might be hiding upstairs. More often than not, he had seen fear lurking in her eyes. She felt unsettled by his presence, and he worried she would try to avoid him. And so, when half an hour passed without any sound from her, Keir decided not to wait any longer. Climbing the stairs, he approached her door and then gave a quick knock. Not waiting for an answer, he called, "Breakfast will be ready in a moment. Be sure to dress warmly." And then he went back downstairs.

At first, all remained quiet, and Keir wondered if he would need to head upstairs once more. Then, however, sounds drifted to his ears. Soft footfalls, and then the gentle creak of a door opening.

A moment later, Loki came charging into the kitchen, his large amber eyes trained upon Keir. "Where have ye been all night?" Keir inquired, stroking the cat's head. "I admit I was a wee bit worried."

"He was with me. I'm sorry. I didn't know you would worry for him."

Lifting his head, Keir found Sarah standing in the doorway, dressed in a simple wool dress, her fair hair pulled back into a braid that hung over her left shoulder. Wisps of hair still danced along her temples, reminding him of the first time he had seen her face in the moonlight. "There's no need to worry, lass," Keir assured her, relieved when she met his gaze without flinching. "'Tis nice to have company on a cold night." He winked at her, wondering if he could make her blush.

As though on cue, her cheeks blossomed to a bright red and she quickly averted her gaze, her fingers fidgeting with her right sleeve.

Keir laughed. "Oh, little wisp, ye would make a most dreadful liar." He moved toward her, and she tentatively lifted her gaze. "Every thought seems to be written all over yer face."

Pinching her eyes shut, Sarah shook her head in dismay. "I know. It is most awful."

"Is it truly?" Keir inquired, intrigued by the many different emotions that flitted across her face.

Sarah's eyes opened, and she looked at him with a rather incredulous look upon her face. "Of course, it is," she replied in a surprisingly strong voice. "I can never quite do as I am told because everything I feel is so visible upon my face that I constantly disappoint." A look of self-reproach came to her face. "Mother always says gentlemen wish to be flattered, to be admired and made to feel important. But how can I do that when I do not even possess the ability to care for what they wish to speak to me about?"

Keir was amazed by the flood of words suddenly spilling from her lips. "The ability to care?" he challenged. "Or the ability to pretend to care?" He lifted his right brow, watching her most carefully.

Sarah paused. "Is there truly a difference? Does it matter whether I truly care so long as the suitor believes it to be so?"

"Then let me ask ye this," Keir replied, encouraged by the soft spark in her blue eyes, "would ye want such a man? One who does not truly care whether ye pretend?"

Her lips parted, yet no sound came out. Her gaze became distant for a heartbeat or two before it returned to him. "It does not matter what I want. It never did." Sadness weighed heavily upon her voice. "As a dutiful daughter I ought to have...I should have..." Her eyes pressed shut for a split second before they flew open once more and stared into his. "What am I doing?" she gasped breathlessly, the expression upon her face frozen in a moment of utter shock and disbelief. "They will never forgive me. I will never forgive myself. How could I—?"

Keir grasped her by the shoulders, his touch cutting off her words. He watched her draw in a shuddering breath, watched her thoughts abandon guilt and remorse and return to the here and now, to him. Aye, he unsettled her, but he also drew her attention in a way that seemed to shut out everything else. "Ye are not wrong to demand respect, Sarah," Keir told her in a voice that brooked no argument. "Yer parents are wrong in denying it to ye. Ye're doing nothing wrong."

For a long moment, Sarah stared at him. Then she shook her head.

"My parents would disagree. As would society." She heaved a deep sigh. "This is the way of the world. These are the rules we live by, and I broke them."

Keir nodded. "Ye did." Her eyes widened at his words. "Yet these rules are man-made. Is it truly wise to accept them without question? Is it not our duty to ourselves, to mankind, to test them, to see if they uphold against doubt?"

Sarah's head was spinning. Keir could see it in the way her eyes moved. Clearly, she had never dared call the rules she had grown up with into question. He knew few women ever did. Except for the Whickerton sisters, of course. Keir almost grinned at the memory of Harriet challenging one of London's most infamous rakes to a duel. She had been determined to defend her honor, and she had been equally determined to do it herself.

And she had bested him. Keir doubted it was a lesson the young lord would ever forget.

"The man ye are to marry," Keir began, and his words instantly brought Sarah's attention back to him, "he is not yer choice, is he?"

Sarah shook her head, and Keir could sense every fiber of her being cringing away from that thought.

"Did yer parents ask for yer opinion?"

"They did not," Sarah admitted with a heavy sigh.

Keir gave her shoulders a slight squeeze. "Then why should ye ask for theirs?"

For a moment, Keir thought Sarah would continue to argue her point. She clearly believed she was in the wrong, had been taught to believe so from the moment she had been born. Still, part of her wanted him to be right, wanted to believe him.

"Are ye hungry, lass?" Keir asked with a smile.

A relieved chuckle left Sarah's lips. "Yes. Yes, I believe I am."

"Good. Then let me show ye how to boil eggs." Without waiting for her reaction, Keir grasped her hand and tugged her forward. He handed her a bucket still half-filled with water and told her to pour it into the pot. Sarah did as he asked, and it was as though he could watch the dark clouds above her head slowly dissolve. Her muscles seemed to relax, her eyes focused on the task at hand, her breath evening.

When the water was boiling, Keir handed her the basket of eggs and a spoon, instructing her not to let the eggs drop into the water if she did not wish to burn herself again. Listening intently, Sarah did as instructed, a childlike eagerness in her gaze that broke Keir's heart. Indeed, it seemed she had never once in her life been made to feel worthwhile, valuable, competent. It was a disheartening thought, and Keir vowed he would do what he could to prove her wrong, to make her see herself in a different light.

The way he saw her.

The way the Whickertons saw her.

After breakfast, they bundled up warmly and then stepped outside. The sky shone in a bright blue, and the sun rose just beyond the canopy of trees. It was a bright, beautiful day, and Keir could see the effect of it upon Sarah's face.

Closing her eyes, she turned toward the sky, lifting her face, as though she were savoring each and every ray of sunshine, feeling its warmth upon her skin. The cold reddened her cheeks, their color for once not due to embarrassment.

"Can I introduce ye to some friends of mine?" he asked with a grin, enjoying the puzzled look upon Sarah's face.

"Friends?" she asked carefully, her gaze moving left and right, as though she were expecting people to step out of hiding at any moment.

Holding her gaze, Keir moved toward her, watching the anticipation built within her. "Well, perhaps not friends. More like acquaintances." Then he reached out and grasped her hand. "Come. I'll show ye."

Even through the fabric of her mittens, Keir could feel her tense at his touch. After all, young ladies of the *ton* were not accustomed to physical contact. Still, a touch could mean so many things. It could simply be a means of offering comfort and companionship, and Sarah was in dire need of both.

"Where are we going?" she asked in a tentative voice as she allowed him to drag her onward. "I thought you were going to show me how to fetch water."

"I will," he reassured her, then he pushed open the door to the shed-turned-stable. "I assume ye remember Scout and Autumn."

At the sight of the horses, Sarah stumbled in her step, and Keir could feel her reluctance to continue onward. It was not terror that seized her but a deep sense of unease. Her breath lodged in her throat, and her gaze became distant, no doubt drawn back to a day in her past.

Keir did not push her closer. Clasping her hand, he moved her along past the two small stalls and toward the back where the chickens were located. "May I introduce ye to Cluck, Eggatha, Peep, and Attila the Hen?" He grinned at her. "Ladies, this is Sarah. She will take care of ye from now on."

Sarah laughed. "Eggatha? Attila the Hen?" She paused. "Wait! What did you say?"

Keir was relieved that she was too distracted to realize that there were six instead of only four chickens in the pen. The other two, however, were not intended for egg-laying and would not remain under Sarah's care for long.

"Here. This is how ye feed them." Keir handed her a bowl with some grain. "Always make sure the pen is locked up after ye leave. There are quite a few predators out here who would love to sink their claws into a plump chicken."

Sarah stared at the bowl in her hands then up at him. "You...You want me to...?"

Keir nodded, disliking the doubt he heard in her voice. She was not appalled by the suggestion because she thought such a task beneath herself. No, that was not it at all. The problem was that she did not trust herself to fulfill this task. "Ye'll be fine. I'll show ye everything ye need to know." He placed a hand upon her right shoulder, meeting her eyes. "Ye'll do fine."

A tentative smile touched her lips. "All right." She nodded in agreement then turned toward the chicken pen.

Keir watched as Sarah fed the chickens, her hands trembling with nervousness and her eyes wide with fascination. A part of her clearly wanted this, while another was terribly frightened. But she did well, even addressed the chickens by their names, turning to look at him in order to assure herself she had the right one. And when she finally stepped out of the chicken pen and locked the door behind herself, a proud smile lingered upon her face.

"To the well then!" Keir intoned, like a general about to lead his troops into battle.

Sarah chuckled. "To the well!"

Leading Sarah around the house, Keir stopped near the barren vegetable patch where the well was located. He handed her a bucket and showed her how to attach it to a rope and then lower it down. Her face shone rosy as she turned the handle, waiting for the sound of water splashing. "In winter, sometimes the surface is frozen over. Before ye can get any water out, ye'll first need to break the ice." He grinned at her. "A good-sized rock will do."

With her hands on the crank, Sarah looked up at him. "Is that what you did when you brought in the water this morning?"

Keir nodded. "Getting the full bucket back up will be a bit more strenuous." He chuckled. "Ye might still feel it tomorrow."

With an expectant look upon her face, Sarah peered down into the well, waiting until the bucket was submerged. Then she began cranking it up, a look of surprise upon her face when she felt the strain in her arms. "It is heavy," she remarked, trying to brush a strand of hair from her face with the side of her arm. Unfortunately, the strand continued to swing back, as did others. With every turn of the crank, more and more wisps of hair escaped her loose braid. *Aye, it suits her!*

Keir watched as Sarah's face became flushed with exertion. Doubt sneaked into her features, and Keir could see that she was losing faith. "Keep going, lass. Ye almost have it."

For a split second, her eyes darted to him before her teeth sank into her lower lip and she doubled her efforts. When the bucket finally appeared, Keir stood back and let Sarah wrestle it out of the well on her own. She half-drenched herself in the process, her face flushed and her arms trembling. She looked exhausted and disheveled and deeply discouraged, and yet there was this glow upon her face that made Keir think she had never in her life felt quite so alive than she did in that moment.

"'Tis hard now, I know, but it will get easier," he promised her, watching as she wrestled with her hair, trying to pin it back up and away from her face. "Let me help ye," Keir said as he stepped closer, lifting a hand and catching a stray curl between his fingers.

Sarah's eyes snapped up, her breath lodging in her throat, and suddenly, Keir wondered what it would be like to kiss her.

Chapter Ten

IN THE PRESENCE OF A STRANGER

Sarah's body still trembled from the effort it had taken to haul up the water. At the same time, she could feel half the bucket's contents soaking through her skirts, her hands roughened from turning the crank. She felt like a fool, like an incompetent fool!

Or, at least, she had a moment ago.

Now, all of a sudden, Sarah felt...other things.

"See how I braid my hair away from my face?" Keir murmured as he stood in front of her, so close that she felt his warm breath brush against her lips. His eyes were a dazzling blue, and they were focused on her in a way that made her insides flutter. "Let me show ye how."

'The audacity of that man!' Her mother's voice snapped in her head, interrupting the moment. And yet, instead of cringe under the lash of her mother's tongue, Sarah felt...annoyed, for a part of her... wanted to know...what Keir would do.

Nevertheless, for a second, Sarah thought she would faint on the spot when Keir reached for her loose strands. She could feel his fingertips brush against her skin as he gathered up her hair, then undid her braid. "It...It is not easy without Molly, my...my lady's maid," Sarah stammered, desperately searching for something to say, utterly shocked by the fact that her voice had not completely deserted her.

Keir chuckled, a low, rumbling sound deep in his throat. "Aye, it'll take some practice, like everything else in life." He combed his fingers through her hair, and the soft touch sent a shiver down Sarah's back. "Turn," he murmured, urging her to stand with her back to him. "Start smaller braids at yer temples," Keir explained then.

His fingers moved swiftly, and Sarah felt a soft tug upon her scalp here and there as he worked. It reminded her of when her lady's maid styled her hair for a ball; however, Molly's practiced hands had never made Sarah's heart skip a beat nor caused her breath to become uneven.

"Perhaps 'twould have been better to show ye in front of a mirror," Keir remarked with a hint of self-reproach in his voice before he stepped back to admire his handiwork. "What do ye think?"

Sarah lifted a hand and ran a finger over the small braids running backward from her temples. They met in the back of her head where they combined into one large braid that hung down her back. Indeed, the flimsy curls that always hung into her face were gone.

Chancing a glance at Keir, Sarah asked, "Where did you learn that?"

For a brief moment, a shadow seemed to pass over his face. "My sister taught me." Then the shadow passed as quickly as it had come. "Do ye like it?" he asked with a wicked grin.

Sarah felt herself blush as the look in his eyes brought back the memory of his touch.

Keir chuckled. "Ye're blushing again, lass."

Turning away, Sarah wanted to bury her head in the snow. *Indeed, he is right. I am an awful liar!* Her face immediately betrayed any lie she might speak. It betrayed her even when she spoke not a word at all.

"Why are ye blushing?" Keir asked, his tone now serious, as he placed one hand upon her shoulder, urging her to look at him. "Does yer lady's maid not do yer hair?"

"Of course, she does," Sarah replied, feeling her fingernails digging into her palms even through her mittens. "But you...you're a man."

Keir had the audacity to grin, and Sarah felt her face burn even hotter—red-hot like a beacon. "I assure ye, little wisp, I have no ulterior motive. Ye needna worry."

Sarah wanted to die on the spot! Indeed, her mortification was complete now! Of course, he had no ulterior motive...at least, not *that* kind of an ulterior motive. No one ever had...with the exception of Lord Blackmore, her betrothed! He had—

"Are ye all right, lass?" Keir asked, his voice suddenly gentle and his blue eyes holding concern. "Have ye ever met a man with...ulterior motives?"

'Gentlemen don't have ulterior motives!' Her mother cried indignantly in Sarah's mind. 'Gentlemen always treat a lady with respect!'

Surprising them both, Sarah laughed. Tears spilled over her cheeks abruptly, making her wonder where they had come from. "Of course, I have! The world is full of people with ulterior motives. It is the very reason I am here, is it not? Everyone wants something. Everyone—" She clamped her lips shut as she felt her tears touch the corners of her mouth and tasted their saltiness upon her lips. This was a mistake. She ought not have lost control like this. She ought not have spoken to him like this, revealed so much about herself, about...

Exhaling a deep breath, Sarah closed her eyes, willing her thoughts to stop, willing everything to simply go away and leave her be. She could no longer bear this burden, these thoughts tormenting her every day. Once, the thought of her future had been a wonderful dream; however, with time, that dream had changed. It had been altered and shaped by experiences she had not seen coming. Now, it was no longer a dream but a nightmare instead.

And it had been for a while.

For too long.

Before Sarah even felt Keir's hand upon her shoulder, she sensed him draw closer. She felt his presence, his warmth, his concern. "I promise ye, Sarah," he murmured softly, and her eyes opened to meet his, "that my only motive is to see ye safe." He stilled, and that shadow seemed to return, casting something dark across his face. "As I hope that...somewhere out there another is doing the same for my sister." He exhaled slowly and then took a step back.

Sarah stared into Keir's face, wishing she knew more. She wanted to ask him, ask about his sister, ask about what he had meant, but he stepped away, the look upon his face hardening. Yes, even a man like

Keir, who knew how to smile like no other, understood the meaning of pain...and loss, probably.

As Sarah watched him walk away, she wondered what had happened to the sister he clearly loved. *Had they simply quarreled? Drifted apart because of some silly argument?* Indeed, Sarah knew what that felt like. After all, years ago, she and Kate had been not only sisters but the best of friends. Now, however, she knew frighteningly little about her own sister's life. They had not seen each other in a long time, and Sarah wondered if that would ever change. They had not even quarreled. Nothing had come between them...but life itself. Kate had married and moved away, her life now circulating around the duties of a wife and mother. Was she happy? Her letters indicated she was, and yet for some time now, Sarah thought the letters did not sound like the sister she had once known so well.

Picking up the bucket, Sarah carried it back into the house, careful not to spill any more of its contents upon herself. She left it in the kitchen and then ventured back upstairs to change. Of course, this task was easier said than done. After all, Sarah had always had a lady's maid to assist her. If only Molly could be here right now; however, no one could know. Sarah knew that. It was paramount that no one ever found out what had truly happened, how this *kidnapping* had come to be.

Once more in a dry dress, Sarah moved over to the window, her gaze drawn outside. She wondered where Keir had gone the very moment he reappeared, crossing the small yard before disappearing once more in the stable. No doubt he was seeing to the horses.

The look upon his face had still been somewhat tense, Sarah thought. *Is he, too, still thinking of his sister? Is his loss perhaps more permanent than mine? Did his sister pass away...in childbirth or because of some sort of illness?* The thought of losing Kate that way was unbearable for Sarah, despite the distance that now existed between them. Clearly, Keir loved his sister, and her passing would have been equally painful for him, would it not?

The sound of a door creaking open drew Sarah's attention back to the snow-covered yard below. She saw Keir leading Scout outside before tying the gelding to a post. He held a basket with an assortment of brushes under one arm, which he sat down upon a large rock nearby. Then Keir turned toward the horse, his hands running down Scout's neck and along his back. He checked the horse's legs and hooves, all the while murmuring something. Sarah could see his lips move, his breath billowing out into the cold air, and Scout's ears twitched, moved as though he was straining to listen to each and every word that Keir spoke.

Then Keir suddenly looked up and saw her watching him from the window.

Sarah flinched, heat shooting up into her face at being discovered. She pulled back and hid behind the curtain, reminding herself that she had no right to watch him so unabashedly. No doubt he thought her a silly girl, inwardly laughing about her struggles to find her place in this world.

The moment the thought crossed Sarah's mind; she could not believe it to be true. Indeed, Keir did not strike her as someone who ever made light of another's struggles. Thus far, he had always been understanding. Or was that only a mask he wore? Yes, so many people these days wore masks. Lord Blackmore did. In public, he came across as a kind and considerate man. A true gentleman. However, in private, he had revealed a very different side of him. One Sarah wished she had never known existed. Yet if she had not, she might not have been desperate enough to undertake this adventure.

Peeking around the curtain, Sarah saw that Keir was now brushing down Scout. He was still speaking to the animal, and Scout turned his head, rubbing it affectionately against Keir's shoulder.

Sarah smiled. No, she could not imagine Keir any differently than he was right now. *He cannot possibly be wearing a mask, can he?* Of course, her opinion was influenced by the very fact that such a possibility terrified her to her core. After all, she was dependent upon him. If he chose to, he could—

Pausing, Sarah squinted against the bright winter sun, trying to look closer, trying to see Keir's face, the look in his eyes. Indeed, this moment, here, right now, was private. There was no one else around. No one to judge him. No consequences to be feared should he act

75

without decorum, without respect toward her. No, he was not wearing a mask, Sarah concluded, and her body sighed with relief.

As much as he enjoyed teasing her, she felt safe with him. How that had happened, Sarah did not know. She had not expected it. Indeed, the thought of spending days, perhaps even a week alone with a stranger had immediately made her doubt the wisdom of this endeavor. Now, she was utterly relieved she had not reconsidered.

Over the next few days, a relaxing routine developed between them. They both rose early, and while Keir saw to the horses, Sarah fed the chickens. They were amusing creatures, and their names brought her great joy, especially Attila the Hen. She was a fearsome little bird with light brown feathers and a tendency for dramatics. The moment she saw Sarah coming, she would cluck and squawk in a very agitated manner, as though Sarah had come to wring her neck for tonight's supper. At the same time, Sarah could not help the thought that Attila the Hen was not truly afraid. Her movements were swift but not panicked, and she had a look in her eyes that made Sarah think that there was more to her than met the eye.

"She's a bit of a warrior, is she not?" Keir remarked with a chuckle from the stall next door.

Sarah laughed. "She seems very...formidable." Setting down the bowl of grain, Sarah stepped out of the chicken pen and latched the door. "Why did you give her the name?" she asked, cautiously venturing a little closer toward the horses' stalls.

Running a brush along Autumn's back, Keir shrugged, his blue gaze darting over to the chicken pen. "That I canna say. It seemed appropriate."

"I cannot fault your observation." With a grin, Sarah watched as the chickens attacked the grain in the bowls, as though it were their last meal.

"Would ye give me a hand?"

Sarah flinched. She could not help it. It was one thing to be standing out here with a sturdy wooden wall between her and those hooves. Yet the thought of stepping inside was—

"'Tis all right," Keir murmured in that soft and reassuring voice of his that never failed to put Sarah at ease. He stepped around the mare and came to stand at the wall, his arms resting upon the door. "It still haunts ye, doesna it?"

Sarah swallowed hard as she stared at Autumn. Indeed, there was nothing threatening about the young mare. Still, at the mere sight of her, Sarah's heart clenched painfully. Her lungs ceased, unable to draw air into her body. Her head began to feel light, her gaze becoming unfocused. Soon, she would—

Reaching out, Keir placed a hand upon her shoulder, his eyes searching hers. "Ye're safe," he whispered. "The moment is of the past."

Clasping her hands together against the trembling that suddenly seized her, Sarah nodded. "I know."

"Yer mind does but yer heart has yet to learn." He smiled at her, and it was a smile that spoke of kindness and understanding, not of reproach and superiority. "Go on ahead inside and prepare breakfast. I shall be there shortly."

Relieved, Sarah nodded and then rushed from the stable. The moment she stepped out into the cool winter air, she breathed in deeply, momentarily overwhelmed by the feeling of air rushing back into her lungs. When she reached the door, she remembered she had forgotten the basket with eggs she had collected that morning. Try as she might, she could not bring herself to turn around. Perhaps Keir would bring it when he was done with the horses.

Entering the kitchen, Sarah busied herself setting the table. Only days ago, the notion of doing such work would have seemed other-worldly. If her mother could see her now, she would faint at the mere thought of it. Only Sarah had come to realize that she loved this kind of domestic work. Of course, it was not much. It was not the kind of hard work kitchen maids did. Yet with everything that Sarah did for herself, she found she stood a little taller. It was a good feeling, one that she cherished, for it was a feeling that stood against the tidal wave of fear that constantly threatened to drown her.

Only this morning, Sarah had woken to a sense of contentedness and realized that it had been a long time since she had felt this at ease.

Here of all places.

In the presence of a virtual stranger.

Away from home.

Sarah could not help but wonder what that meant. Only she did not dare try to find an answer to the question, for deep down, in the far recesses of her mind, she knew its meaning.

And it terrified her.

Chapter Eleven

LOSS OF A SISTER

Keir had seen the change in Sarah. It was subtle, and if he had been a less attentive observer, it would have certainly escaped his notice. Yet he had always been blessed with watchful eyes, and therefore, the soft glow that lingered in Sarah's eyes these days drew him closer like a beacon in the night sky.

Aye, she was still a fearful creature. Fortunately, though, she had found joy in the many small tasks that needed doing around the house. She seemed eager to learn, doubtful of her own abilities, but most willing. The chickens delighted her, and Keir loved to hear laughter bubbling out of her as she watched them. Aye, when his little wisp laughed, it affected him.

He could not say why—after all, they were barely acquaintances—but he could tell that laughter was a rarity for her. For Sarah to find it here in this place in this moment was something very unexpected.

Almost a treasure.

Aye, perhaps even better than treasure.

Keir knew that something had happened in Sarah's past, something that had made her fearful of horses. He had watched her closely, had seen that wistful look upon her face and knew that whatever had happened had not merely frightened her but taken something from her she had once, long ago, held dear.

As though to bless this risky and utterly insane adventure they had embarked upon, the weather remained fair. Temperatures remained low, but the sun shone brilliantly in a clear blue sky, unable to melt the snow but warming their faces the moment they stepped outdoors.

Autumn stood tied to a pole in the yard while Keir was brushing the mare down, cleaning her hooves and slipping her a treat. Scout was already out in the meadow behind the house.

Out of the corner of his eye, Keir watched Sarah step into the stable to feed the chickens. He knew it would not take her long, for he had seen her gaze linger upon the mare. Aye, as much as Sarah feared horses, she was also very curious. She had once loved them; he was certain of it.

Keir waited until Sarah once more stepped out of the shed. She kept her distance but did not hurry away. Again, she watched him and Autumn, a deep yearning in her blue eyes.

"I'll take her out to the meadow," Keir called over his shoulder as he untied the rope. "She needs to move a bit." Then he led the mare down the small path that snaked around the house and toward the back meadow. He did not look at Sarah nor invite her to follow them. He did not want to pressure her, make her feel as though he expected something. Instead, he wanted to put her at ease and let her make her own decisions, certain that curiosity would get the better of her.

With a gentle slap to the mare's rear, Keir sent her charging out into the meadow. Her hooves kicked up snow, and she greeted Scout cheerfully. Keir closed the gate behind her and then leaned against it, his arms resting upon the top beam. He had always loved watching horses. It had helped him realize that if he watched people just as closely, he could learn more about them than by asking questions directly. Most were completely unaware how much they gave away when they spoke not a word. Certainly, words were helpful. They added layers and conveyed a deeper meaning. They filled out the past and shaped the future, but they often fell short when it came to what lived in a person's soul.

The sun shone warm upon his head and shoulders, and Keir

breathed in deeply the winter's air. Aye, it was a beautiful place, free and untamed, a secret spot out in the woods, untouched by the industriousness of mankind. It reminded Keir a bit of the Highlands, of the endlessness and the far horizon. It always made him think of endless possibilities, of adventures and the cresting of a new day. *Aye, it also reminds me of Yvaine.*

The other day, Keir had not even realized he had spoken of his sister before he had seen his words reflected back at him in Sarah's eyes. He still cherished the many wonderful moments he had had with Yvaine, and to speak of those brought joy to his heart. Only to think of her loss was something he had not yet shared with anyone outside of his family. He spoke only of her disappearance when it could not be avoided. After all, her life meant nothing to someone who had never even known her.

As he gazed out at the grazing horses, their noses lowered to the snow-covered ground, searching for a blade of grass here and there, Keir wondered if he would ever see Yvaine again, if he would ever find out what had happened to her.

The soft sound of a twig snapping drifted to Keir's ears, and he turned to see Sarah walking toward him. Slowly, he dropped his hand, which had gone to the knife at his belt out of reflex. "'Tis a beautiful day, isna it?"

Offering him a shy smile, Sarah nodded. She moved closer but stopped a good distance away, leaning against the fence as he did. Keir could see that something was on her mind, and yet her lips remained sealed.

"Ask what ye wish to know," Keir prompted her with a bit of a grin. Aye, she was utterly adorable when her cheeks flushed red and she averted her eyes in mortification. "Ye're blushing again, little wisp," Keir added for good measure.

If possible, Sarah's cheeks darkened even further, and she rested her forehead upon her crossed arms to hide her face.

Abandoning his own post, Keir ventured closer. "Why is it that ye blush so often?" he asked with a chuckle.

Sarah did not lift her head, but he saw her shrug her shoulders. "If only I knew," she whispered in a tentative voice. "Then perhaps I could stop it from happening."

"Why would ye want to do that?"

Her eyes met his, a hint of incredulity in them. "Why would you ask me that? Isn't it obvious?"

Keir heaved a deep sigh, remembering the many lies and confusions he had met throughout his own life. "In my humble opinion," he told her, "honesty is a rare treasure. Cherish it instead of wishing it gone."

A thoughtful expression rested upon her face, and yet Keir could see that she did not completely agree with him. "If the same were true for everyone else, I'd certainly agree," Sarah remarked, then she shook her head. "Only it is not. Everyone can see what I'm thinking, what I'm feeling, but I do not have the same advantage." Her eyes swept over his face. "I have not the slightest inkling what goes on in your head right now, but you see me with such accuracy that it frightens me."

"Ye're right," Keir replied, holding her gaze before he took a step toward her. "Then ask me what ye wish to know, and I promise I shall give ye the truth."

For a moment, Sarah regarded him doubtfully. "People often speak of the truth, and yet I wonder if there is even such a thing."

Keir smiled. "I suppose there is no such thing as an ultimate truth. There are only versions of the truth depending on our own point of view. After all, no two people experience the same situation in quite the same way. We are all shaped by what came before and look at things differently, see them in a different light." He held her gaze, hoping that she could see he was being honest with her. "Ask me anything ye wish, and I will give ye the truth as I see it."

"Promise?" Sarah dared him, something almost mischievous in her blue eyes that Keir had never seen in them before. He could not help but wonder who she had been as a child and what had made her so fearful. He could not help but wonder who she could have been and who she still longed to be.

Keir nodded. "Promise."

Sarah's smile of triumph faded quickly when she realized she would now need to reveal what was on her mind. Keir saw her hesitate, doubt returning to her gaze. For a second, he feared she might change her mind. Then, however, her right hand tightened upon the fence as determination swept through her and she lifted her head in a rather defiant gesture. Yet, almost absentmindedly, her left hand rose, and she ran the tip of her forefinger along the small braid that held back her hair. Indeed, Keir had been surprised at Sarah's attempts these past few days to replicate the braids he had shown her that day by the well.

"What happened to your sister?" Sarah finally asked as Keir had known she would. Aye, her face was easy to read. She was like an open book, and he liked that about her. "I'm sorry," Sarah added before he could answer, shaking her head. "I shouldn't have asked. It's none of my concern, of course."

"Perhaps not," Keir replied, "but I promised ye the truth." He cast Sarah a smile, and her shoulders relaxed. "My sister's story is a bit of an unusual one," Keir began, recalling how he had last spoken of her to Troy, only son and heir to the Whickerton clan. It had not been too long ago, and yet a part of him felt as though a lifetime had passed since. Even then, Keir had not meant to speak of Yvaine's disappearance. However, the conversation had taken a turn and then Troy had asked.

Keir had never been one to lie, and so he had answered.

Sarah watched him with curious eyes as she waited for him to continue.

"My sister was not born to my parents like my brothers and I were," Keir told her with all the honesty he had promised. "She was only a little girl—barely three years old—when we found her."

Sarah's expression stilled. "Found her?"

Keir nodded, although he could barely remember the day. He had been a child himself at the time, barely eleven years of age. "We were out riding, and...there she was. Of course, we searched for her family, asked around, but no one ever claimed her." A wistful smile came to his face as images of long ago drifted back into his mind. "I think my mother saw in her the daughter she had always wanted the moment she first laid eyes on Yvaine." He chuckled, and his gaze moved back to meet Sarah's. "We gave her our name and our hearts, and that was it. We thought it would be forever."

"What happened?" Tension came to Sarah's face. She knew he would speak of loss, and that was something that she knew herself.

Keir shrugged, that helpless feeling sweeping through him once more. "I dunna know," he finally said, knowing that was the worst of it. "One day she was simply gone." Aye, the wound in his heart was still there, aching fiercely with every word he spoke. It also served as a reminder that Yvaine had truly existed, that she had been his sister and would remain his sister until the end of time.

Sarah's face had gone pale, and she looked at him with an anguished expression upon her face.

"Yvaine had always been a free spirit," Keir told her, once more folding his arms and leaning upon the fence. His gaze moved out to the two horses and the distant horizon. "No one could ever hold her back. She did what she wanted to do; her spirit unbroken by whatever tragedy had delivered her to us. She loved to ride." Keir could sense Sarah tense beside him. "Sometimes, she would ride out in the morning and not return until nightfall. Of course, my parents tried to dissuade her, but whenever Yvaine had set her mind on something, there was no talking her out of it." A chuckle rumbled in Keir's throat, and it felt good. It felt good to remember her this way. Perhaps he should speak of her more often. After all, her memory would forever remain with him whether he spoke of her or not.

A wistful smile played across Sarah's features, as though she, too, had once known Yvaine. "She reminds me of my own sister," Sarah remarked with a sideways glance. "Kate used to be so...vivacious. Of course, she was far from free to do as she pleased, and yet she often found little ways to be herself, to do precisely as she wanted." Sarah looked up, and their eyes met.

"And ye?" Keir asked, seeing the faint echo of the girl Sarah had once been flash across her face.

As though her burden suddenly returned, Sarah turned away, her shoulders now slumped as she leaned heavily against the fence. "Oh, I've never been daring," she murmured with a feigned smile, feigned lightheartedness. "I was never more than I am now."

"Even if I'd only met ye today," Keir told her earnestly, "I wouldna have believed that." He looked deep into her eyes and saw a spark of pride. He knew she was hiding a part of herself and wondered if perhaps she had all but forgotten about that part, as though it had been buried as dead.

For a long time, neither one of them spoke until a deep sigh left Sarah's lips. "Sometimes I feel as though I lost her," she murmured, a faraway look in her eyes. "Sometimes my heart aches, as though it fears that she will never return." She blinked, and her eyes met his once more. Instantly, that adorable blush returned, and she clamped her hand over her mouth, her eyes going wide. "Oh, I'm so sorry. I didn't mean to say...I shouldn't have..." She shook her head, disappointed with herself. "I mean, I know precisely where my sister is. It is not the same. She's not lost to me. I—"

Keir stepped closer and gently placed a hand on her arm. "Loss can have many faces," he told her, his gaze searching hers. "What happened to Kate?"

Sarah scoffed, as though still chastising herself. "Nothing happened to her. We grew up, and she was married while I..." A shy smile came to her face, and she averted her eyes. "She was married and now has a life of her own."

Keir frowned at Sarah's choice of words, as though a life was only worth living if one was married. Of course, that was the general opinion! Especially where women were concerned. However, Keir thought it was a dangerous way of looking at the world and at oneself.

"And yet ye feel as though ye lost her," he said, watching her carefully. Somehow, Keir could not shake the thought that Sarah's fear of horses was tied to the loss of her sister.

Sarah sighed. "Well, I no longer see her every day. Surely you know what it is like to grow up with another, to speak to them every day, to know their face better than you know your own." Sadness darkened her eyes. "And then, from one day to the next, they're suddenly gone and all the things you want to say to them continue to circle through your head with nowhere to go."

Keir nodded, remembering all the many conversations he had had with Yvaine after her disappearance. How often had he played through moments in his mind, imagining what she would say, how she would respond? "If she's only married," Keir asked with a hint of a teasing grin, "why then dunna ye go and see her, speak to her?"

Sarah shrugged. "At first, there simply never seemed to be a right moment. After Kate was married, my parents were determined to see me equally well situated." She glanced up at him, that rosy bloom once more gracing her cheeks. "You see, Kate caught the eye of an earl in her first season, and my parents hoped I would be...just as successful." Her gaze moved outward again, past the horses and toward the horizon. "And by the time it became clear that no one wanted to marry me, Kate was already a mother of two beautiful girls. Her time was no longer her own, and we had less in common than ever before." A slight frown came to her face. "I saw her only a few times, and when I did..."

Keir nodded. "She seemed different?"

Nodding, Sarah looked at him. "Not like herself. I tried to speak to my mother about it, but she simply waved it away. The last time I visited, Kate was distant. She was no longer the sister I remembered. Of course, I know that people change, that being a mother changed her, and yet I cannot help but think that..."

Keir felt his muscles tense. It was as though a deep sense of foreboding fell over him, as though he could see a storm approaching. Perhaps it was the look in Sarah's eyes or the hopelessness in her tone, but whatever it was he could not shake that feeling of dread. "That something is wrong," he finished for her.

Again, Sarah nodded. "Perhaps it is nothing. Of course, she would be different now; after all, she's living a different life. She's a mother of two girls, and...her husband demands an heir." A sharp edge came to her voice as she spoke, the muscles in her jaw hardening. "She's with child yet again."

Knowing there was nothing to be done, Keir wished for nothing more but to ease Sarah's mind. "My father always wanted a daughter," he told her with a chuckle, "and when we found my sister, he was elated. He always said that women have more sense than men."

An honest smile came to Sarah's face, and the look in her eyes held wonderment. "Truly?"

"Aye. My father wouldna be the man he is without my mother by his side," Keir told her freely, surprised by the longing for home he suddenly felt in his chest. "He always says that they are two halves of a whole, each special in their own way and yet lost without the other. Incomplete. He always says that he wouldna know what to do without his wife's counsel."

A longing glow came to Sarah's face. "And what about your mother? Does she believe the same?"

Keir laughed. "Oh, she would never admit it! She's a fierce one, like Yvaine. Perhaps they were always meant to be mother and daughter. She has always been determined to prove to the world that she is not some weak female. But deep down, I know she thinks as my father does." He leaned closer conspiratorially and winked at her. "Dunna tell her I said that."

Sarah laughed, the sound pure and simple, and he realized that until this very moment he had not yet truly heard her laugh. "The Whickertons are like that," she said all of a sudden. "They have this family tradition to always marry for love." A wistful expression came to her eyes, one equal parts longing and envy. "And they did. All of them." *She envies them!*

Keir nodded. "Aye, they are a remarkable family, aware that happiness can only be found through respect."

Sarah stilled, her eyes narrowing as she looked at him curiously. "Do you know them?"

Keir gritted his teeth, only now realizing how much he had given away. Indeed, he could imagine Grandma Edie's chiding look. After all, she had implored him not to betray his identity and had been right to do so. After all, better than anyone, Keir knew now that Sarah was an awful liar. Even without meaning to, she could easily endanger his life by revealing the wrong thing at the wrong time in front of the wrong person. No, he needed to be more careful.

"I've heard of them, of course." Keir felt himself cringe at the half-truth. He despised lying and wished he could simply speak honestly.

Autumn's soft nicker drifted to his ears, and he and Sarah both turned to look at the mare. She stood halfway down the meadow, her head angled toward them, as though she was listening intently.

Keir smiled. "She's clearly curious," he remarked, nodding toward the mare, now approaching with careful steps. "Curious but hesitant."

He glanced back at Sarah. "She's not one to trust people easily, and I believe she appreciates it that ye dunna rush at her but give her time to get to know ye."

Slowly, Sarah's gaze moved from the mare to him, something thoughtful there, something that rang with memories, with recognition.

Keir nodded. "That...is respect."

A deep sigh left Sarah's lips when she redirected her attention back to the mare. Both eyed each other warily. Both grateful for the distance between them. Both hoping that perhaps the day would come that the distance might shrink.

Nodding his head, Keir moved back, thinking that it might do both of them good to have some time to themselves. And so, he turned around and walked back to the house, knowing that sometimes good things happened if one let them come at their own pace.

Chapter Twelve

BETWEEN FRIENDS

With a tight knot in her stomach, Sarah watched Keir ride away. Her eyes followed him until the world around swallowed him up, leaving her not even a glimpse. Instantly, cold crawled up and down Sarah's back, and she realized how vulnerable she felt without him. As much as he had been a stranger that first day, as much as his unconventional ways had frightened her in the beginning, she now felt perfectly safe with him.

Don't be a fool! She chided herself. *He will be back in a matter of hours!*

Looking down, Sarah felt a smile tug upon the corners of her mouth when she found Loki looking up at her with his wide amber eyes. He had taken to following her around, as though he sensed somehow that she needed company. He was not Keir, but his presence made her feel better, more at ease. And so, she reached down and scratched him behind his ears before straightening and walking back into the kitchen.

Loki, of course, followed her eagerly.

Three days had passed since the night she had fled London. Three days since her parents had to have found the letter she had left behind in her bedchamber. The letter that had been supposedly written by her kidnapper. It had said to wait for further instructions, and Sarah knew that Grandma Edie had planned to send yet another letter a day or two later, providing such instructions, details for the ransom to be paid.

As Sarah began washing vegetables and cutting them the way Keir had shown her, her mind trailed off. She no longer saw Loki sitting beside her, watching her curiously. No, her mind drifted to one single question. Had her ransom already been paid? Was that the message Keir would find at the inn? Would this adventure end today?

As much as Sarah longed for everything to be resolved, for her life to be her own, the feeling that swelled in her chest at the thought of going home was not one of relief. Indeed, as odd as it was, Sarah felt regret and even a small measure of grief.

Shaking her head, she looked at Loki. "I must be mad," she whispered to the cat, who eyed her with that familiar look of curiosity and bewilderment, as though he could not make sense of her as much as he tried. "Why should I not wish to go home? Why should I now feel regret?"

Moving closer, Loki brushed his head against her arm, purring softly as he rubbed it back and forth. Then he looked up at her with wide eyes, and Sarah could not shake the feeling that he had just provided her with advice she ought to take seriously.

Scratching the feline behind his ears, Sarah chuckled. "I wish you could tell me what to do or that I knew why I felt like this. I did not expect it. Not for a moment." She thought back to all the doubts she had had the night of leaving London. "I was so terrified. I wanted nothing more but to stay where I was, to have everything that was familiar and not dare venture out into the unknown." She swept her eyes around the small kitchen, and a smile came to her face. "Only the unknown is no longer unknown, is it?" Again, she met Loki's gaze. "And Keir is no longer a stranger."

A bit of a chiding meow left Loki's throat.

Sarah chuckled. "Of course, neither are you. I have not forgotten you." Or Autumn, she thought, thinking of the mare out in the meadow. "In a strange way, I found a life here I never expected. It is simple and common, and yet it is beautiful."

And I've only been here a total of three days! How is this possible?

Hanging the large pot over the fire, Sarah filled it with water and then slowly began adding ingredients for another stew the way Keir had shown her. Every small task made her feel wonderful. She felt accomplished in a completely new way, able to do things that mattered. Never before had Sarah felt quite like that. Never had she been good at any of the tasks her parents had set for her. In truth, she had never truly wanted to do the tasks, only seeing them as her responsibility. Only a life lived solely for responsibility was not one that brought joy, was it? Oddly enough, Sarah had never quite considered her own heart. Not in earnest. Yes, of course, she had always dreamed of love as any young girl did. And yet a part of her, deep down, had never quite imagined a happy life for her, a life filled with joy and shaped by her own hopes and dreams.

Indeed, Sarah felt certain that if Lord Blackmore had not advanced on her that night after supper, if he had not stepped too close and frightened her far beyond everything she had ever experienced, she would not have dared go against her parents' wishes. She had always known her duty, and only panic had been able to make her act against it. Perhaps she ought to be grateful for what Lord Blackmore had done, for the way he had looked at her, for forcing a kiss on her.

'Do not exaggerate!' The voice of her mother snapped in her head. 'A kiss is only a kiss, and certainly no reason to behave in such a dishonorable way.'

Sarah disagreed with her whole being, for the thought alone, the thought of Blackmore's approach made her shudder and bile rise in her throat. Only if he had not, she might not be here.

With Keir.

To Sarah's surprise, she no longer felt reluctant to use his first name. Somehow, it felt perfectly natural to address him in such an intimate way.

Little wisp.

Sarah smiled at Keir's nickname for her. She had come to cherish not only the name itself but also the way he said it. Whenever he spoke it, his voice always rang with...something more than they ought to be to one another. They had known each other for those *same three days*, and yet in some moments Sarah felt as though they had known each other forever. He looked at her, and she knew he understood even when she did not find the words to explain herself.

Only the day before, Keir had helped her look at Autumn and truly see the mare. In that moment, Sarah had not faced an unpredictable creature but someone she could relate to. A being with fears not unlike her own, with hopes that felt familiar and curiosity pushing her forward despite the dangers that might linger nearby.

Indeed, Keir was a man unlike the gentlemen she had grown up with. But perhaps that was a good thing. After all, was Lord Blackmore not also one of these gentlemen. Perhaps the world could not be divided into black and white, good people on one side and bad people on the other. Gentlemen were not always true gentlemen, and commoners, or criminals even, were not always bad to the core.

Sarah smiled, for she had a truly hard time seeing Keir as bad in any way. Yes, she knew he was a criminal of some sort. Still, the way he treated her with respect and kindness spoke of a good man. Could one be a criminal and a good man? Was that possible? More than ever, Sarah felt confused about herself, about the world and the people in it. She had hoped to reach some sort of clarity by freeing herself from the future her parents had planned for her, by stepping out of their shadow and claiming the right to choose for herself. Only now, Sarah had no idea how to choose or even what to choose.

"What do I want?" she whispered into the stillness of the kitchen before her gaze drifted lower to where Loki still sat upon the table, his large amber eyes watchful. "What is it you want?" she asked him with a chuckle.

As though he understood her, Loki lay down and then rolled onto his back, one paw reaching up, touching her hand.

Sarah laughed and stroked his fur, scratching his belly as he purred contentedly. "If only my life could be as simple as yours." She frowned. "I never thought having a choice could feel like a burden. What if I choose wrong?" With a heavy sigh, Sarah dropped down onto the chair beside her. "If I choose wrong, I will have no one to blame but myself." She met Loki's gaze. "What is it I want?"

Indeed, it was a question Sarah had given far too little thought to. Somehow, foolishly, she had always assumed that once she had a choice, she would know what to do. If, indeed, Lord Blackmore paid the ransom to see her returned, if Sarah then found herself once again in her parents' house, finally free of any pressure to marry—after all, what gentleman would want a bride who had been in the hands of kidnappers for days?—what then?

At a loss, Sarah pushed to her feet and returned to her preparations. As her mind circled the same question again and again, her hands moved, worked. She added vegetables and the chicken Keir had prepared earlier that morning to the pot before adding spices. Sniffing each one, she carefully added a little before adding more. She tasted the stew a few times, never quite certain if she was doing it right. Still, Sarah was no longer afraid of making a mistake. She no longer felt the need to be perfect, crushed by the knowledge that she was not. All of a sudden, it was all right to get something wrong, to make a mistake, to err. Still, it was one thing to make a mistake while preparing food, to season wrong and ruin a meal. It was quite another to make a mistake with her life, her future. What if it could not be undone? Like a marriage vow? Once spoken, it would seal her fate.

Once the stew bubbled happily in the pot over the fire, Sarah removed the apron and smoothed out the wrinkles of her dress. Then she pulled on her fur-lined winter boots and wrapped the thick woolen cloak around herself before stepping outside into the brisk winter air.

As always, Loki was right by her side, his little paws sinking into the powdery snow. He shook himself, and Sarah laughed, delighted with his antics as he tried to keep his paws dry.

"Perhaps you should stay inside," she suggested, holding the door open.

Loki looked at her as though she had lost her mind, then he shook himself again and proceeded onward. How he knew where she wished to go, Sarah did not know. Yet she followed him, glad to have his company, to not find herself completely alone.

Together, they walked through the snow, following the small path that led around the house back through a cluster of trees and then up and around toward the meadow where Autumn still grazed. The moment Sarah stepped toward the fence and her eyes found the mare, Autumn lifted her head and turned toward her.

For a moment, Sarah felt a flicker of apprehension. Her muscles tensed, and inside her mittens her fingers curled into tight little fists. She could feel the air get stuck in her lungs, and before her eyes images of the past began to flicker.

Gritting her teeth against the onslaught, Sarah pinched her eyes shut. However, that only brought back the memories with full force as apprehension turned to panic.

Oh, I ought not have come! Somehow the other day had been different. After all, Keir had been by her side. He had a way of calming her, easing her thoughts and her emotions. With him by her side, she felt safe...as unbelievable as that sounded.

A soft nicker drifted to Sarah's ears, and her eyes blinked open.

Across the meadow, still quite a distance away, stood Autumn. Her ears flickered back and forth, and then she took a tentative step forward. Her gaze remained upon Sarah, and she could not shake the feeling that the mare was as apprehensive as she was herself. Did Autumn truly feel as she did? Or did the horse simply sense Sarah's tumultuous emotions? Was Autumn wary because Sarah was?

Gathering her courage, Sarah stepped up to the fence, grasping the top beam. Her gaze remained upon Autumn, watching the mare, trying to see her as she had the day before. "Hello there," Sarah said tentatively, her voice barely able to carry to where Autumn stood.

The mare's reddish-brown coat shimmered in the morning sun, off-setting the deep black of her mane and tail. As she moved, taking one cautious step at a time, Sarah felt her heart beat wildly in her chest. Yet it was not only panic or even dread she experienced. Now, there was a touch of excitement as well.

Once, years ago, Sarah had loved horses. She had loved riding out across the meadows, the wind in her hair and her eyes upon the far horizon. She had felt free and utterly weightless in these moments, her mind unable to think of possible dangers or pitfalls. If she had, perhaps *that day* would not have happened.

"Hello, Autumn," Sarah greeted the mare as the horse stopped only a few paces in front of her. "I came to see you today," she whispered, watching the mare's ears move along to the sound of her voice. "I want you to know that it is not you that makes me uneasy. It is my past. You see," with a deep sigh, Sarah all but slumped down onto the tall fence, "when I was little, I had a pony. Her name was Sunshine." She smiled at the memory of Sunshine's golden coat, glittering in the sun as though she had been touched by Midas. "I loved her dearly, and I rode her every day. Even when my parents forbade it."

Closing her eyes, Sarah remembered that day. As a child, she had put little stock in her parents' decisions. Somehow, back then, she had sensed that their interest in their daughters had not been genuine. They had only ever been concerned with reputation and appearance.

Looking back today, though, Sarah knew she ought to have heeded their words.

"My sister Kate had a pony, too," she continued as her eyes began to blur with tears. She wished them away, but they had a mind of their own. "Her pony's name was Storm, and he was a fierce one. But he and Sunshine loved one another just as Kate and I loved one another." A sob left her lips, and she rested her forehead upon her crossed arms. "Life was perfect then. It truly was. I cannot remember a single dark cloud. It was all sunshine and flowers and wind and freedom."

In an odd way, Sarah's childhood stood in stark contrast to her life as a young woman. And it had been that day, that one day, that was the marker between them. Before, Sarah had been a child, a girl, untouched by the harshness of the world. And after, she had grown up in every way that mattered, her mind filled with thoughts of conse-quences and how her actions would influence her own life and those of others.

Yes, she had grown up in a single day.

With her head still buried, Sarah felt more words spill forth like a flood she could no longer control. "Kate and I used to love to race one another. We had done so countless times, and so we did not listen as our parents forbade us from riding out that day." Sarah remembered her mother's stern face, the way she had scrunched up her nose at the thought of her daughters muddying their clothes after the downpour the day before. Indeed, she had not been concerned for their safety, had not spoken out against their endeavor out of concern for *them*. No, she had only ever felt concern for their appearance, the way they were perceived by others, the way their behavior would influence the family's reputation. "Kate and I pretended to return to her chamber, but then later when everyone was busy, we sneaked back downstairs to the stables. We saddled Sunshine and Storm and took them out beyond the gardens to a meadow where we knew we could not be seen from the house. The ground was soft and...and..."

Reliving that day tore heartbreaking sobs from Sarah's throat. Somehow, she could not distance herself from what had happened. It attacked her as much now as it had that day.

The fear.

The panic.

The pain.

Words failed her. Her voice died in her throat. But images kept coming, bringing with them everything Sarah had hoped to forget.

Once again, she saw Kate racing ahead, Storm's gray coat shimmering in the tentative rays of the sun, forcing its way through the clouds above. She felt Sunshine galloping with eagerness, determined to catch up. Wind whipped her hair from her face and tore on her dress, yet it felt wonderful.

Free.

Glorious.

Perfect.

And then, the day had darkened in a way Sarah had not seen coming. Everything had happened so fast, that her mind could not quite recall the events in order. Somehow, Storm had to have tripped, his hooves caught in a muddy part of the meadow or perhaps in a hole in the ground dug by an eager rodent. In any case, his front legs suddenly went down, the movement flinging Kate out of the saddle. Sarah had watched her sister flying through the air as Storm had crumpled to a heap on the ground.

How Sarah herself had been flung from the saddle and ended up on the muddy ground, she could not say. It was as though something had ripped a hole into her memories. Perhaps it had happened the very same way. Perhaps Sunshine had tripped. Sarah could not be certain. However, in the end, it did not matter.

What she did remember was coming to, disoriented for a moment, feeling nothing but the warm sun upon her face. And then pain had ripped through her, pounding in her head like a hammer on an anvil. She had groaned, clutching her hands to her face, and felt warm blood running down her temple. Her riding habit had been soaked through and muddied, and only when the shivers had set in, had Sarah been able to push herself to her feet.

Only then, had she seen the two ponies on the ground, frightened and confused and in pain. Storm had barely moved, blood staining his dapple-gray coat in a terrifying way. Sarah knew she would never forget the sight of it.

Almost paralyzed, Sarah had spun toward Sunshine, instinctively seeking comfort. The young mare, however, had been on the ground as well, one of her front legs at an odd angle. Yet she had tried to get back up, her eyes wide with pain and fear, looking at Sarah as though pleading for help.

Sarah had screamed for her sister then, her legs carrying her to Sunshine's side, then dropping her into the mud beside her pony. Kate had not answered, though. She had lost consciousness, her right arm broken and blood streaming down the side of her face.

Sarah remembered all that had happened that day, and yet the one moment she still relived in her nightmares was the one when she had stood alone in the meadow, staring down at the carnage before her. She could still see Storm's broken body and Sunshine's twisted leg as well as her sister's pale face.

Never would she forget that moment. Sarah was certain of it. After all, every time she saw a horse—any horse!—this very moment returned to her, bringing with it that deep sense of pain and guilt and regret. Oh, dear God, what had she done?

Warm breath brushed over the side of Sarah's face, and she lifted her head to find Autumn standing right in front of her. Her soft nose nudged Sarah gently, and an encouraging nicker rumbled in the mare's throat.

Sarah smiled through the tears that still streamed down her face, and without thinking, she reached out and ran her hand down the column of Autumn's nose. "Thank you for listening," she whispered, remembering what Keir had said about respect. "Thank you for helping me."

The horse nickered again, softly bumping her head against Sarah's arm.

Running her hands over the mare's neck, Sarah leaned into her, breathing in deeply. "Thank you," she murmured once more. "Would you mind...if I came to visit you again tomorrow?" She looked up and saw the mare's ears flicker excitedly.

If there will be a tomorrow, Sarah thought, wondering what news Keir would bring back. Was today their last day?

Sarah prayed that it was not.

"I'm some hostage, am I not?" she said to Autumn, a chuckle leaving her lips. "I don't even want to go home."

The horse neighed softly, and Sarah smiled.

Chapter Thirteen

UNCHAPERONED AND ALONE

" I thank you, good man," Keir said to the innkeeper in what he hoped was a casual English accent. It might sound a touch stilted as he had not used it in a while, but he was fairly certain that it sounded convincing. After all, his own grandmother had enriched many wintry evenings around the fire with—granted, humorous!—instructions about *proper English*. She herself was a duke's daughter and had grown up in England, instructed in the proper way of things from the day she had been born.

Nevertheless, as much as Keir tried, he could not imagine his wild, carefree grandmother in a ballroom full of snobbish lords and haughty ladies.

Tucking the letter Keir had received from the innkeeper into his coat, he sat down in the taproom for a drink, allowing his gaze to drift casually around the room. He saw a family seated in one corner, no doubt stopping at the inn for a bite to eat on their way elsewhere. Two elderly men sat at a table near the back window, arguing about the fastest route to London.

Over the course of the next half hour, Keir watched people come and go, but he saw no one suspicious. He sipped his ale, trying his best to blend in while keeping his eyes and ears open, watching, listening. It was paramount that should anyone discover Sarah's whereabouts or possible whereabouts, he become aware of it as soon as possible. Fortunately, so far no one appeared in any way suspicious, and Keir exhaled in relief.

Downing the last contents of his mug, he pulled the letter from his coat and opened it. His hands were tense, his eyes eager to catch the words upon the parchment. What had Grandma Edie written? It was the one question that had gone through Keir's head on his ride to the inn.

Three days had passed since they had left London. Three days in which all could have been resolved. The ransom could have been paid, and now Grandma Edie was writing to tell him to return Sarah home.

Much to Keir's surprise, he suddenly found himself somewhat reluctant to open the letter, to find out what was written there. Aye, Sarah and he had settled into a comfortable routine together, and the idea of it all coming to an end...bothered him.

Chuckling under his breath, Keir shook his head about himself. Aye, he had grown to like her. More than that, he had come to admire her. He could not quite put his finger on it, but there was something about his little wisp that made him feel proud to know her, to assist her in her endeavor to claim freedom for herself. She was not a bored, pampered lady who was acting out of the desire to get her own way, to spite everyone else and win a battle of wills. She was not spoiled or selfish or mean. No, she was genuinely frightened of the world, of everything that she had seen, and she simply wished to find a smidgen of happiness. *That wasna wrong, was it?*

In Keir's book, it was not. Society would most definitely disagree; however, he did not care. He wholeheartedly approved of her motivation, of her solution to the troubles she faced. Of course, when Grandma Edie had first told him of this feigned abduction, he had shaken his head, thinking her absolutely mad. Yet Grandma Edie's special sort of madness had often proved to be invaluable in procuring another's happiness. And so, Keir had gone along with it, and now, here, in this moment, he was utterly glad he had.

Inhaling a steadying breath, Keir finally pulled the parchment from the envelope only to discover that it was not a parchment at all, but rather two thinner, smaller envelopes. One was addressed to Sarah—or rather to S., in case the letter fell into the wrong hands—and the other to him (aka *My dear boy*).

Keir frowned. The letter addressed to Sarah bore a feminine, somewhat artistic handwriting, and he suspected it might be from one of the dowager countess's granddaughters. Most likely, from Christina. It seemed the old lady had finally decided to share the truth about Sarah's kidnapping with the rest of her family.

Keir chuckled. He would have loved to be there and see their reaction!

The other letter bore the dowager countess's handwriting, and he quickly slipped it open, his eyes falling to the words upon the parchment.

My dear boy, (Keir chuckled)

I am pleased to inform you that all is well. Our endeavor has, of course, been noted, and reactions were as expected. Payments have not yet been made but are expected shortly. I shall keep in touch.

GE

Keir had to admit that this was not what he had expected, but he could not deny the sense of relief that swept through him. "Our journey does not seem to be over after all," he murmured, thinking of Sarah and the radiant glow that sometimes lit up her blue eyes, as though she were still a child, a child who had never seen the world in its true beauty. Aye, she had not lived yet, not truly, and Keir loved watching her as she discovered small joys. There was something utterly honest and genuine in her expression, and Keir liked the fact that he could read her so easily, that she did not possess the ability to lie. He knew she felt embarrassed by it, and it made her utterly endearing.

Tucking the letters back into his coat, Keir rose to his feet. He nodded to the innkeeper and then strode from the room, stepping back outside into the frosty air. Retrieving his horse, his eyes still watchful, he swept his gaze over the building, from window to window, taking note of every person who passed him, walking in and out of the inn. Yet all remained quiet. No one seemed to follow him or pay him any undue attention.

Slowly, Keir made his way back down the road toward a grove of trees that would help him disappear. He swept his gaze over his shoulder, first left, then right, ensuring that no one was nearby, that no one was watching. Then he urged Scout off the road and into the thicket. They proceeded until Keir was certain they could no longer be seen from the road, Scout's coat as well as his own hiding them amongst the brownish underbrush. There, Keir dismounted, peeking through a tangle of branches while he stroked Scout's nose and neck to keep the gelding calm.

For at least half an hour, Keir watched the road, needing to make certain that no one had taken note of him or the direction he was headed. Once he was satisfied that the coast remained clear, he remounted Scout and headed deeper into the woods.

By the time Keir spotted the cabin, the day was already drawing to a close. Smoke wafted out of the chimney into the darkening sky, and a faint glow of light shimmered in the few windows. Keir inhaled a deep breath of winter's air, surprised at this odd feeling in his chest, as though he were coming home. As though Sarah were...

Clearing his throat, Keir shook his head, trying to clear his mind of these unexpected musings. Then he pushed onward, jumping out of the saddle as he reached the yard. He led Scout into the shed, removed his bridle and saddle and gave him a thorough brush-down. Then he headed out toward the meadow to retrieve Autumn as well, and only after ensuring that both horses were settled and fed did Keir step toward the house.

Warmth engulfed him as he stepped across the threshold, and a delicious aroma lingered in the air. Craning his neck, Keir tried to see into the kitchen but could catch no glimpse of Sarah. He shrugged out of his coat and removed his snow-covered boots before moving down the hall. The sound of soft footsteps as well as someone humming under their breath drifted to his ears, tugging the corners of his mouth upward. *Aye, I'm glad to be back!*

Stepping into the kitchen, Keir's eyes swept over the table set for two with Loki perched on one end of it, a small bowl in front of him. Sarah stood by the stove, spoon in hand as she tasted the stew she had undoubtedly been working on all day. It smelled delicious, and although Keir felt his insides tense with hunger, he remained where he was for a moment longer, enjoying looking at her.

Once again, she had braided her hair away from her temples and then down her back the way he had shown her. Yet a few unruly wisps lingered, determined not to yield. Keir smiled. He liked that about her. As much as she tried to comply, part of her simply refused to bow down. A rosy glow lingered upon her cheeks, one that spoke not of embarrassment but rather of pride and accomplishment. Indeed, she looked radiant, like a woman utterly sure of herself, like the woman Sarah could have been had she grown up with support and understanding instead of indifference and burdensome expectations.

A startled "Oh!" left Sarah's lips when she turned around and spotted him standing in the doorway. "You're back!" A joyous smile came to her face that resonated within Keir. She started toward him but then stopped, the expression upon her face sobering. "How did it go? Is everything all right?" Her eyes swept over him, as though she feared he had been injured in some way.

Keir moved toward her. "Everything is fine," he assured her, glancing down at Loki, who had hopped off the table and was now rubbing his head against his leg in a feline greeting. "It smells wonderful in here," Keir remarked, glancing behind her at the stew simmering quietly in the pot. "I admit I'm rather famished."

Nodding, Sarah brushed a nonexistent curl behind her ear, her hands aflutter as the rosy glow upon her cheeks once more turned to one of embarrassment. "I hope you like it," she said tentatively. "I tried to make it as you said, but I'm uncertain if it is any good." She gestured toward the table. "Please be seated."

Keir's initial impulse was to assist her. After all, she had clearly put a lot of work into it all day and deserved a moment of rest. Yet he realized that this was something she wanted to do. As nervous as she was about disappointing him, about disappointing herself, she still looked hopeful. She had tackled a task unknown to her, had done her best, and now needed to know that it had all been worthwhile.

And so, Keir seated himself, brushing a hand over Loki's head as the cat settled beside him on the table, casting an expectant look at his own little bowl. "I hope ye took good care of her," Keir murmured to the feline. "'Tis not a task to be taken lightly."

In answer, Loki purred, then he ducked his head under Keir's hand, begging to be scratched.

Sarah chuckled as she walked over, setting a full bowl of stew in front of Keir. "He's been keeping me company all day," she said with a wide smile, reaching out a hand to brush over Loki's head. "Haven't you?"

As Keir pulled back his own hand, her fingertips brushed his skin, and a deep blush shot up Sarah's cheeks. She instantly yanked back her hand, her eyes everywhere but on him.

Keir smiled. "Ye're blushing again, lass," he murmured, then he reached out and took her hand.

Sarah's eyes widened and snapped up to meet his.

"I'll not bite ye," Keir teased, cradling her hand within his own. "There's no harm in a simple touch." He held her gaze, then tenderly ran the pad of his thumb over her knuckles. "Unless it makes ye feel uncomfortable." His brows rose questioningly as he looked up at her.

Sarah swallowed, her lips slightly parted as her breath rushed in and out of her lungs fast. Her blue eyes looked into his before darting to their linked hands.

"Does it?"

For a terrifying moment, Keir feared he had misread her, that he had, in fact, overstepped. Then, however, she gave a quick shake of her head, and her fingers returned the soft pressure of his.

Keir smiled at her. "Good." Then he released her hand and rose to his feet. "Seat yerself, lass. I'll get ye a bowl as well." Gently, he urged her to sit, then stepped up to the large pot and ladled stew into another bowl. "Here ye go." He set it down in front of her, and she smiled up at him shyly, her eyes once again flitting about without truly settling anywhere.

"And yer highness?" Keir asked the feline, trying to relieve the tension that lingered. "Would ye care for a bite as well?"

As though Loki understood him, the cat padded over to his bowl, a look of utter disappointment coming to his face when he found it empty. He looked up at Keir with a chiding look, and a plaintive *meow* spilled from his mouth.

"Not to worry, yer highness," Keir told the feline. "I'll see to ye immediately." He poured a bit of milk into Loki's bowl, and the cat eagerly lapped it up, now completely oblivious to everything else.

Sarah chuckled. "Sometimes I cannot help but wonder if perhaps he is a person trapped in a cat's body." She looked up at Keir, and her blue eyes sparkled as before. "Sometimes I ask him a question and then I actually catch myself waiting for an answer."

Seating himself, Keir grinned. "Loki may not be able to speak the way we do, but he can understand what's important." He brushed a hand down Loki's back. "It makes him a good companion, does it not?"

Sarah nodded, a touch of sadness coming to her eyes. "It does," she whispered before her eyes moved from Loki and settled upon Keir. "I shall miss him...when I go home."

Keir stilled as they looked at one another, a deeper meaning lingering in the air between them. "I shall miss him as well," he murmured, knowing that he was not merely speaking of the cat. "More than I thought possible."

Another heartbeat passed, and their eyes remained locked. Then, however, Sarah once more became overwhelmed by the intimate moment between them and dropped her gaze. "I hope you like it." She gestured to the stew before reaching for her spoon. "I hope it'll—"

"I'm certain it'll be delicious," Keir assured her before ladling a spoonful into his mouth, aware that Sarah was looking at him expectantly, a touch of apprehension upon her face. He chewed intently, slowly, savoring the warmth as well as the aroma. *Aye, 'tis good.* Not perfect, but for someone who had never cooked before in her life, it was delicious.

Keir could tell that Sarah was nervous. She glanced up at him from below her lashes, unable to look at him directly and equally unable to look away completely. Her lips parted slightly, and he knew she wanted to ask for his opinion...but did not dare. *Is the thought of disappointing someone truly so terrifying to her? To disappoint me?*

Swallowing his bite, Keir turned to smile at her. "Ye did a fine job, lass. 'Tis exactly the kind of meal I needed after a day outside in the cold." He lifted another spoonful of stew to his mouth. "Ye should be proud of yerself."

Although Sarah tried to hide the smile that came to her face, pride and a sense of accomplishment made her glow. She found such joy in small things that Keir found himself appreciating them more as well. "I'm glad you like it," she said shyly, dipping her own spoon in the bowl. "Perhaps you can tell me what other herbs I should've used...or if I used too much...or too little." She turned to look at him, a hint of alarm slowly crawling onto her face.

He reached out and placed his hand upon hers. "Breathe, lass. Ye did well. The same dish cooked by two different people will still not taste the same. And it isna meant to. That is the beauty of life. Small differences that are unique and refreshing." He smiled at her, waiting until he saw the expression upon her face relax. "Eat now. Ye've earned it."

For a few minutes, they ate in silence, the only sounds the soft clinking of their spoons against their bowls as well as Loki lapping up his milk. It was a peaceful silence, and Keir felt the strain of the day fall from him. Aye, everything had gone according to plan—*was* going according to plan!—and yet Keir could not deny that he worried about Sarah.

Now more than ever.

"How did it go?" Sarah asked, as though she had read his mind. Her hand held the spoon a little tighter, and the blue in her eyes had darkened as she looked at him, waiting for an answer. "What did she write?"

Keir smiled at her reassuringly, needing her to know that there was nothing to worry about, needing her to believe that. "Everything is as expected," he told her, reaching to pull the letter from his pocket before realizing that it was still in his coat out in the hall. "She writes that yer disappearance has been noted, but that no payment has been made yet."

Sarah frowned. "That is all?"

Running a hand through his hair, Keir shook his head, chuckling. "The woman is not one to share details." Of course, one reason for keeping things short had been to protect their identities should her letter fall into the wrong hands. However, Keir doubted it had been her only reason for keeping things short. "However, I suppose 'tis safe to assume that yer father has contacted Lord Blackmore, sharing with him the news of yer kidnapping. Dunna worry, lass. The dowager will take care of everything. No doubt, the ransom will be paid soon...and then ye can go home."

Heaving a deep sigh, Sarah nodded. "Home," she murmured, her gaze becoming distant.

Keir watched her carefully. "Are ye all right?"

Sarah cast him a tentative smile. "I wonder..." She sighed and shook her head. "I wonder what my parents thought when they found me gone, when they found the note. I wonder how...Lord Blackmore," her eyes met his and then quickly darted away again, "reacted when he was told." She swallowed hard, her hands tensing upon the bowl and spoon. "I wonder if anyone else found out or if they managed to keep it a secret."

Keir frowned, uncertain which possibility unsettled her. "'Twas never meant to be secret, was it?" he asked, observing her. "If it was to be a secret, perhaps we should have picked a different night then, not the one before yer wedding."

Sarah nodded. "You're right. It was never meant to be a secret. Of course not! It can't be! It's part of the plan that everyone knows..." She blushed a crimson red and then almost frantically continued to eat her stew.

From the first, Keir had wondered what it would accomplish to have Sarah kidnapped only to return her once the ransom was paid. Would that not place her right back in the same spot, namely on the brink of matrimony to Lord Blackmore? Still...

"Why is it so important that society knows?" Keir asked, thinking out loud. "The dowager countess said 'twould be almost impossible to keep something like this quiet, and clearly keeping it quiet isna what she had in mind. Why then?" His mind reeled with all those unwritten rules of society, every misstep punished harshly. And then everything fell into place, and Keir finally understood the other half of Grandma Edie's plan.

Clearly, Sarah was aware of it as well, judging from the deep blush upon her cheeks. "Ye want this kidnapping to become known," Keir murmured quietly, his gaze fixed upon Sarah's bowed head, "to ensure that ye will be ruined in the eyes of society, is that not so?"

Sarah's hand clamped tightly around the spoon; her gaze still fixed upon her bowl.

Reaching out a hand, Keir grasped Sarah's, and her eyes flew up to meet his, her breath coming fast. "Ye want everyone to know that ye spent days in the company of ruthless criminals, unchaperoned and alone. Ye want people to imagine all the things that could have happened to a young lady in such a situation, so that Lord Blackmore will no longer want to marry ye." Keir's words were not a question, and yet he could see the truth of them upon Sarah's face. Aye, never before had Keir seen Sarah look this mortified. Her cheeks were ablaze, and her pulse was hammering in her neck. She looked close to fainting, and yet, for once, she did not drop her gaze.

"I'm sorry," Sarah whispered unexpectedly, shame mingling with the mortification upon her face. "It is not right to suggest you would ever..." She swallowed hard, her mouth opening and closing and opening again as she searched for words. "Only Grandma Edie insisted it had to be this way. She said it was necessary so he would lose interest, so he would be relieved once I suggested ending our engagement."

Keir nodded. "Of course, she's right. From what I've seen of yer world, I know she is." He gently squeezed her hand, trying his best to relax his own muscles because, truth be told, the suggestion that he would harm her in any way was painful. It made him angry, for a part of him worried that a small part of her thought it possible.

"Would you like some more stew?" Sarah asked, all of a sudden, before her eyes darted to his half-full bowl. Instantly, she stilled, her mouth opening once more, her mind searching for something to say.

Keir held onto her hand, giving it a slight tug to draw her attention back to him. "Sarah, ye need to know that ye needna fear me." He held her gaze, needing to know that she believed him. "No matter what happens, ye will always be safe with me."

Sarah looked at him with wide open eyes. Then she nodded, the ghost of a smile tugging upon the corners of her mouth. "I know."

Keir exhaled a deep breath, surprised by the depth of his relief to hear her say so. He sat back in his chair, then finally released her hand. "I have a letter for ye," he said abruptly, determined to draw the conversation to safer terrain. "'Twas sent along with the dowager countess's." He pushed to his feet. "Wait here, I'll fetch it."

As Keir strode out into the hall, he prayed that they could reclaim that sense of comfortable silence, of easy companionship that had been between them before. She had felt safe with him before, had she not? Keir felt almost certain of it, and he hoped it was still true.

Chapter Fourteen

A MARVELOUS TIME

Feeling the breath lodge in her throat, Sarah stared after Keir. Her heart was still pounding in her chest, and she felt a little lightheaded. Indeed, this conversation was one she could have done without. Her head felt as though it was on fire, suggesting that her cheeks burned in a crimson red. Sarah closed her eyes, mortified by all her face constantly revealed as much as by the direction their conversation had taken.

Keir had been hurt by the suggestion that he would...take advantage of her, had he not? Sarah was certain of it. She had seen a shadow fall over his eyes and his jaw tense in response to her words. Whoever he was, he was a good man. Indeed, Sarah had never felt more certain of another's character than she did about Keir's. They had known each other only a matter of days, and yet there were no doubts in her mind nor in her heart. *How is this possible?*

The sound of approaching footsteps drew Sarah's attention back from her inner musings, and she looked up to see Keir step toward the table, a letter in his hand. "Do you know who it is from?"

Seating himself, Keir shrugged. "I canna be certain, but my guess is one of the dowager countess's granddaughters."

Sarah frowned, once again surprised by how well Keir seemed to know the Whickerton family. Yet he kept insisting that there was no close connection. Was he lying to her? That thought struck a nerve, and Sarah almost shied away from it. No, she did not want to believe it. She did not want to believe that there was something dishonest about Keir. She felt so safe with him, safe in the knowledge that he was a truly good and decent man. But if he was lying to her, what then?

Taking the letter he was offering her, Sarah dropped her gaze to the short address decorating its front. "Christina," Sarah murmured, instantly recognizing her childhood friend's handwriting. "Why would she...? Does she know...?" She lifted her eyes to Keir. "I thought it was from Grandma Edie as well. I thought no one knew that..."

Keir shrugged. "Well, nothing remains a secret forever, especially where family is concerned." He chuckled. "Especially where *that* family is concerned." Then he suddenly snatched the letter from Sarah's hands. "Eat up, lass. Then ye can read yer letter."

Sarah stilled, confused, her hands still where they had been a moment ago when they had held the letter.

"Dunna look so shocked, lass," Keir remarked with a grin, the usual ease between them returning once more. "Ye need to eat. After all, ye've been working hard all day." He gave her spoon a slight push, bringing it closer to her hand, then reached for his own.

Together, they finished their bowls. And yet all the while, Sarah's gaze strayed to the letter Keir had placed upon the opposite end of the table. *Does Christina truly know what happened? Does she know of our plan? Did she find out somehow? Or did Grandma Edie tell her?*

Sarah's head began to spin. She remembered well all the warnings Grandma Edie had uttered, urging her to keep quiet about everything, urging her not to let anything slip in the presence of another. Still, Christina was her best friend, and she was one who knew how to keep secrets. She would never betray this endeavor by speaking of it to anyone.

The moment Sarah's bowl was empty, Keir handed the letter back to her. "Go on ahead into the parlor. I'll clean up." He stood and took her bowl with his right hand while his left casually brushed over Loki's head before he reached for his own. Sarah made to object, determined to help clean up the kitchen; Keir, however, shook his head, a determined look in his eyes. "Go and read yer letter."

Casting him a grateful smile, Sarah reached for the piece of parchment, almost hugging it to her chest and then headed down the hall and into the small parlor. There, she seated herself in one of the armchairs by the fireplace and then slowly unfolded the letter. Before she could focus her attention on the words written there, though, Loki strode into the room in that majestic way of his. He eyed her curiously and then jumped up onto her lap, like a king settling upon his throne. He curled up into a tight little ball, a soft purring sound drifting from his throat as Sarah began to stroke his head.

Smiling at the feline on her lap, Sarah then unfolded the letter, her eyes seeking the words upon the page, her heart and mind eager.

Dearest S.,

You might be surprised to receive this letter just as I was surprised to hear of your current endeavor. I wish you had told me, but I understand the need for secrecy, and I assure you I'm not angry in the least. In case you were worried.

Sarah exhaled deeply, only now realizing that she had, in fact, been concerned. Christina was her oldest friend, and they had always shared everything with one another. Yes, she had been worried Christina might be angry with her for going behind her back.

I must say I am proud of you. This is truly the most daring thing you have ever done, and I am so glad you found it within yourself to go upon this adventure. I am certain you shall not regret it, and I'm looking forward to hearing everything about it once you return. Please, my dearest friend, enjoy yourself. Enjoy this moment of utter freedom. Stop worrying. For once do not concern yourself with anything. Simply enjoy this little adventure. You deserve it.

. . .

Your friend (oldest and closest, I might add),

C.

Sarah chuckled, easily imagining Christina's bright blue eyes lit up with excitement. Oh, her friend had always had a daring spirit and, in truth, would have been much more suited to such an adventure than Sarah.

"Something amusing?" Keir inquired as he strode into the room. In two large strides, he had crossed the small parlor and then seated himself beside her in the other armchair, his gaze expectant as he looked at her. "Good news? Who is it from?"

"It is from my friend Christina, one of Grandma Edie's grand-daughters," she told him, then frowned. "But you already suspected that, didn't you?"

At the tone in her voice, Keir's eyes narrowed slightly, their blue growing darker, as though he could guess the direction of her thoughts. "And what she wrote made ye smile?"

Sarah nodded, glancing down at the letter in her hands. "She reminds me to enjoy myself," she told him with a laugh, one hand still stroking Loki behind the ears.

Grinning at her, Keir wiggled his eyebrows. "I, for one, am having a marvelous time." He paused, then regarded her with a hint of feigned concern upon his face. "Are ye not?"

Sarah laughed, realizing in that moment that she had done so quite a few times in the past few days. And yet the weeks, months and even years before had not seen much laughter, had they? "Yes, I suppose I am."

Keir regarded her curiously. "Ye sound surprised."

"I am," Sarah said slowly, trying to sort through the many thoughts racing through her head, trying to look at them more closely. "I suppose I never expected to enjoy," her gaze moved to meet his, "being kidnapped."

And there it was again, one of those moments when reality seemed far away, when Sarah found herself looking into Keir's eyes...and felt at peace. She did not feel nervous or embarrassed. She did not feel like a fool or concerned about the future. Yes, she felt at peace, for this was truly a perfect moment.

A perfect moment in the company of a man who should terrify her to the core. And perhaps he had, in the very beginning. Before she had gotten to know him. Yet looking at him now, Sarah could not imagine ever truly being afraid of him. She knew what it meant to fear a man. Every time her thoughts strayed to Lord Blackmore, she shuddered. Yes, she feared *him*. She feared what would come after the ransom had been paid. She feared meeting him again.

And she would. She would need to. Grandma Edie had instructed her quite clearly on what she needed to do. She knew what the plan was. She knew she needed to suggest to Lord Blackmore that...her kidnapper had taken advantage of her. She needed to make it clear, so he would not object when she cried off.

And she needed to cry off in order to be free.

"May I ask a favor of ye, lass?"

Keir's voice jarred Sarah from her thoughts. She blinked her eyes to focus them, and then cleared her throat. "C-Certainly."

"I just ripped my sleeve," he said, holding up his right arm and showing her the visible tear in the fabric. "It got caught when I hung up the apron on the small hook by the door." Shaking his head, he chuckled. "My mother taught me how to cook, but she never managed to teach me how to sew. Would ye know how?" His brows rose teasingly. "After all, I've heard it said that young ladies are such accomplished creatures, taught to dance, converse and sing."

Sarah felt herself return his smile. "And you believe that includes sewing?"

Keir grinned. "I thought I'd try my luck."

"Well, for your information, it does not include sewing," Sarah informed him in a most haughty tone.

Keir's face fell but not in a way that suggested true disappointment. Indeed, this was a game. He was teasing her, and for the first time, Sarah was enjoying it.

"But," Sarah continued before Keir could say anything, "it did include embroidery."

His gaze narrowed, and yet that sense of humor never left his face. "Those are fancy stitches on handkerchiefs or pillowcases, are they not?"

Sarah chuckled, nodding her head.

"Well, I'd be grateful if ye could try stitching up my sleeve," he told her as a bit of a wicked grin came to his face. "But, please, no little rosebuds if ye please."

'Now, the wicked man has you doing seamstress work!' Her mother snarled. 'Where will it end? The indignity of it all!'

Ignoring her mother's comment in her head, Sarah laughed, delighted with their conversation, with her own reaction to him. Yes, she was enjoying Keir's company, and she hoped he was enjoying hers as well...at least a little.

Loki finally abandoned his post on her lap, clearly annoyed with their noisy laughter. He tiptoed over to the fireplace and curled up in front of it. Resting his head upon his paws, he closed his eyes.

Pushing to his feet, Keir turned toward the hall. "I'll be right back," he told her over his shoulder, then disappeared from view, and she heard him climb the stairs to the upper floor.

For a moment, Sarah was confused before she realized that he meant for her to stitch up the tear in his sleeve now. As expected, only a moment later, Keir reappeared, a fresh shirt pulled over his head and the torn one in his hands. "Ye sure ye don't mind, lass," he asked, holding out the garment to her. "'Tis only a small tear. I can still wear it the way it is."

Sarah shook her head. "Not at all." She stood and took the shirt, the fabric still warm to the touch. Her fingers tingled at the feel of it, and she felt herself warm at the thought of it upon his skin. She even caught a faint scent of him and was tempted to bring the shirt to her nose and breathe in deeply.

"Are ye all right, lass?"

Blinking, Sarah looked up. Keir stood only an arm's length away, his blue eyes intense as he looked at her, something thoughtful, almost knowing in his eyes.

As always, Sarah's face heated with mortification, and she instantly dropped her gaze. *Can he guess my thoughts? Oh, dear, he most certainly can! He always seems to know precisely what*—

Keir chuckled. "Ye're blushing again, lass," he murmured, moving closer. His right hand settled under her chin; his fingers gentle as he urged her to look at him. "Why are ye blushing?" he asked when their eyes met, his voice suddenly serious.

Sarah wished she could sink into a hole in the ground. Obviously, she had experienced embarrassment and mortification more often than she could count; and yet, she was certain that this moment right here was the worst of them all.

No words made it past Sarah's lips, which was not at all surprising, considering that her thoughts were hopelessly entangled. Her pulse thudded wildly in her veins, and she began to feel a little lightheaded again. Clear thoughts were impossible, and even if she had been capable of them, Sarah doubted they would have been of a nature to share them with Keir.

"Ye're a bonny lass," Keir murmured, his gaze intense in a way she had not seen before. "Ye deserve a husband who appreciates everything ye are." The pad of his thumb slowly skimmed over her chin, its tip nearly touching her bottom lip.

Sarah could do little else but stare at Keir. Even breathing was almost beyond her. His blue eyes held her captivated, and she felt herself drift toward him, as though there were an invisible hand at her back, urging her closer.

And then Keir's gaze dropped to her lips, and Sarah almost expired on the spot. A jolt went through her that shook her entire body, almost making her rock back on her heels.

Keir blinked, and his hand fell from her chin. He took a step backward, clearing his throat. "How...How about I tell ye a story," he suggested in a voice that sounded far from relaxed, "while ye mend my shirt?"

Unable to utter any kind of comprehensible sound, Sarah merely nodded, relieved to retreat to the safety of the armchair at her back. Fortunately, her sewing kit—because, of course, she knew how to sew! One of her few accomplishments!—still lay on the small table beside her chair from when she had stitched a tear in the hem of her own dress earlier today.

Busying her hands, Sarah was relieved to focus her gaze on her own hands. Still, she could not keep herself from glancing at Keir out of the corner of her eye every so often. He stood by the window, his gaze directed out into the dark night, a faint white glow visible as the moon shone overhead. His hands were linked behind his back, and for a moment, Sarah wondered about the tense set of his jaw. Then, however, he exhaled slowly, and all tension seemed to fall from him.

"There's an island up at the northwestern coast of Scotland," Keir began in his rolling Highland brogue that Sarah was coming to love. It made her think of a world far away, a place utterly different from the one she knew. "'Tis rich in farmland and timber, and its people rely on trade. Their ships sail the seas towards ports in England as well as the Continent." He turned to look at Sarah over his shoulder, a bit of a wicked grin upon his face. "But, of course, sailing the seas is a dangerous endeavor, for ships whose hulls are filled to the rim with precious cargo are favored prey for pirates and privateers alike."

Sarah felt a chill run down her arms as she tried to picture such a moment, a ship on its way south suddenly overtaken by criminals. It made her shudder, and her hands stilled, the needle stuck in the fabric, her hands tensed upon it.

Slowly, Keir turned from the window, his gaze intense, his features mirroring the emotions of the story he was telling. "The sea is a perilous place," he murmured, his voice quiet, his blue gaze fixed upon Sarah's as he slowly moved toward her. "It brings many dangers to ships and land alike, and people know it. They fear it." With quiet movements, Keir crossed to the other armchair, seating himself, his gaze never leaving hers. "Yet the people who settled on that island know of a secret, a secret as old as time." He paused, silence stretched between them.

"What secret?" Sarah whispered breathlessly, unable to break eye contact, unable to even blink. Transfixed, she clung to Keir's every word, every trace of emotion darting across his face or sparking in the depth of his eyes.

Casting a cautious glance around the room, as though he feared to be overheard, Keir leaned toward her, and Sarah mimicked him instinctively. "Something lives in the waters around the island," he murmured in hushed words, his face so close to her own that Sarah could see flecks of green in his dark blue gaze. "Something that moves below the surface. Something that protects the island and those who dwell there."

Sarah swallowed hard, imagining something dark moving below the waves, never seen, always out of sight, but there, nonetheless. "Something?" she whispered, her heart contracting, uncertain if she wished to know the answer. Would it haunt her? Her dreams? Or reassure her? Bring her peace?

Keir's gaze darted toward the door, once again an expression of caution upon his face, as though he were about to reveal a secret that had been kept for the past millennia and more. "Legend has it," he whispered, and Sarah could feel the faint brush of his breath against her lips, "that a sea serpent lives in a cave below the island."

Sarah swallowed hard, her eyes widening as she stared at Keir. "A sea serpent?" A bit of the daze that had fallen over her retreated, and she could feel her rational thoughts reawakening.

A wicked gleam came to Keir's eyes as he shrugged. "Well, 'tis a legend, nothing more, nothing less." He sat back, and yet his gaze remained upon hers. "Do yer people not have legends?"

Inhaling a deep breath after what felt like an eternity, Sarah leaned back in her chair, stretching her fingers and feeling her tense muscles ache. "I suppose so. I always loved the stories of Arthur of Camelot and the Knights of the Round Table and, of course, the Greek myths." Indeed, it had been a long time since she had last thought of stories. As a girl, she had loved nothing more than to escape to other places, to meet other people and join them on their path for a little while, a path her own feet would never find.

"Are there not also strange creatures in these stories?" Keir asked with a grin.

Sarah nodded, conceding the point. "Yet I wonder why would a sea serpent protect the people on that island, why would it protect their ships." She raised a questioning brow, daring him to provide her with a satisfying answer.

Keir shrugged, clearly feeling no pressure to support his claim by a reasonable argument. "Why do we protect our own?" He returned the question to her instead. "Why do we fight for those we love?"

A fierce expression burned in his eyes, and Sarah felt a shiver dance down her spine. A touch of fear leaped up in her heart, but the look in his eyes made her feel special and safe and protected above anything.

Our own.

Those we love.

In that moment, Sarah wanted nothing more than to belong, to be a part of a people who stood together no matter what, to feel safe in the knowledge that she was never alone. Yes, she had family. She had parents, and yet Sarah had never felt as though she belonged. She had always wanted to, and often dreamed of being one of the Whickerton sisters. Every once in a while, she had closed her eyes to everything she knew and allowed herself to live in this dream. Only morning and reality had always found her, eventually. No, no one had ever been willing to protect her at all costs, determined to see her safe. Sarah knew that there was no one in this world who loved her with such fierceness, and in that moment, it made her almost unbearably sad.

Blinking away tears, Sarah dropped her gaze to the fabric and needle in her hands. "Why would a sea serpent consider people its own?" she asked, willing her voice not to waver. "Why would it care?"

At first, Keir said nothing, and Sarah was tempted to raise her eyes and look at him. Yet she knew by his silence that he could sense her turmoil, and if she were to look at him, if their eyes were to meet, he would know.

Surely, he would know.

Somehow he always did.

"Does it matter?" Keir finally asked, the tone in his voice betraying deeper emotions than Sarah would have expected. She looked up and in his eyes she saw memories lurking...of someone he loved. "Why would the dowager countess go to such lengths to see ye safe, Sarah? What reason does she have? Ye're not her kin. Ye're not family, and yet her efforts suggest she cares. She cares for yer well-being, yer safety and happiness." He shrugged, looking at her with expectant eyes. "Why should she?"

Keir's words severed Sarah's hold on the present. Her mind moved backwards through time, replaying moments before her inner eye she had not thought about in a long time. Moments of companionship. Moments of friendship. Not only with the dowager countess but also with Christina and her sisters. Yes, they had always been at her side, had they not? After all, it had been the Whickertons who had again and again stepped up to protect her from an unwanted marriage that would have broken her heart. Without them, she would have been married long ago and to a man who frightened her no less than Lord Blackmore.

Warmth swept through Sarah, and she felt the corners of her mouth lift into a tentative smile, one that grew with each memory to pass before her eyes. "I'm not alone," Sarah whispered to herself, overwhelmed by that sudden sense of belonging that grew in her chest. "There is someone who cares for me." Through a curtain of tears, Sarah looked up and met Keir's gaze.

"Aye, there is, lass. There is." His eyes, dark and inscrutable, looked into hers, and once again, Sarah felt the inexplicable urge to move closer. It felt like a hand at her back, pushing her toward him, like something tugging her forward.

Subtle.

Fleeting.

Overwhelmingly powerful.

Oh, I shall miss him! I shall miss him so very much! Sarah thought as her tears spilled over and her vision blurred.

Chapter Fifteen

IN THE MEANTIME

Back in London

The world lay in the grips of winter. Frost framed the windows, and even the air outside looked icy. Snow had draped itself across every bush and tree, every wall and fence. Every house lay wrapped in a blanket of snow, ice crystals dangling from the roofs.

And inside, a warm fire burned in the hearth as the dowager countess sat in her favorite armchair, a thick woolen blanket wrapped around her legs and her grandchildren gathered around her.

My rather loud and inquisitive grandchildren!

"How long does it take to pay a ransom?" Harriet demanded with an impatient tap of her foot. Her red hair danced like the flames in the hearth, her limbs unable to keep still. "Should we not have heard something by now?"

Stepping forward, now standing shoulder to shoulder with her younger sister, Christina nodded eagerly. "I agree," she stated vehemently, her blue eyes fixed on Edith, demanding an explanation. "What if something went wrong? What if Blackmore somehow discovered what is going on?"

Edith sighed, thinking that perhaps it had been a mistake to reveal her plan to her grandchildren. Indeed, they could be quite the nuisance when they thought one of their own was in peril! Yet Edith had to admit that was precisely what she loved about them.

Their fierceness.

Their loyalty.

Their devotion.

Indeed, perhaps she ought not have said anything. However, she had had little choice. After all, after hearing of Sarah's kidnapping, they had been beside themselves with concern. Edith would never forget how Christina's face had paled, fear widening her blue eyes in a way she had rarely seen before. Yes, it had been right to tell them the truth, and yet it made things so much more complicated.

"But how could Lord Blackmore possibly find out?" Juliet asked from the settee, exchanging a questioning look with Leonora. Both girls were of a quieter sort, careful in their considerations before voicing their thoughts.

Christina shrugged. "I don't know, but it is a possibility, is it not?" She whirled back around, her eyes once again fixed upon Edith. "Grandmother, tell us where they are?"

"Where who is?" Edith inquired with a yawn, blinking her eyelids in a rather fatigued fashion. "Oh, what a dreadfully cold day! Would you mind ringing for some tea, my dear?"

"Don't try to distract me, Grandma!" Christina exclaimed, hands on her hips. "It won't work."

Quietly, Juliet rose from the settee and rang the bell. A moment later, a maid appeared and was sent back out with a request for tea and biscuits.

"Keir is with her, is he not?" Harriet asked with a sly look in her green eyes. "He's the one who *kidnapped* her, am I right?"

Edith sighed, well-aware that Louisa—the granddaughter who was in many ways most like her—was eyeing her most curiously, not a word leaving her lips. Indeed, *that* was reason for concern, for the girl rarely held her peace! "Is it not enough when I assure you that Sarah is safe?"

Harriet and Christina instantly shook their heads no. While Christina's eyes mostly sparked with concern, the look in Harriet's portrayed that she hated being kept unawares.

"Perhaps it should be," Louisa remarked in an unusually reasonable tone. Indeed, motherhood had calmed her spirit, made her more observant, soothed her mind's eagerness.

All heads swiveled around, staring at her with varying degrees of surprise.

"You cannot be serious!" Christina demanded, beginning to pace the length of the room. While she had initially been relieved to hear of the plan Edith had concocted to keep Sarah safe from yet another unwanted marriage, that first calm had now blown over.

Louisa shrugged as her gaze moved from one sister to the next. "Think about it," she urged cautiously. "Sarah's kidnapping will soon be the talk of London. It is impossible to keep something like that a secret. The whispers have already begun." She paused for effect. "Every time we speak of it, there is a chance that someone overhears, that something leaves this room and is carried past the safety of these walls." Again, she paused, waiting for her words to be absorbed, and Edith smiled, proud of her granddaughter. Indeed, Louisa was becoming a fine meddler! A term, Edith had come to see as a compliment after years of hearing it applied to herself. What would the world be without meddlers? Where would Sarah be without those who dared to interfere?

With a heavy sigh, Christina slumped down in a chair, the expression upon her face one of displeasure. "I suppose you're right," she admitted, resignation in her voice.

Louisa nodded. "It is of the utmost importance," she reminded the others sternly, "that none of what is truly happening, of this plan reaches the ears of Lord Blackmore or those of someone who works for him."

Leonora frowned. "What are you suggesting?"

"Do you think he seeks to unearth who stole Sarah away?" Juliet inquired, a shadow falling over her face as she wrapped her arms around herself, as though to ward off the cold.

Louisa scoffed. "I would not in the least be surprised." She looked from Juliet to Christina. "He's a proud man, one who does not take kindly to those who speak out against him, those who interfere in his plans. He no doubt considers this a personal attack against him and would like nothing more than to get back at whoever dealt him this blow."

"I could not have said it better," Edith said into the silence that followed Louisa's assessment. She leaned forward, her eyes seeking those of her granddaughters. "I know you're concerned, but I assure you that there is no need. Sarah is perfectly safe and will be returned to us shortly."

"Shortly?" Harriet inquired, a wicked gleam in her scrutinizing eyes. "What, to you, is shortly? How long does it take to pay a ransom? Why is she not back yet?" A slow smile spread over Harriet's face. "You're planning something, are you not, Grandmother?"

Sighing, Edith leaned back in her chair. "I don't have the slightest idea what you're speaking of," she murmured, then closed her eyes and pretended to fall asleep, smiling inwardly.

⁘

"Enter!" Albert snapped upon hearing the knock on his door, fixing his entering butler with an icy stare. "What is it? Is Hartmore finally here?"

His butler gave a quick nod, then took a step sideways and gestured for someone to enter. The moment Hartmore stepped across the threshold into Albert's study, his butler quickly withdrew, unable to hide the sense of relief that came to his face.

With marked reluctance, Hartmore stepped forward, his gaze unfocused and fleeting, never quite daring to meet Albert's. Albert could not deny that he enjoyed that fact, that he enjoyed seeing the other man squirm. Still, the reason that had brought them here together once more was less than amusing. "Is there anything...I can do?" Hartmore asked tentatively, his hands trembling. He quickly linked his arms behind his back and straightened his shoulders, clearly hoping to appear confident...and failing to do so.

Miserably!

Slowly, ever so slowly, Albert rose to his feet, his gaze fixed upon the other man, savoring the silence in the way it weighed heavily upon Hartmore's shoulders. Then he lifted his chin and regarded his visitor with a look of utter disdain. "There is something...off about your daughter's kidnapping," Albert remarked, observing his fiancée's father. "It has been days, and her kidnappers seem in no hurry to receive their ransom."

Hartmore's gaze narrowed, a look of utter incredulity upon his face. "I do not know what you mean. Have they not made their demands clear?" He swallowed hard. "I–I simply assumed that—"

"That is precisely it!" Albert snapped, feeling his hands ball into fists, wishing he could put them through a wall or rather connect them with the other man's face. "The exchange of messages is tedious. Days pass until another letter arrives, none of which has yet stated clearly what ransom is demanded and how it is to be paid." He scoffed darkly. "It is almost as though the ransom is not their true goal." He narrowed his gaze. "In fact, this seems personal."

Hartmore wrung his hands, not so oblivious to not understand what Albert was suggesting. "I assure you I do not know who took her from our home. I know as much as you do. All that was left was the single note upon her vanity. Beyond that, I—"

"Who do you owe money?" Albert thundered. "Who holds a grudge against you? Who would seek to prevent this marriage?"

"No one," Hartmore assured him instantly, shaking his head from side to side as though that might convince Albert of his truthfulness. "I assure you I know of no one who would—"

"I've heard it whispered," Albert interjected impatiently, "that your daughter has been on the brink of matrimony before. Is that true?"

After a moment of reluctance, Hartmore nodded.

"Why did these unions not come to pass then?"

Hartmore inhaled a deep breath, clearly unwilling to discuss this matter. Shame shimmered in his pale eyes, and yet Albert thought to detect a hint of anger as well. "There were...unfortunate circumstances...which prevented—"

"Be specific!" Albert thundered, bringing his fist down hard upon his desk. "Who was she to marry and what prevented it?"

Hartmore cleared his throat uncomfortably. "A little more than a year ago, my wife and I intended to see her matched with Lord Barrington." His lips thinned momentarily before he swallowed his anger and continued. "However, a former neighbor of ours, Lady Louisa, daughter to the Earl of Whickerton, stole him away, securing the match for herself."

"I see," Albert murmured, aware that all of Lord Whickerton's children had married this past year. It had, in fact, been a much-discussed topic among the *ton*. "And was that the only match you had sought for your daughter?"

Again, Hartmore shook his head. "It was not," he replied, his voice growing harder as latent anger resurfaced. "We also sought a match with a wealthy merchant; however, once again one of Lord Whickerton's daughters interfered."

Albert felt the hairs on the back of his neck begin to prickle. "How so?"

Hartmore scoffed. "She married the man herself." He shook his head in disbelief, a rather dark laugh falling from his lips. "Lady Christina used to be my daughter's oldest friend. There was a time when the two girls were inseparable, and yet when my Sarah's happiness was at stake, her so-called friend stole it."

Another Whickerton, Albert mused, and his gaze narrowed even further as he once more turned to Hartmore. "Do I dare ask if there was a third union planned?"

"There was," Hartmore replied, his shoulders straightening with righteous anger. "In fact, I was in negotiation with Lord Gillingham when the man mysteriously disappeared and was later found dead."

Albert paused, rummaging through his mind as Hartmore's words echoed within him. "It was a duel, was it not?" he mused, trying to recall all the details he had overheard. "Yes, I believe it was said to have been a duel." He paused, fixing Hartmore with a hard stare. "Was it not whispered that it was, in fact, Lord Pemberton, husband to yet another one of Lord Whickerton's daughters, who put that bullet in the man's brain?"

"I heard those whispers as well," Hartmore confirmed. "However, as I was not present, I cannot say with certainty who killed Lord Gillingham."

Albert scoffed, annoyance as well as amusement warring within him. Of course, he despised anyone who sought to cross him, who prevented his plans from being realized. Still, he had to admit that he felt a certain sense of admiration for the Whickertons' obvious scheming. If only they did not stand against him!

Seating himself, Albert wondered if perhaps the Whickertons had interfered once more. He failed to see what reason they could possibly have to prevent Miss Mortensen's marriage, but, ultimately, their reasons were insignificant. What mattered was finding out who had taken his fiancée and determining how best to seek revenge for this affront against him. After all, the news of her abduction was currently spreading through the *ton*.

Albert heaved an annoyed sigh. It was one thing to wed a penniless chit. It was quite another to wed an openly ruined one. Indeed, his reputation would suffer, and yet the same were true if he were to end their engagement. Or would society forgive such an affront on his part? Albert rather doubted it.

Ringing for his butler, Albert sent Hartmore away, certain that the man had served his usefulness. "Send for Mr. Smith," Albert instructed his butler as the man stood awaiting his orders. "It is most urgent."

Indeed, something had to be done, Albert mused as he leaned back in his chair, elbows comfortably on the armrests and his fingers steepled in thought. It seemed rather obvious that somehow and for some reason the Whickertons were involved. Only that did not tell him where they had brought the girl nor what they hoped to achieve by stealing her away the night before their wedding.

Albert hoped that Mr. Smith would be able to unearth further information. In fact, he had no doubt. After all, the man was very resourceful. It was only a matter of time before Albert finally knew more.

That thought pleased him greatly.

Chapter Sixteen

TENDER HOPE

Keir saw at first glance that something had changed between Sarah and the mare. There was something different in Sarah's gaze when she walked into the stable the next morning to feed the chickens. Before, she had always glanced over at the horses with a hint of caution in her eyes, her posture tense, as though she feared she might need to flee at a moment's notice.

This morning, however, the look upon Sarah's face whispered of curiosity mixed with a hint of hopeful expectation. Keir had seen it right away, and to his surprise, his heart sped up in excitement. He disliked seeing fear in her gaze as it always reminded him of the many things she had suffered, of how people—her family!—had failed her. Her fear of horses, to him, was only one of many and was representative for everything that terrified her.

Everything that was wrong with the world.

With Sarah's world.

After leading the two horses out of the stable and up the snow-covered path around the house and onto the meadow, Keir was not surprised that when he turned around after closing the gate his gaze fell on Sarah. She simply stood there at the fence, arms resting leisurely upon it and her blue gaze directed at Autumn, a tentative smile upon her face.

Keir moved to stand beside her. "The two of ye spoke, did ye not?" he asked with a grin.

Sarah blinked and then turned her head to look at him. "Spoke? You mean...?" Her gaze traveled back to Autumn.

"Ye look at her differently, lass," Keir elaborated, watching her face most intently. He saw a myriad of emotions flicker across it. Some sparked in her eyes while others tickled the corners of her mouth. She seemed uncertain, and yet no longer afraid.

Sarah smiled at him. "I did as you suggested. I...I looked at her," her gaze returned to Autumn, "and tried to see not simply a horse, but *her*."

As though the mare knew she was being discussed, Autumn tossed her head, giving off a slight neigh.

Sarah's smile widened in a deeply enchanting way, the look in her eyes mesmerized as she looked at the horse. "I spoke to her," she whispered absentmindedly, and Keir wondered if she was even still aware of his presence. "I told her what happened when I was a child. I told her what made me afraid." For a moment, her teeth teased her lower lip. "She listened. She truly did. I could tell." With her gaze still fixed upon Autumn, Sarah shook her head. "I don't recall if I ever spoke to Sunshine like that when I was a child. I don't remember if we ever looked at one another like this. Too much time has passed, and for too long I tried not to remember those times at all."

Keir smiled as he watched them, saw the connection that was slowly developing between the two. Then he stepped back, allowing them this moment. Indeed, over the next few days, Keir watched the bond between Sarah and Autumn grow. At first, only whispered words were exchanged as the distance between them grew smaller and smaller. Again and again, Sarah reached out to touch Autumn's nose and brush her hands down her neck. As though they had known each other forever, girl and horse leaned into one another, communicating in a way that needed no words.

Then, Keir took note of the fact that apples and carrots began disappearing from the kitchen. It was an observation that made him smile, and he resolved to tease Sarah about it, wondering what it would take to make her blush again.

"I was planning on making a vegetable soup," Keir told Sarah one night over supper, fully aware of the way she stilled the moment he spoke. "Oddly though, I canna seem to find any vegetables. I thought I had gathered enough supplies for our stay here. However,..." He trailed off, turning inquisitive eyes on her.

Indeed, a faint rosy blush began to bloom upon her cheeks as her blue eyes flitted around the kitchen before she worked up the nerve to meet his gaze. "That cannot be. They cannot all be gone. I only took a few and—" She stilled, her blue eyes fixed upon his face. Slowly, they narrowed, searching, contemplating. "You're teasing me!" she suddenly exclaimed, a look of utter astonishment upon her face. "Yes, you are! Why would you do this?" Laughing, she touched her hands to her cheeks, no doubt feeling the heat there. "You know what happens when—" Her eyes grew wide, and her jaw dropped. "You're doing this on purpose!" Daring as Keir had never seen her, Sarah reached out and slapped him playfully on the arm. "How dare you?"

Keir laughed, raising his hands in surrender. "I apologize," he assured her, unable to look away. Indeed, she was radiant!

Sarah's eyes narrowed as she regarded him. "Then why did you do it?"

Unable to hide a grin, Keir shrugged. "Quite frankly? Because I wanted to see if I could make ye blush."

Again, Sarah's jaw dropped, and her eyes grew as round as plates. "That is...That is..." At a loss for words, she shook her head at him. "That is so...so..."

"It suits ye," Keir told her earnestly before she could find an appropriate word to hurl at his head. "When ye blush like that, ye seem more alive than in any other moment. It becomes ye. It truly does, lass."

Again, Sarah stilled. Only this time, there was no amusement, no laughter in her eyes. No, this time she stilled in a way that told Keir that no one had ever spoken to her like this before. He could see that she did not believe him or perhaps that she wanted to but did not dare. "How are ye not married?" he blurted out without thinking.

As though on cue, Sarah's blush deepened, and she averted her eyes. "The story of my life," she murmured, her hands fidgeting with the nonexistent curls at her temples. Indeed, she still braided her hair back the way he had shown her; only now, it revealed how uncomfortable she felt at his comment.

Keir reached out and took one of her hands in his, waiting until her gaze rose and she finally looked at him. "I am not speaking of yer current fiancé," he all but growled under his breath, surprised at the spark of anger he felt coursing through his veins. "I'm speaking of before. I canna believe that—"

"Our fortune is gone," Sarah rushed to explain, her words all but rehearsed, as though she had spoken them a thousand times before. Perhaps only to herself. "My father...likes to gamble. Unfortunately, he has no affinity for it. As a consequence, we are in severe debt, a fact that has not escaped the *ton*'s notice." Pushing to her feet, Sarah began to pace the kitchen, repressed anger sparking in her eyes.

At first, Keir thought it directed at the parents who had disappointed her time and time again, placing a burden upon her shoulders that was never meant for her to bear. He silently applauded her, hoping that venting her anger and giving it voice would help set her free. Unfortunately, Sarah's anger was directed at another.

Herself.

"I should have secured a match during my first season the way my sister did," Sarah grumbled under her breath, her eyes closing for a moment before she shook her head at herself. "I should've taken this more seriously. I should've done my duty and saved my family." She suddenly spun around and looked at him, tears misting her eyes. "It was the one thing they asked of me. It was all I was meant to do. And yet," she shrugged helplessly, and despite the tears rolling down her cheeks, her eyes burned with anger, "I could not even do that." With a frantic movement of her hand, she wiped the tears from her face. Then she spun around abruptly and strode from the kitchen, her harsh footsteps echoing on the wooden floorboards.

For a moment, Keir was too shocked to react at all. He had always been good at reading people, and yet he had not seen this coming. He could not believe that she would lay blame at her own feet, that she would even for a second believe that any of this was her fault.

Then, however, when the truth sank in, Keir felt his own blood begin to boil with anger. How dare her family do this to her? She was a kind, good-hearted young woman, determined to do anything within her power to right a wrong she had never committed. Nevertheless, nothing she did was ever good enough for them.

Surging to his feet, Keir stormed after her. He had no idea what he would say or do; however, he knew beyond a shadow of a doubt that he needed to shake her out this...this stubborn belief that she was at fault, was responsible, had failed in her duty.

Entering the parlor, Keir found her standing by the window, eyes downcast. Her shoulders trembled with silent sobs while her fingers dabbed at her eyes, desperately trying to stem the flood. She looked miserable, and Keir doubted that this was the first time she had felt like this. How often before had she been on the brink of despair, then reeled herself back in, lifted her head, squared her shoulders, and once again tried her best to do right by her family?

Yet they never see the need to do right by her, do they?

"I'm sorry," Sarah whispered, her back still to him, her head slightly bowed. The tone in her voice held mortification, and she kept her gaze firmly fixed out the window at the dark night. "I shouldn't have said anything. I should have—"

"Why are ye here?" Keir demanded in a harsh voice, large strides carrying him across the room. "Why?"

At the sound of his voice, Sarah spun around, her eyes wide with fear in them, as though she no longer trusted she was safe in his company.

Keir felt his insides twist and turn at the sight. Honesty was needed, and perhaps fear could aid it. "Why are ye here?" he repeated as his arms shot forward and his hands grasped her by the shoulders. "Why this feigned kidnapping? If all ye want is to solve yer family's problems, then why are ye here now?"

Sarah gasped, wide eyes staring up at him. She seemed almost stunned witless, like in the beginning of their *acquaintance*—a mere few days ago—when no word had made it past her lips, and Keir wondered if he had gone too far.

"The...The ransom," Sarah began, her voice wobbling as she fought to voice her thoughts, "is to pay for my father's debts." She swallowed hard. "Then my family will not need me to find a good match." Her wide blue eyes fell from his, and Keir felt her entire body slump, as though she had finally realized that the fight was lost.

Keir gave her a quick shake, and Sarah's head flew back up, surprise widening her eyes once more. Slowly, he pulled her closer, lowering his head, his gaze drilling into hers. "Then why did ye not simply agree to marry Lord Blackmore?" he demanded in a whisper. "Ye could be married now, yer family's problems solved." His brows rose questioningly, demandingly.

Sarah's lower lip trembled as she looked up at him, her eyes misted with tears. Keir could see how hard she fought to hold them back. "I... I..."

"Why?" Keir demanded once more, giving her yet another shake, wanting her to wake up and face him, face this moment.

"Because I..."

"Tell me, lass. The truth! Why did ye run?"

Her brows drew together. "I did not run. I—" She swallowed hard, and the look of shame on her face grew deeper as realization slowly sank in. "I ran," she breathed, her gaze distant, stunned disbelief in her eyes.

"Ye did," Keir confirmed with a sigh of relief. "Ye ran, and I'm proud of ye for it."

Sarah blinked. "Proud? How could you—?" Her lips sealed shut, and tears spilled over running down her cheeks.

"Lass," Keir called softly, waiting until her eyes dared to meet his. "Why did ye not marry Blackmore?"

Her lips quivered. "I did not want to," she admitted in a barely audible voice. "He frightened me, and he..." She shook herself in disgust, and Keir felt himself tense. A part of him wanted to ask what had happened, and yet he did not dare. Now, was not the moment. "I betrayed them," Sarah continued on. "I failed them. It was my duty as their daughter to—"

"'Tis yer duty to yerself to find yer place in this world, to find happiness," Keir implored her, anguished by the vulnerability he saw in her eyes. "And it clearly isna at Blackmore's side." He offered her a tentative grin. "What is it that ye want, lass? What secret dreams live in yer heart? If ye had no one and nothing to worry about, what would be yer choice?"

Sarah stared at him, as though he had suddenly sprouted wings.

"Ye dunna know, little wisp, do ye?" Keir murmured, saddened by the thought that she had never been inspired to dream. "Ye never dared ask yerself that question." He sighed. "Then ask yerself now. What do ye want? When ye return, what will ye do then? What do ye want to do?" He frowned. "Marriage?"

Sarah flinched ever so slightly. "I told you," she murmured, her gaze not daring to stray higher than his collar, "Grandma Edie said Lord Blackmore will no longer want me, once he learns of..."

Keir nodded. "I remember what ye said, lass, and I wasna speaking of Blackmore." He lowered his head and tried to peek into her eyes. "But another? Do ye hope for marriage?"

Why am I asking her this?

A heavy sigh left Sarah's lips, and when she finally lifted her head and met his gaze, a wistful smile teased her lips. "I always dreamed of a marriage like that of Lord and Lady Whickerton, the kind of marriage each of their children found in the past year."

"Ye want love," Keir murmured, suddenly wondering if he was standing too close. Still, it felt perfectly natural to be holding her like this.

With lips pressed into a thin line, Sarah nodded, then bowed her head, a heavy sigh leaving her lips. "It is foolish, I know. What they found is rare. I know I shall never—"

"Never settle for anything less, little wisp," Keir murmured. "Ye deserve to be loved and cherished, and I know that one day ye shall have it."

Slowly, Sarah lifted her chin, her eyes brimming with tears as she looked up at him, the expression upon her face marked by disbelief. "You're kind to say this," she replied in a hoarse voice. "Yet I know the truth. I know that I shall never marry. I know that no one would ever want to marry me...at least not for honorable reasons." She swallowed hard, then shrugged. "After all, no one ever has and...no one ever shall." A forced smile appeared upon her features. "I have nothing to offer and I...I..." Again, those words sounded like something she had been told over and over again. Exhaustion descended upon her features, and all tension seemed to leave her body.

Keir chuckled in disbelief. "Do ye truly believe that, lass?" he asked, reaching out to grasp her chin. When her eyes met his, he leaned closer, noting the way she drew in a trembling breath. "Do ye want to know what I see when I look at ye?"

For a long moment, neither one of them moved. Sarah held herself perfectly still, as though time had stopped. Yet the look in her eyes betrayed her desire to hear his words, to have someone look at her and not only see faults. Eventually, she gave a quick nod, the pulse in her neck thudding nervously.

A slow smile teased Keir's lips when he saw it, and he knew that neither one of them would ever forget this moment. *Perhaps, though, 'tis not wise to speak to her like this!*

Chapter Seventeen

WITHOUT FLAWS

e is standing too close! A familiar, generally chiding voice warned Sarah. *You should not allow him to put his hands on you!*

Sarah knew that the voice was right. Yet she had already broken countless rules by simply being here with Keir that this one seemed rather insignificant right now. And besides, it didn't...*feel* wrong, did it?

Yes, when Blackmore had stepped too close, that had most definitely felt wrong. Very, very wrong! Terrifyingly wrong! But Keir? Sarah knew she ought not feel the way she did. After all, he was a criminal and Lord Blackmore was a peer. Still, she could not help but welcome Keir's presence.

His touch even.

He was sweet and kind and gentle, and he never did anything that frightened her. Even now, as he held her in his arms, his fingers upon her chin, ensuring that she would not turn away, Sarah felt...safe.

More than that.

She felt...

She wanted...

She wished...

Keir's dark blue eyes reminded Sarah of a darkening sky and an approaching storm; his voice, though, was calm and he spoke in a way that held her mesmerized. "Ye are like a pixie, little wisp," he murmured, gently brushing the pad of his thumb across her chin. "Ye seem like a creature not from this world, strong and daring and kind, and yet also vulnerable and shy. Ye often remain hidden, like the stars during the day, but when night falls, ye shine brightly, yer light warm and beckoning like a flame in deepest winter."

Sarah felt her eyes mist with tears as Keir's words washed over her like a warm summer's rain. Her cheeks warmed, and she felt the urge to avert her gaze but could not. She wanted more. More of these beautiful words. Never had anyone looked at her like this, spoken to her like this, and every fiber of Sarah's being wanted to believe him. Oh, who would she be today if her parents had ever looked at her with trust and spoken to her with kindness and faith? What sort of person would she be if they had ever seen more in her than a bargaining chip?

"Ye have a strong mind," Keir continued, a slow smile revealing faint creases at the corners of his mouth, "and an even stronger heart. Ye show others kindness, even when they dunna deserve it. Ye never give up, no matter how heavy yer burden. And when ye smile, little wisp, truly smile, the world comes alive."

Keir's face blurred as tears ran down Sarah's face, an endless stream of emotions too long held at bay. She wanted nothing more than to sink into his arms and sob helplessly, comforted in the knowledge that there was someone who looked at her and saw...

...something beautiful.

"Yer life is yer own," Keir murmured, the look in his eyes imploring as he gently brushed the tears from her cheeks. "Think long and hard on what it is that ye want, lass, and then," he paused, and the corners of his mouth quirked upward into a grin, "go and get it. And dunna dare let anyone stop ye, ye hear me?"

Sarah smiled as her heart began to feel lighter. She could not recall ever having looked toward the future without any form of dread. Was that even possible? But if her life was truly her own—or would be once she returned to London—what then? In truth, Sarah had not even thought that far ahead, her focus solely on ending her engagement. *But once I am free, truly free, what shall I do then? What is it that I want?*

Sarah blinked, and Keir came slowly back into focus. Indeed, he did not look like a gentleman, and yet he had behaved like one in every way. He had been hired to take her away from London and keep her safe until the ransom was paid. Still, he had done so much more for her.

For the first time in her life, Sarah felt...hopeful. She felt a strength deep inside she had not known she possessed and knew she ought never allow it to slip through her fingers again. She needed to stand tall, find her own path and...

"Thank you," Sarah whispered, looking up into Keir's eyes. "Thank you for..." She shrugged, unable to put into words what this had meant to her.

Keir smiled, giving her chin a playful pinch. "I did nothing but speak the truth, lass." He paused, and for a moment, Sarah wondered what he was thinking. He always spoke with such honesty that Sarah rarely felt the need to question his words. Yet in that moment, she could not help but think that he did not wish for her to know his thoughts.

"What is it?" Sarah asked as an unexpected tingle trailed down her spine.

Another moment passed before Keir shook his head, as though to chase away a thought that continued to linger against his will. He made to step back but then paused. His gaze fixed upon hers before he abruptly dipped his head and...

...placed a kiss upon her forehead. "Good night, little wisp. Go on up to bed. I shall see to everything." He smiled at her and then turned and walked back to the kitchen.

For a long moment, Sarah remained where she was, the sound of clattering dishes and heavy footsteps drifting to her ears. She stood as though transfixed, and without thinking, her hand rose and her fingers touched the spot upon her forehead where Keir had kissed her. The memory sent a wave of longing through her. *If only he—*

Sarah's head snapped up at the direction of her thoughts, and she all but rushed from the parlor, almost flying up the stairs to her chamber. After closing the door behind herself, she leaned against it, breathing heavily as the moment downstairs replayed in her mind.

Again and again.

Making her smile.

And wish.

And dream.

And when Sarah had finally calmed enough to lie down and close her eyes that night, the memory even followed her into her dreams. Only now, Sarah was not in the parlor of the little house in the woods. No, in her dreams, she stood in a ballroom, her gaze sweeping over all those in attendance, their expressions unseeing, their minds unaware of her presence. Sarah felt her heart sink, that familiar feeling of unworthiness filling her chest when she suddenly found herself looking into a pair of dark blue eyes.

Keir.

Her heart knew who he was before her eyes even took note of his face. He was looking at her, not in passing, but as though he had been searching for her, waiting only for her. And then he moved closer, his hand extending, and before Sarah knew what was happening, he was twirling her across the dance floor.

Then the moment suddenly changed, and they were outside, the moonlit night wrapping them in silence. Again, Sarah stood in Keir's arms, his dark gaze fixed upon hers as he slowly lowered his head. Only this time, she knew he would not place a kiss upon her forehead. This time, she knew he would—

With a start, Sarah woke, her head spinning and her heart thundering in her chest. For a moment, she felt confused before the memory of her dream returned with shocking clarity. Instantly, Sarah's cheeks heated, and she buried her face in her pillow, cursing her wayward mind. *Oh, how foolish I am to think of him thus! We are worlds apart. Nothing can ever—*

And yet Sarah could not even bring herself to finish the thought, her heart tensing, shying away from it at the mere contemplation.

When morning came, Sarah hesitantly moved downstairs and into the kitchen, willing her mind to think of anything but her dream. She tried her best to think of the chickens, of fixing breakfast, of Autumn. But the second her gaze fell on Keir, the moment in her dream came rushing back, elbowing every other thought out of the way and pushing to the forefront of her mind.

Of course, her body reacted in the only way it could: by sending a wave of heat into her cheeks.

Sarah cringed, averting her gaze the second she saw that knowing smile come to Keir's face. *Oh, of course, he knows what I'm thinking! He always does!*

Rushing to the other side of the small kitchen, Sarah busied herself by pouring a bowl of milk for Loki. *He can't know what I'm thinking, though, can he? Not truly. He might know I'm embarrassed about...something, but—*

As she was setting Loki's bowl onto the floor, Keir asked, "Are ye all right, lass?"

At the sound of his voice, Sarah shot to her feet, her heart once again hammering in her chest. "Y-Yes, of course." Reluctantly, she forced herself to meet his gaze but then quickly turned away, rushing to seat herself. That, however, proved her undoing because only a moment later Keir sat down in the chair opposite her, his knowing gaze sweeping her face, as though she were an open book.

Unfortunately, he said nothing, which proved even worse because it allowed Sarah to imagine all sorts of knowing remarks while she kept her gaze fixed upon her plate, her fingers tearing a slice of bread into pieces.

Keir chuckled. "Why is it, lass, that ye suddenly canna meet my eyes? What did I do?" He paused, and when Sarah continued to rip her bread to shreds, he leaned forward and reached out to stay her hands.

At the feel of his touch, Sarah flinched and her eyes flew up, ignoring the warnings of her mind without a second thought.

Keir's gaze held hers, and she could all but *feel* him reading her mind as her cheeks burned ever more brightly. "Did ye dream of me?" he asked with deadly accuracy, his voice teasing and his blue eyes sparking with mischief.

Groaning in agony, Sarah closed her eyes, praying that *this* was nothing more than a dream. The bad kind. When she opened them once more, all her hopes were dashed.

Keir chuckled, his hand still upon hers, his fingertips now drawing lazy circles across her skin. Then he leaned forward, his gaze sobering, and asked, "What happened in yer dream?"

With panting breath, Sarah stared across the table at Keir, her mind sluggish and her heart overwhelmed. Yet when Keir's hand tightened upon hers and he made to push to his feet, Sarah's body, at last, knew to react.

Without a second of hesitation, she fled the kitchen, barely possessing the presence of mind to pull on her boots and cloak before rushing out into the cold. Behind her, Sarah dimly heard Keir's voice calling her name. Only she did not stop nor pause. Quick steps carried her away from the house and down the path that led to the meadow. With a furtive glance, Sarah noticed that Keir had yet to bring the horses outside and then hurried onward, her eyes all but blind to her surroundings. She knew not where she was going, possibly round and round in circles, but she knew she could not stop, her feet moving as though of their own accord.

She walked and walked and walked.

I'm such a fool! Sarah chided herself as she came to realize that she could not possibly escape Keir's presence for good. Of course, she would have to return.

Eventually.

And then he would look at her again in that way of his, and she would blush to the roots of her hair, utterly humiliated because, of course, he knew precisely what had happened in her dream the night before.

Or almost happened, Sarah corrected herself, still feeling a good bit disappointed she had woken at that most inconvenient moment.

Yet perhaps she ought to be relieved. The more she allowed her thoughts to dwell on Keir, the harder it would be to bid him farewell. And just as she would have to return to the cabin, she would eventually have to bid him farewell. Once the ransom was paid, she would never see him again.

The thought brought tears to Sarah's eyes, and she stomped ahead, once again chiding herself for her wayward thoughts. Indeed, she *was* a fool! She ought never have allowed herself to feel something for Keir!

She ought never have called him by his first name to begin with! She ought never have—

"Deidre, darling," Keir suddenly called from somewhere on her left, "will ye join us for a spell?"

Confused, Sarah turned toward Keir's voice. Had he just called her Deidre? And...darling? Why would he—?

Sarah stilled when she spotted Keir standing a little ways down the snow-covered path, a stranger by his side.

A man Sarah had never met before.

A man with a rifle slung across his shoulder.

A man whose gaze sent icy shivers down Sarah's back.

Oh, no, who was he?

Chapter Eighteen
THE HUNTER

Keir eyed the hunter in front of him carefully, uncertain what put him on edge. Aye, the man was dressed for hunting, his rifle well-kept and in his grasp with practiced ease. Yet without his gear, Keir would never have pegged the man for a hunter. He moved...differently, his attention not on the breathing world around him. Was it possible the man was merely posing as a hunter? Had he been sent perhaps? By Blackmore?

"I did not expect to find another soul out in this weather," the man replied with a good-natured laugh before casting a look overhead at the overhung sky.

"Neither did I," Keir replied with a matching laugh, trying his best to gauge the man's character, still wondering why he struck him as odd.

"Well, I—" the man began, then abruptly broke off when the sound of a snapping twig drifted to their ears. In a flash, the rifle was in the man's hands, aimed in the direction from which the sound had come.

Catching a glimpse of Sarah's golden hair, Keir moved quickly, stepping into the rifle's path. "'Tis my wife," he told the hunter, lifting his hands in warning. "I'd appreciate it if ye chose a different target." He added a good-natured chuckle, his muscles tense as he considered what to do should the man prove hostile.

Fortunately, he need not have worried, for the hunter quickly lowered his gun, a look of stunned surprise coming to his face. "I apologize," he said quickly, shouldering his rifle once more. "I suppose old instincts die hard."

Keir knew that to be true.

With no other option, Keir called out to Sarah. "Deidre, darling, will ye join us for a spell?" After all, the other man would no doubt find it odd if Keir did not introduce his wife—now that he had identified Sarah as such. In addition, if he could convince the man that they were a married couple traveling from Scotland, it would help shield Sarah from nosy inquiries should Blackmore have, indeed, sent out men to look for her. Why else were the ransom negotiations going so slowly? Keir wondered for the hundredth time. Perhaps Blackmore was stalling for time to protect his fortune.

Confusion creased Sarah's forehead as she slowly made her way down the path toward them, her eyes going back and forth between him and the hunter.

With a smile, Keir waved her closer and then told the hunter, loud enough for Sarah to hear, "My wife is mute." Again, he met Sarah's gaze, imploring her to remain quiet.

With an uncertain look in her eyes, Sarah moved to his side, and Keir put an arm around her shoulders, pulling her closer.

"Good day," the hunter greeted her with a friendly nod. "It is not the best day for a walk, is it?"

Sarah hesitated, then offered a quick nod, the hint of a smile upon her lips.

Keir exhaled the breath he had been holding, his arm tightening upon Sarah's shoulders. He felt her shiver and wondered if it was because of the potentially dangerous situation they were in or because of his touch. Aye, the direction of her thoughts earlier this morning had been more than obvious, and he had been tempted to—

Jarring his thoughts back to the here and now, Keir met the hunter's gaze. "We've come down to visit kin but had some trouble with our wagon." He looked down at Sarah, trying for an intimate exchange between husband and wife. "I hope we'll be able to continue our journey soon."

Sarah's eyes were wide and fearful, and yet Keir enjoyed the way she clung to his side. Her right hand slipped beneath the folds of his coat, and he could feel it coming to rest above his hammering heart. Keir wondered if she was merely playing along but doubted it. After all, Sarah was the most awful liar he had ever met in his life. It was more likely that she was simply distracted by this unexpected moment, completely unaware how tightly she was now clinging to him.

Still, Keir could not rightfully say that he minded. Not at all.

"I wish you the best of luck," the hunter said jovially, interest sparking in his eyes as they lingered upon Sarah a moment too long.

Keir could feel his muscles tense. He could also feel Sarah draw in a shuddering breath before she leaned closer into his embrace. *Did she see it, too? Is the hunter simply taken with her? Or is it possible that he has an ulterior motive?* Keir could still not shake that odd feeling in the pit of his stomach. Something simply did not add up.

"Thank ye," Keir replied kindly. "Good luck to ye as well." He nodded toward the man's rifle. "What are ye hunting?"

The man shrugged, an amused grin coming to his face. "Whatever I find." He tipped his hat and then turned away, marching back down the path, leading him away from the cabin.

Keir exhaled a slow breath, watching the hunter. He wished he could pursue the man to see where he was headed but did not dare leave Sarah out here on her own. He shifted from one foot onto the other, then grasped Sarah's hand, pulling her in front of him. "Stand here and look up at me," he murmured, meeting her eyes before casting another glance above her head at the hunter's receding back.

"Why? What is it?" Sarah asked in a quivering voice, her blue eyes wide.

Keir was about to answer when he saw the hunter glance over his shoulder. He kept his own gaze lowered, his attention focused on Sarah so as not to give the other man the impression that he was being watched. "Perhaps nothing," Keir replied as he reached out and tugged a golden curl back inside Sarah's fur-lined hood. "I just want to see where he's going without him thinking he's being watched."

Sarah nodded, then stilled suddenly when the backs of Keir's fingers brushed the side of her neck. Her eyes flew up, and she held her breath, her muscles tensing.

Keir stilled as well, his gaze fixed upon hers, his fingers lingering against the side of her neck. He could feel her pulse hammering there, her skin warming as a deep blush stole across her features. Keir felt his own pulse quicken, knowing without a doubt where Sarah's thoughts lingered.

Not far from his own.

Instead of stepping away, Keir slipped his hand inside her hood, his fingers tracing her skin, then running through her hair. Cupping the back of her neck, he pulled her closer, once again utterly tempted to bridge that small distance between them and steal a kiss as he had been the night before. Yet he knew that would be far from wise. He needed to keep his thoughts focused in order to protect her and kissing her would definitely shift his focus.

Keir was certain of it.

Perhaps later.

Perhaps...

Dipping his head, he placed another kiss upon her forehead, feeling her warm breath against the hollow at the base of his throat. "Embrace me," Keir whispered as he cast another furtive glance at the hunter. He could no longer make out the man's face, and yet it was clear that the hunter's attention still lingered on them, for he once more angled his body to glance back at them over his shoulder.

Keir tensed, again wishing he could pursue the man.

"W-Why?" Sarah asked, sounding out of breath, her lashes fluttering rapidly as she kept her gaze fixed on his collar.

Keir could not suppress a smile at the sight of her fluttering nerves. He would love nothing more than to press her for an answer about the dream she had had the previous night or why she blushed so often when he stepped closer. However, once again, he refrained, knowing it to be unwise under the current circumstances.

"So, he'll believe us to be husband and wife," Keir murmured, catching Sarah's eyes for a brief second before she dropped her gaze, her blush deepening. Keir chuckled. "Should anyone ask him about a kidnapped English debutante, he'll not think of ye."

Sarah nodded in understanding; yet her eyes never rose to meet his. Hesitantly, she lifted her arms and then placed her hands upon his shoulders in an awkward embrace.

Keir chuckled. "Ye're adorable," he murmured without thinking, then reached to grasp her waist and tugged her closer. She all but fell into his embrace, and his arms tightened around her. *Aye, utterly tempting!*

Sarah drew in a shuddering breath, and to Keir's surprise, her eyes rose to meet his. "Why...Why did you tell him I was...your wife?" Her gaze darted from his for a brief second.

Keir smiled, delighting in her reaction to his teasing. "To hide ye," he whispered, slipping his hands farther onto her back. "After all, people do think it odd for a young unwed woman to be out in the woods with a man not of her family. Alone...and unchaperoned." He lifted his brows meaningfully.

Hurriedly, Sarah dropped her gaze, her head bobbing up and down. "Yes, of course. That was...That was quick thinking." She swallowed, her head slightly bowed as she waited, silence stretching between them.

Keir heaved a slow sigh, forcing his gaze past her head and toward the hunter. Only now, the path was empty. The man was gone, and Keir knew he ought to have paid better attention. Indeed, Sarah was proving to be an awful distraction, drawing his thoughts at all times of the day. She drew him near with her shy glances and blushing cheeks, her daring words and nervous hands.

Aye, I've come to care for her.

More than is wise.

Reluctantly, Keir stepped back, releasing her. "He's gone," he told her, watching her sigh with relief as she looked past him down the path. "We should return to the house."

Sarah nodded, and despite the rosy glow of her cheeks, a shiver shook her body, making her pull her cloak more tightly around her.

"Are ye cold?"

Sarah shook her head, her gaze fixed upon the path beneath her feet, her teeth digging into her lower lip, as though she feared a secret might fly past without her consent.

Keir smiled, utterly tempted to reach for her and pull her back into his arms. Aye, he wanted to kiss her. In truth, the thought had been lingering nearby for the past few days, and although Keir knew that right now was not the time to break the rules, he vowed that before their time together was up he would steal a kiss.

Wise or not.

Chapter Nineteen

TARGET PRACTICE

Walking back to the house, Sarah could feel Keir's gaze upon her. Yet he did not say a word, and the silence that lingered chased goosebumps up and down Sarah's back. Keir was not the kind of man who hesitated to share his thoughts. He said whatever came to his mind, and she could not help but wonder what thoughts he was so suddenly unwilling to voice. Was he concerned about the man with the rifle? Although she had been terrified upon first spotting him, Sarah had found his easy smile reassuring.

"Who was that?" Sarah finally broke the silence.

Keir shrugged. "That I canna say for certain. He said he was a hunter, out looking for game."

Sarah chanced a careful glance at him. "You don't believe him?"

Again, Keir shrugged, not a word passing his lips. They walked on another few steps before he suddenly shifted his gaze to her. "Ye played along very well."

Sarah tensed at the teasing note in his voice. "Thank you," she mumbled then, quickening her steps. *Oh, will this awkwardness between us never wane!*

"Have ye ever used a pistol?" Keir inquired, his large strides easily keeping up with her. "Or a dagger?"

Sarah drew to a halt, her heart pausing in her chest as she looked up at him with wide eyes. "Why?" She looked back down the path they had come. "Do you think that...that—?"

Keir reached out and drew her hands into his, his touch effectively cutting off all rational thought. "Ye needna worry, lass." He squeezed her hands, an easy smile back on his face. "I'll teach ye."

"W-Why?" Sarah stammered, wondering what that odd tingling was she felt where Keir's hands held hers.

"Just in case." He pulled her arm through the crook of his, and they turned back down the path. "Tomorrow I'll need to go back to the inn."

Sarah felt a cold shiver run down her back at the thought of being on her own. "Do you...Do you think he will come back? The hunter, I mean."

Keir shook his head. "I wouldna leave if I thought so."

Sarah exhaled a slow breath, welcoming that sense of relief that washed over her. Yet, she could not help but think that if Keir meant what he said, he would not want to teach her how to wield a weapon, would he? She wanted to ask him but feared the answer, and so later that day, she found herself in the yard with a rifle in her hands.

"'Tis the first time ye're holding a rifle, isna it?" Keir asked with a grin.

Sarah chuckled, desperate for that sense of ease between them to return. "Is it that obvious?" Indeed, the clunky weapon felt utterly wrong in her hands, and she wished she could simply set it aside.

In two large strides, Keir was suddenly standing at her side, his arms coming around her, his hands showing her how to hold the weapon, setting it against her shoulder. Every single one of Sarah's muscles tensed, and her breath lodged in her throat as she felt his brush by the side of her neck. He spoke, his words soft and oddly tantalizing, and yet Sarah could not grasp their meaning, her mind strangely muddled. "Go ahead, lass. Try it," he urged, then stepped back.

Sarah's mind reawakened, holding onto those last few words. "Are you certain?" she asked tentatively, trying to remember his instructions. Unfortunately, her mind came up empty.

Grinning as though the scoundrel had once more read her thoughts, Keir nodded. "Aye, lass. Pull the trigger and see what happens."

Squeezing her eyes shut and praying that she would not accidentally wound herself, him, or some other unfortunate creature to step into her path, Sarah did as Keir asked.

The power of the shot slammed into her shoulder and shoved her backward, a dull pain radiating through her limbs. Her eyes jerked open, and she fully expected to see blood stain the crisp white layer of snow covering the ground.

"Well done, lass," Keir complimented with a proud grin. "Ye actually hit the target. That I didna expect."

Sarah stared at him. *There was a target?* She wondered, still unable to recall his instructions. Then her head spun around, trying to see what she had hit.

All her eyes could see, though, were trees.

And more trees.

Ignoring Sarah's confusion, Keir showed her how to reload, then once again pointed toward the trees. "Try to hit the same one again," he said, gesturing toward a tall, bare oak tree.

Sarah nodded, her breathing coming fast as she carefully took aim, quite certain that she had no idea what she was doing. "Beginner's luck," she murmured under her breath, and Keir laughed good-naturedly.

Yet when she fired her second shot, another chip of the oak tree's bark flaked off, and beside her, Keir nodded in approval, mild surprise marking his features. "Ye're a natural, lass," he remarked with satisfaction and then proceeded with his instructions.

By the time they finally returned inside, the sun was setting, and Sarah knew not only how to load and shoot a rifle but also the pistol Keir carried on his belt. Furthermore, he had insisted on showing her how to wield the dagger he also carried on his belt, issuing precise instructions on how to best wound a possible opponent. Sarah could not say that she had cared for the somewhat nauseating details of his explanations. Still, she had enjoyed—if one could call it that considering her fluttering nerves—the way he had stepped closer once again, his hands guiding her own, his breath warm against her skin.

Of course, Sarah's mind had once again blanked on most of his instructions, which made her wonder even more about her apparent success when it came to hitting a target. Perhaps Keir was right, and she was a natural. Oddly enough, that thought stirred a warm glow in Sarah's chest. Never had she truly been good at anything, and thus the sense of having accomplished something was utterly unfamiliar to her.

It had been the same when Keir had taught her how to cook. It had not been a task meant for a young woman of Sarah's station, and yet she had succeeded at it. And now, the same had happened with firing a weapon. Shaking her head, Sarah hid a smile. *Oh, I'm a fairly odd woman, am I not?* Then again, she had always known that. She had never felt like other young debutantes, but she would never have guessed just how much set her apart from them.

"Do you truly think that...that...?" Sarah asked stuttering, uncertain how to put into words what it was she feared.

Seating himself in his usual spot opposite her at the table, Keir met her gaze. "'Tis very unlikely that anyone should find us here," he said, his voice calm and confident and thankfully reassuring. "Believe me. Everything will be fine, lass."

Sarah nodded, and yet her thoughts remained with today's encounter. Had it truly been a simple coincidence? Had the man spoken the truth? Was he a hunter with no intention of tracking her down? Had he not been sent by Blackmore?

Sarah wanted to believe so, but her wayward mind circled endlessly, recalling moments she had spent in Blackmore's company. From the first, even as a child, the man had struck her as cold, and then later as she had grown up, also as dangerous, his only focus on securing his own interests. There had been no kindness, no compassion in his gaze, and it had been that more than their difference in age and the fact that she did not find him appealing that had made her realize she could never marry him.

Pacing the parlor, from window to window, Sarah stared out into the black night. Shivers ran down her back, and she rubbed her hands up and down her arms, the fire in the hearth behind her unable to send warmth through her being. Loki wound around her legs, threatening to upend her balance and send her sprawling onto the floor. His eyes looked up at her with concern, and she could see that he did not care for her fluttering nerves nor the hectic movements they inspired.

"Sit down, lass," Keir instructed sternly, pointing to one of the armchairs near the fireplace. Sarah hesitated, and he raised his brows, as though issuing a challenge. Heaving a deep sigh, Sarah complied.

Snatching up Loki, Keir deposited the feline into her lap, then stroked his head and said, "Keep her there." He flashed Sarah a grin and then seated himself next to her, stretching out his long legs.

Clearly taking Keir's instructions seriously, Loki curled up comfortably in her lap, poking his head at her hand until Sarah began stroking his fur. Oddly enough, she began to relax as she listened to the sound of Loki's purring. Her breathing evened, and her pulse no longer hammered in her veins. Sighing deeply, she closed her eyes and leaned back her head.

"Shall I tell ye another story of my people?" Keir asked into the soft stillness of the parlor. The only sounds were Loki's purring and the soft crackling of the fire in the hearth.

Sarah felt a smile come to her face, and she nodded her head without opening her eyes, determined to cling to the sense of peace that fell over her. She listened to Keir's softly spoken words, and with each one, her mind calmed a bit more. Abandoning its concern for her safety, it simply listened, reveling in the story of a water nymph and a wood nymph who fell in love against all odds. It was a story of hope and faith, of life's unpredictability and beauty, and it made Sarah wonder where Fate would lead her.

That night, Sarah slept peacefully, Keir's comforting words keeping away the nightmares she had feared after the day's events. Yet when she woke in the morning, the bright winter's light once again brought with it the harshness of the world. Gone was that warm glow that had soothed her rattled nerves, and when Keir pulled himself onto Scout's back, Sarah's knees shook so hard, she feared she might fall over face-first into the snow.

And then he was gone, and she was alone, her fears and uncertainties the only things to keep her company.

Except for Loki, of course.

Yet the warm purring feline no longer seemed to possess the ability to put her mind at ease without Keir by her side, and she spent the day in a nervous jitter. Every little noise spooked her, and she kept Keir's rifle by her side throughout the day.

Just in case.

Indeed, Keir's absence made Sarah realize how much his presence put her at ease. She had come to feel so content in the last few days, greeting every day with an unburdened heart despite the tense situation she found herself in. Most days, she had been all but able to forget the threat Blackmore posed to her life, her happiness, living in the here and now, savoring each moment. Yes, before, her life had been full of concerns. She had always carefully weighed every step before taking it, constantly afraid to err, to displease.

To displease her parents.

To disappoint them.

To prove herself unworthy.

To her surprise, Sarah realized that she no longer felt nervous to disappoint. At least, not Keir. He had never made her feel awful for failing at a task. He had never made her feel unworthy.

Yet he made her feel.

He made her feel nervous...only for a completely different reason. A reason Sarah cherished and dreaded all the same, and as she sat in the parlor, her hands wrapped tightly around his rifle, she once again heard his voice echo in her mind, asking her what she would do once she returned home.

Only Sarah could not think of home, of *after*. She could not think of the possibilities she would have once she returned to London. All she could think of was that home meant a life without Keir.

And her heart had never felt so heavy.

Chapter Twenty

APPLE OR PLUM?

Keir held back once the inn came into view, remaining half-hidden in the underbrush, his eyes scanning the comings and goings. Due to the season and the thick layer of snow coating the country lanes, travel had slowed and fewer people than usual drove by or stopped at the inn for a bite to eat or a change of horses. When nothing suspicious caught his eye, Keir urged Scout onward, granting the gelding a deserved reprieve in the inn's warm stable. Then he stepped into the taproom, brushing snow from his coat as he moved toward the innkeeper's desk. "Any letters for me?" he asked, once again shifting to an English accent—something that never failed to make him think of his grandmother. He missed her, realizing that more than half a year had passed since he had left his home. Soon, it would be time to return.

The innkeeper gave him a friendly nod, then handed him an envelope.

Keir retreated to a small table in the corner near the hearth and ordered a mug of ale and a quick meal. Only a few tables were occupied this time of day, and Keir was able to identify a few of the travelers. Some were locals while others seemed to pass through—just as he did—on a regular basis, tending to their business. A young couple sat near the door, arguing in hushed voices, while a burly but tired-looking man had taken a seat on the other end of the large room, his hands wrapped around a mug of ale. Every once in a while, the man sighed deeply, his eyes glazed and the scar cutting through his right eyebrow moving up and down in rhythm.

Turning his attention to the letter in his hands, Keir paused when he found only a handful of words. Once again, the dowager countess assured him that all was well and going according to plan.

That was it!

Nothing about how to proceed, about the ransom having been paid, about returning Sarah to town!

Keir frowned. *What is going on? Are we supposed to remain hidden away in the woods forever?*

Not that Keir minded, he thought with a chuckle, surprising himself. Aye, he would miss the blushing lass! He would miss her fiercely!

Clearing his throat, Keir forced his attention back to the letter in his hands, turning it back and forth, as though that might reveal a hidden message.

It did not.

Asking the barmaid for a piece of parchment and a quill, Keir quickly penned a message of his own, careful to keep it unobtrusive should it happen to fall into another's hands. He assured Grandma Edie that all was well—as she had done in her own letter—and then asked with as much urgency and sternness as he could convey in a few brief lines what was going on. He could easily imagine the old lady's amused chuckle upon receiving his message. No doubt she would disregard his demand for an explanation completely and simply continue on with her plan, as though he had never written to her.

Keir was tempted to return to London—with or without written consent from the dowager. Yet he knew he would never do anything to endanger Sarah, and he had no way of knowing what had transpired in their absence. Obviously, *something* had to have happened considering this massive delay!

Again, not that Keir minded.

The sweet scent of cooked fruit drifted to his nose, and Keir lifted his head. The barmaid was setting down two small tarts in front of the arguing couple near the door, who now seemed to have buried the hatchet, smiling at one another before savoring the treats.

Thinking of Sarah, Keir smiled and then waved the barmaid over, ordering two tarts to take back to the cabin. After finishing his meal, he rose to his feet, nodded toward the innkeeper and stepped back out into the cold. Scout seemed reluctant to leave the warm stables but followed Keir out into the yard without much fuss.

The ride back to the cabin was overshadowed by heavy snowfall, all but obscuring Keir's view as he leaned low over Scout's neck. He could barely see anything in his path and resolved to trust in the gelding's instincts to carry them safely back home.

Home? Keir wondered, picturing the small cabin in his mind, a warm fire in the hearth and Sarah seated in one of the armchairs, Loki curled up in her lap and a rosy blush upon her cheeks. Instantly, his pulse quickened, and he felt a deep longing to reach her side.

Of course, Keir was concerned about the hunter. Not enough to have stayed, but try as he might, he could not shake the feeling that the man had been no mere hunter. Was he still in the vicinity? Had he been watching the cabin? But why? Keir could not imagine the man having been sent by Blackmore; after all, if the baron knew where his fiancée was, he would have no doubt come for her or rather had her brought to him. Still...

When the snow finally let up and the cabin came in sight, Keir breathed a sigh of relief. Everything looked as it always did, except for that extra layer of snow covering everything from the ground to the trees and the roof. Smoke billowed out of the chimney, and a warm light shone out into the darkening day. Keir pulled Scout into the stable where they were greeted by Autumn's soft neigh. He quickly brushed down the gelding and ensured that both horses and the old goat had enough food and water. Then he hastened toward the house.

The door creaked open noisily, and Keir stepped across the threshold. Aside from his own footfalls, no sound met his ears, and he felt the hairs on the back of his neck rise with apprehension. His eyes swept the hall, then glanced up ahead into the kitchen.

Yet he saw nothing.

"Sarah?" Keir called softly, his hand moving to the pistol at his belt.

No reply came, and the shiver of apprehension turned into an icy grip that tensed his muscles and lodged the breath in his throat. Had he been mistaken about the hunter?

Drawing his pistol, Keir edged forward, his pulse hammering in his ears. *I shouldna have left her alone! I should never have gone! What if—?*

Glancing around the corner into the parlor, Keir spotted Sarah's slumped figure. She lay slack in her armchair, her head rolled sideways and her eyes closed...his rifle on the floor by the side of the chair.

Instantly, all manner of horrific images assailed Keir as his mind tried to fill the gap of what had happened to her in his absence. Almost dropping his pistol, he rushed toward her, then fell to his knees and reached out to grasp her by the shoulders. "Sarah!" Keir called, giving her a shake before his right hand moved to her neck and his fingers sought her pulse.

Before he could, though, Sarah's eyes suddenly flew open, and she jerked upward with a sound of alarm leaving her lips.

A breath of relief rushed from Keir's lungs. "Are ye all right, lass?" he demanded as his eyes swept her body, searching for injuries. "What happened? Are ye hurt? Is someone here?" He briefly glanced over his shoulder toward the open door leading out into the hall.

But all remained quiet.

Except for a soft *meow* as Loki rose from his spot by the hearth, stretching and yawning and looking at Keir with such a head-shaking expression upon his face that Keir momentarily had to close his eyes. "Nothing happened, did it?" he asked Sarah with a relieved laugh. "Ye simply fell asleep."

Rubbing a hand over her eyes, Sarah nodded. "I suppose I did," she replied, trying her best to suppress a yawn.

Exhaling a deep breath, Keir returned the pistol to his belt. "Ye just took years off my life, lass," he told her with a chuckle, then he rose to his feet. His eyes fell upon the rifle, and he frowned. "Is something wrong?"

Sarah followed his gaze, a deep sigh lifting her shoulders before she bent down to pick up the weapon. "I was merely..." She moved away and set it down in a corner of the room, leaning it against the wall. "I suppose I was a little...nervous," she finally said, still not looking at him as she moved over to the hearth and began to stoke the fire.

Only now did Keir see how pale Sarah was, her shoulders tense and the rosy glow that so often graced her cheeks gone with not even a trace left of it. "What happened?" he asked, moving closer. He could see that she was trying to evade him, but he would not allow her. "Sarah!" He reached for her hands, pulling her around to face him.

Her blue eyes were downcast, and for a moment, she seemed to sway on her feet. "Yer hands are ice-cold," Keir murmured disapprovingly before reaching out to grasp her chin, forcing her to meet his eyes. "Have ye eaten anything at all today?"

As though in answer, Sarah's stomach rumbled loudly and a fetching and utterly reassuring blush stole across her features. "I...I might have forgotten," she stammered, her eyes flickering away from his.

Keir smiled, relieved to see the woman he had come to know return. "I've brought ye something," he said, then pulled her over to her armchair and all but pushed her back down. "Here. Go ahead and eat," he instructed sternly after handing her the small bundle containing the tarts. "I need to change first, but I'll be down shortly." He stepped away, holding her gaze. "Ye're not alone, Sarah."

A grateful sigh left her lips, and he could see that she was blinking back tears as her head bobbed up and down, as though she needed the movement to convince herself of his words. "Thank you."

Hanging his snow-soaked coat in the hall, Keir headed upstairs and quickly changed into dry clothes, unable to shake the image of Sarah's pale cheeks. Aye, she had been afraid! Terrified even! Terrified enough to be spending the entire day with a rifle in her hands. He ought to have seen it. He ought to have never left her alone. Not today. Not so soon after encountering the hunter.

Resolved not to be gone too long, Keir quickly found his way back downstairs, feeling a small measure of relief when he found her still seated by the fire, a calm expression upon her face. Indeed, the linen cloth lay open upon her lap and both tarts...were gone.

Keir grinned, for he knew precisely what to do...how to distract her from today's unrest.

"Oh, I'm famished," he said, walking into the parlor. "Which tart did ye eat? Apple or plum? I wasna sure which fruit ye liked so I thought I'd give ye a choice."

As expected, Sarah's expression stilled in that telling way of hers before a rosy blush of mortification rose to her cheeks. "I...I...," she stammered, quickly folding up the now empty cloth before pushing to her feet, her gaze anywhere but on him.

Keir knew he ought not tease her, but it was the surest way to distract her. "In general, which do ye like better, apple or plum?"

"I liked them both," Sarah replied before quickly correcting herself. "I mean, I *like* them both." She moved to stand by the fire, holding out her hands, as though to warm them.

Keir made a show of looking around the parlor, as though searching for his tart. Then he paused and turned to look at her. "Did ye eat them both?"

As though slapped, Sarah spun around, her eyes wide. "No!" The word flew from her lips as she took a step back, the look in her eyes revealing that she was just as surprised by her answer as he was.

Keir grinned, slowly advancing on her as she continued to back away. "Are ye certain?"

"Yes!" Again, the word felt like the snap of a whip, and Sarah's eyes widened alarmingly while the pulse in her neck continued to hammer wildly.

Strolling closer, Keir watched her. "First, ye almost give me a heart attack by appearing to have been attacked," he said with a mildly accusing tone in his voice as he boxed Sarah into a corner of the parlor.

"I did not—"

"Then ye eat my tart," Keir interrupted her, watching her jaw drop and her blush deepen. "And then ye lie about it."

Swallowing hard, Sarah bowed her head, her back pressed against the wall. "I'm sorry. I did not mean to... I thought... I..."

Keir leaned closer, bracing one hand on the wall, and Sarah's head snapped up, alarm coming to her wide blue eyes. "Admit it," he whispered, well-aware of the way Sarah was watching him, confusion mingling with the mortification still in her gaze. "Did ye eat my tart?"

Her mouth opened, and yet no sound came out, her gaze searching his face before venturing lower, her cheeks now all but on fire.

Keir stilled, feeling reminded of the morning when she had confessed to having dreamed of him. He still did not know what had happened in that dream. Perhaps something not unlike this very moment.

Perhaps...

Keir reached out and slipped an arm around her waist, gently urging her closer, and although a startled gasp left Sarah's lips, she did not object. Neither did she drop her gaze. No, for once, her eyes remained upon his, her breath coming fast, warm and sweet against his lips as he slowly lowered his head.

His eyes looked deep into hers as the distance between them shrank, his hands upon her waist, her arms hanging limply at her sides. Keir knew this to be ill-advised. He certainly had not planned this. He had only meant to tease her, to distract her. *Aye, this is certainly distracting.* He no longer saw even a flicker of fear in Sarah's eyes but something else instead.

As aflutter as she was with nerves, Keir knew Sarah wanted this as much as he did. That she, too, had pictured this moment in her mind. Aye, that she had dreamed of it.

And now, there was no turning back.

Dipping his head, Keir captured her lips with his.

Chapter Twenty-One

OUT INTO THE NIGHT

Absentmindedly, Sarah wondered why her mother's voice failed to chime in. After all, was this not precisely what parents tended to warn their daughters about. Yet only silence met her, which was all good and well because Sarah felt absolutely certain her knees would give out any moment now. At the very least, they shook so hard that her mind began to spin. All that anchored her to the here and now was the way Keir's dark blue eyes looked into hers, holding her in place. She could not even blink, let alone avert her gaze.

Oh, she felt tempted to do so! Certainly! *Why is he looking at me like this? It almost seems as though he intends to—*

And then Keir moved closer, his hands upon her waist, his arms tugging her toward him.

Rather absentmindedly, Sarah wondered if this was a dream. It had to be, did it not? It certainly felt like a dream, like the moment she had strolled with Keir beneath the stars. Only she had woken before his lips had touched hers, a fact that had disappointed Sarah to the very core of her being. She had wanted that kiss! Dream or not, she had wanted it!

Keir's breath fanned warm against her lips as he leaned closer, his eyes holding hers, as though he wanted to be certain that he was not overstepping, that she wanted this as well.

For a brief moment, Sarah's body tensed, and her mind flashed back to another such moment...with another man. A man who had not been concerned with what she wanted. Who had not asked permission. Who had not complied when she had tried to stop him.

Lord Blackmore.

Sarah shuddered inwardly at the memory of that kiss. Fortunately, it had only been a brief encounter, meant to teach her that he was the one in control and that she had no choice but to comply. It had terrified Sarah, had made her realize she had to take whatever risk necessary to prevent that marriage.

And it had led her to Keir.

To this very moment.

A moment she wanted.

A kiss she wanted.

A kiss she had dreamed of.

More than once.

Banishing all memories of Lord Blackmore, Sarah did her best to savor this unexpected moment. Yes, her nerves were still aflutter and her knees felt weaker than ever before. But there was a spreading warmth in her chest that seemed to heat every inch of her, not only her cheeks. A light tingling buzzed beneath her skin where Keir's touch lingered, where his warm breath brushed against her skin. She felt him lean closer, his tall frame blocking out the rest of the world until it seemed to have disappeared. Yet all the while, the look in his eyes vowed that she was safe with him.

That she would always be safe with him.

Overwhelmed by this moment, Sarah felt a flicker of panic. *What am I to do? How does one kiss? What am I—?*

And then Keir's mouth captured hers and her thoughts vanished, as though they had never been.

His lips were a soft pressure against hers, gentle and tentative, as his hands upon her back urged her closer. The moment Sarah complied, taking a step toward him, her hands reaching up, her fingers brazenly curling into the fabric of his vest, Keir's kiss grew bolder. He slipped a hand into her hair, cupping the back of her head, and kissed her with a fierceness Sarah had not expected.

It stole the breath from her lungs and made her head spin in delicious circles. *Oh, my!* Sarah thought as she clung to Keir, wishing this moment would never end. *I had no idea a kiss could feel like this! So...So...So...*

Indeed, there were no words!

And then, Keir stilled, as though he had suddenly realized all the things Sarah had told herself many times over.

That they were from different worlds.

That they would have to bid each other farewell soon.

That they should not be doing this.

Lifting his head, Keir met her gaze, his own overshadowed, and for a split second, Sarah thought to see...regret.

Not regret over what they had just done. Not regret for a kiss that had felt heavenly. But regret for what they could never have, what they could never be.

In the next instant, a teasing grin flashed across Keir's face, though, and the hand that had been in her hair moved to pinch her chin. "Ye wee liar, ye did eat both tarts!" Keir exclaimed in a whisper. Then he took a step back, and his hands fell away, leaving Sarah swaying on the spot.

For a moment, Sarah stared at him dumbfounded, her mind slow to catch up before her body did what it always did when she felt mortified to the very tips of her toes. Heat shot into her head, and she felt her cheeks flash red-hot the moment she realized Keir had to have tasted the tarts upon her lips.

Backing away, Sarah dropped her gaze. "I'm s-sorry," she stammered, glancing up at him as the calm of the previous moment was swept away by an all too familiar feeling of utter uncertainty. "I didn't think. I was famished, and I—"

Keir's hand settled upon her shoulder, and slowly Sarah lifted her chin. "Dunna fash, lass," Keir murmured, a good-natured gleam in his eyes. "I only meant to tease ye. I'm not upset. After all, it gave me an excuse to kiss ye." Again, he stilled for the barest of seconds, as though he was not quite certain how to continue on from here. Then, however, he cleared his throat and a moment later, that easy smile of his was back in place. "Go on up to bed, lass. Ye look ready to fall asleep on yer feet."

Sarah nodded, even though she did not feel the least bit tired. Had she not just slept half the day away? Still, her nerves were restless, her pulse thudding so wildly that her eyes had trouble remaining focused. Keir's face blurred every now and then, and so she accepted his suggestion and, after reaching for a candle to light the fire in her chamber, slipped from the parlor, Loki upon her heels. Perhaps they could both do with a bit of distance to sort out this moment. Clearly, it had caught them both unawares.

After changing into her nightshift, Sarah contemplated slipping under the covers; however, her limbs still buzzed with energy, making her absolutely certain that sleep would not come any time soon. And so, she donned her robe and draped a heavy blanket upon her shoulders to keep the chill of the night away and then proceeded to pace up and down the length of her chamber. On each turn, the warmth of the fireplace reached out its fingers toward her, and yet Sarah barely noticed, her mind locked on the moment downstairs in the parlor.

An odd joy coursed through her veins, and Sarah pulled to a sudden halt, realizing with perfect clarity that she had made the right choice. Doubts had been there before, but no more. No, she had done right. Had she married Lord Blackmore, she would have regretted it for the rest of her life! Indeed, Keir's kiss had proved to her that she needed more than rank and title, fortune and societal approval. Happiness cared very little for those things but depended on others instead. Yes, it was built upon affection—love if possible—on trust and respect, on feeling at peace in the other's presence. And as much as Keir unsettled her sometimes, Sarah never felt even the smallest part of her rebel against his presence, wishing he were not there. Quite on the contrary, when he was gone, she longed to have him back by her side.

Was that how the Whickerton sisters felt about their husbands? Sarah wondered, seeing her question instantly answered when she remembered the look upon Christina's face the last time they had spoken. Indeed, her friend had been unable to hide her affections for her future husband. There had been something in her gaze, something intangible but powerful all the same. Sarah could not name it, but it resonated within her, a feeling she now understood.

"I cannot marry without love," Sarah whispered into the stillness of her chamber, and Loki's head poked up from where he lay curled up on her bed, lazy eyes traveling to her. Yet standing in front of the fireplace, Sarah's gaze remained distant, almost unseeing, her body warmed by the heat of the flames dancing in the hearth. "I simply cannot. I want...I want what Christina has. I want what they all have." She sighed deeply, imagining her mother's chiding look for thinking only of her own desires and not of her family's needs. *Am I being selfish?* Sarah wondered. *After all, I abandoned my family when I chose this path. But how could I have chosen differently?*

Her mind conjured an image of Lord Blackmore, and Sarah instinctively shied away from it. As though in answer, the image shifted, and she found herself looking at Keir, his kind eyes and good-natured smile, a mischievous spark lighting up his features.

Sarah smiled involuntarily, and that familiar yearning welled up in the very core of her being. Keir was only downstairs, and still, she missed him with a fierceness that took her breath away. "I'm in trouble," Sarah whispered to herself.

Instantly, a cautious voice piped up in the back of her head, reminding her that there could be no future for them.

Keir was not of the peerage. He was not a suitable match for her. He was in all likelihood even a criminal—although Sarah could not imagine that being true. Yet was he not here? Had he not assisted in a feigned kidnapping?

Sarah frowned. *Although, does that not make me a criminal as well?* Oddly enough, the thought was not repellent but made her smile instead. Criminal or not, a kiss was only a kiss. Of course, it could hold meaning, but as sheltered a life as Sarah had lived, she knew that not every kiss spoke of love. And although Sarah felt relatively certain that Keir had grown to like her, she would be a fool to think that there was a sliver of love for her in his heart. After all, this was a job for him. Nothing more.

The heaviness that descended upon Sarah's heart at the thought felt utterly crushing, and she was about to bury her face in her pillows, tears already misting her eyes, when a dull thud echoed to her ears from outside.

Sarah stilled, listening.

Thud!

In two steps, Sarah stood at the window, squinting her eyes as she peered outside into the dark. A few stars shone overhead, and from the faint silvery glow that fell over the yard, Sarah guessed that, at least, a crescent moon hung in the sky somewhere above the cabin. Yet her eyes spied nothing.

No movement of any kind.

Had she imagined the sound?

Thud!

Neigh!

At the sound of Autumn's call, Sarah flinched, for it had a distinctively fearful note. Her muscles contracted, her fingers digging into her arms as an ice-cold chill raced itself up and down her spine. Had something spooked the mare? Had an animal gotten into the stable?

Sarah's heart stilled. "The hunter!" she whispered breathlessly.

Neigh!

Spinning upon her heel, Sarah burst out of her chamber and rushed down the stairs as fast as her feet would carry her. Panic tightened her limbs, and yet she knew she could not simply ignore what she had heard. She needed to—

"What are ye doing up?" Keir demanded as Sarah came rushing toward the front door. "Go back up to yer chamber," he instructed, pulling on his boots and donning his coat, "and take the rifle with ye." He handed her the weapon, thrusting it into her trembling hands as his blue eyes met hers imploringly. "And bolt the door."

Staring at him, Sarah nodded, her ice-cold fingers clamped around the slim weapon. The sign of alarm upon Keir's face terrified her, and as she watched him walk out the door, closing it behind him, every cell in her body urged her out into the night after him. Indeed, the thought of staying behind, not knowing what was going on, was the worst torture. If she followed him, perhaps...she could help? After all, whoever had come had come for her, was that not so? What if something happened to Keir?

For a small eternity, Sarah simply stood there, her gaze fixed upon the closed door. Then Autumn's neigh shattered the night's stillness yet again, and all of a sudden, Sarah was moving. Trembling hands pulled on her boots and reached for her cloak. Then she rushed toward the door, the rifle in her hands, and burst out into the night.

Chapter Twenty-Two

WHISPERS

Back in London

T he dowager countess watched her second-youngest granddaughter pace the drawing room nervously while she herself sat settled comfortably by the fireplace. "Will you not come sit with me, my dear?"

Christina eyed her contemplatively and then shook her head and resumed her pacing. Her blue eyes held concern, and she turned them out the window time and time again, as though the soft snowflakes falling down from the heavens held a message for her.

Edith sighed. "There is no need for concern," she assured her granddaughter. "Trust me. Sarah is well."

Turning to look over her shoulder, Christina nodded. "I believe you."

"Then why are you so agitated, my dear?"

Sighing, Christina shrugged. "Because I miss her." She stepped away from the window and finally seated herself at her grandmother's side. "It's been so long since we spoke. After I prevented her marriage to Thorne, her father forbad her from seeing me." Sadness clung to her features, her eyes forlorn. "It's simply been…too long." A heavy and deeply wistful sigh left her lips.

Edith reached out and patted her granddaughter's hand. She remembered well how infuriated Lord Hartmore had been when Christina had married the man he had intended for his own daughter. Of course, Sarah had been relieved. She would have never been a good match for Thorne. Neither would he have been a good match for her.

Christina, however, was perfect for him.

And he for her.

All had gone well.

All had gone according to plan.

"Did you not write to her?" Edith inquired, knowing it to be so. "Did you not send a letter to her alongside my own?" Her brows rose challengingly.

Christina chuckled. "How is it you always know everything, Grandma?"

Edith shrugged noncommittally. "A little more patience," she whispered, once again patting her granddaughter's hand. "Sarah will be back in your life soon."

Christina nodded, yet the downcast look in her eyes remained. "What if something goes wrong? What if Lord Blackmore becomes suspicious?"

"I would be utterly surprised if he were not already."

With eyes widening in alarm, Christina sat up straight. "What? Then we have to do something! We cannot allow—"

"All will be well," Edith assured her, well-aware how agitating Christina found these vague statements of hers. "Sometimes risks must be taken. Sometimes they serve a greater purpose."

Christina frowned. "What purpose?" Her blue eyes swept over Edith's face. "You are not going to tell me, are you?"

Edith smiled. "Not right now, dear. Not right now."

A knock sounded on the door, and a moment later, the butler entered. "There's a visitor for you, my lady."

Edith nodded, gesturing to him to show the visitor in. Then she turned to her granddaughter. "Go and see to your child and husband," she said gently, brushing a stray curl from Christina's face, "and leave the rest to me."

Christina heaved a deep sigh but complied. However, before she left the drawing room, she cast another contemplative look at her grandmother.

Edith smiled, pulling the blanket tighter around her legs. "You'll see, my sweet. All shall be well."

A moment later, the door opened anew, and the butler showed in her visitor. "Mr. Garner, how good to see you," Edith greeted him as the door closed once more. "I hope you bring good news."

Still dressed in simple clothing made for a prolonged stay in the outdoors, Mr. Garner moved into the room, his watchful eyes sparking with triumph. *Ah, he* does *have good news!* Edith thought, pleased to see a good-natured smile touch the man's face.

Offering a respectful nod, Mr. Garner linked his hands behind his back. "I believe so, my lady."

Edith nodded. "You saw them?" she inquired carefully. "Together?"

The man nodded, and the corners of his mouth quirked, as though he remembered something amusing. "I encountered Mr. MacKinnear near the cabin and Miss Mortensen soon joined us."

"What reason did you give for your presence there?" Edith asked, wishing she could have been there. Oh, her curiosity truly was a curse upon occasion!

"Hunting," Mr. Garner replied with a chuckle.

"What is so amusing?" Edith demanded as she regarded the man through slightly narrowed eyes. "What happened? Why, Mr. Garner, you almost look as though you found a pot of gold!"

Chuckling, the man shook his head. "Not quite like that, my lady, but as I am aware of your hopes for the outcome of the current situation, I must say what I observed seemed quite promising."

Edith rolled her eyes at him, huffing out an impatient breath. "And what *did* you observe? Are you going to make an old lady go to her grave without ever knowing?"

The man's smile faltered at her bold words, and Edith smiled inwardly at seeing him unsettled. *Serves him right for not coming right out with it!*

Clearing his throat, Mr. Garner quickly regained his composure. "Clearly considering me a potential threat and wishing to hide her true identity, Mr. MacKinnear introduced Miss Mortensen to me as his wife."

"Did he now?" Edith murmured, delighted to hear it. "And Miss Mortensen, how did she react?"

"I thought she looked momentarily surprised," Mr. Garner elaborated, "but she did not contradict him. In fact, Mr. MacKinnear informed me within earshot of his...*wife* that she was mute; a ruse to not see his story contradicted, of course. You see, he had told me that they were not only man and wife, but both Scots traveling to visit kin."

Edith nodded, yet again regretting that she had not been there to see it herself. "And did they...appear like husband and wife?" she asked carefully, arching her brows meaningfully.

Mr. Garner chuckled again, amusement lighting up his eyes. "They appeared...intimately acquainted."

Edith frowned, her gaze drilling into the man, willing him to speak plainly. "Meaning?"

"Mr. MacKinnear embraced her," Mr. Garner finally elaborated with a grin, "and Miss Mortensen did not object. In fact, they appeared quite comfortable with one another." He frowned, then nodded. "Quite like husband and wife."

Edith smiled. "That is good to hear. Indeed, good to hear." She sighed, contemplating how to proceed when she took note of Mr. Garner's face sobering. "What is it?"

"I believe it possible that their location will soon become known to Lord Blackmore."

Edith straightened. "What led you to this assessment?"

"My colleagues reported to me that Lord Blackmore has men not only poking into Lord Hartmore's past and gambling habits, but that he is also making inquiries into locations and connections linked to your family, my lady."

Settling more comfortably into her chair, Edith nodded, considering Mr. Garner's words. "I see. Well, I have to admit I expected that; although, I had hoped it would not be quite so soon."

"If he learns the cabin is in your name, then—"

Edith scoffed. "It is not in my name! I assure you it has no official association to my family."

Mr. Garner considered her with an expression of stunned surprise.

"What?" Edith challenged. "Do you think me an imbecile, Mr. Garner? Believe me, this is not my first dance." She chuckled, equally amused and annoyed that she had been underestimated yet again.

Mr. Garner paled ever so slightly and a touch of alarm came to his eyes. Mostly, however, he maintained his composure. "Not at all, my lady. I assure you." He allowed a grin to play across his features. "In fact, with each passing day I'm becoming more and more aware of your...capabilities."

Edith returned his smile, pleased by his reply, understanding it to be genuine. "That being said, the cabin not being in my name does not prevent Lord Blackmore from drawing unwanted conclusions, of course." She sighed, then nodded to Mr. Garner. "Return to your post. I shall see to everything."

Mr. Garner took his leave without question, and Edith remained in her favorite chair for the next half hour contemplating how best to proceed. Cautiously, she considered the situation from all angles, trying her best to predict each individual's next step. Blackmore, of course, was the wild card! Who knew what he would do if he truly discovered Sarah's whereabouts?

Edith sighed. "I wish I could give the two of you more time," she murmured under her breath, thinking of Keir and Sarah pretending to be husband and wife, "but I hope it was enough."

Chapter Twenty-Three

DANGERS

In certain places, the night was pitch-black. In others, it shimmered in a faint silvery glow. Keir moved slowly across the yard, back firmly pressed to the cabin wall, gaze sweeping his surroundings, flickering from shadow to shadow. The air was still icy, and his breath wafted out in front of him in little puffs.

Everything seemed peaceful, and yet something was not right. Keir could feel it. Again, he listened, and although Autumn and Scout remained quiet, he could sense the horses' agitation. What had upset them?

Long ago, Keir had learned to trust in his horses' instincts. If otherwise calm and relaxed horses became suddenly agitated, they had a reason for it! One he ought not discount as simple skittishness!

His boots sank into the deep snow, leaving large prints, tracing his path from the front of the cabin to the stable. Fortunately, his boots' indentations were the only ones Keir saw. There were no others. No other tracks or disturbances of the snow blanket that had fallen since his return from the inn.

Keir breathed a momentary sigh of relief, and the small cloud danced away on the icy north wind. Only that feeling of dread still lingered, and Keir wondered if perhaps someone had approached from the back, bypassing the cabin and sneaking up from the direction of the meadow.

Of course, anything was possible. Perhaps Blackmore had somehow learned of Sarah's whereabouts—through the hunter or a spy Keir had yet to lay eyes upon. Or the hunter himself had returned, either on Blackmore's orders or for other nefarious reasons. Perhaps it was something entirely different.

Quietly, Keir pushed open the door to the stables. The air inside lacked the familiar icy chill and smelled pleasantly of hay. His eyes quickly adjusted to the near darkness, and he slipped inside, closing the door behind himself. Scout and Autumn turned toward him without delay, sensing his approach, their need for reassurance palpable.

Keir moved toward them, stroking their necks and noses and murmuring words of comfort under his breath as he listened for signs of an intruder, his eyes sweeping over the old goat and over to the chicken pen. Yet he saw or heard nothing suspicious. *Am I wrong?*

Instantly, the little hairs on the back of his neck rose, sending an icy chill down his spine. What if whoever had come had sought to lure him away from the cabin to get to Sarah?

At the thought, his heart tensed painfully, and Scout nervously tossed his head, as though the gelding could sense his distress. "Be calm," Keir whispered to the bay. "All is well." He desperately hoped that his words rang true.

Then Keir hurried back outside, careful to stick to the shadows. The blanket of snow covering the yard was still undisturbed except for his own prints and the door to the cabin seemed firmly closed. He could only hope Sarah had heeded his advice and was locked upstairs in her chamber, his rifle in hand.

Slinking around the stables to the back, Keir reminded himself not to be too long. The thought of Sarah alone in the cabin worried him. After all, what if someone were to sneak back into the house while his back was turned? *Aye, this endeavor has gone on far too long! I ought to have taken Sarah back to London, to the Whickertons, days ago! With the dowager's permission or not!*

Quickening his steps, Keir peered into the darkness, that feeling of impending doom needling him like never before. The woods loomed before him, bushes and brambles nothing but a black void that swallowed up all light. The meadow lay deserted, and yet Keir could not shake the feeling that he was being watched.

Ensuring that the back door to the cabin was also firmly locked, Keir paused when he suddenly heard a slight rustling in the underbrush. Of course, it could have been the wind...but Keir doubted it. He turned slowly, eyes watchful, and moved along the side of the cabin, then farther past the stables, all the while listening to every sound carried to his ears. Aye, he was certain that someone was nearby...or perhaps something. Could it be that—?

With a grunt, a dark blur shot out of the underbrush and came barreling toward him. It moved with incredible speed, and Keir barely managed to fling himself sideways, instantly rolling over into a crouched position. Another grunt met his ears, and he spun around, his eyes locking onto the creature as it once again charged him with vicious intent.

A boar! His mind screamed the moment a searing pain shot through his left arm and the animal's attack knocked him off his feet.

Gritting his teeth, Keir once more hurried to right himself, his hand moving toward the knife at his belt. He had no intention of killing the creature, but if he could wound it, it might feel persuaded to leave him be.

With another intimidating grunt, the boar came at Keir once more, its sharp tusks catching the moonlight for a bare second. Keir moved quickly, still gritting his teeth against the pain in his arm. He spun sideways out of the animal's reach, swiftly moving his blade in a backward motion, feeling its tip graze the animals hide just deep enough to cause pain.

The boar squealed and instantly retreated to a greater distance, its huffed breaths like little clouds rising into the night sky.

Keir felt his heart pounding in his ears, his hand gripping the dagger tightly. He could feel warm blood running down his arm as he kept his gaze fixed on the creature, trying to gauge its reaction. Would it charge again? Or retreat?

For a long moment, nothing happened. The boar remained where it was, not moving closer, and Keir stood his ground, his stance signaling his readiness. Then, the animal abruptly turned away and within a heartbeat or two disappeared in the underbrush.

Keir exhaled audibly, then carefully resheathed his blade. The pain in his arm had subsided to a dull ache; however, the moment he moved it, his muscles protested, sending a sharp jolt of pain through him.

Holding his injured arm close to his body, Keir retreated back to the cabin, relieved that no real threat lingered nearby. However, the moment his gaze fell on the cabin's door, his heart nearly stopped.

It stood wide open!

Keir almost keeled over in shock, his breath stuck in his throat and the pain in his arm forgotten. Then he blinked, and his mind shook off the unexpected shock, finally able to focus on what he was seeing.

Footprints!

Small, dainty footprints...

...leading away from the cabin...

...and over to the stable.

Keir closed his eyes, his chest rising and falling with a deep breath. Then he changed direction and hurried over to the stable, not in the least surprised to find the door open. "Sarah?" he called into the darkness, stepping inside.

Sarah stood by the far wall, her arms wrapped around Autumn, her head resting against the mare's forehead. When she heard Keir's voice, though, she looked up. "Keir!" Utter relief swung in her voice. "What happened? Where did you go?"

Still holding his arm, Keir approached slowly. "'Twas a boar," he told her with a wince when another stab of pain sliced through his arm.

"What's wrong?" Sarah asked alarmed, her face half-hidden in the dark. Still, Keir thought to see a deep frown come to her face as she released Autumn and turned toward him.

"I thought I told ye to stay inside," Keir admonished, fear for her darkening his voice and giving it an angry edge. "With the door bolted and the rifle in yer hands." He lifted his brows, demanding an answer, before he realized that, in all likelihood, she could not see it in the dim light.

"Are you hurt?" Sarah demanded in turn, ignoring his question completely. Gentle hands reached for him, careful and tentative, as though terrified of causing him more pain. Keir almost smiled at the thought. She could never hurt him...

...and yet he was beginning to suspect that she could wound him like no other.

"'Tis only a scratch," he replied, then he drew in a sharp breath when her hand accidentally touched his wound.

Sarah flinched at his sharp intake of breath, jerking back her hand. "That is no scratch!" she stated with an utterly unfamiliar sense of certainty in her voice. "What happened? Did the boar attack you?"

"What are ye doing here?" Keir demanded in return, beginning to like this back and forth, the steel that had come to her voice. *Aye, she can be unrelenting if she wants to, if she has reason to. Was her concern for him reason enough to make her forget her fears? Her uncertainties?*

Keir liked that thought. "I told ye to stay in the cabin."

For a moment, Sarah hesitated. Then she shrugged, easily brushed aside his objection, and said, "And I decided to come out here. I thought perhaps I could help." Again, she stepped toward him, her hands now reaching for his uninjured arm. "Come inside. We need to tend to your wound."

Keir fell into step beside her as she led him out of the stable. "Ye shouldna have come out here by yerself."

As the light of the moon illuminated her face, Keir saw her smile, her eyes dark and yet glowing as she looked up at him. "I did not," she replied, then purposefully dropped her gaze.

Keir frowned, then chuckled when he felt something brush up against his legs. He looked down and saw Loki's upturned face, his eyes aglow in the dark. "Meow," the little devil said with such an indignant expression at having been overlooked that Keir had to laugh. "Aye, ye're a fierce one," he told the feline. "Thank ye for protecting her."

Pacified, Loki tiptoed ahead toward the cabin, leaving little indentations in the snow, matching the indentations Keir had overlooked in his shock upon discovering the door open.

"Come! I need yer help," Keir said with a sideways look at Sarah as they followed in the feline's wake.

"Of course," Sarah replied, her voice steady. Yet she eyed him warily. "I suppose I should boil some water, fetch some clean linens." Her voice rose ever so slightly at the end of the sentence, making it sound like a question.

Keir nodded. "Aye, lass, and yer sewing kit." Sarah's eyes grew wide, and Keir hoped she would have the stomach for what he needed her to do.

Chapter Twenty-Four

A BIT OF STITCHING

A chilling shiver swept through Sarah's middle, and it was not from the cold. Certainly, her toes were starting to go numb, and her cheeks felt as though they were being pricked by little pins again and again. Still, the boulder of ice that had settled in her stomach had nothing to do with the icy north wind. "My sewing kit?" Sarah murmured under her breath, her voice no longer steady, her pulse suddenly too fast.

Keir nodded as he held open the door to the cabin with his uninjured arm. "Aye, I've had enough cuts and scrapes to know when stitches are needed, believe me." A chuckle rumbled in his throat but turned into a wince when he tried to shrug out of his coat.

All of a sudden, Sarah felt utterly overwhelmed and helpless and foolish. This was her fault, was it not? If she had not gone outside…

Heaving a deep breath, Sarah pulled off her own cloak, her mind foggy and circling, reminding her that the only reason Keir had been hurt, the only reason he was here in the first place was because of her. *What if I cannot do what he asks? What if above everything else I am unable to help him? What if—?*

"Lass!" At the sound of Keir's voice, sharp as a whip, Sarah flinched, and her head snapped up. His blue eyes met hers, looking deep. "Stop!"

Sarah frowned, shaking her head ever so slightly in confusion. "What do you mean? Stop what?"

With his coat only hanging upon his left shoulder, Keir chuckled before he reached around with his good arm, doing his best not to move the other. "Ye have that look upon yer face again, little wisp. Aye, I mean it. I can all but read yer thoughts. Ye're concerned, even frightened, but above all, ye're thinking 'twas yer fault." He paused, bringing his head a fraction closer to hers, his deep blue eyes unflinching. "'Twas not. Do you hear me? Dunna blame yerself. 'Twas an accident, nothing more." His brows rose meaningfully and remained there until Sarah nodded her head in acknowledgment.

Gritting his teeth, Keir peeled the coat from his injured arm, revealing a torn sleeve stained red with blood.

Sarah gasped, and her hands flew up to cover her mouth. There was so much blood! Bright red and in stark comparison to his white shirt. It ran down his arm, little droplets of blood tracing a trail down his sleeve, and as she lowered her gaze, Sarah saw blood dripping from the tips of his fingers onto the floor. *This was no mere scrape! This was—*

"Lass!"

Again, Sarah's head flew up, her eyes meeting Keir's, his gaze imploring. "Look at me and nothing else," he instructed, wincing through gritted teeth as he curled his right hand around the wound in his left arm, applying pressure. "Fetch yer sewing kit and meet me in the kitchen, aye?"

More from reflex than anything else, Sarah felt her head bob up and down. Her thoughts were scattered, her body moving of its own accord, up the stairs and into her chamber. Under her breath, Sarah heard herself murmuring, "Sewing kit. Sewing kit," afraid she might forget, completely lose her mind and fail Keir entirely.

Rushing past her bed to the small armoire in the corner, Sarah reached for the small pouch that contained an assortment of needles and threads with trembling hands. She had packed it that night she had left London in case she might tear her sleeve or the hem of her dress. Never had she pictured a scenario in which she would be required to stitch up a wound.

With her sewing kit pressed to her chest, Sarah slowed her steps once she reached the staircase and proceeded carefully, afraid she might stumble and fall, breaking her neck. She certainly would be of no use to Keir then!

Reaching the kitchen without incident, Sarah found Keir seated at the table, a few pieces of cloth stacked beside him on the tabletop. He had also set water to boil and was currently in the process of removing his shirt. Yet that endeavor proved far from easy! His jaw was clenched against the pain that assailed him, and his eyes pinched shut as he awkwardly tried to slip his injured arm out of the sleeve.

"What are you doing?" Sarah asked, rushing to his side. "You'll only make it bleed more."

Keir paused, and a bit of a grin teased his lips despite the pain that still lingered upon his face. "Even with the sleeve torn, ye canna stitch my wound with the garment in the way, now can ye?"

"I...I..." Sarah stammered, disliking the reminder of what he wanted her to do. Her hands tensed involuntarily, her fingers curling into her sewing kit and squashing its contents into a tight ball until one of the needles pricked the tip of her finger. "Ouch!" Dropping the small pouch onto the table, Sarah brought her injured finger to her lips, sucking away the small droplet of blood that had welled up due to her own carelessness.

"Sit!" Keir ordered, pushing the other chair toward her with a swift kick of his foot.

"I'm so sorry," Sarah whispered, close to tears, as she dropped onto the chair, beginning to feel lightheaded. "I never meant for this to happen. I—"

Keir's right hand clamped down upon her arm, yanking her forward until her nose almost touched his. "Ye need to keep yer wits about ye, lass. Ye canna swoon. Not now. I need ye."

Sarah stilled, and her mind cleared at Keir's honest declaration. "I'm sorry," she said again, the words slipping out before she could prevent it. "Yes. I mean, no, I will not swoon. I promise." She swallowed, willing the fog to recede. "What do you need me to do?"

Keir gave a quick nod and then released her arm. He sat back with a heavy sigh, a painful grimace stealing across his face. "Can ye help me remove my shirt?"

The lump of ice in Sarah's stomach grew heavier. "Of course," she mumbled, rising to her feet. She stepped toward him, her hands reaching for the blood-stained sleeve, terrified of causing him more pain. "Wait! Can we not cut it?"

Keir's brows rose doubtfully.

"The shirt, I mean," Sarah rushed to clarify. "Can we not cut off the sleeve? That should be easier, should it not?"

Keir nodded. "Good thinking, lass."

Rushing to fetch the scissors, Sarah could not help but wonder if Keir had truly failed to think of this option or if he had merely allowed her to discover it herself. In any case, the relief Sarah felt at not having to maneuver his injured arm out of the sleeve stilled her hands as she set to work cutting away the fabric.

Unfortunately, the sight of his wound once more turned Sarah's stomach, and she had a hard time keeping her composure.

Keir chuckled. "Ye have never dressed a wound, have ye, little wisp?"

Sarah shook her head, staring at his torn flesh and the blood still seeping out of the wound. "Not once. What if I...?" Her voice trailed off, and she turned fearful eyes to him.

"Ye'll do fine," Keir assured her, his voice steady despite the pain that currently assailed him. "Hand me a piece of cloth, will ye?" Sarah did, and he pressed it to his wound. "Before ye stitch me up, ye need to dip the needle in the boiling water to treat it." He nodded toward the pot. "But be careful not to burn yerself."

Nodding, Sarah rose to her feet, her hands once more trembling as she rummaged through her pouch. "And then...? How do I...?" She met his gaze, then let it fall sideways to where his hand still held the piece of cloth pressed to the wound.

Keir grinned, and Sarah felt the unexpected urge to roll her eyes at him. *The man has the audacity to enjoy this!* He was wounded, bleeding, had almost been killed, and here he was grinning at her with those teasing eyes of his! Were injured people not supposed to look pale and weak and...somehow ill at ease? Quite frankly, in all likelihood, *she* looked worse than he did!

As though to prove her right, Keir laughed. "Every thought is written so clearly upon yer face that I'm afraid ye'll never be a good liar."

Sarah felt her face heat but refused to bow her head. "Well...I...I suppose I'll take that as a compliment."

Keir nodded his head. "'Twas meant as such." His eyes held hers, and Sarah felt a rush of pride well up in her chest.

"Thank you," Sarah murmured in reply, feeling the sudden need to express how much his words meant to her. "Thank you for trusting me with this...although, admittedly you don't have much choice in the matter as I am currently your only option." Where those daring words had come from Sarah did not know, but they made her heart feel lighter and teased a smile onto her face.

Keir's grin broadened. "Why should I not trust ye, lass? Are ladies not taught the art of embroidery?"

Sarah chuckled. "We are not taught to stitch up flesh, and I doubt you'd want a floral pattern stitched onto your skin."

Keir quirked an eyebrow. "Is that a threat?" he teased, then grinned at Loki as the feline came strutting into the kitchen, his usual air of authority about him. "Ah, yer highness, ye've decided to grace us with yer presence."

Loki cocked his head at Keir, then jumped up onto the table and seated himself, watchful eyes trained upon them both.

"Oh, good!" Sarah exclaimed, throwing up her arms. "He's here to supervise me!" Instantly, the shivers returned, and her hands began to tremble.

"Aw, no," Keir objected, meeting Loki's amber gaze. "He's here for moral support, are ye not, wee kitty?"

Loki looked honestly offended at being called *wee kitty*. Still, he did his best to ignore Keir, offering Sarah an encouraging *meow*.

Sarah tried to smile. "I hope you're right." Her eyes swept over the needle and thread she had prepared. "So, how do I—"

With a grunt, Keir reached out his left hand and grasped hers. "Listen, lass," he began, his eyes trained upon hers, "dunna feel for me."

At his words, Sarah's heart paused in shock. *Keir cannot possibly know that I've come to—*

"If ye wince every time I wince, ye'll only hurt me more," he elaborated, and Sarah instantly felt foolish. "Dunna worry about hurting me because ye will. That's a given. Stitches are painful. But believe me, I've felt worse." He paused, and one brow quirked upward in thought. "Unless ye'd prefer to clonk me over the head with a pan." That familiar teasing grin returned, making Sarah's heart feel lighter.

"Is that what you'd prefer?" she asked with a laugh. "It might hurt your head though."

"Well, then perhaps not," Keir replied, giving her hand a squeeze. Then his expression sobered, and he exhaled a slow breath. "Ye can do this, little wisp. I know ye can. Have faith in yerself...and be ruthless," he added with a mischievous grin.

Sarah chuckled, grateful for the lightness in Keir's tone. How he managed to boost her spirits when he was in such pain she did not know, but she knew she could not fail him. Never in her life had anyone ever truly depended upon her, upon her ability, upon her strength. Never had anyone ever truly needed her.

But now, Keir did.

And it was a heady feeling. It swirled in her blood and danced in her belly, steadying her hands while setting her breath aflutter. Determined to prove herself, Sarah dropped her gaze from Keir's face and focused her attention on his wound. Gently, she peeled his fingers away and then removed the stained cloth he had pressed to it. For a moment, her stomach flipped, and she inhaled a slow steadying breath.

The gash was not deep, but deep enough to have bled profusely. Fortunately, the bleeding had slowed. However, the jagged edges of the cut gaped apart, and even to an untrained eye like Sarah's, it was obvious that stitches were needed.

Without looking up, she asked, "Any more advice?"

Keir shook his head. "No floral pattern, please."

Sarah pressed her lips together tightly to stifle a laugh, trying her best to remain focused. She reached for the needle and thread, then carefully touched her fingers to Keir's flesh. It was a startling sensation to feel warm skin and not cool fabric, and for a moment, doubt assailed her anew.

Be ruthless, Sarah reminded herself silently. *You know what to do. This is simply a piece of cloth. Nothing more. Be ruthless.*

Locking all thoughts of Keir away, Sarah held the wound closed with her left hand, ignoring the muffled wince of pain from Keir's lips. Her gaze swept along the line of the tear before she inhaled a deep breath, held it in and then exhaled the moment her needle pierced Keir's flesh.

The needle went through with practiced ease, and Sarah did not dare pause. Her hands moved fluidly, her mind picturing a torn hem or ripped sleeve. She barely took note of Keir's occasional sharp intake of breath or the way his muscles beneath her fingers would tense every so often.

"Breathe, lass," Keir reminded her at some point, and Sarah did, not daring to even glance up at him. Her gaze remained fixed upon her task, and her fingers moved as though guided by invisible strings.

And then the wound was closed, and Sarah cut the thread. For a moment, her gaze remained where it was, her mind suddenly overwhelmed by what to do next. Then a warm hand descended upon her shoulder, giving it a squeeze, and her chin rose.

"Thank ye, little wisp," Keir murmured, giving her one of his smiles. "Ye did well. I always knew ye would."

A bit shaken, Sarah returned his smile. "You should rest," she told him, pushing to her feet and reaching for a bandage. "A wound like that is no—" All of a sudden, the world began to sway, and Sarah felt as though a heavy weight were pulling on her, threatening to throw her off her feet.

"Slowly, lass." Keir's hands grabbed her shoulders, his tall stature suddenly dwarfing her. "Open yer eyes, lass. Open them."

Blinking, Sarah slowly watched Keir's face come into focus, wondering at the same time when her eyes had closed. She could not recall. "I'm fine," she murmured, watching her own lashes flutter up and down. "D-Don't worry. I'm truly f-fine."

Holding her upright, Keir looked down at her, his left hand grasping her chin. Annoyingly enough, *he* seemed perfectly fine, as though *she* had been the one wounded and not him. "Ye're a remarkable woman, little wisp," Keir murmured, the look in his eyes mesmerizing, "and I'm grateful to have met ye."

Sarah's first impulse was to contradict him, to argue against him, but the moment her lips parted, something stilled her tongue. For once, she did not want to doubt or question. For once, she wanted to believe. His words rang true, and Sarah wanted nothing more than to bask in their warm glow.

Tears came to her eyes, and Keir pulled her into his arms, resting her head against his shoulder. "Ye're a fierce one, little wisp. Never forget that."

Sarah closed her eyes and vowed that she never would.

Chapter Twenty-Five

A RELUCTANT PATIENT

T he moment his eyes opened, Keir groaned. His head felt as though it had been split in two and his arm throbbed painfully, like a living creature was trapped inside, fighting to get out. He cursed under his breath, then he pushed himself upright, trying his best to ignore the wave of dizziness that assailed him. He swung his legs out of bed and began to dress. Unfortunately, this simple everyday task suddenly proved rather challenging.

The sun shone in brightly through the window, and Keir had to pinch his eyes to keep the glare from stabbing through his mind. Everything looked too bright, felt too raw, and his mind continued to spin in little circles, threatening to upend his balance at any moment. How he made his way downstairs, Keir did not know. However, the moment his feet stopped in the doorway to the kitchen and Sarah looked up, her eyes finding his, Keir knew he could no longer ignore his current state.

"Oh, you look awful!" Sarah exclaimed, the smile sliding off her face and drawing down her brows into a worried frown. She hastened toward him, her blue eyes searching his face and drifting lower to his arm. "You're not well," she observed, then tentatively reached out her hands and cupped them to his cheeks. Instantly, her eyes flew open wide. "You're burning up!"

Keir offered her a weak smile, once again cursing under his breath when her image blurred before his eyes, and he had to grasp the door frame to keep from keeling over and dragging her down with him. Yet he could not deny that her touch felt soothing. "Perhaps I ought to sit down," he murmured, disliking the breathlessness of his voice.

"You ought to *lie* down," Sarah corrected him with an air of authority he had never seen about her. There was something stern in her gaze, and she moved her hands over him, one to his forehead and the other to the back of his neck, with the practiced ease of a nurse. "I'll help you upstairs. You need rest."

Keir knew she was right. He felt terrible and far from capable of anything. Yet it was his responsibility to protect her, not the other way around. What if someone were to discover her now? Discover her whereabouts? The thought made him shudder, for he knew he would be utterly helpless, unable to prevent anything from happening to her. *Why does this have to happen now? How often do I receive cuts and scrapes? Why does this one now have to bring about a fever?*

Reaching for his uninjured arm, Sarah draped it across her shoulders. "Lean on me," she told him, urging him out of the kitchen and then slowly back up the stairs.

Each step was torture, not only because Keir felt absolutely awful but also because each step felt like one in the wrong direction. The last time he had spent the day in bed he had been a child, nursed back to health by his mother. And even then, Keir had been a dreadful patient, unable to lie still, unable to rest. From the day he had been born, energy had hummed in his bones, urging him to move, to be outside, to chase the sky. Locked up in a room was his idea of torture, and he could not bear it, not even when he was ill. He truly preferred not to be ill; however, right now it did not seem to be up to him.

"You are not to get up under any circumstances, do you understand?" Sarah told him with a stern look as she tucked the blanket in around him. "Do you hear me?"

Keir frowned at her. "I knew ye were a fierce one," he muttered, a touch of disapproval in his voice, "only I never knew how fierce." He chuckled, enjoying the way she tried not to roll her eyes at him. Indeed, he liked this forceful side of her and wished he could see it more often. "Still, there is no need to worry. Perhaps just a moment of rest, and then I shall be fine again."

With her arms akimbo, Sarah looked down at him, then slowly shook her head, a slight twitch coming to her lips. "Admit it, you're one of those people who cannot lie still, who cannot admit that they need help, who cannot allow another to take care of them." Her right eyebrow arched upward in challenge. "Is that not so?"

All but mesmerized, Keir stared at Sarah. Yet he felt a twinge of unease that she read him so easily. *Is that what it is like for her? To have every emotion written upon her face? To have everyone know precisely at every moment what she is feeling and thinking?* He had to admit he did not care for it. It felt intrusive, and it made him feel vulnerable. "Ye might not be completely wrong about that," Keir admitted with a smirk.

Sarah laughed. "You're awful."

"I never claimed otherwise."

Once more adjusting his blanket, Sarah shook her head at him. "Stay in bed," she repeated sternly, then looked over her shoulder at Loki, who had curled up at the foot of Keir's bed, his eyes lazy. "Watch him for me, will you?"

Instantly, Loki's head came up, and he gave her his full attention. For a moment, Keir actually expected the feline to answer. Instead, the little creature pushed himself up onto his paws and then tiptoed over and lay down next to Keir, curling up into his side.

A triumphant smile came to Sarah's face. "Thank you, Loki." Her gaze returned to Keir. "Sleep, and I shall bring you some soup soon."

Keir frowned at her. "I'm not eating in bed like an invalid."

"Yes, you are." Again, her arms rose, and her hands ended up upon her hips.

"I can get up," Keir insisted in part because he truly despised being trapped in a bed and in part because he adored seeing Sarah like this. The blue of her eyes seemed almost stormy and wild like the churning sea, and for once, the rosy glow upon her cheeks did not speak of embarrassment but rather of a woman willing to fight for what she believed in.

A woman willing to fight for someone...she cares for?

"I do not doubt that," Sarah replied in that unfamiliar tone of voice that made her seem utterly sure of herself. "However, you must admit that you are not likely to remain upon your feet for long." Again, her right brow quirked upward in challenge, that amused twitch upon her lips once more.

Keir laughed. "Perhaps ye're right. I must be delirious because I can hardly believe what I'm seeing and hearing. Are ye truly the same woman who barely managed to speak a word to me the day we met?"

At his observation, Sarah stilled, and for a second, the rosy glow upon her cheeks once again reminded Keir of a woman embarrassed. Then, however, she shook her head as though chasing away unwanted thoughts, her golden curls dancing from side to side. "Perhaps I'm not," she finally told him, a smile coming to her face that whispered of pride and accomplishment. "Perhaps..." She broke off and stepped around the bed but paused by the door. "Rest now." And with this last instruction, she closed the door behind herself and Keir listened to the sound of her receding footsteps as she made her way back downstairs.

Beside him, Loki stretched and yawned, then snuggled back down and closed his eyes, purring peacefully.

Keir scoffed. "Traitor," he grumbled under his breath. "I'm not like ye, I canna simply curl up and fall asleep." Indeed, the thought of sleeping during the day was ludicrous and seemed like an awful waste of time. Yet he was forced to lie here and stare at the ceiling with nothing worthwhile to do. Keir heaved a deep sigh, closing his eyes against the blinding glare of the sun.

Strangely enough, when he opened them again, the sun had disappeared, and darkness had fallen over the world. "What on earth...?"

"Oh, you're awake!"

Keir turned his head and found Sarah standing beside his bed, a tray in her hand and a steaming bowl on top. "Awake?" Keir repeated, momentarily confused.

Setting down the tray, Sarah pulled up a chair. "Yes, you slept all day." She chuckled. "You had me concerned there for a second because you were sleeping so deeply it seemed like nothing would ever be able to wake you again. You didn't even twitch when I cleaned your wound." For a second, a dark cloud passed over her head before it was once again chased away by a relieved smile. "How do you feel?"

Running a hand over his face, Keir tried to straighten his thoughts. "I feel..." In fact, he *did* feel better. There was still a mild throbbing behind his right temple and his arm still...well, hurt. Yet it was nothing compared to how miserable he had felt before. "Better."

"I'm glad to hear it," Sarah told him with a smile. "Now, sit up." She leaned forward and helped him up, fluffing up his pillow, as though he truly were an invalid. Once Keir was finally seated in bed, she placed the tray upon his lap. "Careful. It's hot."

Keir rolled his eyes. "There's no need to mother me."

"I'm not mothering you!" Sarah shot back indignantly, a disapproving frown upon her face. "I'm...I'm taking care of you. Is that wrong?"

Keir heaved a deep sigh, regretting the hurt expression in her eyes. He bowed his head. "I'm sorry. I was wrong to snap at ye. I didna mean to but..." He shrugged his shoulders helplessly, gritting his teeth as pain lanced through his arm. "Well, I've always been a rather irritable patient. 'Tis all I can say in my defense."

Sarah's features softened, and she seated herself more comfortably in the chair. "Very well. Apology accepted."

Keir returned her smile, then ladled a spoonful of soup into his mouth. It was hot, but it was also good. "Will ye tell me a story?" he asked on a whim.

A look of surprise came to Sarah's face. "A story?" She shook her head. "I'm afraid I don't know any stories."

Keir frowned, savoring the warmth of the soup. "Yer parents never told ye any stories? Not even at bedtime? Or seated around a roaring fire?"

Regret flashed in Sarah's eyes. "I'm afraid not. My parents were never..." She shrugged, clearly uncomfortable, trying to find the words to explain without betraying her family. "They were always rather busy."

Keir nodded. "Yer sister then. Did ye not share stories?" Even though Loki's head was still resting upon his paws, the tips of his ears began to twitch. "My brothers and I always used to tell each other stories. Before we were old enough to venture out into the world, it was the closest thing we had to an adventure."

At his words, something…meaningful flickered across Sarah's face. Her eyes became distant, and the corners of her mouth quirked upward and slowly grew into a smile. "I suppose we did," she murmured absentmindedly before her gaze once more settled upon him. "We used to pretend that we were princesses," she giggled embarrassed, "trapped in a tower by an evil queen."

Ladling another spoonful of soup into his mouth, Keir nodded for her to continue.

Sarah's cheeks began to glow crimson red, and she placed her hands upon her face to shield herself from him; yet she continued to speak. "Eventually, one of the princesses would be married and went away with her prince to live happily ever after."

"And the other princess?" Keir inquired, wondering which of the two sisters had played the princess to be married and which one had been left behind. *Has life turned out precisely as they imagined? Or are their roles reversed?*

Sarah sighed and met his eyes. "Eventually, the married princess would return and free her sister from the clutches of the evil queen." She stilled, a thoughtful expression in her eyes, before she then shook her head, as though to chase away silly dreams.

"They were loyal to one another," Keir murmured, watching her carefully. "They were one, each of them unable to find happiness without the other."

Blinking back tears, Sarah nodded. "If only life were a fairytale," she murmured, dabbing a finger to the corner of her eye. "I know it is silly, but I suppose a part of me always hoped that Kate would return for me, that she would come to free me." Again, she shook her head, dabbing at her eyes once more. Yet the tears lingered. "It was foolish of me to think so. Life is what it is, and people like us do not have many options."

Setting aside his tray, Keir leaned back against the headboard. "Why would ye say that? Is she not still yer sister? Does her happiness no longer depend upon yers?"

Sarah shrugged. "Perhaps. Perhaps not. However, even should Kate wish to, she is in no position to help me."

"Why?"

Sarah sighed, a sound so defeated and disillusioned that it brought a heavy weight to Keir's heart. "Because her husband is not a prince, and she is not living happily ever after." She stilled; her eyes momentarily distant before they moved to meet his once more. "Perhaps... Perhaps Kate is in need of rescuing as well. Perhaps we both are."

Annoyingly, Keir felt his eyelids begin to droop. "Yet ye found a way to rescue yerself."

"You rescued me," Sarah objected. "Without you, I—"

"I helped," Keir interrupted in a murmur, no longer able to keep his eyes open. His head rolled back, and he sank deeper into the pillows. "I helped, but ye were the one to free yerself from the evil queen's clutches. Ye didna need a prince for that. Perhaps yer sister doesna, either. Perhaps all she needs is ye."

Stillness fell over the chamber, and Keir quickly lost the battle with sleep, his eyes firmly closed and his mind drifting away to a place where Sarah's smile never waned.

Never dimmed.

Never faded.

Chapter Twenty-Six

THE STORY OF YVAINE

S taring at Keir, Sarah watched as his eyes closed and he drifted off to sleep. His chest rose and fell slowly, peacefully, and Sarah was grateful when she saw the paleness vanish from his cheeks and his color return. Indeed, she had feared for him and felt her heart pause in her chest when he had slept so deeply nothing had been able to disturb him.

Now, he looked better.

Much better.

And once again, he had opened her eyes to something she had all but overlooked. Was it true? Had she saved herself? Sarah had never quite thought of it like that. Certainly, she had been desperate, terrified of a future by Lord Blackmore's side. She had told herself that no other fate could be worse, and so she had been daring enough to accept Grandma Edie's proposition, to go along with her outrageous plan. Yet she had done very little herself but gone along with all the dowager suggested. *Did I truly save myself? Was it* my *doing?* Perhaps or perhaps not. What mattered was that all had gone well, and here, right now, Sarah felt safe.

At least, as safe as was possible under the circumstances. After all, tomorrow still loomed upon the horizon, all its uncertainties still as terrifying as before. What if something were to go wrong?

Quietly, Sarah rose to her feet, reaching out a hand to stroke Loki's head. "Watch over him for me, will you?" she asked the feline.

Loki snuggled deeper against Keir, his expression that of one who had accepted a serious mission and was determined to see it through no matter what it might cost him.

Sarah giggled. "Thank you. What would I do without you?" On tiptoes, she slipped from the room, carefully closing the door behind herself. She went to straighten up in the kitchen and then once more stepped outside, her cloak pulled tight around her, and went to check on the horses in the stable.

Everything around her was quiet. The night seemed peaceful, a star-speckled sky overhead and the soft glow of snow beneath her feet. If only life could simply be beautiful! If only there were no threats to health and happiness! If only...

Autumn greeted Sarah eagerly, pushing forward her head to demand her attention. "I'm sorry you were locked up in here all day," Sarah murmured to the horses. "Perhaps tomorrow I can...take you out to the meadow?" She had thought about it before, but she had not dared. She had not wanted to leave Keir for too long and, quite frankly, she had been worried she might not be up to the task.

Stroking the mare's neck, Sarah found her thoughts drawn back to her sister. She could not help but wonder what Kate was doing at the moment. Sarah doubted her sister was truly happy, and yet perhaps she was misjudging the situation. That was, at least, possible, was it not? Yes, Kate had not seemed happy, had not seemed like the sister Sarah had known all her life the last time they had met, but life did change people, did it not? Sarah herself was living proof of that. Since meeting Keir only a little while ago, since going on this unexpected adventure, she herself had changed. Sarah knew it to be true. She could feel it deep inside. She could feel a deep desire to be the person she had always been meant to be, the person she had never dared to reveal to those around her, knowing they would disapprove.

The person she had perhaps once been as a child when the world had still been a magical place full of fairytales and adventures, of dashing heroes and fierce heroines.

Ye're a fierce one.

It was Keir's voice that echoed through Sarah's head and brought a smile to her face. But was she truly? Over the past few years, she had always thought of herself as weak, one who bowed to pressure instead of standing tall. Could she be strong? Could she fight for herself? And perhaps for Kate as well?

Inhaling a deep breath of the cool night air, Sarah bid the horses farewell and then stepped back outside, locking the stable door behind her. Perhaps she truly ought to write to Kate. Perhaps the distance that now existed between them was one of their own making. Perhaps the future could be different.

Perhaps it was not too late.

Keir was still asleep when Sarah quietly tiptoed back into his chamber, finding Loki faithfully by his side. The feline lifted his head in acknowledgment before closing his eyes once more. Sarah smiled, then she turned to go...but paused, realizing that she could not bring herself to leave him. What if Keir woke during the night and needed her?

After a moment of hesitation, Sarah retrieved the blanket from her own chamber and settled herself on the chair by Keir's bed. Oh, her mother would be appalled to see her spending the night in a stranger's bedchamber!

Outraged!

Sarah smiled, realizing that she no longer cared about her mother's opinion. Too much had happened, and her mother had made it unmistakably clear that Sarah's happiness was not her concern. Nevertheless, Sarah was surprised by her own thoughts, by their boldness and finality. Truly, she *had* changed.

Perhaps more than she even knew herself.

Sarah never meant to fall asleep. In fact, she had been determined to watch over Keir throughout the night and then perhaps rest herself come morning. Yet once again, Fate had other plans, and Sarah woke the next morning half-seated, half-slumped over onto Keir's bed, her eyes closed and her hand covering his.

Unfortunately, Sarah was not the first of them to wake.

The moment she lifted her head, she found herself looking into two teasing blue eyes, which seemed to be considering her with the utmost interest and amusement. "Do ye not have a bed of yer own, lass?" Keir asked with a smirk.

Sarah surged upward, blinking her eyes against the bright sunlight. Lately, the days seemed to be brighter than ever before. "I'm sorry. I must have...dozed off."

Keir's expression sobered. "Did ye stay by my side all night?" he asked earnestly.

Swallowing, Sarah nodded. "How are you?" she asked to change the topic, lest she blush again. After all, Keir knew how to make her blush like no one else in the world.

With the exception of Kate, perhaps.

"Better," Keir replied vaguely, then carefully moved his arm to test it. A mild grimace contorted his face. Only it was not nearly as pain-filled as it had been before. "Definitely better."

"I'm glad," Sarah sighed, remembering how afraid she had been for him. "I'll go and fetch you some breakfast."

"I can go," Keir said hastily, hand reaching out to pull back the blanket.

"Don't you dare leave this bed!"

Keir's eyes widened, and Sarah swallowed hard, surprised by her own outburst. "Ye're not as biddable as ye claim to be," Keir observed sternly, yet the twinkle in his eyes betrayed his delight with that observation.

"What about your fever?" Sarah asked, once again to change the topic.

"Gone."

She quirked a doubting eyebrow at him.

"Truly," he assured her, then he reached out, grasped her hand and placed it upon his forehead. "See?"

Sarah felt her breath lodge in her throat, and for the first time since Keir had kissed her downstairs in the parlor, she felt her insides quiver with remembrance. A lot had happened between then and now, occupying her thoughts and focusing them elsewhere. Now, it would seem, all distractions had vanished in the blink of an eye.

"Are ye all right, lass?" Keir asked, his expression unreadable.

Sarah swallowed, then nodded. "I'm fine," she replied, then she slowly retrieved her hand, feeling a pang of regret when Keir released her without even a hint of reluctance. "I'll fetch you some breakfast." And with that, Sarah spun around and hurried from the chamber a bare second before her face caught fire, her cheeks burning hotter than ever before.

Still feeling a bit unsteady upon her feet, Sarah made her way into the kitchen, prepared a simple breakfast and then returned back up the stairs. She prayed that the awkwardness of the previous moment had vanished and that they could face one another again as before. Fortunately, when Sarah opened the door, Loki rose and stretched, eagerly coming toward her, the expression upon his face clearly stating that he considered the breakfast she was bringing to be meant for him.

Keir laughed. "Never in my life have I met such an entitled cat," he remarked, winking at her. "Perhaps he was a king or emperor in a previous life. What do ye think?"

As always Loki ignored their comments with a haughtiness that ought to have been beyond a feline's abilities.

"Perhaps," Sarah replied with relief, "for I cannot think of another explanation." Setting down the tray, she handed Keir a plate with eggs and a buttered slice of bread before setting a saucer of milk on the floor for Loki. "Here you go, your highness."

"Sit down and eat something yerself," Keir insisted, nodding toward the chair she had slept in. "Or soon ye'll be the one falling flat on her face."

Sarah returned his grin. "You didn't fall flat on your face."

He shrugged. "Because ye steadied me."

"True," Sarah agreed with a nonchalant shrug of her shoulders and then laughed when Keir glowered at her. "How are your eggs?"

"Delicious," Keir assured her around a mouthful of them. "Perhaps ye should make breakfast every day." He sighed contentedly, then leaned back and took a bite from the buttered bread. "Will ye tell me another story?"

Sarah scoffed. "I cannot remember ever telling you one."

"Last night."

"That was not a story. That was..." Sarah shrugged. "That was noth-ing." She shook her head, trying to clear it. It seemed the more she thought of Kate lately, the more she got the distinct feeling in the pit of her stomach that something was wrong. She could not explain it, and yet it worried her. "You're a much better storyteller anyhow." She settled back in her chair, looking up at him expectantly. "Go ahead, tell *me* another story."

"Very well." Taking another bite from his bread, Keir chewed slowly, a bit of a faraway look coming to his eyes, suggesting that he was all but sifting through a myriad of stories, trying his best to pick out the right one for this moment. "I shall tell ye the story of Yvaine."

Sarah frowned. "Your sister? But you already did. You already told me how you found her and—"

Keir held up a hand to stop her. "No, not my sister, but the woman she was named for." Setting aside his empty plate, Keir turned toward her. "There is a legend among my people of how our clan came to be. Centuries ago, the islands were a wild place, uninhabited and untamed. Yet on the mainland, there lived two clans near the coast. Once, long ago, they had been allies, riding into battle side by side and equally working the fields side by side in times of peace. Eventually, though, as it often does, something happened to tear them apart. Our legends do not tell what it was, but one day friends became enemies."

Riveted, Sarah watched Keir, enthralled by his storytelling. He spoke slowly, almost wistfully, and the look in his eyes almost made her believe that he himself had been there to watch events unfold, that he had known the clans, had seen them in times of peace and been heart-broken the moment their bond had been broken.

"Years passed, and the hatred between the two clan chiefs grew. People who had once been friends, allies, no longer even knew how to speak to one another. Each one sought to align himself with other clans, deter-mined to strengthen his ranks to one day overthrow the other." Sadness lingered upon Keir's face, and he shook his head, his blue gaze finding Sarah's. "I often wonder why people seem so utterly unable to learn from the past, determined to repeat the same mistakes over and over again, unwilling to reach out a hand and offer friendship instead of war."

Sarah sighed, overwhelmed by the way her heart ached for those unknown people who had lived long ago. She knew none of their names, and yet the way Keir spoke made her feel for them. "Fear changes people," Sarah said quietly, realizing more and more that many decisions she made in her life, even those her parents' made, had been made out of fear and everything that fear had led to, be it anger or jealousy or mistrust.

Keir nodded knowingly, then breathed in slowly and continued his story. "One day, a woman appeared as though out of nowhere." He grinned at her.

Sarah smiled. "Yvaine."

"Aye, Yvaine." A deep longing blazed to life in Keir's eyes, and Sarah saw plainly how deeply he missed his sister. "One day, she was simply there. No one quite knew where she had come from. Some thought that she had been one of the clan chiefs' daughters, hidden away at birth, only to return when times were dire. Others whispered the fairies had finally been fed up with all this war and strife and had sent her to the people with a message."

"I like that thought," Sarah murmured, wondering if it was that part of her that still remembered her childhood so vividly that wished for a magical solution, something otherworldly to interfere and bring peace and happiness.

Keir grinned at her. "Aye, it does have the ring of a fairytale, doesna it?" He sighed wistfully. "My sister adored the story, even more so because the heroine carried her name."

"That is why your family chose the name, is it not?" Sarah inquired. "Because your sister came into your lives the same way Yvaine appeared out of nowhere."

Keir nodded. "'Twas my mother's suggestion. She thought 'twas the perfect name. Yvaine even muttered it in her sleep one night not long after we found her." His expression darkened. "We never expected her to vanish again, and it broke my mother's heart."

Without thinking, Sarah reached out and placed her hand upon Keir's. "In the stories, does Yvaine disappear as well?"

Keir paused. "I dunna think so. If so, the legends do not speak of it. 'Twas the marked difference between the two Yvaines. One vanished while the other stayed."

Sarah gently squeezed Keir's hand, savoring the feel of his own fingers closing around hers. "You could not have known," she murmured, wondering what it would have felt like had she lost Kate like that. "Do you regret opening your heart to her?"

"No," he replied without a second of hesitation. "She is my sister in every way that matters, and I treasure every moment she was with us."

"Perhaps one day she will return," Sarah suggested carefully, wondering what the odds were of that happening. "Perhaps the fairies will send her back."

Keir chuckled. "That would be grand. If only it were possible." He heaved a deep sigh. "I'd ride to the ends of the earth to be able to speak to her again."

Seeing Keir's longing for his sister, Sarah realized she could no longer ignore that feeling in the pit of her stomach. Once all of this was over, once she was back in London, she would reach out to Kate. She would find out if her sister was, indeed, in need of rescuing, and if her suspicions proved true, she would do everything within her power to save her. Yes, she, too, would ride to the ends of the earth to have Kate back, to see her happy once more.

Before, though, Sarah had never thought to have the power to do so.

Now, I have hope.

"What happened then?" Sarah asked, curious to hear more of the mysterious Yvaine from long ago. "What did she do?"

Keir cleared his throat, clearly pushing away thoughts of his sister and focusing his mind back on the old legends. "For the first time in countless years, someone spoke of peace, she spoke of peace. She visited the clan chiefs and urged them to reconsider."

"And did they listen?"

Keir sighed. "At first, it seemed she would be successful. The old legends tell of a peace summit. The clans gathered, distrustful of one another but, at least, once more willing to speak instead of fight."

"Something went wrong, didn't it?" Sarah asked, wishing it had gone differently.

Keir nodded. "No one remembers who attacked who first or why. All that is known is that the clans nearly destroyed one another that day."

Sarah felt her hand tense upon Keir's, felt his hand squeeze hers with equal measure. "And what of Yvaine? What of your people?"

Keir offered her a small smile. "One of the clan chiefs' had a son. His name was Caelen, and it is said that he and Yvaine fell in love. Once they realized they would not be able to change the old clan chiefs' minds, they began speaking to the people themselves." Hope lit up Keir's eyes. "Even though many perished that day, countless young people followed Yvaine and Caelen, decided against war and hatred, left behind their old homes and began anew. Together, they came to the islands where they built a new home as one clan, free of their fathers' hatred, united in their hope for a peaceful future."

Sarah sighed, her heart torn between joy and sadness. "Thank you for telling me that story. It was...beautiful. Memorable."

Keir nodded. "Aye, 'tis one of my favorites."

"Because it was your sister's favorite?"

Keir grinned at her. "That might have something to do with it." He chuckled. "As a wee lass, my sister used to stand up high on a cliff overlooking the sea, her green eyes fixed upon the far horizon and the mainland beyond, a fierce expression upon her face as she wielded the wooden sword Father had made for her, fighting invisible enemies, defending our people." He shook his head, laughing. "Aye, she was a fierce one, like the Yvaine from the story. Sometimes I wonder if it was that story that made my sister into the woman she became."

Sarah nodded. "Truly good stories stay with us," she replied, remembering the many stories Christina had told her as children, her imagination boundless. "They become a part of us, don't you think?"

Keir met her eyes. "Aye, ye might be right about that, lass."

"Christina once told me a story about a young girl who ventures out into the woods and loses her way," Sarah told him with a wistful smile.

"And does she find her way back?"

"She does," Sarah said with a grin as all the details of that story began to return to her.

Keir eyed her curiously. "How?"

Sarah felt her smile stretch across her face. "Fairies," she whispered, as though speaking too loudly might chase away the magic.

Keir laughed, his eyes lighting up with mirth. "Aye, fairies. Perhaps people are not as different as they think. Perhaps they simply need to pause every once in a while and realize that we're all the same."

Sarah nodded in agreement. After all, outwardly she and Keir could not be more different. And yet she had never felt a stronger connection to another person. Perhaps it should not matter that she was a baron's daughter, and he was a common criminal. Perhaps what did matter was that they both believed in fairies.

Chapter Twenty-Seven

THE AUDACITY!

Back in London

"What is it, Father?"

Albert glared at his son, as though Anthony had been the one to ruin his day and not the ransom note in his hands. Still, Albert could not abide the deep concern he saw in his son's eyes. Instead, Anthony ought to feel outrage at seeing his own father blackmailed, forced to give up part of his fortune in order to see Hartmore's daughter returned. Indeed, it had been a mistake to agree to this union, for it had brought more bad than good. While a young wife was certainly appealing, a mistress would have done as well and would have come with less responsibility.

Especially now that whispers of her abduction were all over London, growing louder with each day. It was a disgrace! Albert wished he had never accepted Hartmore's offer, and yet he had never been one to bow out. He would not surrender in defeat, no matter what it would cost him.

"It's a ransom note," Albert growled, fighting to resist the urge to tear it to pieces and toss it into the flames.

Anthony exhaled a deep breath of relief. "That is good," he sighed, one hand pressed to his chest, as though his heart now truly felt lighter. Albert suspected it did, which angered him even more. "I must say I was concerned that we had heard nothing for so long. That is unusual, is it not?"

Albert shrugged. "How would I know?" he snapped, giving into the urge to, at least, crumple the note into a tight little ball. "No one has ever dared blackmail me before."

That thought still needled Albert like none other ever had. *The audacity! The—!*

Inhaling deeply, Albert forced his pulse to slow, reminding himself that he needed to remain calm in order to remain in control. "Have Hartmore informed of this development," Albert instructed his son, and Anthony flew out the door to comply as though time was of the essence. Quite clearly, the boy's late mother's influence proved harmful after all!

Seating himself at his desk, Albert jotted down a message to Mr. Smith, urging the man to expedite his inquiries and finally locate the bothersome chit. After all, Albert loathed the idea of paying the ransom for her return. In his book, it was a failure, and Albert Harris, Baron Blackmore, did not fail.

Especially not when they were getting so close.

The chit has to be somewhere near that inn.

If only I knew where!

Chapter Twenty-Eight
NEWS

Keir was bored out of his mind. And annoyed. He absolutely adored Sarah, but the girl's insistence he rest was driving him mad. He had spent three days upstairs in his bedchamber, lying flat on his back for the better part of the day like an invalid. She had even posted a guard in his chamber, and Loki—the little traitor!— had dutifully reported any of Keir's attempts to sneak off.

Meanwhile, Sarah hurried through the house, cleaning and cooking, bringing him food, tending to his wound and, of course, reminding him to rest. Never before had Keir realized what an awful word it was.

Rest!

Hearing the front door fall closed, Keir ignored Loki's protests and slipped out of bed, moving over to the window on legs that felt encouragingly strong. He spotted Sarah vanishing into the stable, only to see her reappear a few moments later, leading Scout by a rope. The gelding tossed his head in delight at being back outside and eagerly followed Sarah down the path and then around the cabin toward the meadow.

Next came Autumn.

Aye, life keeps Sarah busy while deciding to torture me with inactivity. But no more!

Slowly moving his arm, Keir tested its limits, encouraged when he felt barely a small measure of pain. Indeed, the wound was healing well, his head no longer throbbed, and the world had decided to once again remain in its place and not spin loosely upon its axis. All good signs!

After washing and changing into a fresh set of clothes, Keir stepped determinedly toward the door, only to find the little feline in his path. "I promise I'll take it slow, your highness," Keir told the cat with as much sincerity as he could muster. "There is no need to alert your superior."

For a moment, Loki cocked his head, as though in doubt. Then, to Keir's surprise, he stepped aside and moved toward the door himself, demanding Keir open it with a forceful *meow*.

Stepping out into the crisp winter air, Keir inhaled a deep breath. Aye, he had missed the outdoors. This was where he was meant to be. This was where—

"What are you doing out of bed?"

Keir groaned inwardly before turning to face Sarah with a determined expression. "I'm out of bed because I feel perfectly fine," he told her firmly. "And I have been fine for days." *Honestly, that might be a bit of a stretch, but it serves to make my point.*

"Very well," was all Sarah said as she marched off toward the stable, the ropes she had used to lead Scout and Autumn to the meadow slung over one arm.

"Very well?" Keir echoed, hurrying after her. "That's it? Ye're not insisting I return to bed?"

Sarah grinned at him over her shoulder. "Do you want me to?"

"No!" Keir replied quickly, then paused when she opened the stable door. "I'm simply surprised ye're not..." He frowned, starting to feel exasperated. The moment she reappeared from inside the stable, he fixed her with a determined stare. "If ye believe me now, why did ye not before? I've been telling ye that I was fine for days." *Again, perhaps a wee bit of an exaggeration!*

Smirking up at him, Sarah shrugged. "I wanted to see how long you would last," she told him with a devilish look in her blue eyes. "I'm surprised you didn't escape earlier."

Keir felt his jaw drop. "Well, ye posted a guard at the door, in case ye forgot," he all but snapped the moment he had recovered his wits.

As though on cue, Loki tiptoed up to Sarah, seating himself at her feet, like a loyal general in her majesty's army.

Keir glared down at the feline. "So, this is where yer loyalties lie?"

Sarah laughed. "Oh, don't be mad at him. He was merely concerned for you. As was I." The humor in her eyes vanished, replaced by something almost vulnerable. *Was she truly afraid for me?* Keir wondered. *Does she care that much?*

"Well, I assure ye I'm fine," Keir repeated, no trace of humor in his own voice, either. "I promise ye."

Sarah nodded in acknowledgment. "Good." Then she turned and headed back toward the cabin.

Keir looked after her, for the first time noticing that radiant glow that suddenly lingered upon her features. It whispered of someone who had come into their own, someone who felt proud of her own abilities, her own accomplishments. Aye, she had taken care of everything over the course of the past few days, and it had not gone unnoticed.

Not by him.

And definitely not by her.

The next day, Keir informed Sarah that he needed to return to the inn. Although he had expected her to object, she merely nodded her head, the concerned look in her eyes the only sign that she disliked his intention.

"I shall be back by nightfall," Keir told her as he pulled himself into Scout's saddle. His arm protested a bit at the strain, but it was only a pinch, easily forgotten.

"Be careful," Sarah said unnecessarily as she bent down and picked up Loki, cradling the cat in her arms. His highness seemed utterly surprised by her sudden need for closeness but did not protest.

"I will," Keir assured her, then fixed his gaze on Loki. "Look after her in my absence, will ye?"

Loki meowed in acquiescence.

Keir smiled at her, then he pulled Scout around and headed out. A part of him still felt ill at ease at leaving her alone; yet there was no other way. Perhaps it would have been wiser if he were not the only one looking after Sarah as he could not be in two places at the same time. Still, Keir would have disliked to have another guard here with them. If so, they would have never...

Keir shook his head to clear it as the memory of their kiss drifted back into his mind. He needed to maintain a clear head to ensure Sarah's safety. Who knew what had happened over the course of the past few days! Who knew what messages the dowager had sent expecting him to receive them! Keir could only hope that he had not missed something vital.

By the time the inn came into view, snow was falling hard, obscuring Scout's hoofprints and impairing Keir's sight. Still, after the freezing cold, the inn's warmth felt all the more welcoming. As always, Keir resolved to seat himself at a table in the back where he could observe the comings and goings. First, however, he headed toward the innkeeper's desk to see if any messages had arrived since his last visit.

The man handed him a single letter, the dowager's familiar hand-writing gracing its front. Keir felt his heartbeat quicken as he strode across the taproom toward an unoccupied table. Seating himself, he ripped open the envelope.

My dear boy,

Demand for payment has been sent. Be warned, though, (Keir felt his heart still in his chest.), *BB* (Keir supposed that stood for Baron Blackmore.) *has become suspicious and is making inquiries. He might have men nearby. I shall write with further instructions.*

GE

Keir gritted his teeth as he stared at the message. The worst had come to pass. If Blackmore, indeed, suspected something, then there was no telling what he might do. Keir lifted his gaze, sweeping it over the taproom. Was there one of Blackmore's men present here right now?

Keir could not tell, and it worried him. Perhaps his concern for Sarah was clouding his judgment, as, at present, he found it increasingly difficult to assess those around him.

Two elderly men sat only two tables down from his own, arguing about their right to a particular piece of land. Another with a full beard and bushy eyebrows sat by the hearth nursing a large mug of ale. A third muscular one with a scar above his right eyebrow was enjoying a hearty meal near the innkeeper's desk. For a second, Keir thought the man looked familiar, but a moment later, he was no longer certain.

Aye, my concern for Sarah is clouding my judgment! I ought never have kissed her! 'Twas a mistake!

Keir felt the desperate urge to jump to his feet and rush back to her side. Still, if someone was watching, he would lead them right back to her. Yet what could he do? After all, he had promised Sarah he would be back by nightfall. Knowing her, she would be out of her mind if he did not return. Also, his absence did not mean that Blackmore's men could not simply stumble upon the cabin some other way. He could not leave her alone!

Forcing himself to remain calm, Keir surveyed the taproom for another ten minutes. Then he leisurely strolled back out into the cold. On his way, he first dropped a purse of coins and then pretended his hat had been blown off by the wind to allow him an inconspicuous glance over his shoulder when retrieving his lost items.

He saw nothing.

No one followed him.

Still, that was no guarantee.

Pulling himself back into Scout's saddle, Keir headed back down the road, constantly looking over his shoulder. As soon as trees appeared at the side of the road, Keir weaved through them, hoping they might obscure his direction. Still, he saw nothing suspicious.

Keir desperately hoped he was not mistaken.

He desperately hoped Sarah was safe.

And would remain so.

Chapter Twenty-Nine
BRAVING THE ELEMENTS

T he moment Keir proved to be on the mend, the moment
Sarah's concerns for him proved unjustified, she felt her heart
grow lighter, felt her spirits being lifted and a truly genuine
smile return to her face. Indeed, she loved taking care of him, of the
horses, of the cabin, of everything, even the goat and the chickens. She
loved feeling valuable, capable and in charge of her own life. It, too,
was a heady feeling, and she wondered how she could have ever lived
without it.

Yet as she watched Keir ride away on Scout, watched him disappear between the trees, her heart grew heavy again. Perhaps she
simply did not like being alone. Perhaps she simply did not like being
without him. Whatever the reason, the world suddenly seemed...
darker, threatening even. Without Keir's presence, worrisome
thoughts returned, and Sarah did her best to keep herself occupied,
hoping they would simply slip from her mind if she kept it focused on
other things.

All day long, Sarah rushed from one task to the next, sweeping the
entire cabin, cleaning the windows, dusting the rugs and preparing
supper. She tended to Autumn, fed the chickens and allowed them
outside for a few hours before chasing them back in, Loki by her side

at all times. Indeed, the feline had become a loyal companion, making her feel less alone, as though someone was still here watching over her.

By the time the sun began to set on the far horizon, Sarah felt exhausted. Her limbs ached, and her mind felt strangely sluggish. With a deep sigh, she sank into her favorite armchair by the hearth, welcoming the warm glow of the fire. She had not planned to fall asleep; however, slumber had other plans. It took her swiftly and without her noticing, carrying her away to a beautiful place that teased a smile onto her lips.

In all likelihood, Sarah would have slept on for another hour or two if the wind had not grown stronger, if it had not pushed and shoved against the small cabin in the woods, if it had not ripped open a window, banging it against its frame.

With a startled gasp, Sarah shot upright, her eyes blinking into the dark. Her body felt stiff, and she shivered at the icy wind that streamed inside through the open window. Quickly, she was on her feet, pulling it closed and fumbling with the lock before securing it.

Beside her, Loki yawned and stretched, not in the least bothered by the cool air in the parlor.

"Oh, don't worry," Sarah assured him, nonetheless. "I should go and fetch some logs. It will be warm in here again soon." As she turned to leave, her gaze swept over the hearth, and the sight gave her pause. The dancing flames she remembered from before she had fallen asleep had disappeared, leaving behind nothing more but a few glowing embers. Indeed, the cabin slipped more and more into complete darkness as the sun bid the day goodbye for the night. And so, Sarah hurriedly pulled on her cloak and shoved her feet into her boots before rushing outside.

At the back of the cabin, firewood was stacked high against the wall, shielded from most of the elements by the stable nearby, holding off the biting east wind. With her teeth chattering, Sarah reached for log after log, choosing the smaller ones and piling them into the crook of her left arm. However, when she stretched to reach for yet one more, she lost her balance on the slippery ground and fell hard against the wall of the cabin. The logs she had gathered fell from her limp arms, and her legs collapsed beneath her, dropping her into the snow.

Dazed, she blinked her eyes, feeling the cold seep into her bones, before moving to right herself, to get back on her feet.

Before she could, though, the sound of something sliding towards her from up above caught her attention, and she lifted her chin the very moment a cascade of snow came down upon her head, slipping between the folds of her garments and chilling her skin. The breath caught in her throat, and her knees buckled once more, sending her back down into the snow. Her teeth now chattered uncontrollably, and her toes and fingers began to hurt from the cold.

More than anything, Sarah wanted to lie down and close her eyes. She felt her strength wane, her muscles refusing to comply. Exhaustion pulled on her once more, and she exhaled a deep breath, sinking deeper into the snow.

Move! A voice screamed in her head. *Move! You cannot stay here! Get back inside! Now!*

Sarah's eyes snapped back open, and with her last bit of strength, she managed to get her feet back under her. With her gaze fixed forward, she staggered along, but then she paused and reached for three of the smaller logs she had dropped. Cradling them against her chest, Sarah stumbled onward, not daring to stop until she had reached the door. She all but fell through it the moment it swung open, fighting to keep her balance.

Loki greeted her with a sympathetic meow, his glowing eyes slightly narrowed in concern.

"I-It'll b-be w-warm s-s-soon," Sarah assured him, her teeth chattering so badly that she could barely understand her own words.

With her arms still wrapped around the logs, Sarah moved into the parlor and then dropped to her knees by the hearth, her eyes going wide and her heart pausing in her chest. "I-It went out," she murmured under her breath, shock seeping into her bones more and more as she stared at the dead embers. Every bit of glow was gone. Every bit of orange and red extinguished. *What now?*

Sarah looked down at the logs in her arms, overcome by a sudden panic. Keir had shown her how to stoke a fire, how to add more logs, how to make it blaze higher. Yet he had never shown her how to start a fire. He had never needed to. In the evenings, they had always taken candles, lit them upon the fire in the hearth and carried them upstairs to warm their chambers, to light new fires there. Sometimes, the fire in the parlor had gone out overnight; however, they had always been able to light it again come morning, using the remaining embers in their bedchambers.

And I have yet to light the fire in the kitchen! I meant to do it when...

Hanging her head, Sarah closed her eyes. She could not recall the fire ever going out completely. Everywhere! She had a vague memory of Keir lighting the fire in the kitchen the day of their arrival at the cabin. He had used some sort of kit he always carried in the pouch on his belt. It contained a piece of flint, Sarah believed, as well as...

Pain pounded beneath her temples, and the memory slipped away. Even if it had not, it would not serve her. The kit was with Keir, safely secured upon his belt, and even if it were here, right here in her hands, Sarah had no knowledge of how to use it.

Tears pricked Sarah's eyes, and the logs slid from her numb arms. Violent shivers seized her, and the sound of her teeth chattering became almost deafening. Once again, she felt an almost overwhelming need to sink to the floor and lie there.

Simply lie there.

"Meow," came Loki's insistent little voice a moment before he brushed up against her arm. His wide glowing eyes were looking up at her face, and Sarah could all but sense his disapproval of her current lack of determination. Was she truly giving up? It certainly felt like it.

"Meow," Loki insisted with a bit of a haughty expression. He bumped his little head against her arm, as though urging her to her feet.

Sniffling, Sarah nodded, then she slowly pushed herself off the floor. For a moment, she swayed upon her feet but then regained her balance. Slow steps carried her out of the parlor, and then even slower ones carried her up the stairs. She knew she needed to get warm. She needed to change out of these wet, chilling clothes and find some way to warm herself.

As she stepped into her chamber, one glance out the window told her that night was upon them. Had Keir not promised to be back by nightfall? Would he be here soon? Sarah prayed that he would, that he would come and save her. She all but hung her head at the thought, for she did not want to be saved. *No, I want to save myself.* Was that not what Keir had said? Yes, she still remembered that proud expression upon his face as he had looked at her in that moment. Indeed, she, too, had been proud.

She was no longer.

All of a sudden, Sarah did not feel strong and capable and in control of her own life. Instead, she felt miserable and helpless and utterly dependent on others.

Upon Keir.

Changing out of her wet clothes took forever. Sarah's limbs simply would not stop trembling, and her fingers had a hard time peeling the clothing from her body. Her eyes stared into the dark fireplace, her mind imagining dancing flames, their warmth reaching out to her. Yet the dream remained a dream.

Once free of her wet clothes, Sarah staggered over to the small armoire in the corner and pulled layer after layer over her head, praying that they would warm her. She put on, at least, three pairs of stockings, her feet still cold as ice, and then quickly slipped into bed, pulling the blanket up to her chin.

There, she lay shivering, her whole body moving against her will, fighting to warm her. Loki jumped up onto the bed, poking his wet little nose against hers and offering her another compassionate *meow*.

Meeting his yellow gaze, Sarah lifted the edge of the blanket and, as though the little feline knew exactly what she needed, he moved closer and curled up in the crook of her arm. His little body was warm, so very warm compared to her own, and Sarah snuggled closer, grateful.

Her eyes closed, and she could feel her mind grow sluggish. The world around her slowly retreated, and yet the shivers would not stop. Loki was warm, but he was small, and he could not warm her. Not the way she needed. *What if he cools down too much?* Sarah worried before she drifted into a fitful sleep.

Chapter Thirty

A FLAME IN WINTER

The first thing Keir noticed as he approached the cabin was that there was no light. None at all. Not a flicker. Not a spark. Nothing. The windows were completely dark, and he saw no smoke billowing out of the chimney and rising into the star-speckled night. In fact, the cabin looked deserted, as though no one was there.

Keir's heart tightened in his chest as fear slowly crawled up his spine. *Am I too late? Did Blackmore's men somehow find the cabin? Is Sarah already gone?*

Kicking Scout's flanks, Keir urged the gelding the last stretch toward the cabin. Once he reached the yard, he jumped out of the saddle. Everything looked in order, and he saw no signs of forced entry on the front door as he burst through. "Sarah!" Keir called breathlessly, wrenching his head from side to side, trying to listen, trying to decide where to go. *Is there any chance she is still here?*

The cabin was dark, not even a glimmer of light drifting into the hall from the parlor or the kitchen. The air felt completely still, as though no one even dared breathe, and no sounds could be heard beyond those drifting to his ears from the outside.

An owl hooting every now and then.

The push and shove of the wind as it swirled through the trees.

Scout's neigh, and Autumn's answer.

Spinning upon his heels, Keir charged up the stairs, calling Sarah's name again and again. He felt like a fool, acting without thought, without caution—who knew who was nearby?—and yet he could not stop himself. Fear pushed him onward, and he almost stumbled over a small creature at the top of the stairs.

Loki.

"Where is she?" Keir demanded of the feline, who immediately charged ahead toward Sarah's door, a sense of urgency in his movements. Keir did not have time to marvel at the cat's understanding nor his response. His feet carried him onward, and he burst into Sarah's room without a moment of hesitation.

Her fireplace was dark as well, but Keir could make out a faint shape upon the bed, buried under the blanket. He shot toward her, his hands reaching out, his mind trying to understand what had happened here. Had she had a fall? Was she ill? Why—?

Ice cold! Her hands are ice cold!

Keir's hands touched her forehead and then moved to her cheeks and down her neck. He hesitated for a moment and then slipped his right hand over her shoulder and under her dress, right between her shoulder blades.

Cold!

Too cold!

"Sarah!" Keir called, giving her a shake. His eyes flew over her face, her features hidden in shadows. "Sarah! Wake up!"

A soft sigh drifted to his ears, and he thought to see her eyes flutter, opening and then closing again. "Keir?" It was only a faint murmur, weak and barely conscious.

Cursing under his breath, Keir glanced at the dark fireplace and then rushed out of the room. He bounded down the stairs and back outside. Scout greeted him with a friendly neigh, and Keir snatched the gelding's reins and pulled him into the stable. In a few fluid motions, he removed the bridle and saddle and then tossed a blanket over the bay gelding. Then he grasped a few fistfuls of hay and stuffed them in his pockets before rushing back outside toward the back of the cabin where the firewood was stacked.

For a moment, Keir paused, his eyes sweeping over a small heap of snow, uneven footprints all around it and a handful of logs discarded nearby. What had happened here? Had she gone for more firewood? Had she slipped?

Keir shook his head. *'Tis not important right now.* He moved down the line of logs to the driest part and quickly gathered an armload full before turning and rushing back into the house. Up the stairs he went. Then he dropped to his knees in front of Sarah's fireplace. He quickly stacked the logs and gathered some kindling from a basket near the hearth. He added the dry hay and then reached for the small pouch on his belt. Pouring out its contents into the palm of his hand, he struck flint and steel together to create a spark. It fell onto the dry kindling and a flame immediately danced to life.

Forcing himself to go slowly, Keir gently blew onto the flame, coaxing it higher and higher. It flickered and then grew, consuming the hay and dancing from twig to twig, gaining strength before it stretched around the first log.

Keir breathed a sigh of relief and jumped to his feet. He hurried back to the bed and stared down at Sarah, briefly contemplating what to do. Then he grasped the wooden bed frame and pushed and shoved the bed closer and closer to the fireplace.

As close as he dared.

"K-Keir?" Sarah murmured again as her head rose from the pillow. Her eyes blinked and then for a moment focused on him, her teeth chattering. "W-What...?" Too weak to hold herself upright, she sank back down into the covers. "W-What are you—?"

Not bothering to explain himself, Keir removed his boots and his coat. He could feel Sarah watching him, could all but sense her confusion. Yet she said nothing until he pulled his vest over his head and then reached to tug his shirt free.

"W-What are y-you doing?" Sarah stammered, still shivering violently. Her eyes were wide in the dim light, her features pale even in the orange glow from the awakening fire.

"Ye need warmth, lass," Keir replied and tossed his shirt aside.

Understanding dawned upon Sarah's face. "B-But the f-f-fire?"

Keir sat down upon the bed, lifting the blanket to slip underneath. "'Tis not enough," he said, reaching out to pull Sarah into his arms.

Suddenly, Sarah seemed wide awake, all signs of drowsiness gone from her face. "B-But you c-cannot—"

Sarah's voice broke off and Keir drew in a sharp breath the moment her fingers brushed against his bare chest. "Blast, lass, ye're as cold as ice!" Goosebumps rippled up and down his arms and back, but he pulled her closer still, slipping an arm underneath her head and around her shoulders.

Sarah's body grew rigid at his closeness, and she dug her teeth into her lower lip. Still, a contented sigh escaped her lips as he wrapped her in the warm cocoon of his arms.

Keir rubbed his hands up and down her back, and the tension slowly left Sarah's body. She relaxed against him, her palms coming to rest against his bare skin, soaking up his warmth. "Feel better?" Keir asked, his chin resting atop her head.

A sleepy *Mmmh* drifted to his ears, and when Keir looked down, Sarah's eyes were closed. Her breath evened, warm and teasing against his skin, and she slipped into a deep slumber.

As the fire slowly warmed the room, Keir held Sarah in his arms, her head resting upon his shoulder and her heartbeat a constant reminder that she was truly here.

In his arms.

This was no dream, and Keir held her a little tighter, savoring the moment. No matter what happened tomorrow, they would have to bid each other farewell soon. Before long, Sarah would be back in London with her family, her choices her own, and he would return to Scotland.

In all likelihood, their paths would not cross again.

The thought brought a deep ache to Keir's chest, and his embrace grew more daring, more demanding as he pulled the sleeping woman in his arms tightly against him. If only tomorrow did not have to come!

Brushing tender fingers along her temple, Keir wondered if there was any way for them to see each other again. Of course, it was not impossible. Sarah was Christina's childhood friend, and to him, the

Whickertons had become all but family. But would Sarah want to? Or would she be content to return to her old life, shackles removed and freedom granted?

Perhaps he simply ought to ask her.

Chapter Thirty-One

ONCE UPON A KISS MOST DESIRED

Sarah sighed deeply, her body pleasantly languid and warm, nestled somewhere safe and—

She paused.

In the far reaches of her mind, the echo of a nightmare lingered. Something cold and dark and terrifying. She remembered wind and ice and snow, the absence of fire and warmth. The sensation of sinking deeper into a freezing void from which there would be no escape.

She remembered a feeling of utter panic and helplessness.

Only that feeling was gone now.

Replaced by—

Sarah's eyes flew open...and her heart tripped over itself.

Keir.

Right here in front of her. The tip of his nose only a hair's breadth from her own. She could feel his warm breath against her lips as he breathed in and out, his eyes closed in slumber. His arms were wrapped tightly around her, and her head was resting upon his shoulder, his warm skin the pillow she had slept upon.

Shocked, Sarah tensed, felt her body grow rigid as she expected Keir's eyes to fly open at any moment, his teasing gaze sending a blazing trail of embarrassment up her neck and into her cheeks.

Only he did not.

His eyes remained closed, and his breath remained even. He was asleep. Truly asleep. *And I...am not.*

A wicked desire to look at him welled up in Sarah's chest, and so she slowly lifted her head, scooting back only a little to better see his face.

He looked peaceful despite the slight crease upon his forehead that spoke of a lingering concern. Sarah wished she could see the blue of his eyes, and yet the thought that his gaze might meet hers, here, in this moment, was almost terrifying.

Fortunately, Keir remained asleep.

Hesitating for a breath or two, Sarah ran her eyes over his features, along the curve of his brows, down the line of his nose and farther to his lips...currently *not* twitching with teasing amusement.

Instantly, Sarah remembered how Keir had kissed her downstairs in the parlor. Her whole body warmed at the memory, and she stilled as her mind recalled the feel of his lips upon her own. It had felt shockingly foreign, and yet Sarah had known right away that she would never forget it.

Nor want to.

Her gaze traced the curve of his lips as she allowed the memory to replay in her mind again and again. A part of her wished she possessed the boldness to steal a kiss for herself—as he had done. She wished she was daring enough to reach out and press her mouth to his, to feel him again and sear the memory of this kiss into her mind.

Her heart.

Her bones.

Of course, instead of daring boldness, Sarah experienced a depressing moment of shocked disbelief, for in her mind she heard her mother's appalled voice, berating her for allowing Keir to take advantage of her like this.

Only he is not, is he?

He was here to warm her, to save her life, not to...

Sarah sighed, pinching her eyes shut, determined to banish her mother's chiding gaze from her thoughts. After all, this was a once-in-a-lifetime opportunity. Sarah was certain of it. Never again would she feel like this. Never again would she have the chance to be in Keir's arms.

Never again...

The thought made her heart heavy, and yet it also tingled through her limbs with increasing speed, waking every fiber of her being and urging her to take this risk, to reach for something she would cherish until the end of her days.

Tentatively, Sarah's hand moved, closer and closer, until the tips of her fingers brushed against Keir's bottom lip.

Shocked at her own audacity, Sarah stilled, her breath lodged in her throat. Still, when the world did not end, that daring tingle returned with full force and she found herself tracing the curve of Keir's lips, mesmerized.

If only she dared—

Sarah stilled, suddenly overcome by the notion that she was being watched, that someone—

Her eyes rose, and her lips parted on a mortified gasp as she yanked her hand back as though burned.

Keir's eyes *were* open now, and he *was* watching her. *Had been* watching her.

Sarah wanted to crawl into a hole in the ground. She could feel that familiar heat rise to her cheeks and knew she would die of embarrassment if Keir were to laugh at her now. Could he not simply—?

Her eyes rose to look into his, and for once, she saw nothing laughing or teasing there. The corners of his mouth did not quirk, and the expression upon his face held no amusement at all.

Indeed, the look in his eyes was...

Sarah's heart skipped a beat or two, and she felt her breath quickening as her mind blurred and her thoughts became unfocused. Instinctively, she tried to retreat, to put some space between them, but Keir's embrace was unyielding. He held her tightly in his arms, and silently Sarah rejoiced at the feel of it.

And then Sarah's dearest wish came true.

Without saying even a single word, Keir leaned in and kissed her. He kissed her as he had kissed her before. Downstairs in the parlor.

His hand touched her cheek, his fingertips trailing across her skin, as his lips roamed hers, teasingly at first and then with more pressure.

Sarah's head spun, and her hands reached out toward him, tangling in his hair and pulling him closer. If this was all she would ever have of this heady feeling, then she wanted the memory to be all it could be.

The night was still dark. Her chamber illuminated by the warm orange glow from the fire in the hearth. Their breathing and the soft crackling of the dancing flames the only sound drifting to her ears.

"Ye're warm again, little wisp," Keir whispered, his breath teasing her skin as his lips trailed lower, past her ear and down her neck. He placed feather-light kisses upon her skin, each one a blazing fire that made her long for more. "I like ye better warm," he murmured before kissing her again.

Sarah thought to hear a teasing chuckle in those words, and yet she did not mind. Did not care. In fact, she liked it. She liked the way he spoke to her. The way he saw precisely who she was...and did not object. Never had a word of disapproval passed his lips, and Sarah realized in that moment that even though Keir did see her many faults, he did not see them as such.

He liked her for whom she was.

He did not see a reason for her to change.

Tears stung Sarah's eyes, and her fingers dug into Keir's shoulders, holding him close, willing his touch, his gentleness to banish those feelings of inadequacy that had loomed over her head her entire adult life. She dove into the kiss, parting her lips and accepting all he had to give, desperate for one memory of utter bliss.

Oh, it would break her heart to bid him farewell! Sarah knew. She had known it for a while and yet had not allowed the thought to manifest, knowing only too well how it would devastate her. If only there was a way they could—

Keir suddenly stilled.

Confused, Sarah's eyes blinked open, and she saw the furrows that came to Keir's forehead as he held himself completely still, listening.

No sound beyond the crackling of the fire reached Sarah's ears, but she did not doubt that Keir had heard something. *What can it be? Loki perhaps. Where is he?* Sarah glanced around her chamber. *Perhaps down-stairs? Did he knock something over? Or—?*

Looking up into Keir's eyes, Sarah realized she had not had the chance to ask Keir about the inn. Had there been a message from Grandma Edie? Had something gone wrong? Had Keir returned earlier with the intention of taking her away, only to find himself distracted by finding her nearly freezing to death in her chamber?

With a finger to his lips, Keir bade Sarah to be quiet. Then he slipped from the bed, hastily pulled his shirt over his head and slipped his feet back into his boots, reaching to refasten his belt.

Sarah watched him, clutching the blanket to her chest, afraid to speak, afraid to make even a single sound. Yet she burned to ask Keir what he thought had happened. Was there truly an intruder down there? Was that possible? What if Keir went down there and then—?

Sarah shuddered at the thought of all that could happen to him, and for the first time, she felt regret. Regret for having made this choice. Regret for having come here, for having met Keir. Regret for putting him in danger. Her selfish decision, her choice to free herself of her family's obligations, of a marriage that might crush her soul but see her body unharmed, had brought this on him. If he was harmed in any way, Sarah knew she would never forgive herself.

"Stay here," Keir whispered under his breath, "and lock the door." His eyes looked imploringly into hers, reminding her of how he had instructed her to do so before and how she had completely disregarded it. Abruptly, he reached out and pulled her off the bed and into his arms. "I mean it, Sarah." His breath felt harsh against her lips. "Dunna dare come after me."

Swallowing hard, unable to utter even a single word, Sarah nodded her head.

Keir exhaled a slow breath, relief palpable upon his face. Then he stepped back, slowly releasing her, and Sarah sank back down onto the bed. "Take this," Keir whispered, handing her a small blade. "Just in case."

Sarah reluctantly took the knife, its blade cool against her warm skin. Then she watched Keir silently slink from the room, closing the door behind himself.

A feeling of doom settled in Sarah's belly, as though she would never see Keir again, as though their time together had come to an abrupt end and she had not even had the opportunity to bid him farewell.

As tears once more threatened to fill Sarah's eyes, she angrily willed them away. Then she slipped from the bed and locked the door. That done, Sarah searched for her boots. After all, she was already dressed— in multiple layers no less! There was nothing wrong with being prepared, was there? Who knew what would happen? Perhaps Keir would need her help after all! Perhaps they would need to flee quickly! Sarah did not know, and yet it seemed like a good idea to put on her boots.

Once that small task was accomplished, Sarah listened.

The stillness and this almost eerie silence that suddenly hung over the small cabin was unnerving. It brought chills back to Sarah's skin, made her feel cold in such an all-consuming way that she moved closer to the fire, unable to bear it.

Oh, if only Keir would come upstairs any second now, mischievous Loki in his arms and a grin upon his face! *Please let there be a simple explanation*, Sarah prayed fervently. *Please!*

The moment the last word echoed through her thoughts, a muffled grunt echoed to her ears.

Sarah flinched, every muscle in her body tensing as she listened, waiting for more. Had it been Keir? Or someone else? An intruder? Who else was there?

Silent steps carried Sarah over to the door, her hands coming to rest upon the smooth wood, her ear pressed against it. Indeed, she could make out faint footsteps, and then there was the sound of another muffled groan.

A moment later, an almost ear-splitting *thud* seemed to shake the house. To Sarah it felt like an earthquake, a tremor from deep in the ground. Of course, though, it was not, and as time continued on, second after second ticking by, she could make out the distinctive sounds of a fight, of, at least, two men in a small space, colliding with the walls here and there, knocking small pieces of furniture out of their way.

Gritting her teeth, Sarah closed her eyes and rested her forehead against the door. *So, it* is *an intruder!* She thought, and Keir's instructions echoed loud and clear through her head. Yes, he had been very specific, and yet Sarah felt her hand itch with the need to reach for the door handle, to unlock the door, pull it open and rush out of her chamber. She could not simply wait up here and allow Keir to face this danger on his own, could she? What would that say about her? If she saved herself at the expense of another? Someone she...cared for deeply?

Her hand curled around the door handle, gripping it tightly. Her jaw began to ache from the pressure as the two sides of her mind warred with one another. What was she to do?

And then her hands moved as though on their own. The key turned, and the door slid open. Sarah stilled, shocked at herself. The sounds of a scuffle were still there, and with the door ajar she could tell they came from downstairs. Upstairs, everything seemed quiet, and so, Sarah stepped out into the hall, her eyes trained on the staircase. What would she do if someone suddenly were to come up here?

Her right hand still held Keir's knife, clutching it tightly. Yet would she have a chance to use it? Would she even have the courage to do so? Sarah doubted it. In all likelihood, the blade would be of no use to her. She could not imagine having the stomach to plunge it into another's body, to know it would rip and tear and spill their blood. No, she was no fighter. She was someone who bowed her head and accepted what was.

She always had been.

Fortunately, the only one to come upon her was Loki, his glowing gaze visible in the dark. He moved toward her, and some of the cold dread in Sarah's bones waned at his presence. "Shhh," she said, placing a finger against her lips.

Listening for another moment, Sarah tiptoed toward the stairs, then quietly began moving toward the lower floor. Every small creak from below her feet made her flinch, made her pause, certain that people far away in London had to have heard it.

Yet no one came to find her.

And so, Sarah proceeded onward, her eyes wide and searching.

Again, she heard muffled sounds, voices saying words she could not make out, quickly followed by a dull *thud* as though—

Sarah pinched her eyes shut, her hand curled painfully around the banister, unable to imagine another's fist connecting with Keir's jaw, being driven into his stomach. The thought was too much to bear, and Sarah felt her knees begin to tremble.

Perhaps she truly ought to turn back.

After all, she was not a hero. She was a coward. Had been all her life.

Yes, she ought to have listened to Keir.

She never ought to have come.

Chapter Thirty-Two
INTRUDERS

E ven before he saw them, Keir knew it was not a single intruder. He could sense their presence even in the dark. The little hairs on the back of his neck rose, chasing an icy chill down his spine, a sign of what awaited him. After all, he could not simply turn and run, seeking safety elsewhere. *Sarah is upstairs, safe and sound for now, but for how much longer?*

That was up to him.

Keir would never allow anything to happen to her. He had made the dowager a promise, and yet deep down he knew it was not that promise that made him face the intruders without flinching, without a moment of hesitation.

The first one came at him in the narrow hallway, and Keir almost smiled at the thought that the snugness of the cabin prevented his attackers from approaching him from all sides at once.

Forcing his thoughts to focus, he ducked out of the way as a fist came flying toward his head, then spun to the left and drove his own fist into his attacker's stomach. The man groaned and then doubled over, sinking to his knees. Another punch to the jaw knocked the man out, sending him sprawling onto the floor, like a hastily discarded blanket.

Ignoring the dull ache in his arm, Keir looked over his shoulder and spotted two other shadows moving through the cabin. They did not rush at him at once but held back, lingering nearby but out of sight. Gripping his blade tightly, Keir flattened his back against the wall, his eyes slightly narrowed as he tried to see in the darkened room.

For a moment, he contemplated what to do.

"Meow."

Looking down, Keir spotted two glowing yellow eyes as Loki moved toward him in the dark. "Upstairs," Keir murmured to the feline, nodding toward the staircase in his back. "Watch over Sarah." To his surprise, *his highness* complied instantly, his little paws carrying him quietly out of sight.

From where Keir stood, he could still see the staircase leading to the upper floor. If he were to move, he could never quite be certain if someone had slipped past him and found his way to Sarah. Yet at the same time, Keir knew he could not remain here indefinitely. Eventually, the sun would rise, and he would lose his advantage.

Watching the shadows at the other end of the hallway, Keir felt a flicker of recognition. For a split second, he had glimpsed one of the men's faces. Something about it had struck him as familiar, as though he had seen it before. If only he knew wher—

A low groan slipped from Keir's lips when the memory finally clicked into place. Aye, he had seen the man before, but it was not the hunter as he had expected. No, it had been at the inn. More than once, he had seen a man seated at a nearby table, his gaze distant, completely disinterested, staring into a mug of ale. Keir remembered the slashed scar that cut through the man's left eyebrow. Aye, Keir was certain that it was the same man.

Cursing under his breath, Keir felt a sudden intense need to fling himself at that man, to strike him down, desperate to erase the fact that he, Keir, had no doubt been the one to lead the man here. He had not been careful enough. He had made a mistake, and now Sarah would be the one to pay for it.

No! He would never allow this to happen. Even if these men would not harm her, they would no doubt return her to London, to her parents, to Blackmore perhaps. There was no telling what either one of them would do to her. Perhaps the dowager was correct in believing that Blackmore would no longer be interested in seeing Sarah made his wife if he believed her ruined. However, that was no guarantee for her safety. Keir knew men, had encountered those who possessed very little to no honor, who hurt others for the joy of it and considered any word spoken against them as a personal affront.

Inching forward, Keir continued to glance back over his shoulder at the staircase, praying that he would be quick enough if need be. His main focus, though, rested forward, his gaze flickering from shadow to shadow. He could hear them breathing, hear their soft footsteps as they shifted their weight and the almost inaudible way of a blade being unsheathed.

In a flash, someone lunged himself at Keir.

Having heard the man coming, Keir easily sidestepped him, tripping him so he tipped forward, banging his head on the wall as he lost his balance. However, before Keir could spin to face the other, he felt the cold steel of a knife pressed to the back of his neck. "Think carefully now about what you do," the man spoke in a calm yet icy voice. Even though Keir had never heard it before, he knew it was the man with the scar. "There is no need for you to die. All we want is the girl."

Keir remained still, his mind racing with how to react. He said nothing, for he doubted that these men could be reasoned with. While the other two looked like hired thugs, the man with the scar held himself like a professional, one who could not be tempted by promises of monetary nature, and what other option was there?

Allowing his shoulders to slump, Keir gave the impression of a man defeated. He sighed audibly. "Very well," he replied in an English accent, slowly turning to face the scarred man. "But I want a share of the cut."

The scarred man chuckled darkly. "You are in no position to make demands."

Keir met the man's gaze, his own filled with annoyed defeat. "She locked herself upstairs," he said, feeling the blade against the skin of his neck as he spoke. "I can get her to come out."

The scarred man chuckled. "So can we. Might take longer. But in the end the result will be the same."

Keir was not surprised by the man's reaction. Yet he knew he had not given anything away. However, he had bought himself some time, to shift his feet and slide another little dagger out of his sleeve. It now rested snugly in the palm of his hand, hidden not only by the darkness but also by the fact that the men's attention was directed elsewhere. He gritted his teeth, making a show of his defeat, and felt the other man's hold on the blade against his neck slacken. Aye, they thought themselves triumphant.

They are wrong!

Behind him, Keir heard the other man scramble back to his feet, complaining about a throbbing pain in his head. "We should have just shot him," he grumbled, shuffling closer. "If the girl's upstairs, there was no danger of harming her."

The scarred man snapped at his companion. "We could not be certain. Now, shut up!" Anger sparked in his eyes, and for a split second, they flickered sideways, away from Keir and to the man behind him.

It was not long, but it was enough.

Keir's arm shot up to protect his throat from the scarred man's blade as he spun away, his own small knife coming up and slashing at the man's arm. A groan of pain ripped from the man's throat and he dropped his blade, his eyes blazing with fury. But Keir did not hesitate, he landed one punch and then another. The man doubled over and went down onto his knees.

Unfortunately, the man in Keir's back was not a complete coward, for he lunged himself at Keir again. The two of them staggered through the small hallway, colliding with the walls again and again. The small space made it hard to move and gain any kind of advantage. The man shoved Keir against the wall, and his elbow would have been plunged into Keir's middle had he not spun out of reach. Twisting around, Keir brought his own elbow down upon the man's neck, then jabbed his fist into his stomach.

With a loud groan, his opponent went down, panting for breath…

…and Keir heard the unmistakable sound of a pistol being cocked.

Closing his eyes, Keir cursed under his breath, then slowly turned to face the scarred man once more.

"You should not have done this," the man snarled, blood trickling from a wound in his arm. Keir could smell it. "I would have let you live, but now..." He breathed in deeply, savoring the moment, and an evil sneer stretched across his face as he pointed the pistol at Keir's forehead.

Facing death, Keir was surprised by the regrets that assailed him in that moment. He had expected something else. He had expected—

The sneer suddenly vanished from the scarred man's face as his eyes widened with shock. The hand that held the pistol began to tremble, and Keir moved quickly, disarming him a moment before he went down...

...revealing Sarah, a blood-stained blade in her hand and her face pale with fear and shock.

Keir stared at her disbelievingly. If fairies had rushed to his aid in that moment, he would have been less surprised. Although he probably ought to have known, had she not disobeyed him before?

He almost smiled at her. "Sarah, are ye—?" Keir broke off when the other man behind him suddenly fled back through the kitchen, clearly making a run for it. If he were to reach Blackmore, Sarah's life would be forfeit. She had come to Keir's defense, attacking one of her *rescuers* to defend the man who had *kidnapped* her. If Blackmore heard this tale, he would know! He would know it had all been a ruse! He would know she had played him!

Without a second thought, Keir bolted after the man, jumping over a fallen chair and then vaulting over the small table the other man had pushed into his path. The frosty night air engulfed them, slamming into Keir with a startling force. Yet he kept going, his gaze fixed upon the man's receding back as he raced toward the tree line.

Soon, he would be gone, out of Keir's reach and—

A shot rang out, shattering the stillness of the night and bringing the man down. He fell face-forward into the snow and did not rise again.

With his pulse hammering in his ears, Keir pulled to a halt, eyes searching his surroundings. *Is there another? Why then would he fire at one of his own? It makes no sense!*

And then a shadow stepped out of the darkness, a rifle in his hand,

and Keir recognized the face of the hunter. "Ye?" he demanded as the man strode toward him. "Why?" He glanced at the fallen intruder.

The hunter held up a hand, signaling his loyalty. "See to the girl," he told Keir, his voice as kind as before but with a sharp edge of authority. "You need to leave. Tonight." His brows rose meaningfully. "Now. Blackmore knows where you are." He nodded toward the fallen intruder. "I shall take care of them. Go!"

Keir nodded, then he rushed back inside the cabin, loathe to leave Sarah alone with the other two. He could not be certain if the scarred man was dead, and the other one would come to, eventually. He could not say why, but he trusted the hunter. In all likelihood, he had been sent by the dowager. There simply was no other explanation, and he knew that the shrewd woman liked to backup her plans. More than that, she had probably sent the hunter to spy on them, unwilling to be kept in the dark.

Keir almost smiled at the thought of it.

Sarah still stood in the very spot where Keir had left her. She was as white as a sheet, her gaze distant and full of shock. Her hands were trembling, still clutched around the blood-stained blade.

Slowly, Keir approached her. "Sarah?" he addressed her gently, not wishing to startle her.

At the sound of her name, Sarah blinked. Then her gaze cleared, and she looked at him. Instantly, tears welled up in her eyes, and the blade fell from her shaking hands, clattering to the floor. "They came for me, didn't they?"

Keir quickly assured himself that neither of the two men would rise anytime soon. Then he pulled Sarah away and grasped her chin to focus her attention on him alone. "We needa leave," he told her insistently. "I need ye to go upstairs and pack a few things. Dress warmly, and then meet me back down here. Do ye understand?"

Despite her shivers, Sarah nodded, her eyes still filled with tears. "They came for me, did they not?" she asked yet again, and Keir could tell from the look in her eyes that she would not drop the subject.

So finally, he nodded. "They did," he told her honestly. "They wouldna have harmed ye, though. They came to fetch ye back home."

Of course, Keir could not be certain of that; however, there was no need to unsettle Sarah further.

A large tear spilled over and ran down her cheek. "But they hurt you," she said softly, her voice full of anguish as her gaze swept over his face. Her hands reached for him, gently touching his cheeks, shoulders, and arms. Keir did his best not to flinch as his bruises protested against her touch. "Are you hurt badly?" Her eyes rose to meet his again, her vision still blurred. "I'm so sorry. This is my fault. I'm the reason you got hurt. I should never have—"

Keir pulled her closer, his grip on her chin tightening as he looked down into her eyes. "Ye saved my life, little wisp," he told her earnestly, for it was the truth. "If it hadna been for ye, I would no longer be here."

His words tore a sob from Sarah's lips, and she buried her face against his shoulder. "If it had not been for me," she wept, "you would never have been here. I'm the reason you were hurt. I'm the reason you were in danger. If we had never met—"

"I have no regrets," Keir told her gently, needing her to know that he would not have chosen a different path.

Sarah lifted her head to look at him, and Keir knew he could no longer deny how deeply he felt for her. He had done his utmost to ignore the deep longing that had grown day after day. Now, however, he had to admit—at least to himself—that he cared for her.

That she was special to him.

That he would never forget her.

That he had no regrets.

"Neither do I," Sarah suddenly whispered. "I know I should, but I do not." Her large eyes looked into his, and Keir knew that if they did not leave right now, he might forget the world around them and do something unwise.

"Go! Now!" He nodded toward the staircase. "And be quick about it. We need to leave!"

Sarah nodded and then hasted up the stairs. Keir remained below for a moment longer, drawing in a deep breath, before he followed her and went to his own chamber. He dressed quickly and gathered everything essential before rushing back downstairs. Sarah met him there barely a minute later, dressed in her warmest cloak, a small bag slung over her shoulder.

"Can ye ride?" Keir asked, taking her hand. "On Autumn, I mean."

For a moment, Sarah hesitated, old fears sparking up in her eyes. Then, however, she nodded slowly. "Yes, I can," she said, her voice ringing with not so much conviction as determination. It seemed she no longer wanted to be afraid. It seemed she had finally reached that point where facing her fear head-on was no longer the most terrifying thing she could imagine.

And so, without a glance back, they rushed out of the cabin and into the stable, desperate to be on their way, to find safety. Wherever they would find it, Keir could not say. However, he was certain it would be far from here. There was no telling how many of Blackmore's men might linger nearby or would arrive soon. Aye, there was no time to lose. Yet when they led their horses from the stable, Keir could not help but look over his shoulder at the small cabin, remembering the many days Sarah and he had spent here.

Aye, a part of him was sad to leave.

Sad, indeed.

Chapter Thirty-Three
INTO THE UNKNOWN

For a long time, they rode along in silence.

The stillness of the forest felt soothing to Sarah, and the otherworldly glow of the snow-covered landscape was a balm to her wounded soul. She could still feel her insides shaking, her mind unable to abandon the memory of Keir facing death. It felt like a heavy weight crushing her heart and squeezing the breath from her lungs. Again and again, Sarah would shake her head, trying to dislodge the memory. But it always found her again, reminding her of how close she had come to losing him, reminding her of what she had done.

Looking down, Sarah found a small bloodstain upon her right hand, right where her sleeve met her glove. She knew it was there by now, had found it when she had rushed upstairs to her chamber to change. There had been no time to wash, and so it had remained. It was only a drop, and yet it was a constant reminder. Sarah knew she ought not feel guilty, and she did not. But to harm another in such a way had shocked her deeply, and she had not quite recovered.

A soft nicker drifted to Sarah's ears, jarring her from her thoughts, and she leaned forward to pat Autumn's neck. It almost felt as though the mare could sense her distress and meant to offer comfort, more comfort than her softly swaying gait already did.

When Sarah had first pulled herself into the saddle, she had expected to lose her nerve, to feel panic washing over her. Yet none of that had happened. Some old sense of familiarity had fallen over her, as though her body remembered what to do and how good this felt even though her mind and heart had forgotten. Indeed, seated on Autumn's back Sarah felt...safe.

The sun was already rising when Keir slowed his gelding and waited for her to catch up. Concern rested in his gaze, and Sarah could see that he was weighing his next words. He met her eyes, his jaw strangely tense, as though he were torn in two different directions and did not know which one to follow. "There is something I needa say to ye," he finally uttered, a bit of a helpless expression coming to his face. "It makes no sense, but I have to say it, nonetheless." He drew in a slow breath, then pulled Scout to a halt and faced her. "I'm furious that ye left yer chamber, that ye endangered yerself, that ye came downstairs when I told ye not to."

Startled, Sarah blinked. That, she had not expected. "If I had not, you would've...died," she pointed out, unwilling to remember that moment, to draw any attention to it at all.

"I know."

Sarah frowned. "And yet...you're angry with me?"

Keir shrugged, throwing up his hands. "I said it didna make any sense."

"Very well," Sarah replied, not unfamiliar with the feeling of heart and mind running contrary to one another. She knew what it was to deem something right but feel as though it was not. More so than that, Sarah knew the sensation of something being wrong but feeling utterly right.

Keir paused, looking at her, as though he had expected a different reaction. Then, however, he nodded, the look upon his face one of relief that she understood. Still, he, too, seemed unable to drop the subject. "Next time, dunna interfere!" He lifted his brows meaningfully, waiting for her to acknowledge his words.

Sarah felt something inside her snap. *I was brave! In that one moment, I was brave!* She had pushed aside her fears and rushed to his aid! *And what does he do? He—* "I could not let you die!" she retorted, her voice sharp. "And if you're asking me to do so, should we ever find ourselves in such a situation again, then I'm sorry but I'll do the same again!" She held Keir's gaze unflinchingly, wondering what he would do.

Lash out at her?

Chide her again?

He did not.

Instead, he laughed, mirth sparking in his eyes. "Ye're a fierce one, lass. I always knew ye to be." He leaned toward her. "I may not approve of what ye did, but I acknowledge that the choice was yers." A muscle in his jaw twitched, and yet his eyes remained cheerful. "And will be in the future."

"Thank you," Sarah replied, surprised by his words. She had not expected him to disagree with her and still respect her decision. In her experience, people only ever looked at her favorably if she did precisely as they wanted her to.

Sarah cleared her throat, longing to find something else to speak of. "What now? Where are we going?" Her gaze swept over the tall trees surrounding them before she glanced back over her shoulder, half-expecting to see the small cabin that had all but been her home this past fortnight. Would she ever see it again? She doubted it. It was a saddening thought, and Sarah's gaze rose to look upon Keir. Indeed, they were forever linked, the place and the man...

...and the happiest time of her life.

Keir nodded up ahead. "The dowager said, should anything go wrong, I am to take ye to an overgrown spot near a meadow. 'Tis close to a road leading into London." He breathed in deeply, then turned to look at her. "'Tis the very place where I am to return ye to once the ransom has been paid."

Sarah swallowed hard at the mention of their impending farewell. "*Has* the ransom been paid?" she asked, recalling that she had yet to learn what had happened upon his last visit to the inn.

"Not yet," Keir told her as they rode along side by side. "However, the dowager was confident that it would be any day now."

Sarah frowned. "Even after what just happened?" Her mind reluctantly ventured back to the previous night. "The men that... Are they...dead?"

Keir eyed her carefully. "They werena when we left."

"What does that mean?" Sarah asked, feeling a cold chill chase itself down her back. "What if they say something? What if—?"

"They willna," Keir assured her, a look in his eyes that was beyond confident, as though he knew the future. "Ye didna see him, but we had help last night."

Sarah pulled on Autumn's reins, and the mare drew to a halt. "Help? What are you talking about?"

Keir turned Scout around, urging the gelding closer until his knee almost touched hers. "When I pursued that man outside, he was taken down...by the hunter."

Sarah frowned. "The hunter? What—?" Her jaw dropped as recognition flared. "You mean...?"

Keir nodded. "Aye, he was near the cabin last night." He scoffed. "I suppose he has been near the cabin ever since we got there."

Sarah's limbs were trembling. "But why? Who is he?"

Shaking his head in amusement, Keir chuckled, a gesture so reassuring that Sarah felt her pulse begin to slow. "If I'm not at all mistaken," Keir told her, "it was the dowager who sent him."

Sarah stared at him. "To help us?"

Keir laughed. "I suppose mainly to spy on us." He shook his head. "Ye know how she likes to be informed. I have no doubt 'twas the hunter's task to watch us and then report back to her, and only to interfere if need be."

Once again, Sarah wondered how Keir knew the dowager so well. She remembered thinking so before, in the beginning of their time together. Yet Keir had never spoken to her of how he had come to be hired for this task, to protect her, to *kidnap* her. How had Grandma Edie found Keir? How did one go about finding someone trustworthy for a feigned kidnapping?

Indeed, Sarah wished she could ask the dowager a few very specific questions, realizing that she ought to have done so long before agreeing to the lady's plan.

"Ye were brave last night," Keir suddenly murmured, his gaze fixed up ahead. "Ye should know that. Ye're braver than ye give yerself credit for, lass." He turned to meet her eyes. "Never forget that."

Keir's words felt like warm sunshine upon her skin, and yet its warmth rose up into her cheeks and made her avert her eyes in embarrassment.

A deep chuckle rumbled in Keir's throat. "Ye truly ought to learn how to take a compliment, lass."

Ignoring him, Sarah urged Autumn onward, trying her best to regain her composure. She breathed in deeply of the chilling morning air, praying that it would help chase away the warmth in her cheeks. Of course, few people had ever paid her true compliments. They had never had any reason to do so. Never had Sarah accomplished anything of worth. Only last night, she *had* been brave.

Sarah could not deny that she was proud of herself. She was proud that for once fear had not ruled her, that she had been strong enough to overcome it. It had been a proud moment, and she knew she would remember it forever.

"This way!" Keir called, urging Scout down a gentle slope. "Toward the east."

Sarah followed in his wake, allowing Autumn to pick her own path down the slope, trusting in her mare's instincts. After for so long only remembering the horrors she had experienced and forgetting the joys, it truly felt good to do so again. Autumn had become a dear friend, and—

"Loki!"

Keir turned in his saddle, looking at her over his shoulder. "What?"

Sarah brought Autumn to a stop, her heart beating wildly. "We forgot Loki! We left him behind!"

The expression on Keir's face grew tense, and Sarah could see that losing Loki bothered him as well. "We canna go back," he told her calmly, that muscle in his jaw twitching once again. "'Tis not safe. No one will harm him. He's...He's a clever cat, and he will stay out of the way. When all of this is over, I will go back and look for him." His gaze held hers. "I promise."

"Will you bring him to me then?" Sarah asked without thinking, answering that overwhelming desire deep within her to find some way to ensure their paths would cross again.

Keir nodded. "I shall make sure that he is returned to ye."

More than anything, Sarah wanted to wrench a promise from Keir that *he* would be the one to place Loki back in her arms. That *he* would come. *Only his words did not quite say that, did they?*

"How much longer do you think it will be before we hear anything?" Sarah asked, nervous to see their time together come to an end. "How will we know? You don't intend to go back to the inn, do you?"

Keir shook his head. "No, that is not an option. Blackmore might have more men there or somewhere nearby." His shoulders slumped a little, and Sarah could see that he was angry with himself, no doubt considering it his fault that their whereabouts had been discovered by Blackmore's men.

"Then how?"

Keir lifted his head and smiled at her. "Oh, I have no doubt that the hunter will find us when the time comes. After all, the dowager seems to keep him very well informed." He chuckled, shaking his head at his thoughts of the old lady, which once again made Sarah wonder how well he truly knew her. Were they acquainted? The way Keir's eyes lit up when he thought of her made Sarah think that he truly cared for Grandma Edie. How was that possible? She had always assumed that Keir was merely a hired hand, someone who had perhaps been recommended to the dowager for this task. Yet that thought felt unlikely. After all, the dowager could not have inquired among her circle of matrons after a slightly dubious but trustworthy man who might be willing to undertake such a rather outrageous task, could she?

Of course, there was very little Sarah would put past the dowager. The woman was an enigma, and rules did not seem to apply to her as they did to others.

Chapter Thirty-Four

WEE KITTY

Keir's limbs still felt a bit sore, but he knew from experience that the few bruises and cuts he had sustained would heal quickly. He breathed in deeply of the fresh forest air, savoring the sensation of it coursing through his body. Always had he enjoyed being outdoors with no walls around him and no roof over his head. He glanced over his shoulder. Of course, for Sarah, it was different. She might enjoy a ride through the forest or a walk across a meadow, but what would it be like for her to be out here for days?

At midday, they pulled their horses to a halt by a small stream. A quick fire warmed them both, and Keir could tell that Sarah savored the warm tea he put in her hands. Fortunately, he had been prepared for a quick getaway, his saddlebags packed with all the necessities for a trek across country with no inn to stop at.

"How much farther is it?" Sarah asked as they pulled themselves back into the saddle.

"Another day's ride," Keir told her, well aware of the way she paused slightly before nodding. "We shall ride until nightfall and then make camp."

Again, Sarah nodded, not a word of concern or complaint leaving her lips. Keir knew she was worried and felt uncertain, and yet it seemed she trusted him. The thought warmed his heart, making him realize a lot had happened since their first day together. Then, Sarah had been so terrified, so afraid of everything, him included. But now? Now, it seemed she was ready to follow him wherever he led without hesitation.

"What will ye do once the ransom is paid?" Keir asked, feeling the sudden urge to learn more about the future that awaited Sarah. Oddly enough, the knowledge that he would not be a part of it felt utterly strange.

Sighing deeply, Sarah met his gaze. "The plan is to use the ransom to pay my father's debts and pray that he will have learned from this experience."

Keir looked at her doubtfully.

"I know," Sarah replied, a bit of a defeated expression upon her face. "I do not truly believe he will have. However, after...all this, he cannot marry me off again." She exhaled slowly, and a bit of the tension left her face.

"And yer fiancé?" Keir inquired, disliking the word. "Do ye think ye will need to face him?"

A shudder gripped Sarah, but she quickly shook it off and lifted her head. "I do not know. I certainly hope not. However, I might have to... to cry off and end our engagement."

"Ye truly believe he will agree to it?"

Sarah shrugged. "Grandma Edie said he would, and I've never known her to be wrong." She chuckled, no doubt remembering the old lady.

Smiling, Keir nodded. "Neither have I." He paused when the expression upon Sarah's face suddenly changed, became contemplative, her blue eyes watching him in a different manner. Perhaps he had said too much. No doubt Sarah had begun to suspect a deeper connection between him and the Whickertons. After all, how else would he know so much about them?

Still, Keir could not help but worry about Blackmore. How would the man react if after paying the ransom for Sarah's return she then broke their engagement? No doubt it would be a severe blow to the man's pride. *But, will he lick his wounds in peace? Or will he find some way of retribution for the slight against him?*

Keir wished he knew.

When the sun slowly began its descent, Keir chose a spot beneath a small grove and set up the tent he had packed for precisely such a situation. He got a small fire going and once again boiled some water, soon handing Sarah a steaming mug of tea. She was trembling slightly, her eyes wide as she looked past the dancing flames into the dimming world beyond. Darkness was falling, shrouding everything in mystery, creating shadows that seemed otherworldly and frightening.

After a quick meal, Keir bade Sarah climb into the tent and bed down for the night. She nodded and stepped toward it but then paused and looked back at him. "What about you? You cannot sleep out here. It is much too cold."

As though on cue, a handful of snowflakes danced down from over-head, as though the sky agreed with Sarah, working to prove her point.

Keir chuckled. "I will be fine. Dunna worry."

Still, Sarah hesitated. "I...I'm afraid...to be alone...out here." She swept her gaze over their dark surroundings. And once again, as though nature was supporting her, a twig snapped somewhere nearby and Sarah flinched.

"Verra well," Keir relented. "If ye dunna mind."

The corners of her mouth twitched upward into a faint smile. "I do not." Even in the dark, Keir saw a tentative blush come to her cheeks, and he wondered what had caused her embarrassment. Was it the soci-etal wrong of inviting a stranger into her sleeping quarters? Or was it perhaps something else?

Indeed, the thought of sleeping next to Sarah inevitably brought back the memory of how he had drawn her into his arms the night before. Keir still remembered how cold she had been and then how her body had warmed at his touch. She had curled into his embrace, her muscles relaxing, her eyes closing in contented slumber. For a long time, he had simply watched her, enjoying the closeness and marveling at the depth of his feelings in that moment. In truth, they barely knew one another, and yet this time they had spent together so...intimately, there in that cabin, had changed them both. Had brought them closer. *But how much closer? Will more distance between us break the spell?* Keir wondered. *Once Sarah finds herself back with her friends and family, will she still think of me then? Will I, once I'm back in the Highlands?*

Deciding to postpone these thoughts to another day, Keir followed Sarah into the tent. She chose the right-hand side and crawled under the blankets, drawing them close around her shoulders and up under her chin. Keir did the same, keeping an arm's length between them. "Good night," he murmured, hoping she would sleep well.

"Good night to you as well," Sarah replied, closing her eyes and snuggling deeper into the blanket.

For a long time, Keir waited and listened for her breathing, expecting it to even and for her to fall asleep. Yet it did not, even though her eyes remained closed. After a while, the shivers started, and he knew she needed more warmth. A part of Keir cursed the cold, knowing that it was unwise to bring them so close together, while another rejoiced at the thought of holding Sarah in his arms once more.

"Come here, lass," Keir murmured in the dark as he moved closer. "Ye're cold. I can hear yer teeth chattering." He chuckled, holding out his arm to invite her closer.

A quick chuckle left her lips, her voice trembling with shivers. "Y-You m-might b-be r-right." Accepting his invitation without another thought, Sarah slipped closer, her head coming to rest against his shoulder and her body curling into him like the night before.

Keir held her tightly in his arms, rubbing his hands up and down her back. Her skin felt chilled where her forehead touched his jawline, and she still shook from the cold. Willing his warmth into her, Keir began to speak in whispered words, telling Sarah another story of his people, hoping it would lull her to sleep.

Slowly, Sarah's breathing evened, and even Keir could feel slumber tugging upon him. His voice trailed off and his eyes closed. He tightened his arms upon Sarah one more time and then drifted off himself.

To Keir's surprise, they slept until the sun began to rise. As it was winter, it was already late in the day, and Keir wished he had woken sooner. After all, they needed to be on their way.

"Is everything all right?" Sarah asked sleepily as she scooted out of his embrace, that slight blush upon her cheeks once more.

Keir smiled at her. "Ye snore, lass."

Her jaw dropped, and her flush deepened. "I do not!"

Delighted with her reaction, Keir chuckled. "How would ye know that? Do ye often listen to yerself sleep?"

Her mouth opened and closed and then opened again.

"Or do ye often invite others to sleep beside ye?" He had meant to say it lightly; however, the thought of Sarah wrapped in the arms of another stung.

Adorably, Sarah's blush deepened even further. "Sometimes, you're quite horrible," she chided him, pressing her fingers against her cheeks, as though hoping that might wipe away the color. "Why do you always tease me so?"

Keir shrugged. "That I canna say. I suppose 'tis because of that beautiful blush that comes to yer cheeks." He moved toward the opening flap of the tent, smiling at the way she averted her gaze and dug her teeth into her lower lip. "Come. I'll prepare some breakfast." He crawled out into the fresh morning air...only to pull up short when his gaze fell on a familiar brown-gray cat seated beside the remnants of their fire.

"Loki?" Keir mumbled disbelievingly.

The feline all but shook his little head at him, clearly annoyed that Keir had not foreseen his arrival and prepared an appropriate welcome.

Keir laughed. "Sarah, come quick. Ye need to see this." Stepping out of the tent, Keir held out his hand to help her up.

"What is it?" she asked, brushing down her skirts, her knees apparently a bit shaky for her hand tightened upon his. "What do I need to —?" Her voice broke off and her jaw dropped the second her gaze fell on Loki.

For a moment, utter stillness hung over their little campsite, the only sound the chilling breeze as it blew through the fir trees surrounding them or perhaps the faint gurgling of a nearby brook.

Then, however, a wide smile exploded onto Sarah's face, and she swept the feline into her arms. "Loki! I feared I'd never see you again! How did you come to be here?" She looked from the cat to Keir.

Keir shrugged. "Dunna ask me." He grinned at the feline. "*That* is clearly not a normal cat." He stepped toward them and reached out to brush a hand over Loki's head. "But I'm glad ye found yer way back to us, *wee kitty*."

Loki looked clearly affronted at his words whereas Sarah suddenly stilled, a look of sadness washing over her face.

Keir frowned. "Is everything all right?"

Shaking her head, she willed a smile back onto her face. "Of course. Yes. Everything's all right." She exhaled. "Of course, it is."

Keir could not help but shake the feeling that something was, indeed, wrong. Yet he could not fathom what it was. Clearly, Sarah had been overjoyed to see Loki again. What then had suddenly brought her spirits down?

He wished he knew.

Chapter Thirty-Five

A FINAL FAREWELL

The moment the clearing came into sight, Sarah felt her heart wither. Of course, she had known this moment would come, and yet rationally, somehow, a part of her had clung to the belief...that it would not.

"Come!" Keir called, his right hand pointing toward the higher tree line. "We'll make camp up there. It'll give us a good view." He spurred on Scout and rushed ahead.

Sarah followed with Loki in her arms. Of course, she was relieved that the little feline was all right, that he had followed them through the wilderness, and yet all hopes of seeing Keir again after this endeavor ended were now dashed.

The meadow below bordered the woods, half-encircled on one side while the other opened up toward the far country, the road leading up from town farther south. Indeed, it seemed like a good place to hide out. Anyone approaching they could see from far down the road, allowing Keir to stay hidden and then make his escape once Sarah was back with her family. Sarah did not even want to think of what would happen if her father or Blackmore caught sight of him, discovered his identity.

No, what had truly happened on this adventure would forever

remain her secret. She would never speak of it to anyone, cherishing every moment until the end of her days. Sarah heaved a deep sigh, wondering right then and there if she would ever again feel this deeply.

Dejectedly, Sarah watched as Keir set up their campsite. She wanted to help. She knew she ought to help. Yet her feet would not move. Her mind remained distant and foggy, and she felt tears lingering nearby. Loki stayed at her side, crawling into her lap, as though he knew about the sadness in her heart. *Can he sense it? Is he, too, disappointed that our little world in the woods came to an end? Did he miss us when we left him behind?*

As Keir prepared their evening meal, a shadow suddenly fell over them, startling Sarah and making her clutch Loki even more tightly in her arms.

Right there, as though he had risen from the ground, stood the hunter, his clothes not unlike Keir's, colors of the forest, easily hiding him from sight. His rifle was slung over one shoulder, and he pushed back the hood of his cloak as he stepped toward them.

"'Tis all right," Keir told her with a sideways glance. "He is no danger to us." He met the hunter's gaze. "Is that not so?"

The man chuckled good-naturedly. "I thought I'd proved that last night."

Keir shrugged. "In a situation like this, one ought to be careful, would you not agree?" Without waiting for an answer, he stepped forward. "What message does the dowager send?"

The hunter's expression sobered. "The ransom was paid." He glanced at Sarah, and she felt a cold chill descend upon her. "She is to be returned to her parents tomorrow at daybreak. Down there." He nodded toward the meadow below.

Sarah blinked back tears, then lifted her gaze and looked at Keir. He, too, seemed...distressed by this message. *Or am I mistaken? Am I seeing something that is not there?*

"Verra well," Keir finally replied, his jaw tense and his gaze not once meeting hers. "Anything else?"

"Keep yourself hidden once they arrive," the hunter instructed. "I shall remain nearby and watch over her."

"What of Blackmore's men?" Keir inquired, a slight frown upon his face as he watched the other man carefully.

The hunter tried not to smile. "I delivered them to the authorities, and the dowager said she would see to them, ensure that," he paused, clearly considering the right words, "that they would receive fair punishment."

Sarah wondered how the dowager could possibly ensure that. After all, she held no political position. No woman did. Yet—

Keir chuckled. "I have no doubt." He nodded to the hunter in gratitude. "Thank ye for yer help last night."

The man nodded in return, then he moved to leave. "Good luck." A moment later, he was gone, swallowed up by the forest, as though he had never even been there.

For a long time, neither one of them spoke. While Sarah remained seated with Loki in her arms, Keir busied himself around the campsite, ensuring that they would have more firewood than they would ever need.

"I'd love to show ye the highlands," Keir suddenly said, glancing over to her as he stoked the fire. "'Tis beautiful country up there." He paused, then offered her a sheepish grin. "But it does get mighty cold."

Sarah smiled, feeling warmed by his words and the picture they painted. "I would like that."

Keir's hands stilled, and he looked at her for a long moment. Then he said, "Perhaps one day."

Sarah nodded. "Perhaps one day."

Again, silence fell and lingered until Keir spoke up, his warm, deep voice once again telling a tale of his people. And Sarah listened, enraptured, clinging to the peacefulness of the moment and pretending—if only for a moment—that it would never end.

When the sun had finally disappeared and the air had grown colder, they crawled back into the tent. Only this time, Sarah snuggled into Keir's embrace without a second thought, and his arm came around her as though it belonged there. Neither one of them spoke, each lost in their own thoughts, Loki curled up somewhere by their feet.

Outside, an owl hooted, and the wind blew through the trees something fierce while Sarah felt warm and safe...and heartbreakingly sad.

She felt Keir's rhythmic pulse beneath her ear and listened to his slow and calm breaths as he slowly drifted off to sleep. Yet Sarah's mind was wide awake, her fingers curled into Keir's coat as though she could keep him at her side by sheer willpower. How could she sleep now when in only a few hours she would have to bid him goodbye forever? It seemed every fiber of her clung to these last few hours, chasing away her exhaustion.

As she had two nights ago, Sarah turned slowly to look at Keir's face, his eyes closed in slumber. His chest rose with each peaceful breath, and she sighed deeply, allowing his calm to wash over her. Slowly, the uproar in her heart quieted and her mind cleared.

Slipping a hand free from the nest of blankets around them, Sarah reached out to touch Keir, gently tracing the line of his jaw, imagining his lips quirking upward into a teasing smile.

Forever would she remember him like this.

"I shall miss you," Sarah whispered into the stillness of the night. "My heart breaks at the thought of never seeing you again."

Suddenly, a muscle in Keir's jaw twitched and in the next instant, he was on top of her, his mouth claiming hers.

Sarah's senses reeled in shock, unable to adjust to this new reality as swiftly as it had broken over her like a wave rushing onto a beach. Yet her body responded to Keir's touch instinctively, her hands reaching up to pull him closer, her fingers digging into his hair. A part of her could not believe this was truly happening while another simply did not care. Dream or reality, what did it matter? Only this could not possibly be a dream, could it?

After all, it felt so...

He felt so...

Keir kissed her deeply, thoroughly, his right hand trailing up her neck, his fingertips a teasing caress against her skin. She felt him linger where her pulse thundered wildly, and a rumbling hum resonated against her lips. She gasped, and his hand slipped to the back of her neck, cradling her head and holding her close.

So close.

Yet not close enough.

Sarah wished—

A soft weight suddenly landed beside them, and they both flinched, pulling apart, only to find Loki gazing at them, his yellow eyes glowing in the dark.

Sarah's breath came fast, and as she looked up, she saw Keir close his eyes and hang his head. "I suppose I shouldna have done this," he murmured, then he looked down at her before moving to lie beside her once more. "Come, lass," he whispered, pulling her against him, his arm draping around her shoulders. "Sleep now. Morning will be here soon."

If only it wouldn't, Sarah thought as she snuggled into Keir's embrace, disappointed at having this last perfect moment interrupted. If only she were not such a coward! If only she dared take a leap of faith and find out if a similar feeling lived in Keir's heart!

Perhaps tomorrow.

Or never.

Chapter Thirty-Six

GOING HOME

S arah woke the next morning with a heavy weight upon her heart. It was not the kind of waking when for, at least, a few seconds one does not remember what transpired the day before nor the effects it might have upon one's life. No, it was indeed the kind of waking when reality stands all but crystal clear before one the second one's eyes blink open.

Reaching out her hand, Sarah found the place beside her empty. Her heart sank instantly, and she turned her head to confirm that Keir was indeed gone. He had already risen, and as she listened, she could hear him move about outside. Somehow, she had hoped that they would wake up together, perhaps share another close moment, that perhaps he would whisper a few words of farewell.

Now, that was not to be.

Ignoring the deep regret that settled in her heart, Sarah stepped out of the tent, blinking her eyes against the bright sunlight reflecting upon the snow everywhere. Never before had the world seemed so blinding, so much aglow, so beautiful. Yet in that moment, Sarah could not appreciate it.

"Are ye hungry?" Keir asked from where he knelt by the fire. For a moment, his gaze remained fixed upon the dancing flames before he finally looked up and met her eyes. "Ye're finally returning home."

Sarah thought to hear a touch of regret in his voice, wondering instantly if she had truly heard it, if it had truly been there or perhaps if she had simply imagined it. "I don't think I can eat anything," Sarah replied, settling upon the small log she had occupied the night before. "My stomach is in knots." Somehow, she wanted him to know that this farewell weighed heavily upon her, and yet she did not dare speak clearly. *Why do I not dare? It is the easiest thing in the world, is it not?*

Loki came tiptoeing over and settled on her lap, a comforting soft weight, anchoring her to the here and now. He looked up at her, his wide eyes kind and compassionate before he brushed his head against her hand, purring softly.

"What happens now?" Sarah asked, trying her best to speak around the lump that had settled in her throat.

Keir cleared his throat. "We wait here," he said and then lifted his gaze, his eyes finding the meadow down below, the road leading up from London. "The moment we see yer family arriving, ye can go down into the meadow and meet them."

Sarah nodded, her gaze fixed upon the purring cat in her lap, upon the movement of her hand as she stroked his fur. "And you?"

Again, Keir cleared his throat. "I shall remain here. Out of sight." Out of the corner of her eye, Sarah noticed him lift his head and look at her. "Ye dunna need to worry. The hunter is nearby. He will watch over ye. Everything will go as planned."

I want you to watch over me, Sarah thought quietly to herself. *Not him. You.*

If only she dared say these words out loud. In fact, there was so much on her mind, so much to say. Here they were, moments away from never seeing each other again, and yet Sarah still could not find the courage to speak her heart. She did not quite know what it was she felt for Keir, but she knew she felt something deep and all-consuming, something that was growing bit by bit every day. Where it might lead, she could not say, but she longed to find out. She wanted the chance to speak to him again, to laugh with him, to hear him tease her. Yes, she even wanted to feel herself blush again when he cast her one of those looks, one that reached deep inside her very core. Sarah wanted all that and more. And yet...

Silence lingered, neither one of them able to find simple words, easy conversation. Occasionally, their eyes would meet, and the silence that lingered would become uncomfortable. Sarah could not help but wonder if perhaps she had been wrong about the bond that she had felt come into existence between them. Had it simply been the magic of the moment, being locked away together in frosty winter, danger looming over their heads? Perhaps it had been nothing more than that. Perhaps Keir said nothing because he already knew it to be true.

And so, moment after moment passed until Keir suddenly stood, his eyes directed down the road. Before he even spoke, Sarah knew what he would say. "Riders are approaching. A carriage follows them."

Sarah nodded, then sat Loki down on his paws and rose to her feet. As much as she needed the little feline's presence, the comfort he offered, she could not leave without—

Panic swept through Sarah's being as she found the moment of farewell upon her. Each second she hesitated, she found slipping away.

Wasted.

Steeling herself, she looked across the fire at Keir, at the hard contours of his face, for once not softened by humor and mirth. He looked tense. Dangerous even.

Sarah almost smiled when a not-too-distant memory suddenly surfaced. Though it seemed far away, she recalled with ease how she had first looked at Keir, how he had even frightened her. She had thought him a criminal without honor, someone who might pose a danger to her, someone she ought to guard herself from. Oh, she had been so very wrong. After all, now, there was no one else in the world with whom she felt safer.

Casting her a small smile, Keir moved around the fire and came toward her. "I suppose this is it," he said, his words hesitant. He reached for her hands, holding them gently within his own. "'Twas an honor to meet ye, little wisp." His blue eyes glowed brightly as they looked into hers. "I shall always remember our time together fondly, and I wish ye all the best, all the happiness ye can hope for. Ye deserve it." He grinned at her, tilting his head downward to peek deeper into her eyes. "Never forget how brave ye are, how fierce. The rest of the world may not recognize it, but 'tis who ye are."

Tears pooled in Sarah's eyes, and Keir's image blurred. "Thank you," she said in a trembling voice. "Thank you for all you've done. Not simply for helping me with this...this ruse." She heaved a deep sigh, her hands tightening upon his. "Thank you for all your advice and counsel, all your encouragement and...all your faith in me." She sniffed, shaking her head. "I shall never forget it." *Oh, I ought to have said* 'I shall never forget you'. *Why didn't I?*

Sighing deeply, Sarah bowed her head in defeat. "I suppose I should go." She turned away, her mind in a daze and her heart hurting so acutely that she thought it would surely stop.

Keir's hands never released hers. Instead, he pulled her back, pulled her close and kissed her.

And Sarah kissed him back.

This time, his touch did not overwhelm her. No, this time, Sarah knew what she wanted, and although she could not seem to bring herself to say the words, she found she was bold enough to return Keir's kiss most ardently.

Pushing herself up onto her toes, she slipped her hands onto his shoulders and then higher into his hair. She clung to him, desperate to hold on, savoring the feel of his firm embrace, as though he, too, felt as she did.

"Ye need to go, lass," Keir murmured against her lips, his voice breathless, "and try to look shaken." He grinned at her, yet his eyes held sadness. "Ye were kidnapped, remember? By an unscrupulous man!"

Sarah chuckled. *Oh, I will miss him so much!*

Brushing another soft kiss onto Keir's lips, Sarah spun upon her heel and then hurriedly walked away. "Don't look over your shoulder," she whispered to herself as her feet carried her swiftly away. "Don't look at him," she continued to plead with herself. "If you look at him, you will not be able to go." On and on, she went, her vision blurring as tears filled her eyes and then spilled over and down her cheeks. Only Sarah kept walking and walking until the ground slowly leveled out and she found herself down below in the meadow.

Lifting her head, Sarah saw riders approaching quickly, a carriage following close behind. She stopped and waited, watching them draw closer. Soon, she recognized one of the riders as her father, wondering in that moment what he might be thinking. Was he disappointed in her? Had he been worried?

Sarah's gaze moved to the other rider, and although she could not yet see his face, she knew it to be her fiancé. *Oh, how I loathe that word!* It never failed to send chills down her back. He held himself proudly, not like her father, his movements commanding and measured. Sarah shuddered at the thought of standing before him, of coming face to face with him again. *Will he be able to see that I was not truly kidnapped? That the past fortnight was the happiest of my life?*

Wiping the tears from her face, Sarah inhaled a deep breath...and then turned to look over her shoulder. She could not see Keir up on the slope, but she knew without a doubt that he was there. "Farewell," she whispered, knowing that their path would never cross again. How could they? They were worlds apart, after all. She did not even know his full name. In truth, she knew very little about him. Perhaps this had been a dream after all, and now it was time to wake up.

To return to reality.

Lifting her chin, Sarah reminded herself of what she needed to do. Yes, she needed to play the part of the shaken victim, and yet she needed to be strong to shape her own future, to find a way to be free to make her own choices. Yes, Keir would want her to do that.

Chapter Thirty-Seven

EXCHANGE

Albert still could not believe that he had been forced to pay the ransom. After Mr. Smith had failed to make contact as agreed upon, Albert could not refuse to ensure Miss Mortensen's safe return. He still had no notion of what had gone wrong; yet clearly, something had to have gone wrong. It seemed Mr. Smith—generally, a very reliable man—had disappeared from the face of the earth. Neither had any of his associates reported back to Albert.

Perhaps he had underestimated the kidnappers. Had he made a mistake that—? *Oh, I hate finding fault with myself! I much prefer finding fault with others!*

Kicking his horse's flanks, Albert charged ahead, his eyes trained upon the lone figure standing in the clearing. Morning dew still lingered, casting a bit of an eerie atmosphere over the snow-covered meadow bordering the forest. Albert looked up, wondering if any of the kidnappers still lingered nearby. *Are they watching?*

Anger sizzled beneath his skin. Oh, he did not care how long it would take, but he would make them pay! He would ensure that they came to rue the day they had decided to cross him!

"Sarah!" Hartmore called out to his daughter, urging his mare to catch up with Albert's stallion. "Sarah!"

Reaching the girl, Albert pulled the black beast he was riding to a halt. It snorted and stamped its hooves, close to rearing up. Albert greatly approved of the horse's temper as it so clearly matched his own. What Albert also approved of was the way the stallion tended to intimidate others, making them shrink back, their eyes fearful and wary of the beast's hooves.

All the ride here, Albert had imagined seeing such an expression upon Miss Mortensen's face. Indeed, he deserved to see such a look upon her face! After all, had he not just spent a small fortune on procuring her safety?

Yet as Albert's gaze dropped to look at her, he saw neither wariness nor fear of any kind. He saw not even hesitation. She remained where she was, did not even take a step back to put more distance between herself and the stomping beast he sat atop. No, her gaze swept over his stallion with curious interest instead.

In that moment, Albert wanted to ride her down. How could she not even have the decency to grant him this small mercy? Was it truly too much for him to ask to see fear in her eyes?

With his pulse thundering wildly in his neck, Albert dismounted. Then he moved toward her, his gaze hard as it swept over her features. He drew himself up tall, shoulders back and his chin lifted. Looking down at her, he asked, "Miss Mortensen, are you all right?"

The girl's eyes flashed to him before she nodded shyly, her gaze dropping to the ground, as though she were suddenly fearful. Why now? Albert wondered, eyeing her more closely.

"Sarah!" Hartmore pulled to a halt beside him, dismounted as quickly as an indulgent man his age could, then he rushed toward his daughter. He grasped her by the arms, staring into her face, before hugging her to him, almost crushing her in a tight embrace.

To Albert, the girl looked startled. Confused even. It was clear, that her father had never before shown such affection or concern. Indeed, Albert had not known the Mortensens to be a tight-knit family. They were not like the Whickertons.

"Are you all right, Sarah?" Hartmore inquired, cupping his hands to her face and looking into her eyes. "Are you...hurt?"

Still looking confused, the girl shook her head. "I'm unharmed, Father."

Albert took a step closer. "What can you tell us about your kidnappers?"

A shudder went through the girl, and she dropped her gaze, wrapping her arms around herself. "I... I...," she stammered. "I'm afraid not much." Her eyes flashed upward, meeting his for only a split second, before they returned to the ground. "I was blindfolded most of the time, my hands and feet tied." She closed her eyes, as though trying to block out a painful memory. "I'm sorry." Again, she met his gaze for the length of a heartbeat. "I'm sorry I cannot tell you more."

"How many were there?" Albert demanded, annoyed with this lack of information, annoyed even more that the girl clearly did not deem it necessary to express her gratitude for what he had done for her.

Miss Mortensen shrugged. "I'm uncertain. Two or perhaps three. I don't know."

"How did they express themselves?" Albert pressed, moving closer, his gaze trained upon her. "When they addressed you, how did they speak? Were they English? Noblemen? Or commoners?"

The girl stilled, perhaps hesitated, before finally nodding. "English, yes. At least, I think so. It...They did not speak like us. Their words often confused me."

Albert suspected that the men who had taken her might have been common criminals, their language a representation of their low birth. Certainly, the daughter of a baron would be confused by their way of expressing themselves.

"I'm tired, Father," Miss Mortensen said with a deep sigh, her hands reaching out to her father's. "Please, can we go home?"

Wrapping an arm around his daughter, Hartmore led her toward the carriage. "Of course, my dear. Of course, you need rest. Please, do not worry. You are safe now. We shall take you home."

Albert heaved a deep sigh, annoyed with the developments of the day...and it had barely begun. Still, watching father and daughter walk toward the carriage, Albert could not help but frown. Something... struck him as odd.

Something *about Miss Mortensen* struck him as odd.

Indeed, the girl had seemed shaken, frightened, and yet the look in her eyes...

Granted, Miss Mortensen had not dared look at him for longer than a split second. Still, Albert felt certain that he was missing something, that something had transpired that he had no knowledge of. But what could that be?

Albert did not know.

What he did know was that he would find out.

Chapter Thirty-Eight

BACK TO THE WHICKERTONS

Once the riders and carriage had disappeared from sight, Keir packed up their small campsite, doused the last flames of the fire and then mounted Scout, leading Autumn by the reins. Loki had surprised him by disappearing into the forest. At first, Keir wanted to go after him. Yet a part of him could not help but think that the mischievous feline would surely find his way back to him. And so, instead, he made his way back toward the cabin, reaching it the next day a little before sunset.

There, he spent the night, a rather long and wakeful night, before packing up the remaining chickens and attaching the small crates to Autumn's back and tying the goat to Scout's saddle. He knew a nearby farm, perhaps half a day's ride to the west. The farmer had a large family and would certainly appreciate a handful of chickens and a goat.

As expected, Loki returned come morning, demanding his usual saucer of milk, his gaze wide and searching the small kitchen. Then, he looked up at Keir, who could not shake the feeling that the feline was inquiring after Sarah's whereabouts.

"She's not here, *wee kitty*."

Loki glared at him and then lapped up his milk eagerly.

Riding through the snowy countryside, Keir often found himself lost in thought. Oddly enough, he had very little attention for the world around him, a world which before had never failed to draw him in. Only right now, all he could think about was Sarah. He thought about the time they had spent together, and he thought about where she was right now and what she was doing. He prayed she was all right.

More than anything, Keir wanted to see her again, was resolved that he would. Yet he could not have told her so. First, he needed to speak to the dowager. He needed to know what had happened upon Sarah's return to London.

And so, once he had delivered the chickens and the goat to the farmer's family, Keir hastened back toward London, eager for news. He rode straight to the Whickertons' townhouse, handed Scout and Autumn to the stable hands, and then walked inside, demanding to see the dowager.

Loki followed upon his heels, startling the servants.

"He'd like a saucer of milk," Keir translated the feline's overbearing attitude to those unfamiliar with his comportment. Then he was shown into the drawing room.

The dowager sat in her favorite armchair by the fire, a blanket wrapped around her legs and a cup of tea on the small table beside her. Her pale eyes watched him intently as he walked in, Loki at his side, and Keir thought he saw a small smile play across her features. "Welcome back, my boy." She grinned at the cat. "And you've brought company as well."

Keir smiled. "'Tis good to be back," he said, immediately wondering if he even spoke the truth. "This is Loki."

"Is it?" The dowager inquired, momentarily ignoring the feline, which Loki clearly disliked.

Refusing to play the dowager's game, Keir seated himself in the chair on the opposite end of the fireplace while Loki curled up in front of it. "I hope everything went according to plan," he said, trying his best not to give the dowager any reason to be suspicious. Indeed, more often than not, the old woman was like a bloodhound! "I hear the ransom was paid." He lifted his brows meaningfully.

The dowager laughed. "Are you truly surprised I had someone posted near the cabin?"

Keir chuckled. "I was at first," he admitted, "before I realized I shouldna have been."

"You cannot blame me for wanting to ensure your safety," the dowager replied with an utterly earnest expression upon her face.

Keir laughed. "That is one explanation, I suppose. However, an even better one is that ye simply wished to remain informed at all times."

Grandma Edie chuckled, shifting in her seat. "You know me too well, my boy." She sighed and then leaned back, watching him curiously. "Is there something you wish to ask?"

Keir paused and leaned forward, resting his elbows upon his legs. If he wished to know, he would need to be honest. It was the price the dowager demanded. "So, the ransom was paid?"

The dowager nodded, not offering anything more.

A quick knock sounded upon the door, and Loki received his requested saucer of milk. Once the maid had disappeared again, Keir asked, "And was it already used to pay Lord Hartmore's gambling debts?"

"We are in the process of seeing it through right now." Again, not another word passed her lips.

Keir sighed and leaned back. "What will happen to Sa-Miss Mortensen now? Did Blackmore agree to ending their engagement?"

For a long moment, Grandma Edie did not say a word. Then her shrewd gaze narrowed. "Why are you asking?"

Shaking his head, Keir grinned at her. "I might as well ask something else," he told her with a meaningful look in his eyes. "For example, I might ask why it took so long to deliver the final ransom note." He lifted his brows for emphasis.

The dowager chortled, clearly amused. "You noticed that, did you now?" Then she shrugged. "What can I say? Some things can be...made to take time." The corner of her mouth twitched. "What is it you're asking?"

Keir knew very well that by asking, he was also revealing something deeply profound, something he had not even yet accepted himself given the circumstances. Only he had never liked secrets, much preferred honesty and directness to half-truths and lies. It had not been easy tiptoeing along that line over the past fortnight, being honest to gain Sarah's trust while keeping essential details from her in order to ensure their safety. "I suppose what I'm asking is," he paused, holding her gaze, "are ye matchmaking again?"

A slow grin came to the dowager's face. "What can I say? I'm *always* matchmaking."

Chuckling, Keir hung his head. "'Tis not an answer."

"Let me ask you something in return. Should—"

Keir shook his head, once again amazed by the dowager's way of holding a conversation, which, in truth, was not a conversation at all. After all, the woman revealed very little. "Ye would ask me a question without answering mine first?"

There was a twinkle in the old lady's eyes. "It is rude to interrupt the elderly, did your grandmother not teach you that?" she asked teasingly, her eyes lighting up at the thought of her oldest friend.

Keir ran a hand through his hair. He ought to have known that she would answer like this, without truly answering at all. The woman knew how to speak while revealing nothing better than anyone else Keir knew. "Well, she taught me to be honest and helpful," he replied with a chuckle.

"Honest, you say?" the dowager mused. "Well, then tell me," she paused, and her gaze fixed upon his more intently, "should Miss Mortensen require your help in the future, may I call upon you again?"

Keir stilled, feeling a cold shiver trail down his back. "Why would ye ask that?" He frowned. "Did something go wrong? Is Sarah all right?"

With a pleased smile, the dowager waved his concerns away. "Be assured that *Miss Mortensen* is perfectly fine. In fact, I—"

The door flew open, and in stormed Christina, Harriet following close upon her heels. Both young women looked agitated, yet it was curiosity that sparked in their eyes.

"Keir!" Harriet exclaimed, her green eyes lighting up as she rushed toward him. "It is so good to see you! What happened? Tell us everything!"

The dowager laughed. "Harry, will you let the poor man settle in first before you hound him with questions? There will be more time to talk later."

While Harriet looked severely disappointed and close to arguing her point, Christina stepped toward Keir, her blue eyes narrowing in concern. "Is Sarah all right?" she asked quietly. "I mean, while you were...gone. She was not terribly frightened the whole time, was she?"

Keir knew well that the dowager was listening intently, yet he could not deny Christina the relief she needed. "No, she wasna frightened. She was nervous at first, of course, but later she settled in quite nicely."

Closing her eyes, Christina exhaled a deep breath. "Oh, I'm so glad. So, so glad." She grasped his hands. "Thank you so much for looking after her."

"Will you stay for the ball a sennight from today?" Harriet inquired, a shrewd look not unlike her grandmother's coming to her green eyes. "Everyone's invited." Something wicked seemed to tease her lips as they curled upward.

A frown came to Keir's face, and he turned to look at the dowager, who nodded in agreement. "Certainly, stay," she said. "You've been gone awhile, and it will be a wonderful opportunity to reacquaint ourselves."

Keir could all but see the little cogs in the dowager's head turning. *She is up to something!* Keir was certain of it. He only wished he knew what it was! *Can it possibly have something to do with Sarah? Will she be at the ball?*

"'Twill be my pleasure," Keir agreed, nodding his head at the dowager.

Harriet clapped her hands together delightedly. "Splendid!" Then she spun around and looked at her grandmother. "Will Sarah still be marrying Lord Blackmore?"

At Harriet's question, Keir felt himself tense, the suggestion shaking him to his core.

"Of course not!" Christina exclaimed, her face slightly paler than before. "Right, Grandma? She's not going to marry him, is she?"

For a moment, the dowager's contemplative gaze rested upon Keir, and he knew had they been alone in the room, she would not have answered him directly. She would have found some way to be vague, to speak in riddles as she always did. Yet she could not deny Christina either. "Of course not, my child. Don't worry! I'm on my way to see Sarah now." Her gaze met Keir's. "I promise I shall take care of everything."

Christina exhaled a deep sigh of relief, and Keir felt his own body relax as well. He wished he could join the dowager, but, of course, that was impossible. He would have to be patient, for even though Grandma Edie had answered none of his questions, he could not shake the feeling that this journey was not over yet.

Far from it.

He liked that.

He liked that very much.

Chapter Thirty-Nine

CONFRONTATION

Before leaving London, Sarah had expected to feel relief upon returning home after her feigned kidnapping had come to an end. And now, here she stood, back in her own chamber and what she felt was not relief.

Perhaps a small measure of it.

But no more.

Truth be told, if there was any place in this world where Sarah would want to be, it was the cabin in the woods. It was by Keir's side. Not in her wildest dreams could Sarah have imagined such a change of heart. She could never have imagined that her life would be turned upside down by a mere fortnight.

Yet I have changed, have I not? I am no longer the woman I was before. Yes, the essence of her character remained, but there were significant differences now.

Sarah had already penned a letter to Kate, determined to reconnect with her sister. Life had led them in opposite directions, but the Sarah she was today would no longer simply accept what was. No, she would do everything within her power to bring Kate back into her life. Her parents might object—although her father had been strangely thoughtful these last few days—but Sarah did not care. She would not again bow her head and allow them to rule her life.

After all, she was free now, or she would be free soon, as soon as she spoke to her fiancé.

Knocking on the door to her father's study, Sarah waited for him to bid her to enter. Then she inhaled deeply, reminding herself of her purpose, and strode across the threshold.

"Sarah!" her father exclaimed, his face lighting up, as though he were truly happy to see her. He all but jumped to his feet and, rounding his desk, came toward her. "How are you, my dear?"

Sarah did not quite know what to make of her father, of this strange behavior of his. "I'm all right," she told him, then withdrew her hands from his and moved over to the window. What she had to say was not easy, and perhaps it would be best if her father could not see her eyes.

A small smile played over Sarah's features as she recalled the many times Keir had told her she was an awful liar, that every thought was written upon her face. "I came to speak with you about something," Sarah began, casting him a quick glance from over her shoulder before directing her gaze back out the window at the street below. "It is not something...easily spoken of."

Her father's footsteps drifted to her ears, and she listened as he moved closer. "What is it?"

Sarah swallowed hard. "It is about my engagement to Lord Blackmore," she began hesitantly, her voice trembling for real, her hands shaking. "I'm afraid I...cannot become his wife." Linking her arms, she bowed her head and waited.

For a long time, her father said nothing, and Sarah wondered what he might be thinking, what conclusions he might be drawing from what she had said. "Why?" he finally asked, that one word ringing with apprehension and a deep sense of discomfort to discuss this matter.

"Well, I—"

Angry footsteps suddenly thundered out in the hall before the door flew open, connecting hard with the wall, and in walked none other than Lord Blackmore. A sneer rested upon his features, and his eyes were cold as he fixed them upon Sarah's father. "Hartmore, I need to speak with you! I heard that—" He broke off when he took note of Sarah's presence. "Miss Mortensen." He cleared his throat. "Good day to you."

Panic seized Sarah's heart. *I'm not ready for this! I cannot do this, not with him here! Every time he looks at me, I...*

"Good day, my lord," Sarah managed to force past her dry lips, reminding herself not to give in to the panic that throbbed in her heart.

Her father cleared his throat, nervousness lingering in his gaze. "Blackmore, now is not a good time. I was just speaking to my daughter, and—"

"I cannot marry you!" Sarah blurted out before she could lose her nerve. How she could ever have thought she could do this was beyond her. Her hands were shaking so badly she had to dig her fingers into her arms to keep them still.

Lord Blackmore's gaze narrowed. "Pardon me?" Those two words sounded like a threat, conveying all the darkness, all the evil she had always glimpsed in his eyes. "Why ever not?"

Sarah closed her eyes, forcing her mind to recall what she had rehearsed a hundred times. "Our...Our engagement was based on... specific conditions," she began, her voice trembling, trembling even more when Lord Blackmore moved toward her. "These...conditions are no longer met." Unable to stand her ground, Sarah abandoned her spot by the window and moved closer to her father, watching Lord Blackmore circle around her like a hawk cornering its prey.

"What conditions are you referring to, Miss Mortensen?" he all but hissed, his hands linked behind his back, as though he knew himself close to losing control and fought to retain it.

Sarah licked her lips, trying her best to recall what to say. "Well, during my...While I was..." The world began to sway in front of her eyes, and she grasped her father's arm to keep herself upon her feet.

"Blackmore," her father said, placing his own hand upon hers. "Perhaps right now is not the right time. As you can see, my daughter is—"

"She will answer me!" Lord Blackmore growled menacingly, and Sarah was loath to see her father grow smaller under the other man's hateful glare.

Sarah knew no one would come to aid her. Not her parents. Certainly not Keir. No, if she wanted to be free, she would have to free herself. Remembering Keir's words, how he had urged her to remember her strength, Sarah lifted her chin and met Blackmore's gaze. "I apologize, my lord. The last thing I wish to do is disappoint you." The words felt awful upon her tongue, but she managed to say them. "Unfortunately, I must inform you that I am no longer the... innocent woman...I once was." She dropped her gaze briefly, before reminding herself to stand tall. "So, you see, that our union cannot be. It would be unfair to you, and I respect you too much to put this burden upon you." Sarah wanted to retch, but she held herself in place, not flinching under Lord Blackmore's scrutinizing gaze.

The pulse in the man's neck thundered wildly, and fury stood in his eyes. "Is that so?" he snarled, suspicion ringing loud and clear in his voice.

And then he moved.

He moved toward her with threatening speed, every bit of distance that vanished between them sending Sarah's heart into a faster gallop. She shrank back, closer toward the open door in her back, yet her feet would not turn and run. She felt all but frozen, unable to move aside, even though she saw the danger coming.

Then, out of nowhere, a small blur flew past her, flinging itself at Blackmore with a ferocious hiss.

Stunned, Sarah blinked and blinked again, unable to believe her eyes. "Loki?"

The feline was clawing at Blackmore's vest, half hanging upon his arm and half seated upon his shoulder. He snarled and hissed, dodging Blackmore's attempts to throw him off.

Completely caught off guard by Loki's attack, Blackmore all but danced on the spot, flinging his arms and growling under his breath. His eyes went back and forth between narrowed in anger and widened in shock as he tried to grab a hold of his little attacker and fling him aside. Loki, however, was made of sterner stuff, unwilling to surrender, unwilling to accept defeat. His claws dug in deep, and Blackmore howled in rage and pain.

All the while, Sarah's father fluttered around the other man, waving his arms as though trying to shoo Loki away. He looked flustered and completely at a loss as to what to do. He clearly knew that he ought to help, that it would not serve him if he allowed Lord Blackmore to come to any harm; yet the situation was far beyond his abilities to handle.

Sarah knew what that felt like, for she simply stood and stared in shock, unable to move, unable to think. All she could do was watch... until all of a sudden, the soft sound of approaching footsteps reached her ears. The sound was accompanied by another, one that reminded Sarah of a walking cane meeting the hardwood floors.

Before she even turned, an image of Grandma Edie flashed through Sarah's mind, and a moment later, the old lady came hobbling into the room, one hand clasping her favorite walking cane while the other rested upon her grandson's arm. Troy Beaumont, only son and heir to Lord Whickerton, stood beside his grandmother, his scrutinizing gaze taking in the scene, his expression unreadable as always.

"Oh, dear!" Grandma Edie exclaimed, lifting her walking cane off the floor and pointing it—almost accusingly!—at Lord Blackmore. "My lord, I must insist you stop tormenting my poor kitty!" She rapped her walking cane on the floor a couple of times. "Loki, my boy, come here!"

With wide eyes, Sarah looked back and forth between the dowager countess and the brown-gray cat with black stripes and a white line running down his nose, which gave him a continually mischievous expression. *How did this happen? How is Loki here? And how does Grandma Edie know his name?*

Sarah's heart suddenly paused in her chest, and she spun around, her eyes staring out the door and down the hallway. Unfortunately, they came up empty. There was no sign of Keir.

Closing her eyes, Sarah exhaled a slow breath. Of course, she should have known. He had never promised to find her again, only to return Loki to her. It seemed he had found a way. A way that did not include their paths crossing once more.

Small cracks appeared in Sarah's heart, slowly widening and running deeper as that one last hope slipped away.

"Sarah, dear," the dowager addressed her a moment before a soft hand landed upon Sarah's shoulder. "Would you hold my kitty? It seems something about Lord Blackmore agitates him."

Sarah blinked, and then her gaze met the dowager's, and her heart felt a little lighter. Indeed, it felt like coming home. In truth, the Whickertons had always been her family, far more than her own. And only now, having Grandma Edie's eyes look into hers as they always had, full of kindness and compassion, Sarah felt the ordeal of the last few days slowly fall away. Tears came to her eyes, and she hastily blinked them away.

The dowager smiled at her, her wrinkled fingers pinching Sarah's chin good-naturedly. "Don't you worry, my dear," she whispered low enough only for Sarah to hear. "All will be well. I assure you."

In Sarah's experience, many people promised many things. Yet when Grandma Edie promised, it was like a law of nature. Something that could not be shaken. Something that was true. Something she could trust without question.

Returning the dowager's smile, Sarah nodded and then lifted her gaze as the dowager's grandson appeared beside her shoulder, Loki in his arms.

"Grandmother," Troy began, trying to hold on to the squirming feline, "what am I to do with this cat?"

The dowager chuckled. "Give him to Sarah," she said with a pat on his shoulder. "I have something to discuss with Lords Hartmore and Blackmore." She paused, then chuckled. "My, I never quite realized how much alike their titles are. How odd!"

With a sigh of relief, Sarah held out her hands and Loki all but jumped into her arms. The feel of her loyal companion instantly soothed the ache in Sarah's heart, and she held him closely, exhaling a slow breath as he snuggled closer and a soft purring sound drifted to her ears.

While Sarah's father still looked flustered and completely at a loss, Lord Blackmore appeared to be seething with anger, claw marks gracing his neck and cheeks. Even a drop of blood trickled down the side of his face where Loki had dug in his claws. Sarah could not help but hug the cat tighter, grateful that he had come to her defense.

"Lord Hartmore," Grandma Edie began, turning her attention to

Sarah's father, "as agreed, I have come to fetch Sarah. I hope this is not an inconvenient time."

Sarah could tell that her father was confused. Clearly, nothing had been agreed upon. Yet no one in their right mind contradicted Grandma Edie.

"What are you speaking of?" Lord Blackmore inquired when Sarah's father failed to utter even a single word. His voice was a low growl, his gaze hard and full of hatred as it moved from Sarah to her father and then back to the dowager.

Grandma Edie looked surprised. "Oh, you did not know?" She glanced at Lord Hartmore, the expression upon her face suggesting that she had expected him to share whatever information she was referring to. "Of course, after her ordeal, Miss Mortensen cannot be expected to enter into a marriage at this point." Lord Blackmore tensed, his jaw clenching. "Therefore, I discussed with Lord Hartmore the possibility of her becoming my companion." Grandma Edie sighed dramatically, once more leaning more heavily upon her grandson's arm. "At my age, it is a balm to the soul to have a kind and caring young woman at my side who will keep me company." She smiled at Lord Hartmore. "I thank you so much for agreeing to this. I know it will do your daughter good. She needs some time to recuperate, and I treasure her company."

Sarah saw her father's mouth open and close and then open again as he tried desperately to find something to say that would not anger Grandma Edie or Lord Blackmore. Unfortunately, such a thing did not exist.

"But she is to be my bride!" Lord Blackmore growled, and Sarah felt her arms tighten upon Loki. What if he insisted? What then? A new wave of panic once again rose in her chest. *No!* Sarah reminded herself. *Grandma Edie will handle this! All will be well!*

The dowager met Lord Blackmore's gaze without flinching, her own hard and determined despite the polite smile upon her lips. "She *was* to be your bride, my lord. Now, she is to be my companion." A contemplative frown drew down her brows. "What do you even want with a wife? You have an heir! Go and dote upon your grandchildren. I assure you it's great fun! Good day, gentlemen." Leaning upon her grandson's arm, the dowager hobbled toward the door. "Come, dear," she said to Sarah. "We'll send for your things later. My granddaughters cannot wait to see you again."

Casting a last glance at her father, Sarah fell into step with the dowager. "Thank you," she whispered as they walked out of the study, her body tingling with relief. It felt like a low hum beneath her skin, soothing as well as invigorating.

"Of course, dear," Grandma Edie said with a smile, patting her arm. "You're family, and we take care of our own. Sometimes it takes a bit longer and requires great ingenuity," she chuckled, her eyes flashing with amusement, "but we never give up, do we?" She looked up at her grandson.

Troy smiled at his grandmother before looking to Sarah. "Never," he confirmed, the look upon his face no longer unreadable.

"And thank you as well," Sarah murmured to Loki, scratching him behind the ears. Then she looked at the dowager. "How did...he come to be with you?"

Grandma Edie grinned. "Oh, he was delivered to us earlier today. Come now, we'll go home." She heaved a dramatic-sounding sigh. "I'm old, and I need to rest."

Troy chuckled, as though the mere thought of it was ludicrous.

Chapter Forty

POWERLESS

Never in his life had Albert felt so powerless, so humiliated, so furious as when he watched his would-be bride walk away, never to return.

And after I paid the ransom to bring her home!

"What just happened here, Hartmore?" he growled, turning his gaze to the flustered man by his side. "How dare you agree to this?"

Hartmore wrung his hands. "I apologize," he said, fighting to regain some measure of control. "I never meant for this to happen. However, considering the ordeal my daughter has been through, this might be for the best. She would not be an...adequate wife."

Albert's gaze narrowed. "And does that sudden change of heart have anything to do with the fact that someone whose identity I have yet to uncover has taken over your debts?" He lifted his brows for emphasis. "How did that happen? Who was it?"

Hartmore shrugged. "I cannot say. I was as surprised as you."

Albert gritted his teeth, well-aware that Hartmore was ignorant. After all, he did not possess a mind capable of elaborate schemes. *Who then?* Albert's gaze moved to the open door, through which the Dowager Lady Whickerton had just disappeared—with his bride, no less!

Indeed, Albert would not put it past the old woman! But how? And why? He doubted his bride simply decided to cry off because she suddenly felt unworthy of him. No, there had to be more to it! Much more!

Storming out, Albert vowed he would find out and that he would make her pay.

That he would make all of them pay.

Especially his unfaithful bride!

Chapter Forty-One
A CLEAR MESSAGE

It had been a week since Sarah had left her parents' house and gone to live with the Whickertons. To her, it was like a dream come true, something she had always dreamed of and wished for but never thought to see happening. Finally, she was feeling safe, their presence reassuring, their smiles and kind words soothing and heartwarming. Yes, this was family. This was what family was supposed to be, to feel like. Indeed, it felt so good to be here with them, to be seated alongside the family at breakfast, to be asked for a stroll outside in the gardens, to speak with Christina as they had as children, sharing secrets and their hearts' desires.

"You look truly happy," Sarah observed as they stood outside on the small terrace, bundled up warmly against the cold winter's air. Down below, in the garden the next generation of Whickertons played in the snow, making snow angels, and throwing snowballs at one another, their cheerful voices echoing to her ears. "What is it like being a mother?" Her gaze moved from Bash, Juliet and Christopher's son, to little Samantha, Christina's adopted daughter. Her friend's husband had found the child upon his doorstep long before he had even met Christina. Now, however, they looked as though they had always been a family.

Perhaps they had always been *meant* to be a family.

Grinning, Christina shook her head. "No, no, no. We are not here to speak about me." She slipped an arm through Sarah's and then pulled her away from the others. They ventured down a small path and disappeared behind a tall snow-covered hedge. "You asked me for some time to settle in," Christina began once they were securely out of earshot. Then she turned and looked at Sarah. "Now, tell me everything."

Sarah heaved a deep sigh, uncertain what to say, how much to reveal or even where to begin. "Did your grandmother not tell you what happened?"

Christina sighed. "Yes, she told me about the plan. But what I truly am dying to know is every little detail of what truly happened." Her blue eyes twinkled mischievously. "Sarah, please! You cannot tell me you spent—what?—more than a fortnight in the company of a good-looking and utterly charming man and nothing happened!" She lifted her brows meaningfully.

Sarah stared at her friend, overcome by Christina's directness. "Who told you he was...good-looking?"

"You did."

Sarah's jaw dropped, heat shooting into her cheeks as always. "What? I did not!"

Christina chuckled. "Perhaps not in words. But believe me, the look in your eyes every time you try not to think of him says more than a thousand words." Once again, she slipped her arm through Sarah's and pulled her along. "You care for him, do you not?" Christina asked as they continued along the path.

Sarah sighed, grateful that her friend's inquisitive eyes were not directed at her. Yes, perhaps it was easier to talk while walking. "I suppose I do," Sarah finally admitted after spending the past week trying her utmost not even to think of Keir.

"And you miss him," Christina observed.

Sarah nodded, feeling tears gathering in the corners of her eyes.

Christina sighed, then stopped and turned to look at her. "If he means so much to you, why then will you not simply see him again?"

Sarah's gaze widened, her insides grasping the straw Christina was holding out, instinctively reaching toward the idea of seeing Keir again. Yet... "I cannot," she exclaimed, reminding Christina as much as herself. "He is not... And I am..." She shook her head, trying her best to clear it. "We are from two different worlds, and besides, I have no way of knowing how...he feels about me."

Christina eyed her shrewdly. "Did he kiss you?"

Sarah's face went up in flames, and she closed her eyes and bowed her head, wishing to sink into a hole in the ground.

Christina laughed. "You have to see him again!"

"You know as well as I do that not every kiss speaks of a deeper feeling," Sarah objected, afraid of her friend's counsel, afraid of what it might do to her, to her resolve. To her heart! "And even should I choose to believe everything you say, I cannot simply see him again. I don't know who he is. I don't even know his full name. He could be anywhere by now." Sarah heaved a deep sigh.

"That's true. He could be out there abducting the next lady in need of rescuing," Christina suggested with a mischievous chuckle. All the while, her gaze was watchful and remained trained upon Sarah's face, and the moment Sarah felt every fiber of her being revolt against her friend's suggestion, Christina pulled her into her arms, laughing. "See? I told you; you are in love."

Sarah pulled back, staring into her friend's eyes. "I'm not in love! I...I simply like him. That is all." She straightened her shoulders and inhaled deeply of the chilling winter air. "It is not love, and it will go away...with time."

Christina eyed her carefully. "So, you intend to do nothing? You will not see him again?"

Sarah shook her head, knowing that this was not her choice. After all, Keir knew precisely who she was and where she was, and yet he had chosen to deliver Loki to her without meeting face to face. That was a clear message, one she intended to heed. "I will not," she finally said in reply to her friend's questions. "Your grandmother's plan succeeded, and I am now her companion. I'm finally free, free of the threat of marriage. I can live my days in peace, here, with you." Her gaze swept sideways when another bout of childish laughter echoed to her ears. "I can be happy here, and I intend to be." She grasped Christina's hands. "Please, help me be happy here."

A deep sigh left Christina's lips, and for a moment, she appeared to be on the verge of arguing her point. Then, however, she seemed to change her mind and nodded. "Very well. If that is what you wish."

"It is," Sarah replied, reminding herself that she had won more than she ever had dared hope for. Ever since she had come out, Sarah had been terrified of the thought of being married off to a stranger, someone she could not care for, someone who even frightened her. That fear had materialized in Lord Blackmore. And now, that this threat had disappeared, that she was finally safe, Sarah knew she ought to be grateful.

After all, Kate had had no such fortune. She *had* been married off to a stranger, and Sarah burned to find out how she was faring in her marriage. Yes, every few weeks a letter arrived, in which Kate assured her family that she was well and happy. Still, Sarah could not shake the feeling that her sister was anything but well and happy.

In fact, she had already spoken to the dowager countess about her fears, and Christina's grandmother had once again promised to help. Knowing that she was not alone in this took an enormous weight off Sarah's heart. Indeed, if she did not receive a reassuring reply to the letter she had sent to Kate a week past, then Sarah was determined to go and visit her sister.

To see the truth for herself.

Of course, the thought of traveling on her own made Sarah nervous. More than nervous, in fact! For if her sister's husband was truly the kind of man who had no interest in his wife's happiness, then...what could she, Sarah, do? Alone? On her own? More than anything, she wished the dowager countess could accompany her. After seeing her deal with Lord Blackmore, Sarah did not have the slightest doubt that she would be able to handle Kate's husband with equal ease. Yet, of course, the dowager's health did not allow for it. Still, Grandma Edie had promised to find Sarah a trusted companion who would stand at her side should need be. Sarah had no idea who the dowager had in mind, but now more than ever she trusted her.

When Grandma Edie said all would be well, then all would be well.

If only the dowager had told her so with regard to Keir. *If only I had never met him! If only I had never come to feel for him!* For although Sarah was now free of the threat of marriage, her heart suddenly seemed trapped, bound to someone she could never have.

That, Sarah had not expected. Yet she would find a way to live with it.

After all, she would have to.

Chapter Forty-Two

A FAINT MEMORY

After a week of running errands for Grandma Edie once again, Keir returned to London. He had seen to a few more loose strings, paying off potential witnesses and ensuring that nothing could be traced back to the dowager countess. The hunter, too, had been out in the woods, doing his best to clear away all traces of their being there. Their paths had crossed a few times, and Keir had done his utmost to elicit further information from the man. However, it seemed Grandma Edie had been no more forthcoming with him than with Keir himself.

Not knowing was simply something Keir would have to accept when dealing with the dowager. Her intentions were always good, and he was glad he had gone along with her plan in aiding Sarah. Yet those few days had changed him, and right now he did not quite know what to do about it.

The moment Keir set foot back into the Whickertons' townhouse, he was summoned to the dowager countess. Of course, it did not surprise him that she seemed to know about his every move. "Is there yet another task you wish for me to see to?" he asked as he walked into the drawing room, finding her as always seated by the fireplace.

Grandma Edie laughed good-naturedly. "Are you growing tired of my errands?"

Keir settled in the chair opposite her. "Not quite," he said. "However, I wish I had a bit more context."

As always, the dowager ignored such a request. "Guests will start arriving shortly, so I suggest you head upstairs and," she looked him up and down, "dress accordingly." A teasing smirk came to her features.

Smiling, Keir bowed his head in defeat. "Verra well." He rose to his feet and stepped toward the door. There he paused, turning back to look at the dowager. "Is Miss Mortensen all right?" he asked without preamble, knowing that the dowager would draw her own conclusions no matter how he phrased his inquiry. "Did she cry off?"

As expected, a contemplative smile came to the dowager's face. "She is...and she did."

Keir nodded. "What of...the possible aid ye spoke of last time?"

"I shall inform you as soon as the need arises," Grandma Edie promised. "But for now, go and change. It'll take forever to wash all that dirt out from under your fingernails." She chuckled.

Keir shook his head at her and left, returning to the chamber he had been assigned when first arriving from Scotland. Aye, perhaps it was time to head back home soon. He missed his family, his own grandmother, his parents and brothers. "Yvaine," he murmured with a sigh, knowing that she would not be there to welcome him back home.

Only the Whickertons had become family as well, and he would miss them dearly once the time to say goodbye came.

And...Sarah.

Running a hand through his hair, Keir seated himself on the edge of his bed, then began pulling off his boots. The idea of attending a ball filled him with dread. He would much rather head back out into the woods; yet the past week had proven that on his own with no one to distract him, his thoughts tended to linger upon his little wisp.

Aye, I've somehow come to think of her as mine. *After all, for a fortnight, she was mine to look after. Mine to protect. Only she isna truly* mine. *But neither is she Blackmore's, and that, at least, is a relief.*

As darkness fell, guests started to arrive, their voices echoing through the large townhouse. With a sigh, Keir looked at himself in the mirror, his brows drawing down into a frown as he saw himself dressed like a gentleman, his hair the only thing that set him apart. Never would he forgo the little braids that would forever remind him of his sister. "Let them gawk!" he said to his reflection, shaking his head at himself. Honestly, he looked ridiculous!

Without another thought, Keir headed downstairs, hoping for nothing more than a distraction. Aye, it would soothe his mind to see it focused on something other than Sarah. If only he knew what she was doing right now, back home with her parents!

With each step, the noise grew, and the moment Keir stepped into the ballroom, his ears began to ring. After the gentle stillness of the forest, a crowded ballroom felt like a tidal wave of noise, overwhelming his senses and making him wish he could simply turn and walk away.

Then his gaze fell on the Whickerton family, and a compelling urge to join them filled his heart. They stood together beneath an arched window, the dowager seated in their midst, Lord and Lady Whickerton off to her right with their children as well as their children's spouses grouped around them, chatting and laughing. Harriet's fiery-red curls seemed aflame in the candlelight, and Christina's golden-blond tresses glowed like the sun itself. Yet more than their appearance, it was the joy reflected in their eyes, to be together in this place as a family that touched Keir, that made him look and truly see them. He saw not only smiles but also trust and confidence, whispered words passing back and forth, not those of rumors and snide comments passed behind another's back but the good kind. The kind that spoke of loyalty, of unity.

Aye, the Whickerton family stood as one. Certainly, they had their differences, but they never allowed these differences to come between them. Instead, the family continued to grow. Keir allowed his gaze to sweep over Harriet and her husband Jack, the serious Duke of Clements, who had been utterly changed since meeting his young wife. He smiled at Christina and Thorne, Louisa and Phineas, Leonora and Drake and Juliet and Christopher as well as Troy and Nora, all of whom looked utterly happy, just like their parents.

Keir grinned, allowing his gaze to return to the dowager. After all, she had been responsible for all their unions; he knew. He had been witness to, at least, half of them and had been told about the others by the Whickerton siblings themselves. Of course, each and every one of them had complained about their grandmother's meddling, but in the end, each had been grateful to have found happiness because of her, because she had seen something they had missed.

Aye, they are a wonderful family, and I will miss them dearly. I will—

Keir's thoughts jarred to a halt as his gaze fell on a familiar face. Of course, his gaze was sweeping over quite a few familiar faces; only *this one* he had not expected to see.

Not here.

Not tonight.

Sarah!

Keir felt every fiber of his being still as he breathed in deeply, disbelief and joy sweeping through him at the same time. He blinked. Was it truly Sarah? He wondered, allowing his gaze to trail over her as she stood next to Grandma Edie's chair, handing the old woman a beverage.

Aye, she looked different, but it *was* her.

Her hair was styled elaborately and pinned up, the little wisps upon her temples forced into accurate curls, dancing down to her shoulder. She wore an azure gown, its color strangely pale, matching the lack of color upon her face. Indeed, there was no flush, no crimson upon her cheeks. She looked like a shadow of the woman he had come to know, not completely devoid of color but as though all the colors had shifted. Her eyes seemed paler than he remembered them, and her hair glowed almost golden, no longer like it had been touched by sunshine. Aye, she looked very, very different, not like the Sarah with whom he had spent a fortnight in a lonely cabin in the woods. In fact, she looked like...

Again, a jolt of awareness slashed through Keir when a memory returned with sudden force, answering a question he had asked himself long ago. *How do I know her?* Indeed, the first night when he had taken her out of London, when she had fainted and he had laid her down gently upon the forest floor, her face illuminated in the pale moonlight, Keir had paused, thinking that she looked familiar. Yet he had been unable to place her face, to make a connection.

Now, he remembered.

It had been the previous summer.

After meeting Harriet and the Duke of Clements up north in Gretna Green, Keir had returned with them to England. He had been on his way to see the Whickertons anyhow, and it had been sheer coincidence that he had stumbled upon the Duke of Clements and been able to lend a hand in retrieving Harriet after she had been abducted by a disrespectful suitor.

Before riding to Whickerton Grove, they had stopped at Atwood Park, where many guests had gathered for a house party. It had been the place from which Harriet had been abducted, and Lord Whickerton had been intent on speaking to Lord and Lady Atwood about what had occurred under their roof. They had stayed for one night, and that evening, Keir had ventured outside into the gardens.

That was where he had seen her.

Sarah.

Only that night he had not known her name. He had not known who she was. And yet he had been unable to forget her.

Walking deeper into the gardens, Keir had savored the darkness, his mind calming as the noise of the ball inside fell away. He had walked and walked, exploring every inch of the gardens, the trees, the small pond nearby. It had calmed his nerves after everything that had happened, and he had been about to return to the house when he had seen someone slip outside.

One of the terrace doors had opened quietly, and a lone figure had stepped out into the night. Then, she had worn a pale blue dress as well, her hair pulled back into some elaborate style as though she were a doll, her face pale like porcelain, her eyes wide, unblinking. Hurried steps had led her down into the gardens, and he had heard her breath coming fast, muffled sobs tearing from her lips.

To Keir, it had appeared she had no destination in mind, her feet carrying her blindly onward. He had hung back, kept himself in the shadows, unable to leave, feeling the need to watch over her. After what had happened to Harriet, he knew that a young woman out alone could easily come to harm. He had thought of Yvaine, hoping that— wherever she was—someone else might look out for her as well.

Eventually, Sarah had found her way to a lonely bench under an old oak tree. There, she had sunk down, her knees trembling, her hands shaking. Tears had streamed down her face and she had wiped them away, only to find more coming. She had been beside herself, and Keir had been close to revealing his presence, unable not to offer comfort. Yet even then he had known that his presence would not have been of any comfort to her. In all likelihood, she would have been mortified.

He had no notion of what had happened to her, what had brought on the tears. His gaze moved back up to the terrace but no one followed. No one seemed to be missing her. Eventually, the young woman had calmed, her face pale in the moonlight, as pale as her gown and her hair. She had seemed as though not of this world, yet the sadness in her eyes had been too real to ignore.

Too real to forget.

Aye, I've never forgotten that moment.

Eventually, the young woman had calmed enough to return inside, her eyes dry once more and her cheeks free of tears.

In the days after, Keir had often found himself wondering if the young woman had ever spoken to anyone about what had happened that night. He had often wondered if anyone had noticed her absence. And he had often wondered who she was and where she might be today.

A smile teased Keir's lips as he looked at her now, deep joy springing to life in his heart to find her here, so close. Only the woman he remembered from that night as well as the woman he saw with his own eyes right now did not quite resemble the woman he had spent that fortnight with in the woods, did she? Something was different. Something—

And then all of a sudden, Sarah's eyes met his, and Keir felt it like a punch to his midsection. He felt it as though he had been knocked off his feet. He felt it in his heart and soul.

As did she.

Upon beholding him, Sarah stilled completely, shock at finding him here written all over her face. Her lips parted on a gasp, and her right hand grasped the backrest of Grandma Edie's chair tightly.

Keir smiled, for he could not help it, holding her gaze with a knowing look, waiting to see if...

A deep blush darkened Sarah's cheeks, and she quickly dropped her gaze, only to meet his eyes once more a second later. Yet her own narrowed in confusion, and she slightly shook her head, perhaps believing herself trapped in a hallucination.

Delighted with her blush, Keir raised one brow in challenge, wanting to—

Sarah's blush deepened, and the blue of her eyes grew more intense as her fingers began to fidget with one of the styled curls dancing down from her temples.

Keir all but held his breath as the perfect little curl disappeared before his eyes, picked apart by nervous fingers, revealing the little wisps Keir had come to love. They curled in all directions, wild and untamed, and somehow they brought back the woman he knew.

Suddenly, the perfect porcelain doll was gone, in her place a woman of flesh and blood, her large blue eyes fixed upon him and her teeth nervously digging into her lower lip. Her cheeks shone crimson, and her breath came fast as she still clung to Grandma Edie's chair.

Keir caught the old woman's knowing gaze, not at all surprised to see the dowager wink at him conspiratorially. She nodded for him to approach, and without a moment of hesitation, Keir complied. His feet moved, carrying him across the ballroom, his gaze fixed upon Sarah, her eyes growing wider with each step he took.

Aye, perhaps tonight willna be a waste of time after all.

Far from it.

Chapter Forty-Three

A MEETING MOST UNEXPECTED

Sarah could not breathe. She could not think, barely knew what she felt. Her knees threatened to buckle at any moment, her hand clamped around the backrest of Grandma Edie's chair. However, her heart seemed to dance in her chest.

Keir!

Not in her wildest dreams would Sarah ever have expected to see him here. In the Whickertons' townhouse. At a society ball. Among peers of the realm. *What is he doing here? How does he come to be here?*

Sarah's initial shock, though, was quickly infiltrated by joy...slowly followed by confusion, which soon turned to concern. What was the reason for Keir's appearance here tonight? After all, he knew who she was. He had always known, and yet he had returned Loki to her without asking to see her. Had she completely misread him?

Indeed, throughout all their time spent together, Sarah had allowed herself to see him not as a mere protector, someone who had been tasked to look after her, but as someone who cared. Truly cared. She had come to trust him more than anyone. More than even herself. Had she been a fool? Why would he be here now? Knowing who she was?

Yes, since Sarah's return to London, she had not been unaware of the whispers. She knew that her abduction had not been kept a secret. Of course not. After all, it had been part of the plan in order to encourage Lord Blackmore to accept her ending their engagement. Only he believed her to have been a victim of another's scheme.

Keir's appearance here at tonight's ball could mean nothing good, could it? Was he here to demand additional payment in exchange for his silence? Was he truly such a man? What would happen if Lord Blackmore found out that she, Sarah, had orchestrated this whole thing?

Sarah felt herself sway on her feet. The mere thought of that happening turned her stomach and sent ice-cold shivers of panic down her back.

Yet looking at Keir, her instincts refused to yield to thought. Her instincts still rejoiced at the mere sight of him, urging her across the ballroom and toward him. *I still feel safe with him, but am I right to do so?*

And then, all of a sudden, Keir started toward her, his blue gaze fixed upon her. She saw intent in his eyes and wished she knew what it was he wanted.

"Don't worry, my dear," Grandma Edie murmured softly, reaching for Sarah's free hand. "All is well."

Sarah's gaze dropped from Keir's, and she turned to look at the dowager. "How can you say that? What is he doing here? What if he...?" She glanced around, well-aware of the way people were eyeing her, had been eyeing her since the moment they had taken note of her presence. Of course, they all knew what had happened. Every chance for making a match was now certainly gone, and although Sarah was relieved to have it so, it still stung to be judged by her peers in such a harsh way. Even as a companion to the dowager countess, Sarah wished they would look at her favorably. No one wanted to be a societal outcast, forced to live with the very people who considered one disgraced and ruined. And if Keir were to reveal the truth of what had happened...

Sarah pinched her eyes shut, unable to even imagine such a scenario. But was it not the only explanation for his being here?

And then, Keir suddenly stood right in front of her. He looked odd, dressed so formally. Yet the little braids upon his temples remained, and Sarah's hand absentmindedly traveled upward to her own. The moment her fingers found her own braids absent, deep sadness filled her, and a part of her felt as though somehow she had betrayed him.

"Good evening, my lady," Keir said with an utterly familiar grin, meeting the dowager's eyes with such frankness that Sarah once again felt the air knocked from her lungs. Something strange was going on! She looked at the dowager, seeing the old woman's eyes sparkle with mischief.

"It is good to have you here tonight, my boy," Grandma Edie replied in greeting, her words as well as the tone of her voice suggesting a deeper connection than one would have with a mere acquaintance. *Is it truly possible that they know one another?* Sarah wondered yet again, remembering similar musings during her time in the woods.

For a long moment, silence lingered, and Sarah became aware that, at least, to the Whickerton family they were suddenly the center of attention. All eyes were on her and Keir, suppressed smiles upon their faces and curiosity glittering in their eyes. *What is going on here?* Sarah wondered. *What do they know that I do not?*

And then, Keir held out his hand to her. "May I have this dance?" His blue eyes looked at her teasingly, dimples showing at the corners of his mouth as he waited patiently for her reply.

Sarah was at a loss. Had Grandma Edie not earlier today promised her she would not have to dance? Had she not assured her that as her companion Sarah would be free to simply observe in peace?

"Go on ahead," Grandma Edie urged her with a nod of her head. "Young people ought to dance." She winked at Sarah with her right eye, then nodded to her, urging her to accept Keir's offer.

Utterly bewildered, Sarah stared at the dowager, unable to move, unable to utter a single word. Never before in her life had she felt so confused, desperate to understand. And then she felt Keir's hand take her own, and her head snapped around, her eyes meeting his.

His fingers curled slowly, gently around hers, urging her toward him, and all the while he looked at her as he had before, his blue gaze open and honest.

Instinctively, Sarah moved toward him, allowing Keir to pull her onto the dance floor. She barely noticed the whispers that followed them, or the curious glances stolen in their direction. Indeed, all her attention was focused upon the man holding her in his arms.

So unexpectedly. *Is this perhaps a dream?*

"Are you truly here?" Sarah asked, as they began to move to the music.

Keir grinned at her. "Does this not feel real?" His hand moved a little lower on her back, tugging her closer.

Sarah gasped. "But w-why?" she stammered. "Why are you here?"

His gaze remained locked on hers, his hand holding hers a bit more tightly. "Isna it obvious?"

Not to me, no! Her mind spun, as the world seemed to turn in alternate directions. "You do know them, do you not?" She glanced past his shoulder to the Whickertons, who were observing them with great interest.

Keir nodded. "Aye, I do."

Sarah frowned, her eyes searching his face. "Who are you? Truly?"

Keir grinned wickedly, leaning closer until she felt his breath tease her lips. "Come with me, little wisp," he whispered, "and I shall tell ye everything." For a long moment, Keir held her gaze, then he took her hand and led her off the dance floor.

Unable to stop herself, Sarah allowed him to pull her along, wondering if perhaps she had fallen asleep and was merely dreaming that Keir had come.

For her.

TO BE CONTINUED

Of course, Sarah and Keir's story does not end here. How could it? There is more to come...so much more! Too much for a single novel! So, stay tuned for the next part of their story as Grandma Edie asks Keir to watch over Sarah yet again when she travels to her sister's home, determined to find out if Kate is well...or if she, too, is in need of rescuing.

Get *Shield of Fire* now!

Acknowledgement

A great big thank-you to all those who aided me in finishing this book and made it the wonderful story it has become. First and foremost, of course, there is my family, who inspires me on a daily basis, giving me the enthusiasm and encouragement, I need to type away at my computer day after day. Thank you so much!

Then there are my proofreaders, beta readers and readers who write to me out of the blue with wonderful ideas and thoughts. Thank you for your honest words! Jodi combs through my manuscripts in an utterly diligent way that allows me to smooth off the rough edges and make it shine. Thank you so much for your dedication to my stories! Brie, Zan-Mari and Mary are my hawks, their eyes sweeping over the words to spot those pesky errors I seem to be absolutely blind to. Thank you so much for aiding me with your keen eyesight!

About Bree

USA Today bestselling and award-winning author, Bree Wolf has always been a language enthusiast (though not a grammarian!) and is rarely found without a book in her hand or her fingers glued to a keyboard. Trying to find her way, she has taught English as a second language, traveled abroad and worked at a translation agency as well as a law firm in Ireland. She also spent loooong years obtaining a BA in English and Education and an MA in Specialized Translation while wishing she could simply be a writer. Although there is nothing simple about being a writer, her dreams have finally come true.

"A big thanks to my fairy godmother!"

Currently, Bree has found her new home in the historical romance genre, writing Regency novels and novellas. Enjoying the mix of fact and fiction, she occasionally feels like a puppet master (or mistress? Although that sounds weird!), forcing her characters into ever-new situations that will put their strength, their beliefs, their love to the test, hoping that in the end they will triumph and get the happily-ever-after we are all looking for.

If you're an avid reader, sign up for Bree's newsletter on www. breewolf.com as she has the tendency to simply give books away. Find out about freebies, giveaways as well as occasional advance reader copies and read before the book is even on the shelves!

Connect with Bree and stay up-to-date on new releases:

 facebook.com/breewolf.novels

x.com/breewolf_author

instagram.com/breewolf_author

amazon.com/Bree-Wolf/e/B00FJX27Z4

bookbub.com/authors/bree-wolf

Printed in Great Britain
by Amazon

44022208R00179